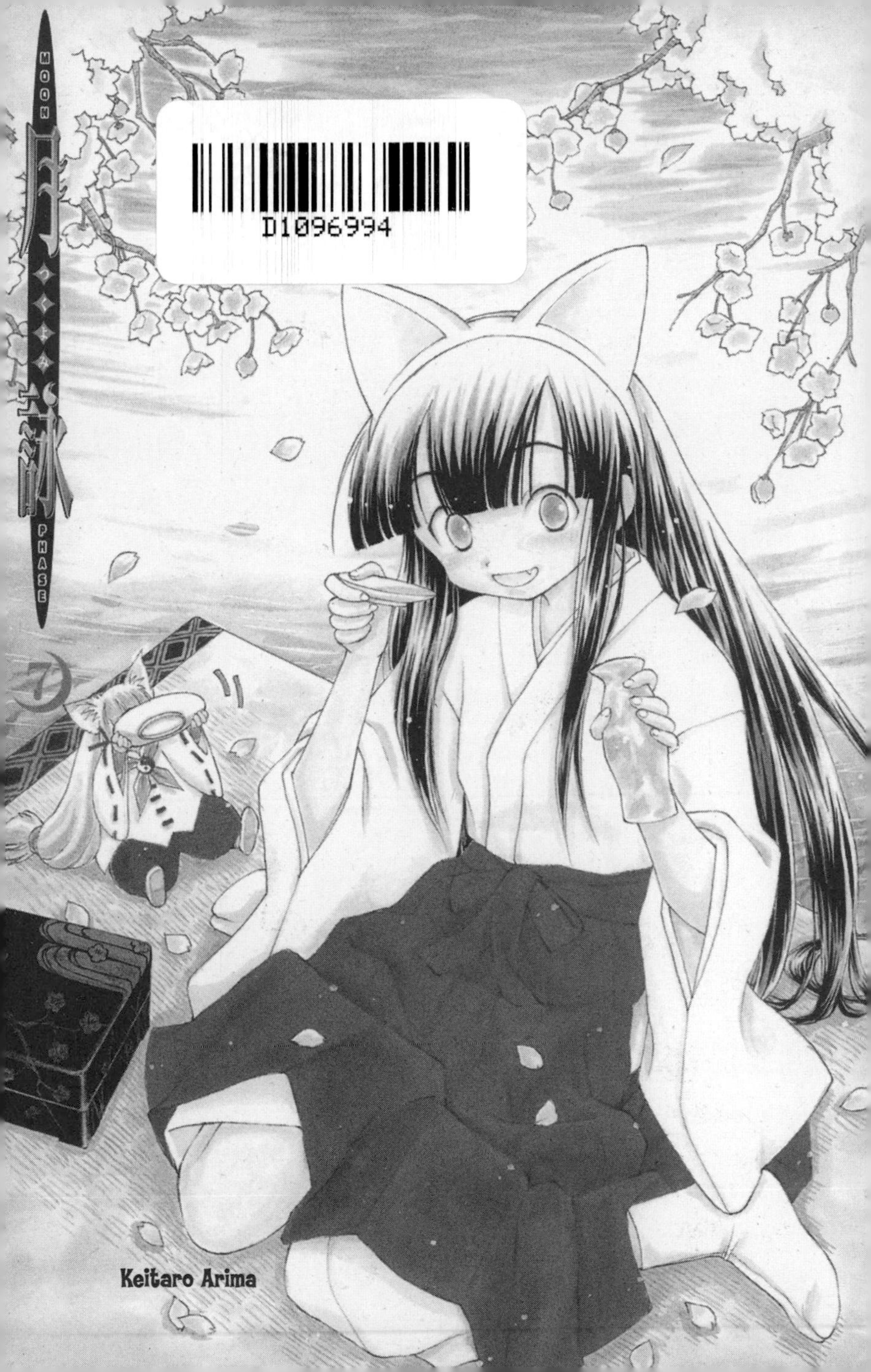
MOON
月詠
つくよみ
PHASE
7
Keitaro Arima

STORY SO FAR

Kouhei Mido has never had a close encounter with the supernatural kind, so why are ghosts showing up in every picture he takes? It all makes sense when he meets the adorable vampire girl, Hazuki, at an old German castle. After a treacherous battle against Count Kinkle, who was bent on capturing Hazuki for himself, Kouhei and his family thought they were finally safe. However, behind the shadows, "Oyakata-sama" orders Mario to seek Hazuki out once more! With all the danger Kouhei's been through, he's more determined than ever to train and be able to protect Hazuki. But will it be enough...?

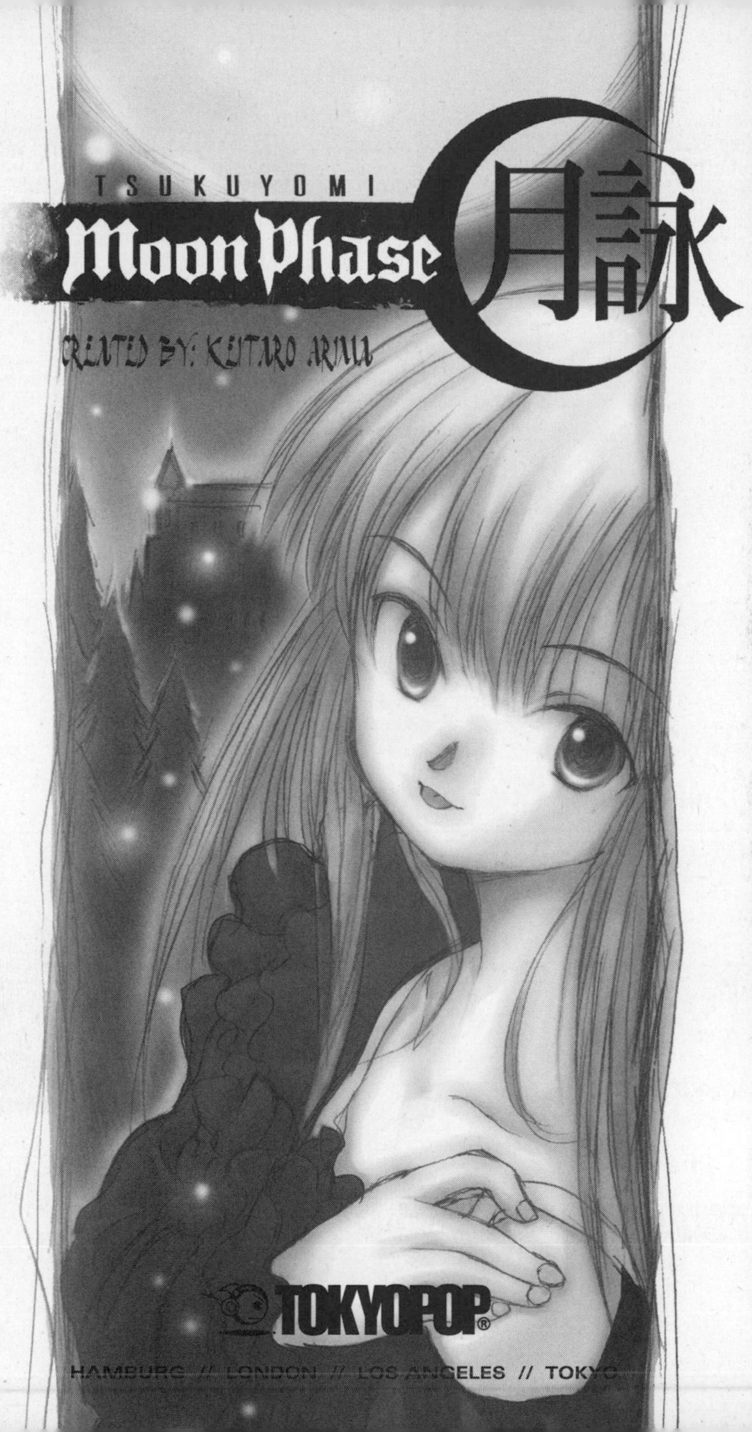

TSUKUYOMI

Moon Phase 月詠

CREATED BY: KEITARO ARIMA

TOKYOPOP®

HAMBURG // LONDON // LOS ANGELES // TOKYO

Tsukuyomi: Moon Phase Volume 7
Created by Keitaro Arima

Translation - Yoohae Yang
English Adaptation - Jeffrey Reeves
Retouch and Lettering - Star Print Brokers
Production Artist - Courtney Geter
Graphic Designer - Fawn Lau

Editor - Katherine Schilling
Digital Imaging Manager - Chris Buford
Pre-Production Supervisor - Erika Terriquez
Art Director - Anne Marie Horne
Production Manager - Elisabeth Brizzi
Managing Editor - Vy Nguyen
VP of Production - Ron Klamert
Editor-in-Chief - Rob Tokar
Publisher - Mike Kiley
President and C.O.O. - John Parker
C.E.O. and Chief Creative Officer - Stuart Levy

A  Manga

TOKYOPOP and are trademarks or registered trademarks of TOKYOPOP Inc.

TOKYOPOP Inc.
5900 Wilshire Blvd. Suite 2000
Los Angeles, CA 90036

E-mail: info@TOKYOPOP.com
Come visit us online at www.TOKYOPOP.com

ISBN: 978-1-59532-954-7

First TOKYOPOP printing: June 2007
10 9 8 7 6 5 4 3 2 1
Printed in the USA

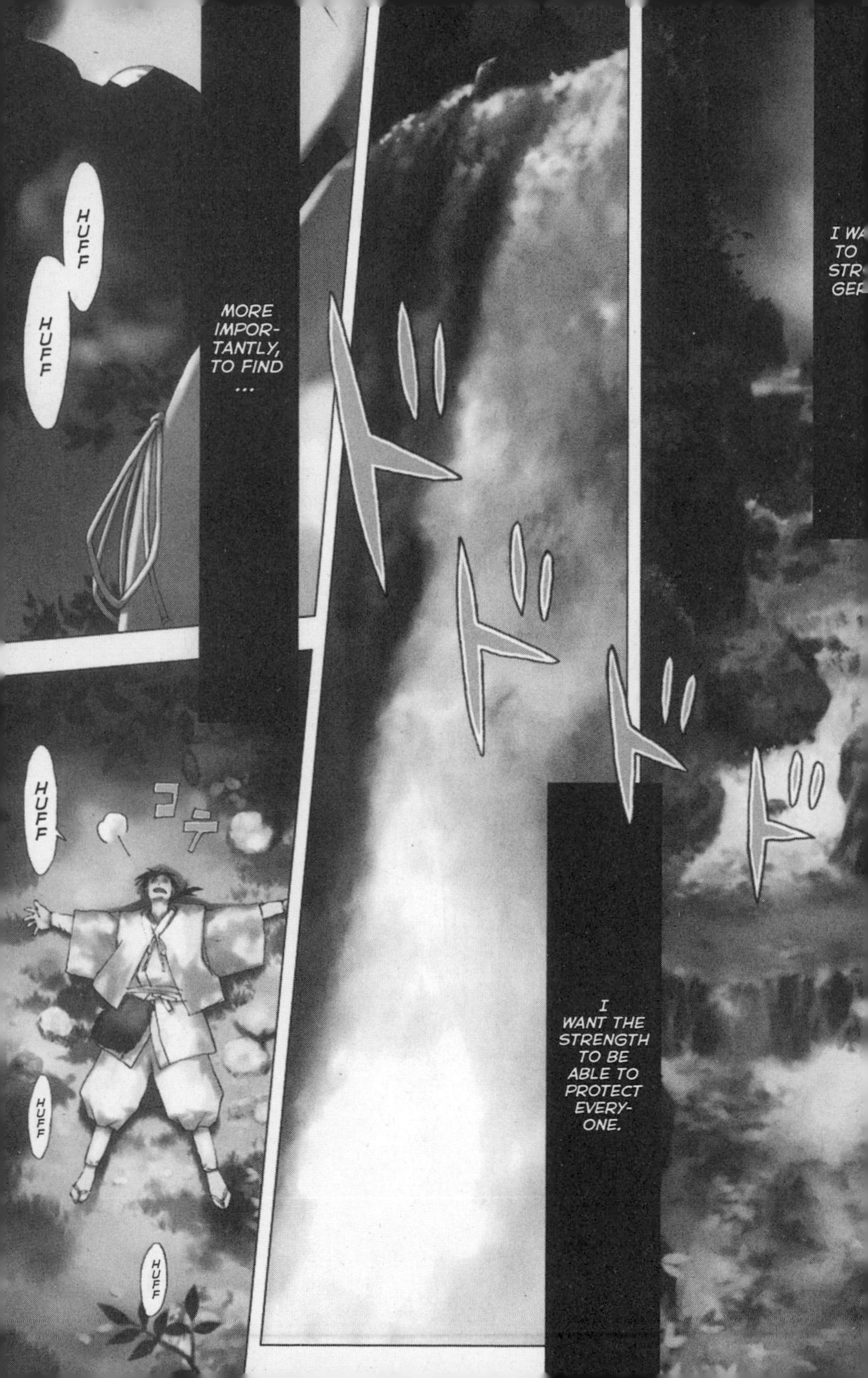
I WA TO STR GER
ドドドド
I WANT THE STRENGTH TO BE ABLE TO PROTECT EVERYONE.
MORE IMPORTANTLY, TO FIND ...
HUFF
HUFF
コテ
HUFF
HUFF
HUFF

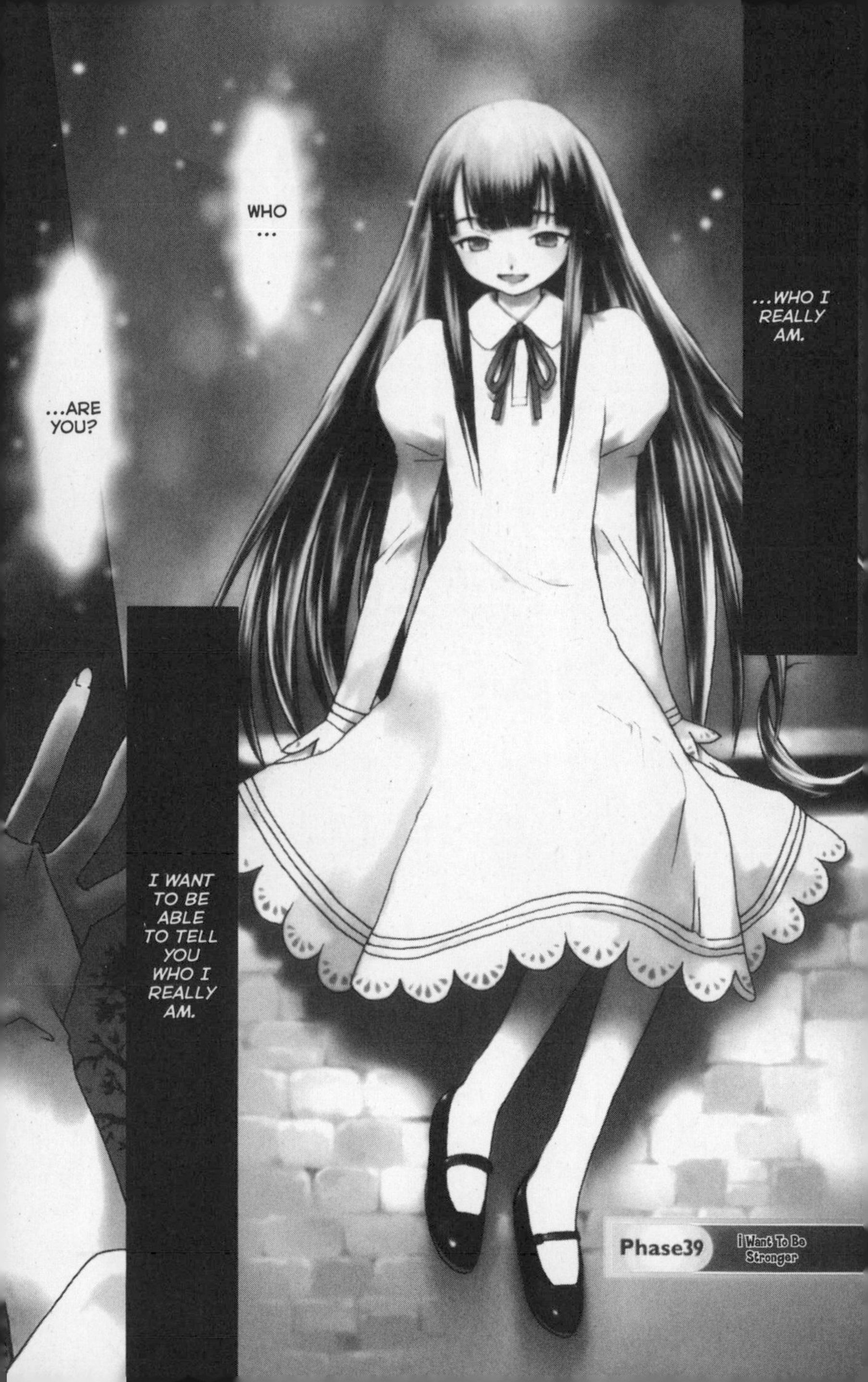
...WHO I REALLY AM.
WHO ...
...ARE YOU?
I WANT TO BE ABLE TO TELL YOU WHO I REALLY AM.
Phase39
I Want To Be Stronger

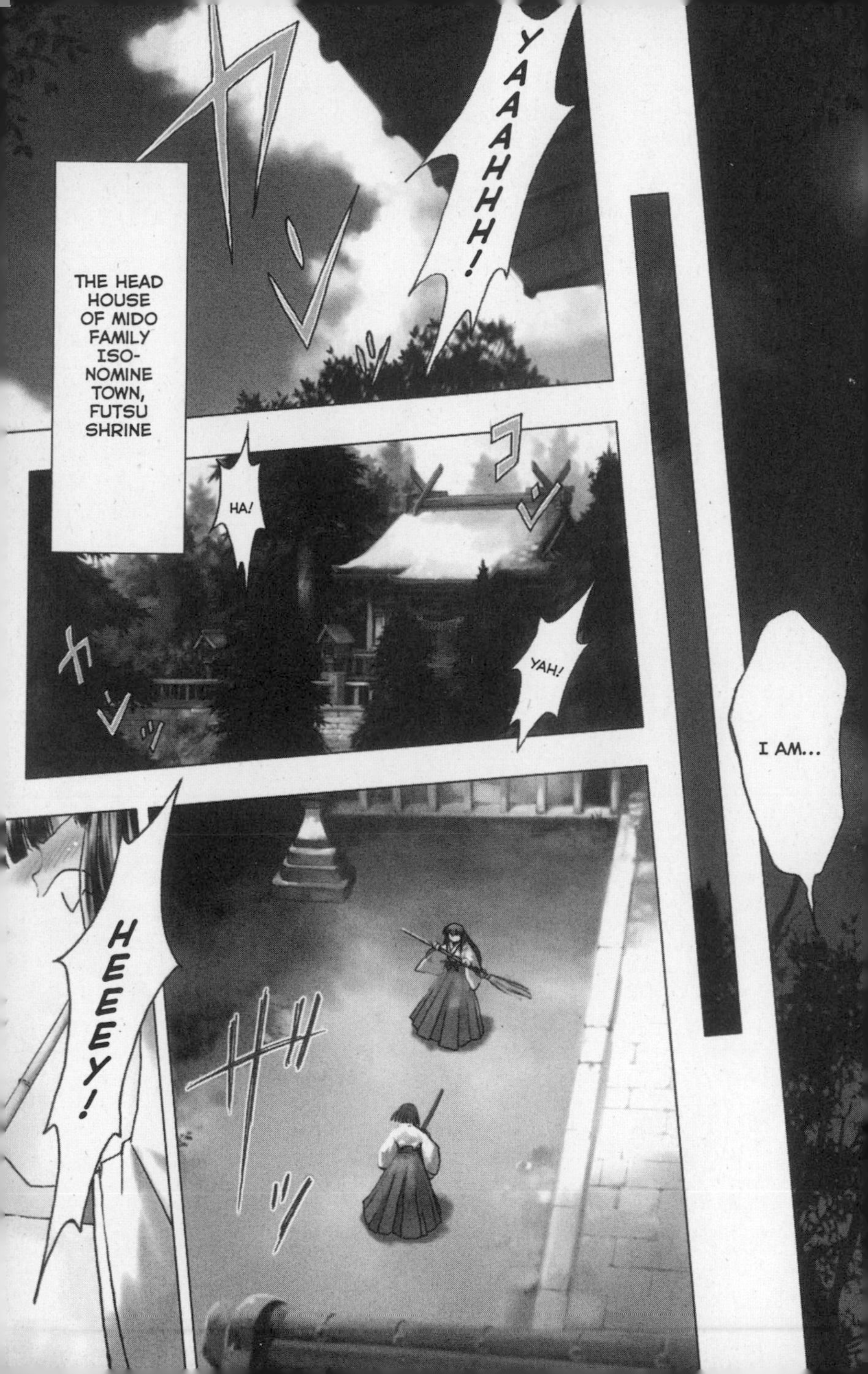
I AM...
YAAAAHHH!
THE HEAD HOUSE OF MIDO FAMILY ISO-NOMINE TOWN, FUTSU SHRINE
YAH!
HA!
HEEEY!

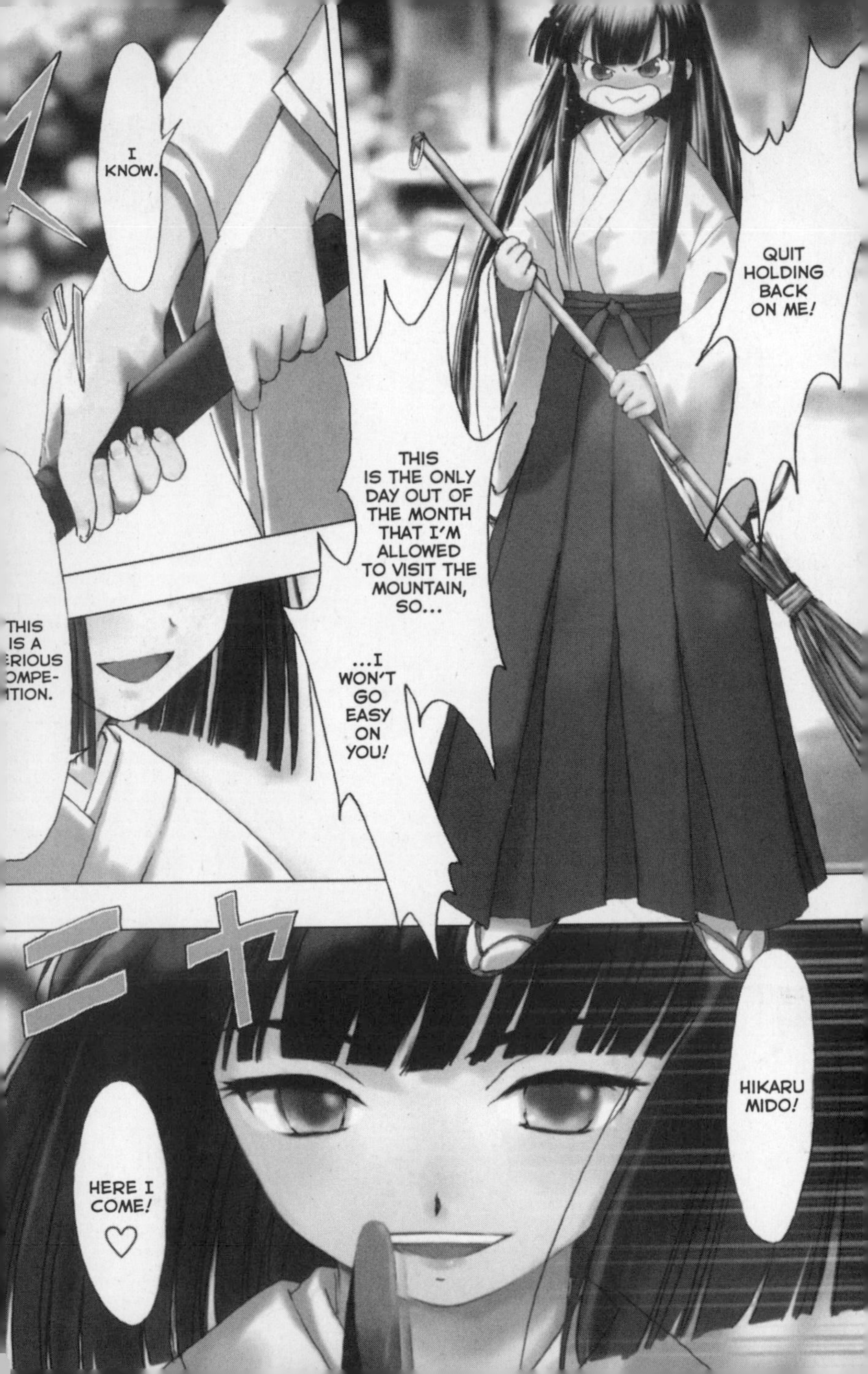
QUIT HOLDING BACK ON ME!
THIS IS THE ONLY DAY OUT OF THE MONTH THAT I'M ALLOWED TO VISIT THE MOUNTAIN, SO...
...I WON'T GO EASY ON YOU!
I KNOW.
THIS IS A ERIOUS OMPE- ITION.
HIKARU MIDO!
HERE I COME! ♡

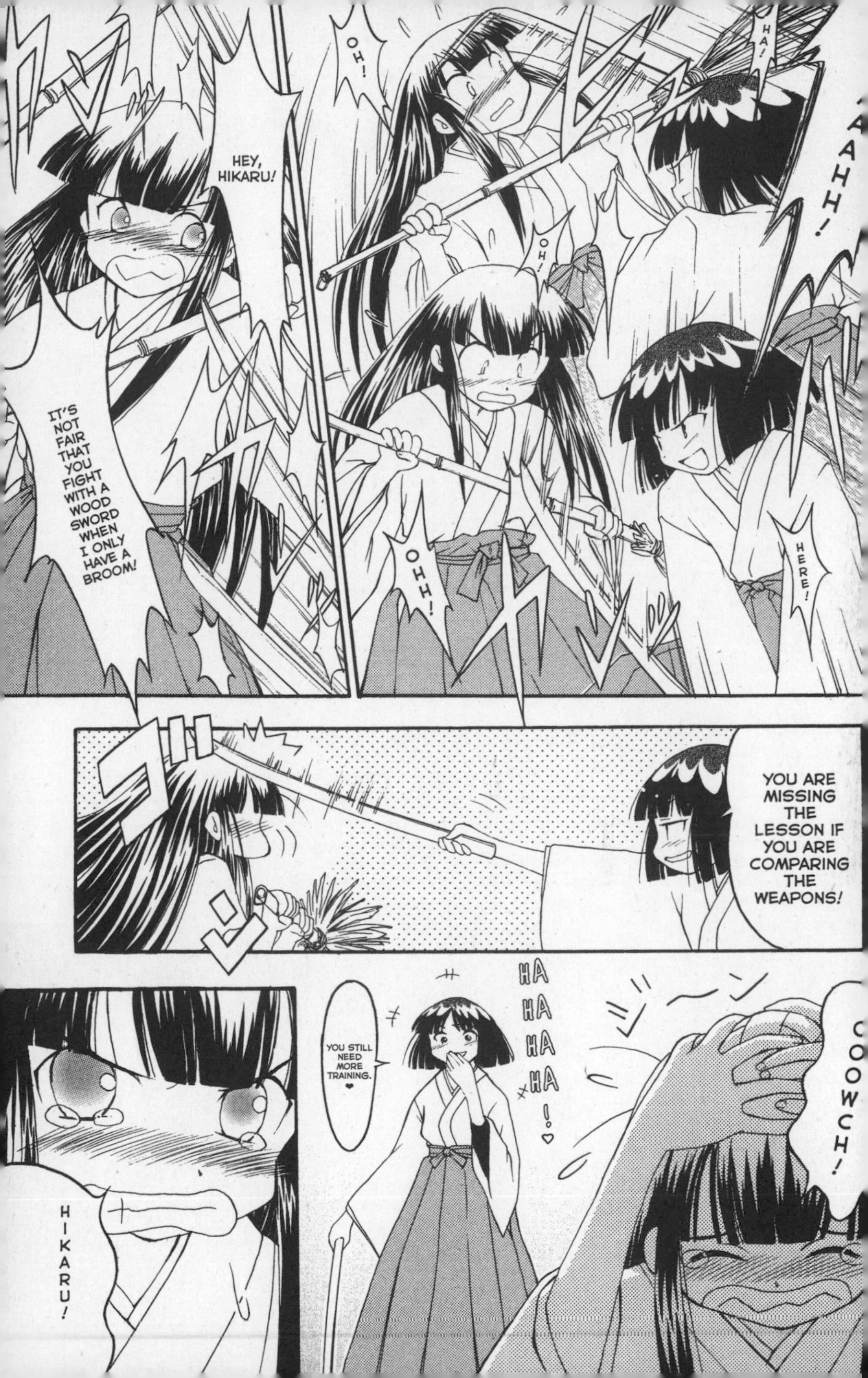
HA!
AAHHH!
OH!
OH!
OHH!
HERE!
HEY, HIKARU!
IT'S NOT FAIR THAT YOU FIGHT WITH A WOOD SWORD WHEN I ONLY HAVE A BROOM!
YOU ARE MISSING THE LESSON IF YOU ARE COMPARING THE WEAPONS!
OOOWCH!
HA HA HA HA HA!
YOU STILL NEED MORE TRAINING.
HIKARU!

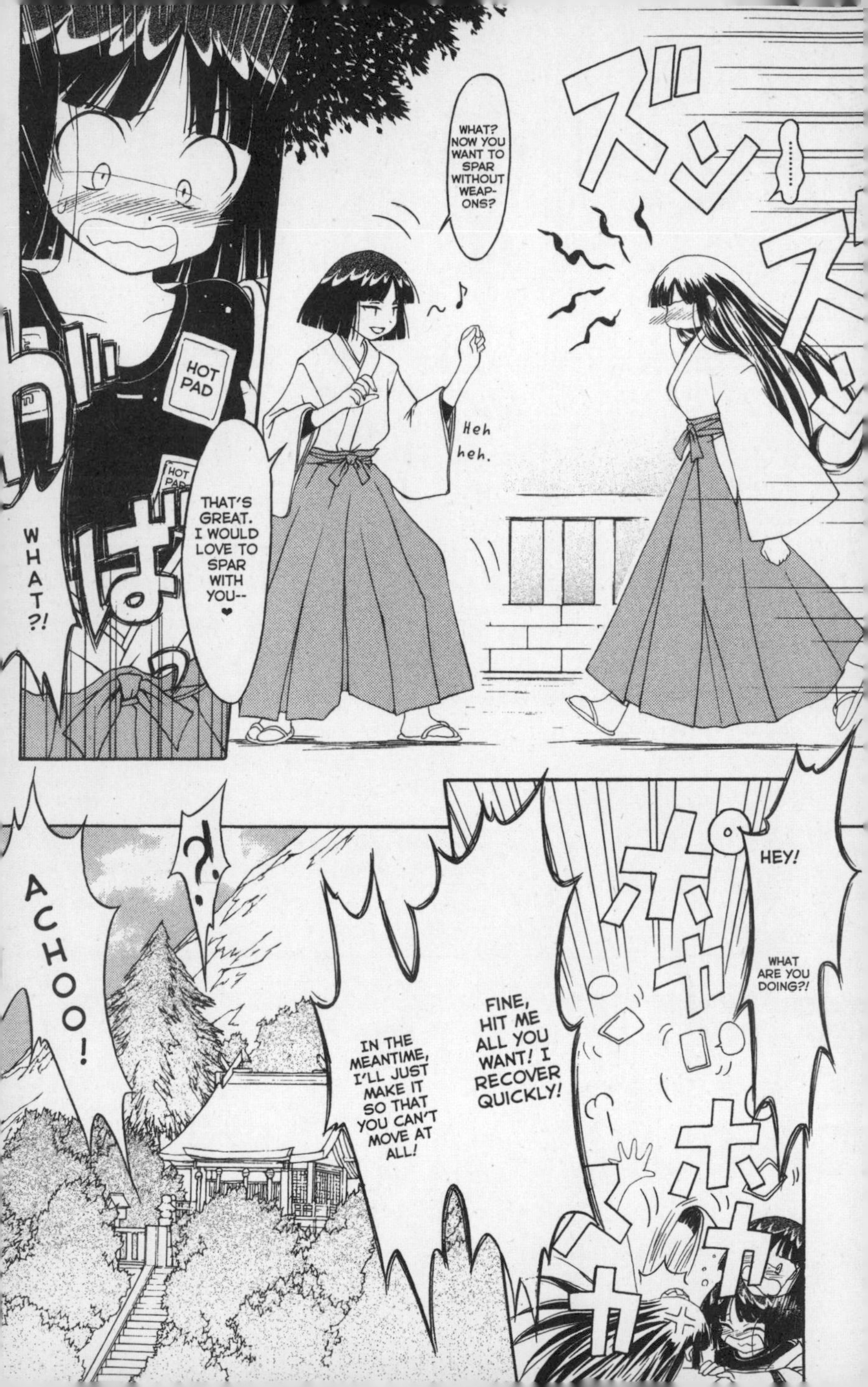
......
WHAT? NOW YOU WANT TO SPAR WITHOUT WEAP-ONS?
Heh heh.
THAT'S GREAT. I WOULD LOVE TO SPAR WITH YOU-- ❤
HOT PAD
HOT PAD
WHAT?!
HEY!
WHAT ARE YOU DOING?!
FINE, HIT ME ALL YOU WANT! I RECOVER QUICKLY!
IN THE MEANTIME, I'LL JUST MAKE IT SO THAT YOU CAN'T MOVE AT ALL!
?!
ACHOO!

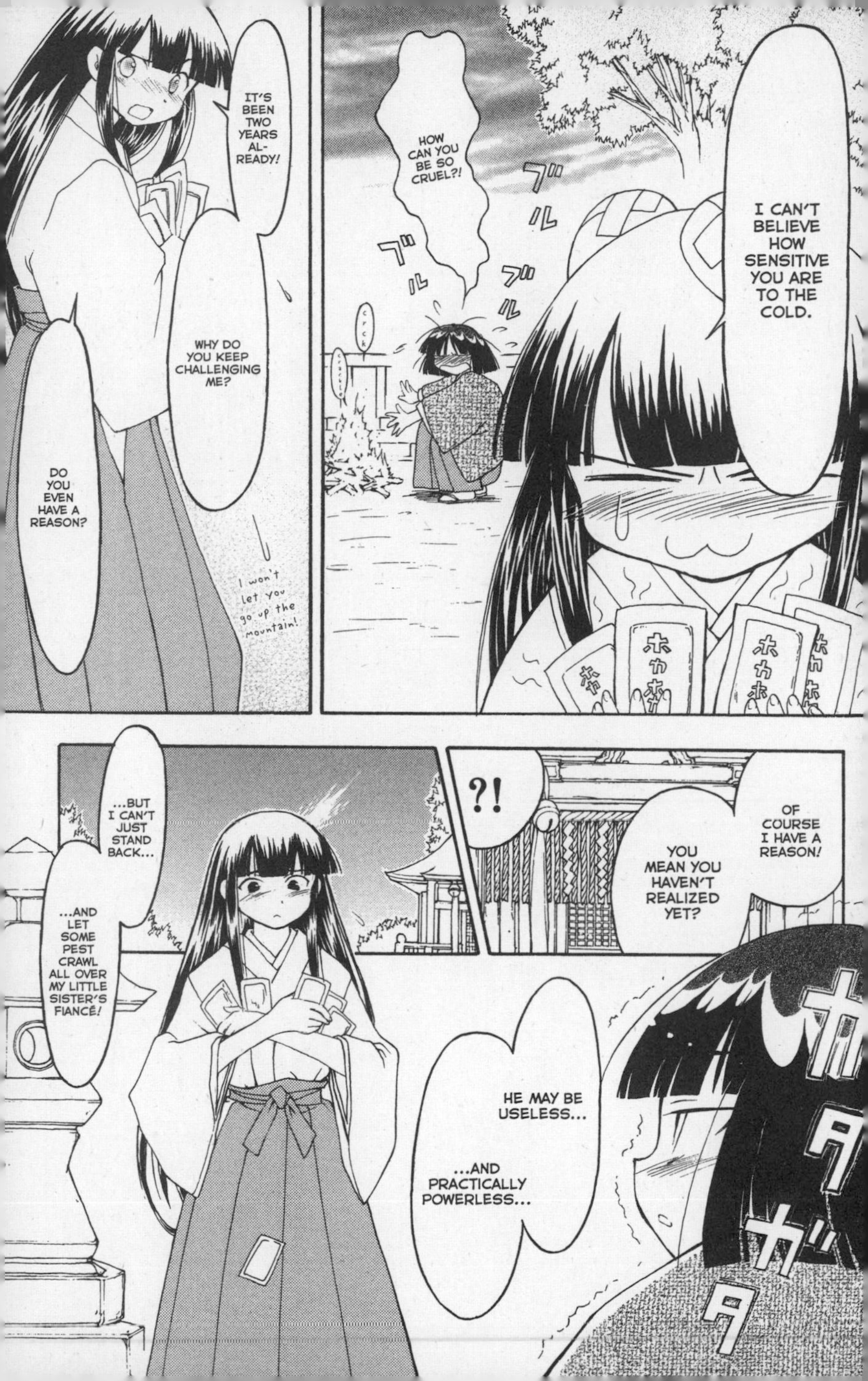
I CAN'T BELIEVE HOW SENSITIVE YOU ARE TO THE COLD.
ブル
ブル
ブル
HOW CAN YOU BE SO CRUEL?!
crck
crackle
IT'S BEEN TWO YEARS AL-READY!
WHY DO YOU KEEP CHALLENGING ME?
DO YOU EVEN HAVE A REASON?
I won't let you go up the mountain!
OF COURSE I HAVE A REASON!
YOU MEAN YOU HAVEN'T REALIZED YET?
?!
HE MAY BE USELESS...
...AND PRACTICALLY POWERLESS...
...BUT I CAN'T JUST STAND BACK...
...AND LET SOME PEST CRAWL ALL OVER MY LITTLE SISTER'S FIANCÉ!

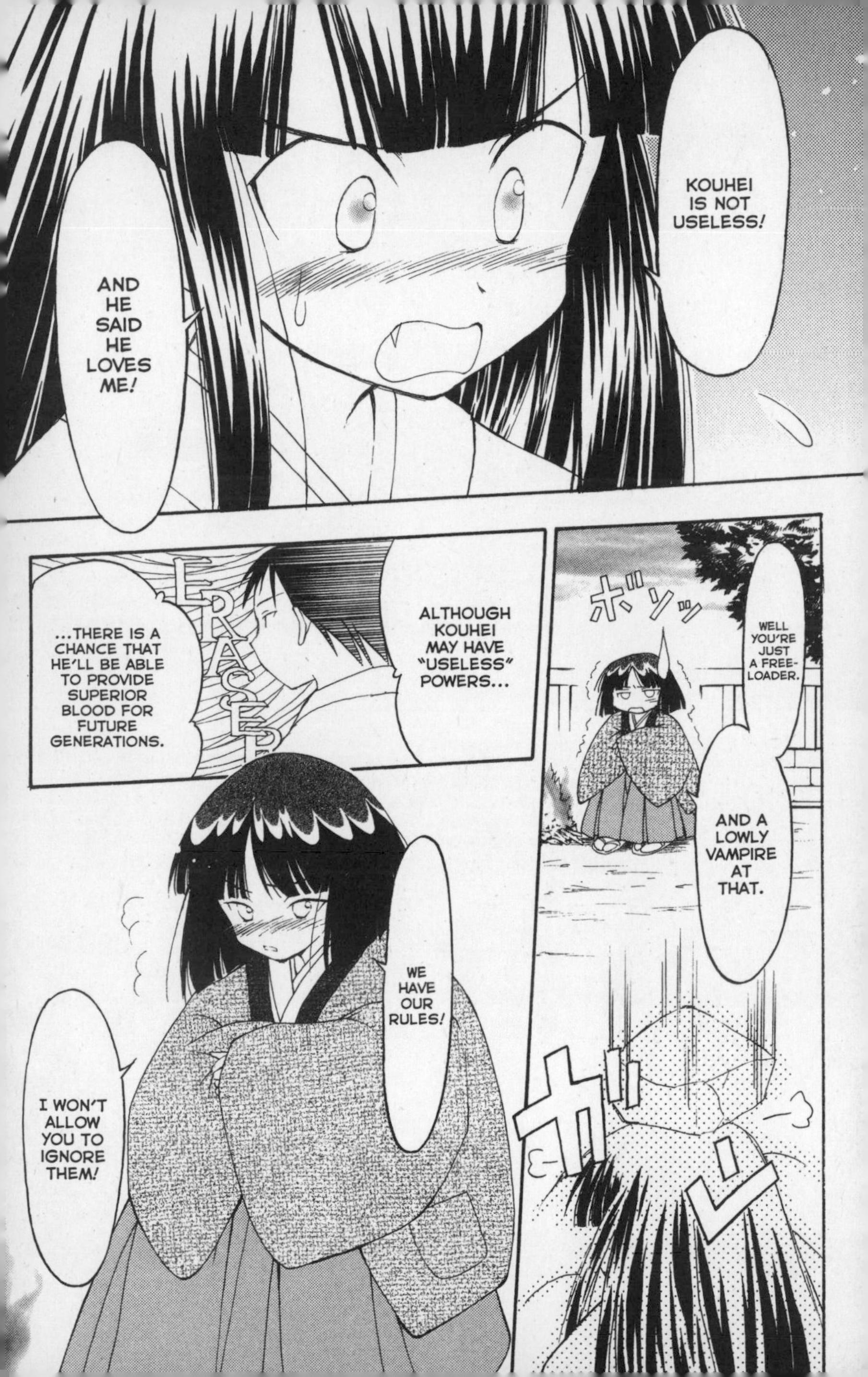
KOUHEI IS NOT USELESS!
AND HE SAID HE LOVES ME!
ボソッ
WELL YOU'RE JUST A FREE-LOADER.
AND A LOWLY VAMPIRE AT THAT.
ガーン
ALTHOUGH KOUHEI MAY HAVE "USELESS" POWERS...
ERASER
...THERE IS A CHANCE THAT HE'LL BE ABLE TO PROVIDE SUPERIOR BLOOD FOR FUTURE GENERATIONS.
WE HAVE OUR RULES!
I WON'T ALLOW YOU TO IGNORE THEM!

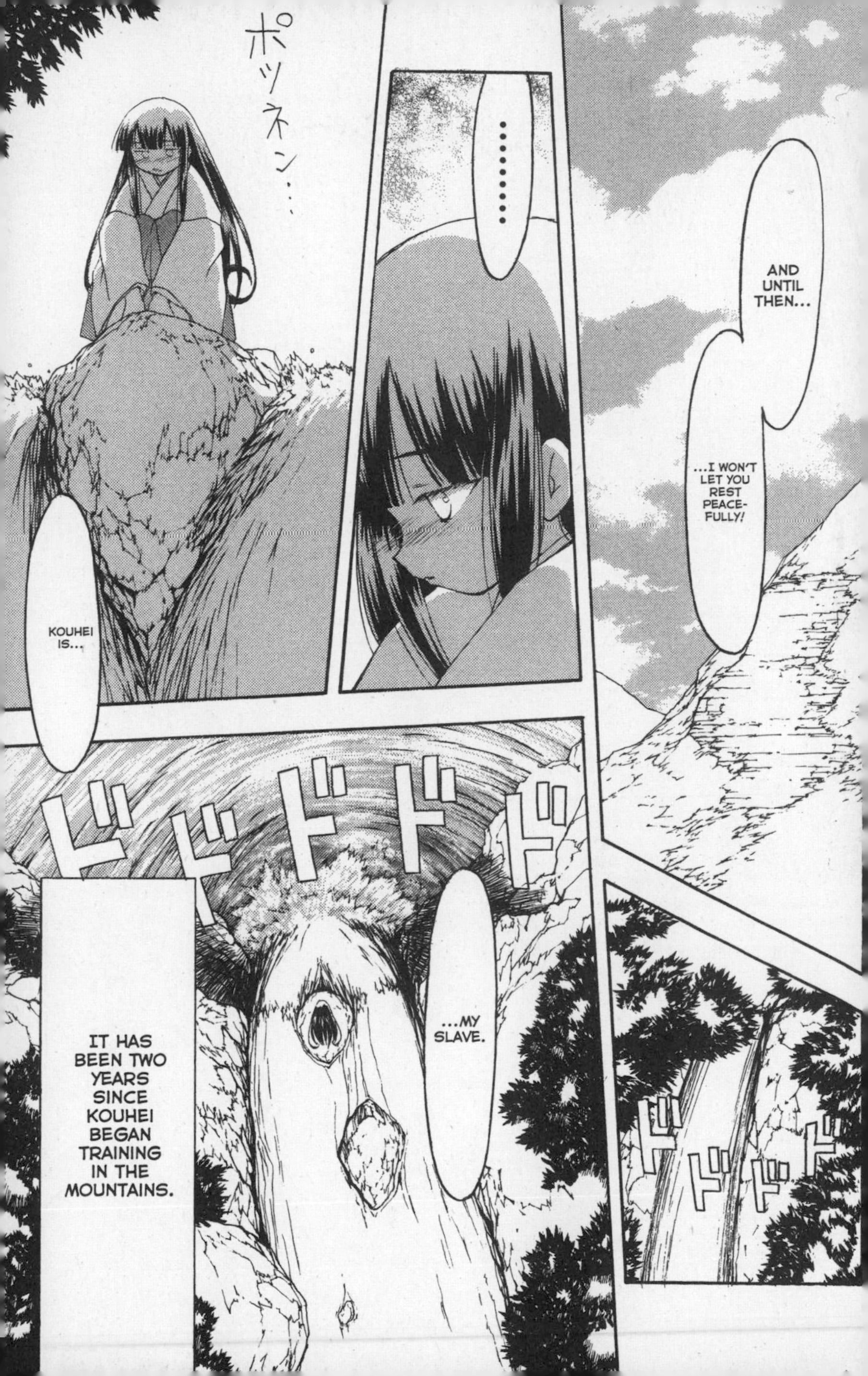
AND UNTIL THEN...
...I WON'T LET YOU REST PEACE-FULLY!
......
ポツネン...
KOUHEI IS...
ドドドド
ドドドド
...MY SLAVE.
IT HAS BEEN TWO YEARS SINCE KOUHEI BEGAN TRAINING IN THE MOUNTAINS.

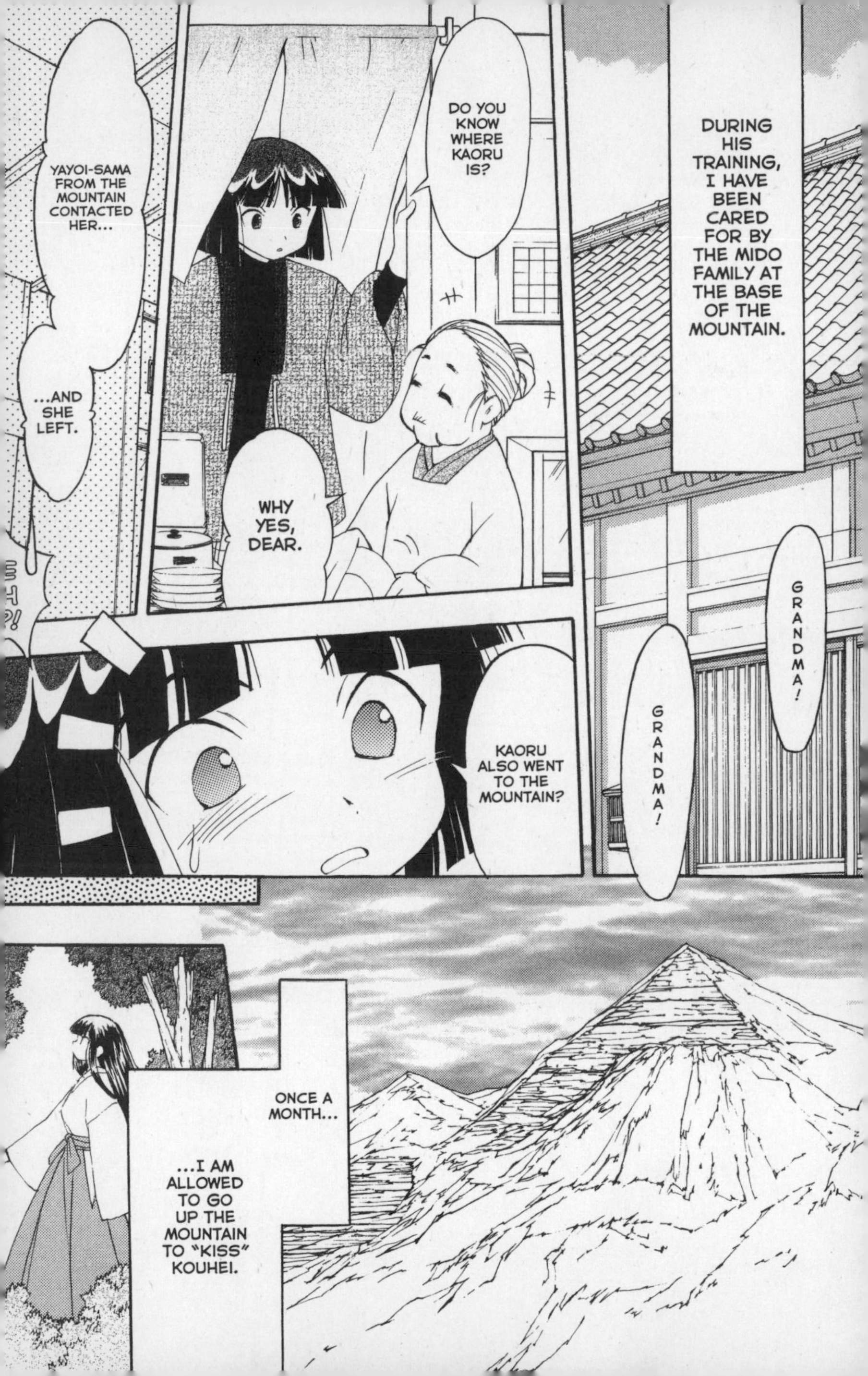
DURING HIS TRAINING, I HAVE BEEN CARED FOR BY THE MIDO FAMILY AT THE BASE OF THE MOUNTAIN.
GRANDMA!
GRANDMA!
DO YOU KNOW WHERE KAORU IS?
WHY YES, DEAR.
YAYOI-SAMA FROM THE MOUNTAIN CONTACTED HER...
...AND SHE LEFT.
KAORU ALSO WENT TO THE MOUNTAIN?
ONCE A MONTH...
...I AM ALLOWED TO GO UP THE MOUNTAIN TO "KISS" KOUHEI.

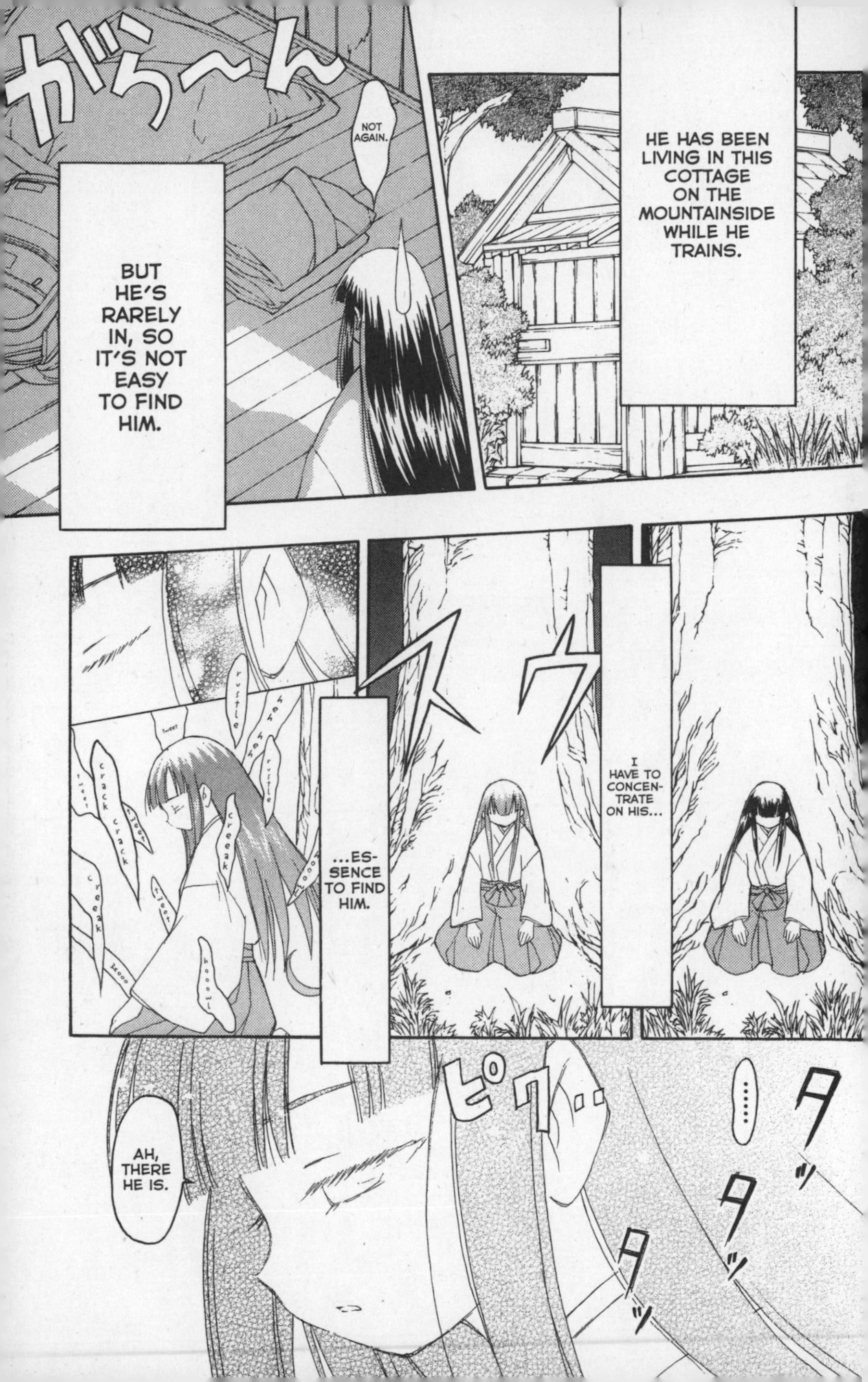
HE HAS BEEN LIVING IN THIS COTTAGE ON THE MOUNTAINSIDE WHILE HE TRAINS.
がら～ん
NOT AGAIN.
BUT HE'S RARELY IN, SO IT'S NOT EASY TO FIND HIM.
I HAVE TO CONCEN-TRATE ON HIS...
スゥ
...ES-SENCE TO FIND HIM.
rustle
heh heh
rustle
crack crack
creeak
creeak
tweet
hooowl
タッタッタッ
......
ピク..
AH, THERE HE IS.

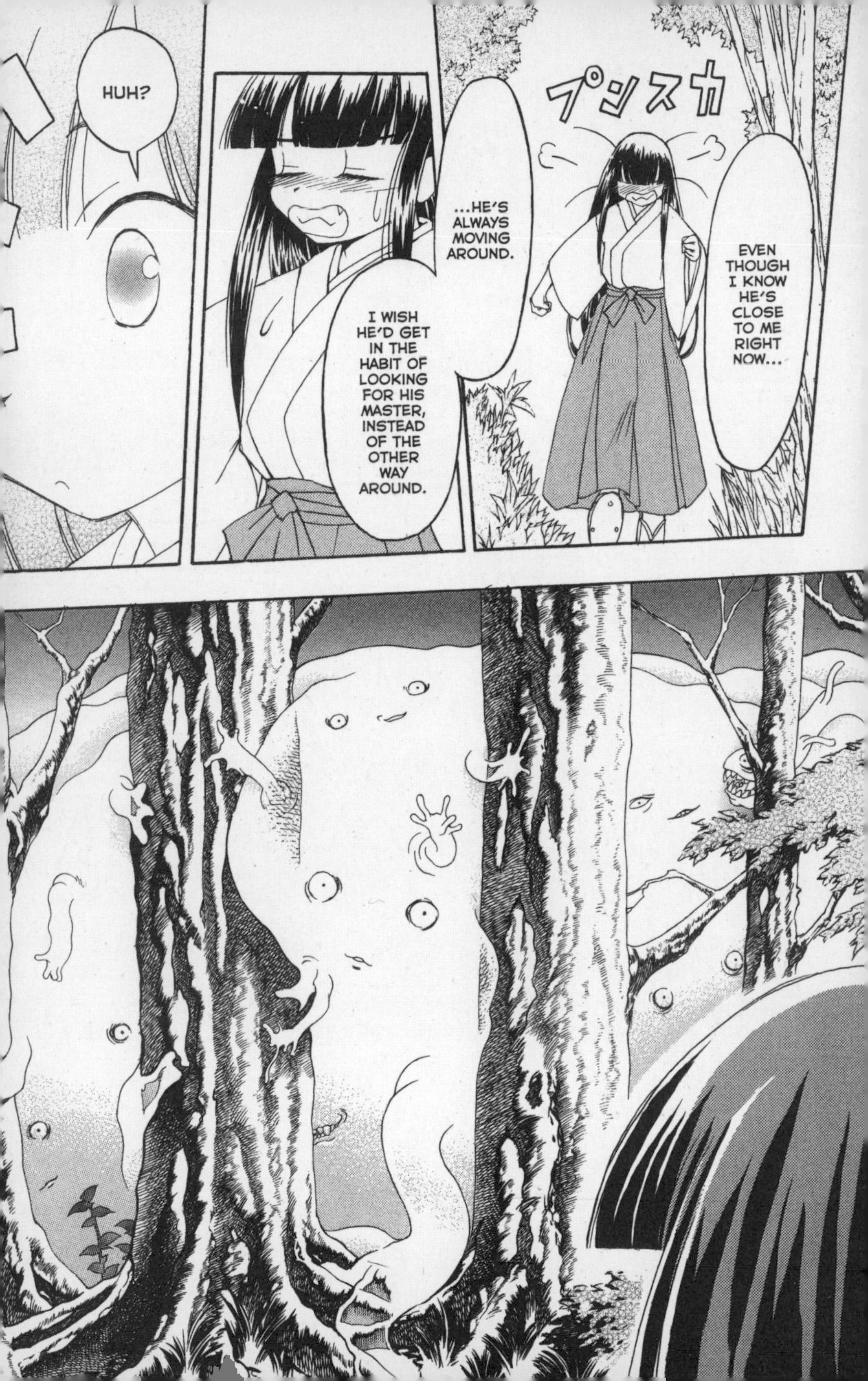
プンスカ
EVEN THOUGH I KNOW HE'S CLOSE TO ME RIGHT NOW...
...HE'S ALWAYS MOVING AROUND.
I WISH HE'D GET IN THE HABIT OF LOOKING FOR HIS MASTER, INSTEAD OF THE OTHER WAY AROUND.
HUH?

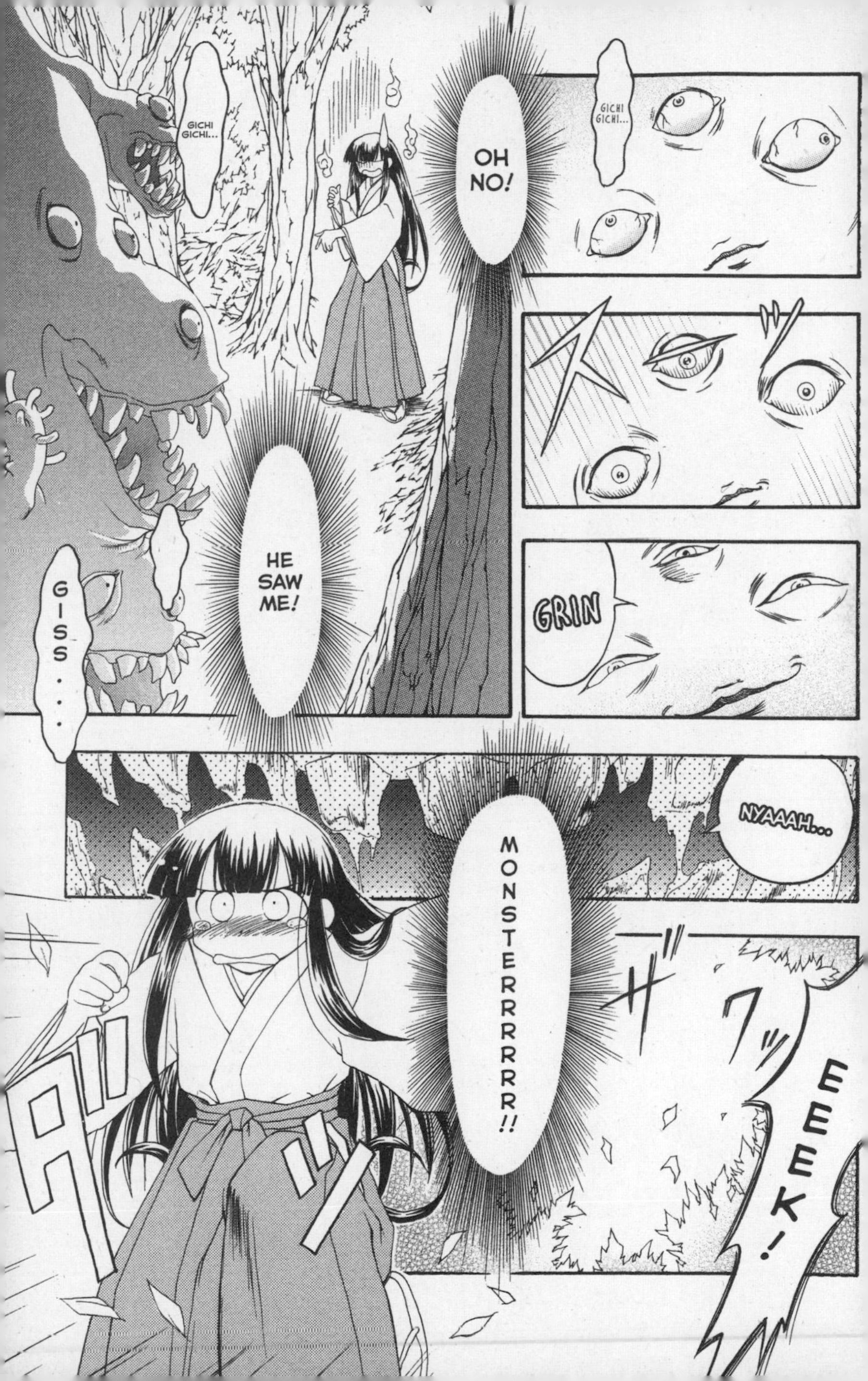
GICHI GICHI...
GRIN
OH NO!
GICHI GICHI...
HE SAW ME!
GISS...
NYAAAH...
MONSTERRRRRR!!
EEEK!

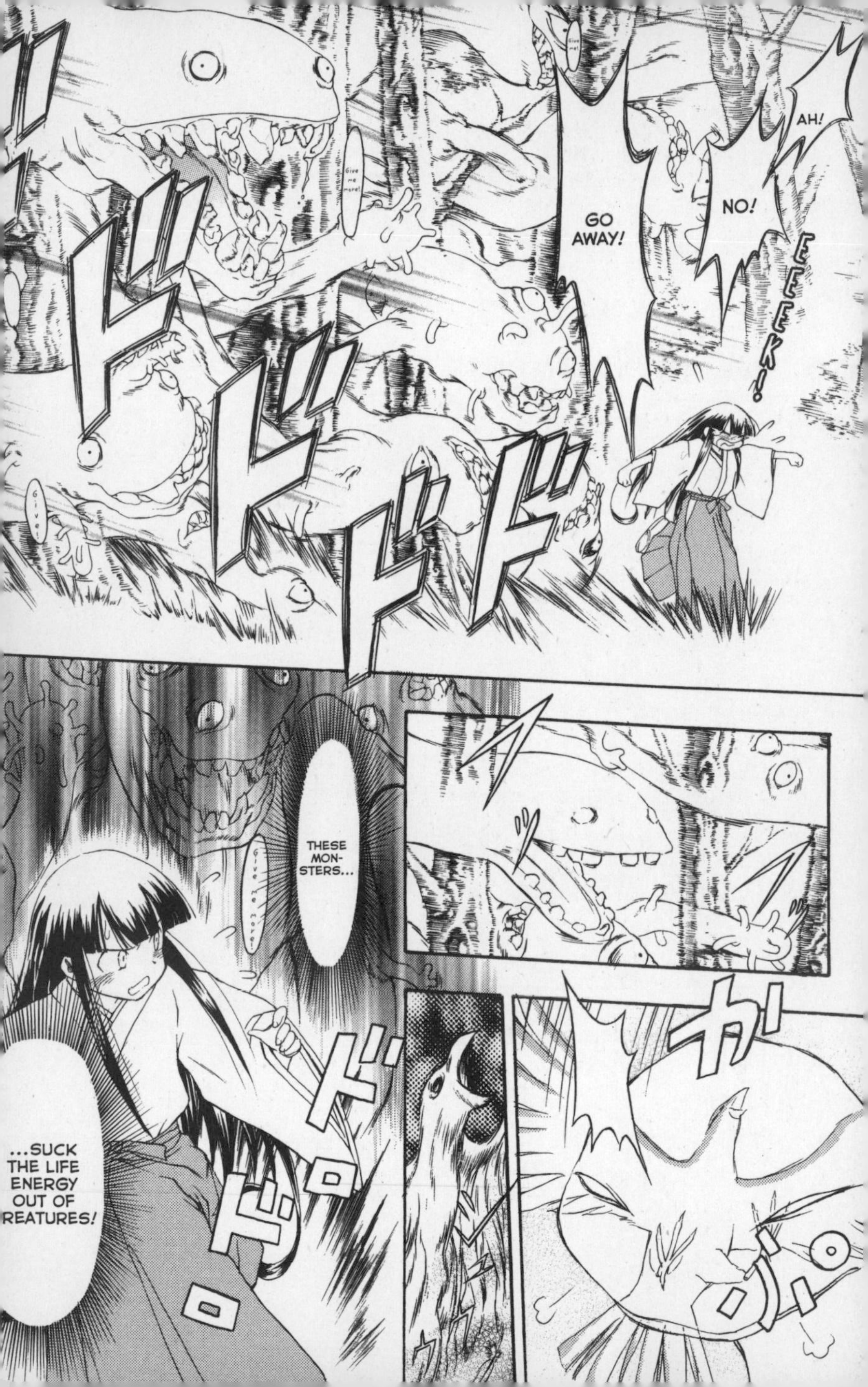
AH!
NO!
EEEEK!
GO AWAY!
Give me!
Give me more!
Give!
THESE MONSTERS...
Give me more!
...SUCK THE LIFE ENERGY OUT OF REATURES!

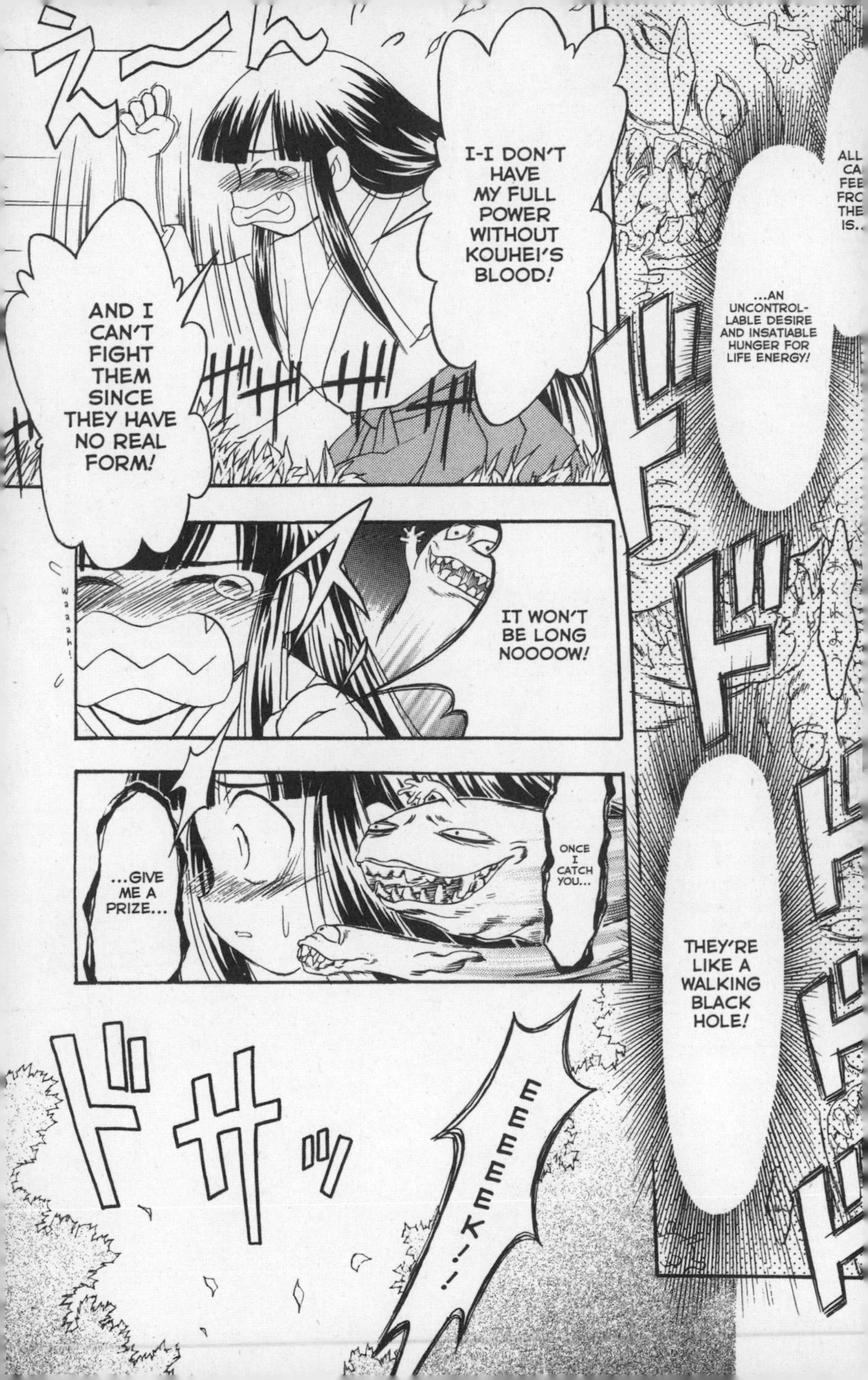
...AN UNCONTROLLABLE DESIRE AND INSATIABLE HUNGER FOR LIFE ENERGY!
THEY'RE LIKE A WALKING BLACK HOLE!
I-I DON'T HAVE MY FULL POWER WITHOUT KOUHEI'S BLOOD!
AND I CAN'T FIGHT THEM SINCE THEY HAVE NO REAL FORM!
IT WON'T BE LONG NOOOOW!
Waaah!
ONCE I CATCH YOU...
...GIVE ME A PRIZE...
EEEEEEK!!

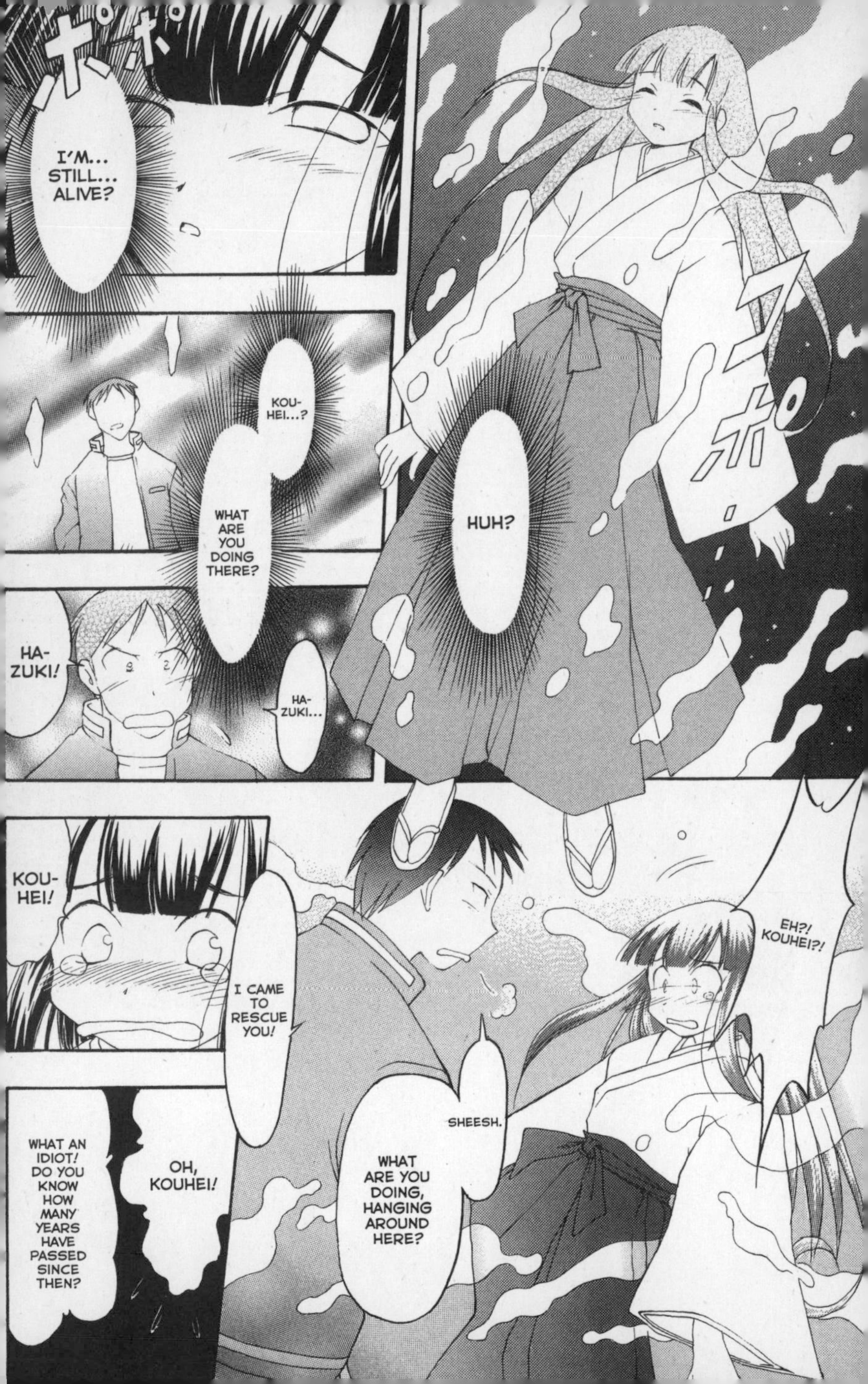
HUH?
I'M... STILL... ALIVE?
KOU-HEI...?
WHAT ARE YOU DOING THERE?
HA-ZUKI...
HA-ZUKI!
EH?! KOUHEI?!
I CAME TO RESCUE YOU!
SHEESH.
WHAT ARE YOU DOING, HANGING AROUND HERE?
KOU-HEI!
OH, KOUHEI!
WHAT AN IDIOT! DO YOU KNOW HOW MANY YEARS HAVE PASSED SINCE THEN?

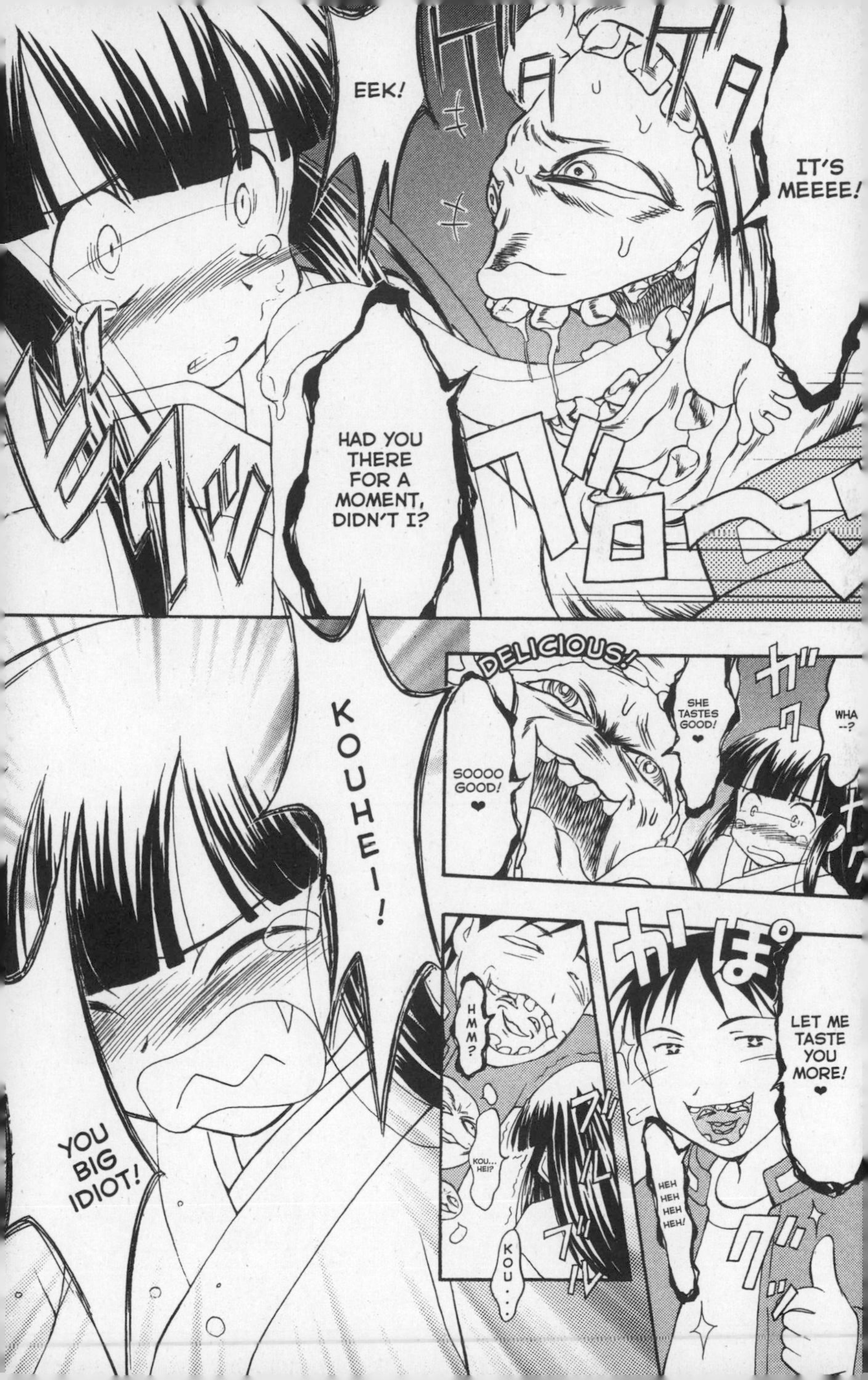
IT'S MEEEE!
EEK!
HAD YOU THERE FOR A MOMENT, DIDN'T I?
WHA --?
SHE TASTES GOOD! ❤
DELICIOUS!
SOOOO GOOD! ❤
LET ME TASTE YOU MORE! ❤
HEH HEH HEH HEH!
HMM?
KOU... HEI?
KOU...
KOUHEI!
YOU BIG IDIOT!

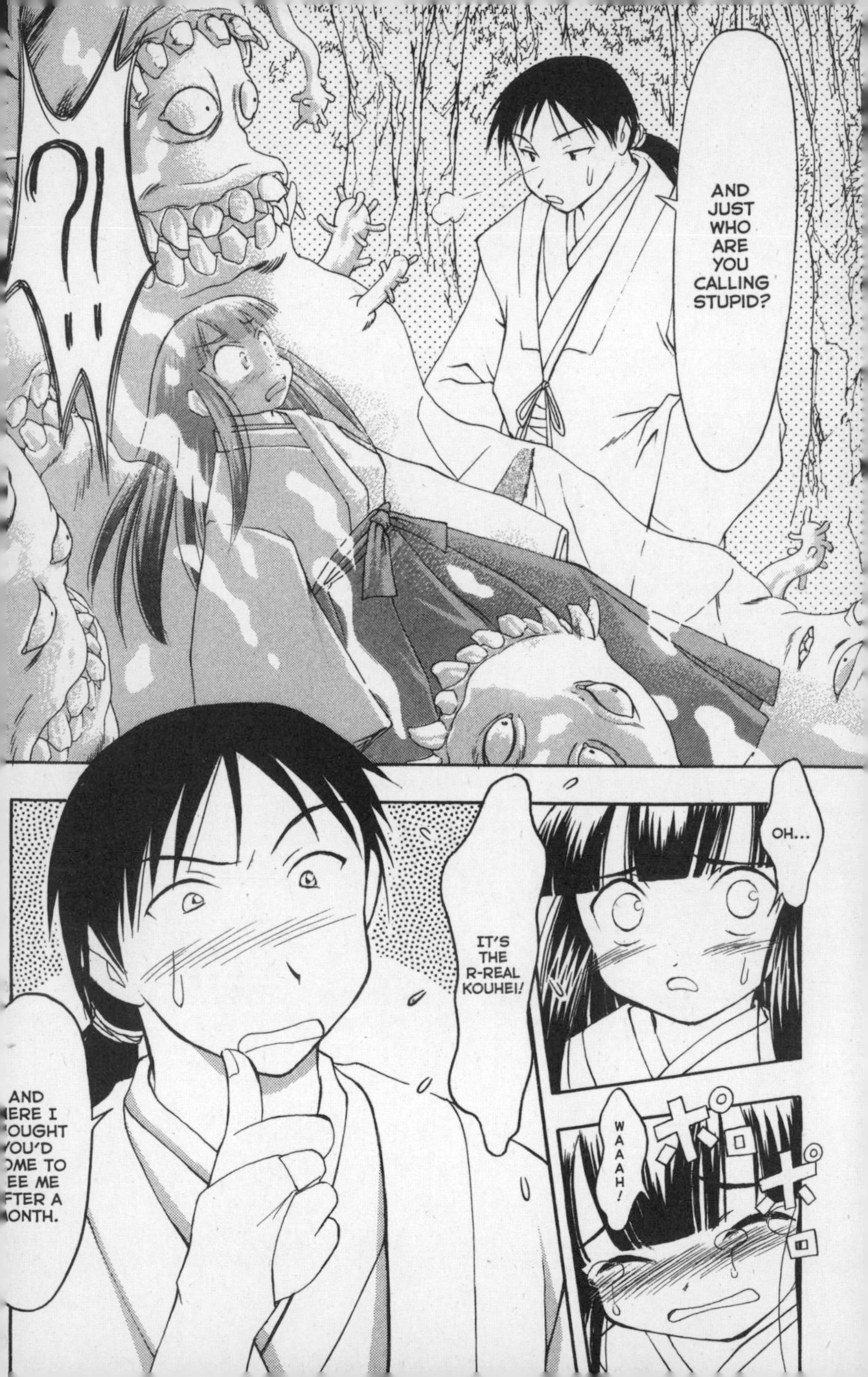
AND JUST WHO ARE YOU CALLING STUPID?
?!
OH...
IT'S THE R-REAL KOUHEI!
WAAAH!
AND
ERE I
OUGHT
YOU'D
OME TO
EE ME
FTER A
ONTH.

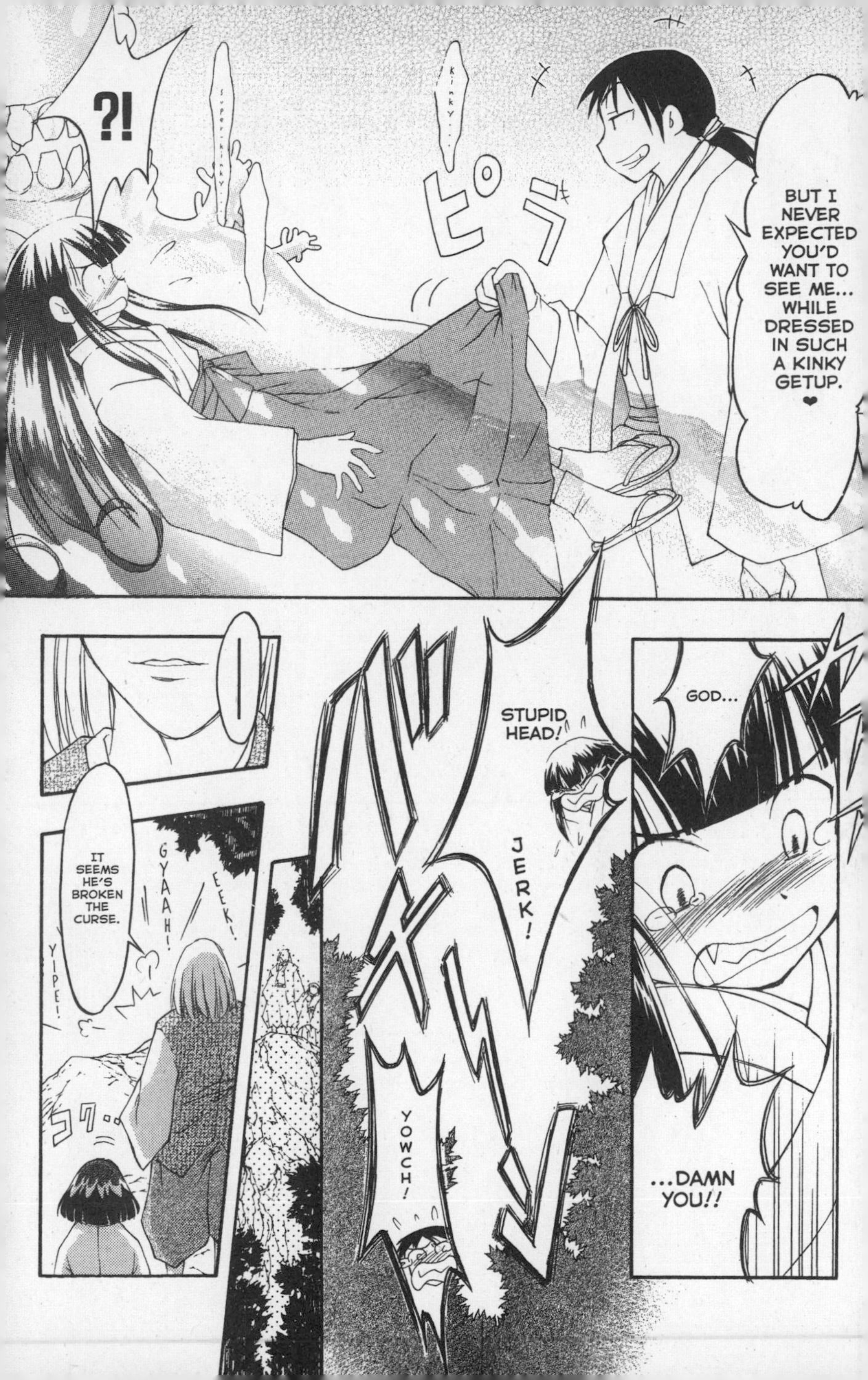

BUT I NEVER EXPECTED YOU'D WANT TO SEE ME... WHILE DRESSED IN SUCH A KINKY GETUP. ❤
kinky...
ピラ
super-kinky...
?!
GOD...
...DAMN YOU!!
STUPID HEAD!
JERK!
YOWCH!
IT SEEMS HE'S BROKEN THE CURSE.
GYAAH!
EEK!
YIPE!

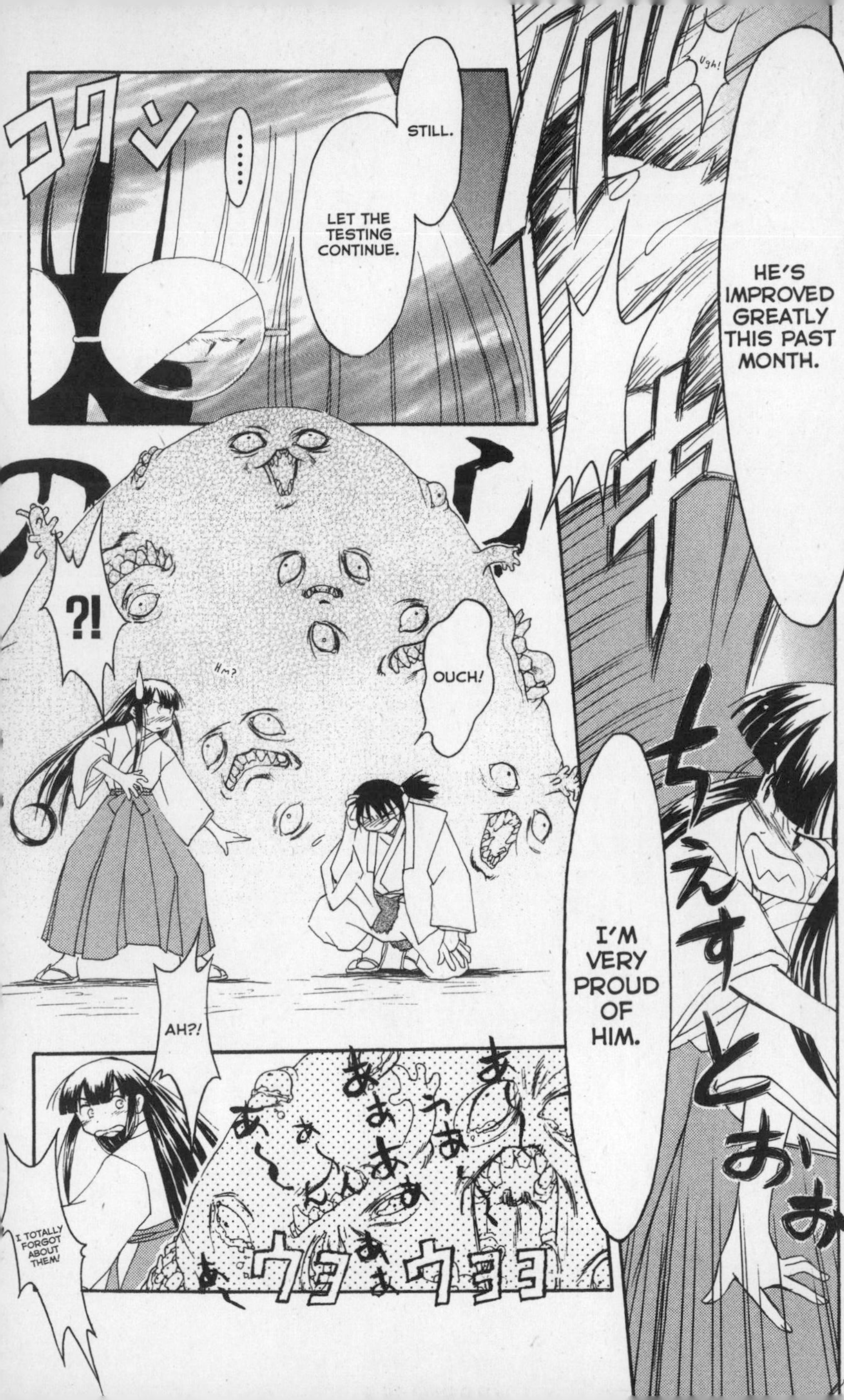
Ugh!
HE'S IMPROVED GREATLY THIS PAST MONTH.
I'M VERY PROUD OF HIM.
......
STILL.
LET THE TESTING CONTINUE.
?!
Hm?
OUCH!
AH?!
I TOTALLY FORGOT ABOUT THEM!

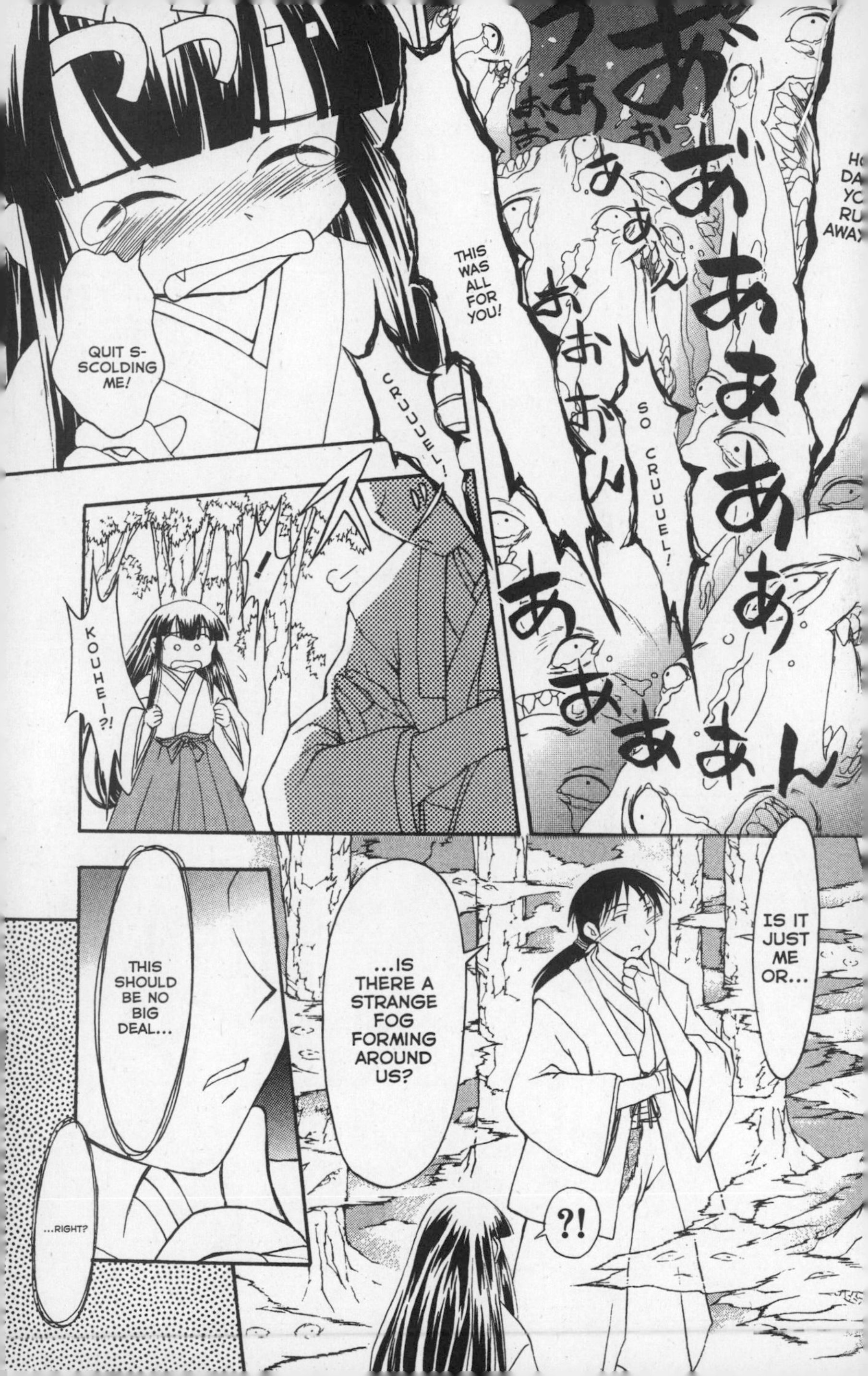
THIS WAS ALL FOR YOU!
SO CRUUUEL!
CRUUUEL!
QUIT S-SCOLDING ME!
KOUHEI-?!
!
IS IT JUST ME OR...
...IS THERE A STRANGE FOG FORMING AROUND US?
?!
THIS SHOULD BE NO BIG DEAL...
...RIGHT?

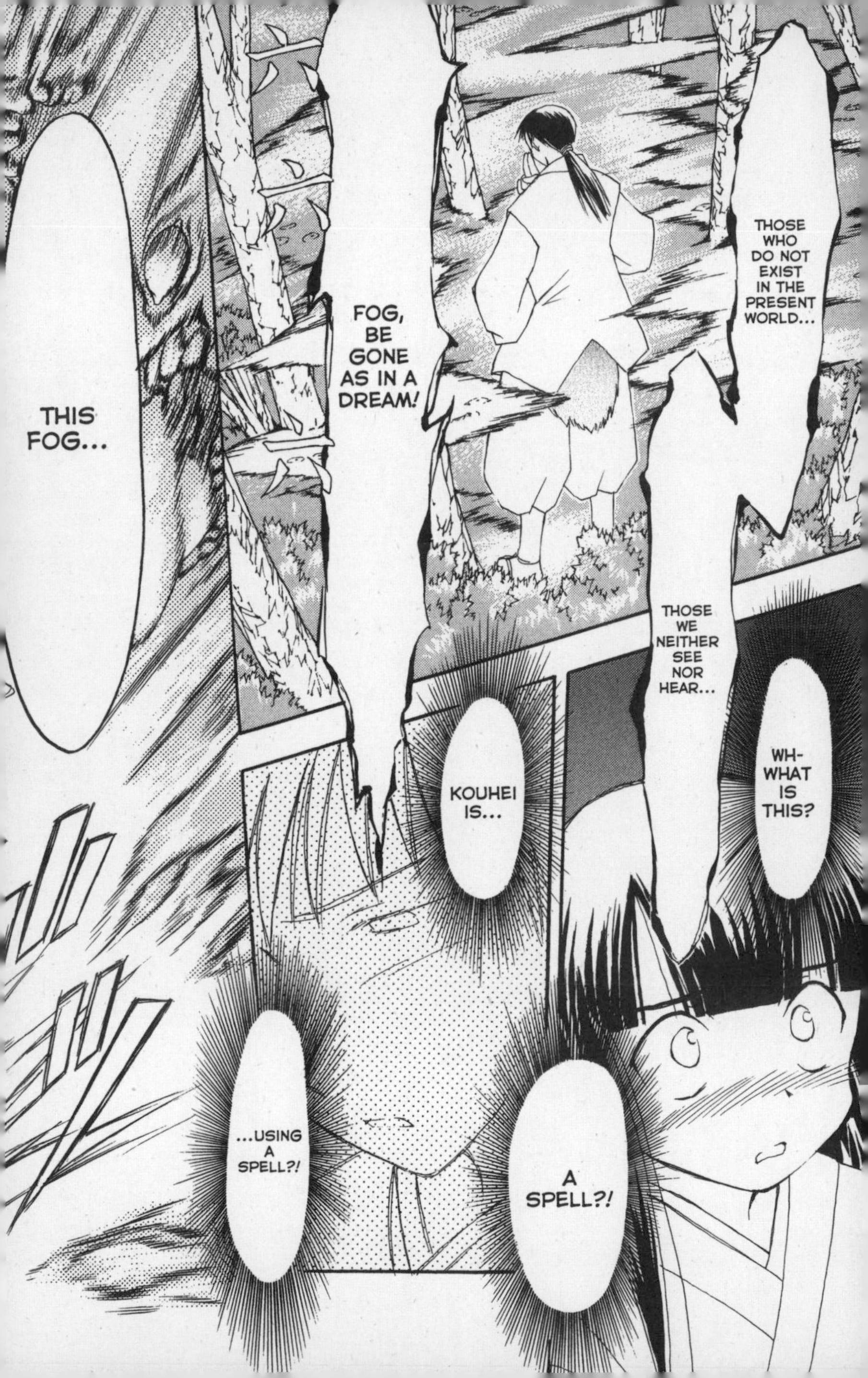
THOSE WHO DO NOT EXIST IN THE PRESENT WORLD...
THOSE WE NEITHER SEE NOR HEAR...
FOG, BE GONE AS IN A DREAM!
WH-WHAT IS THIS?
A SPELL?!
KOUHEI IS...
...USING A SPELL?!
THIS FOG...

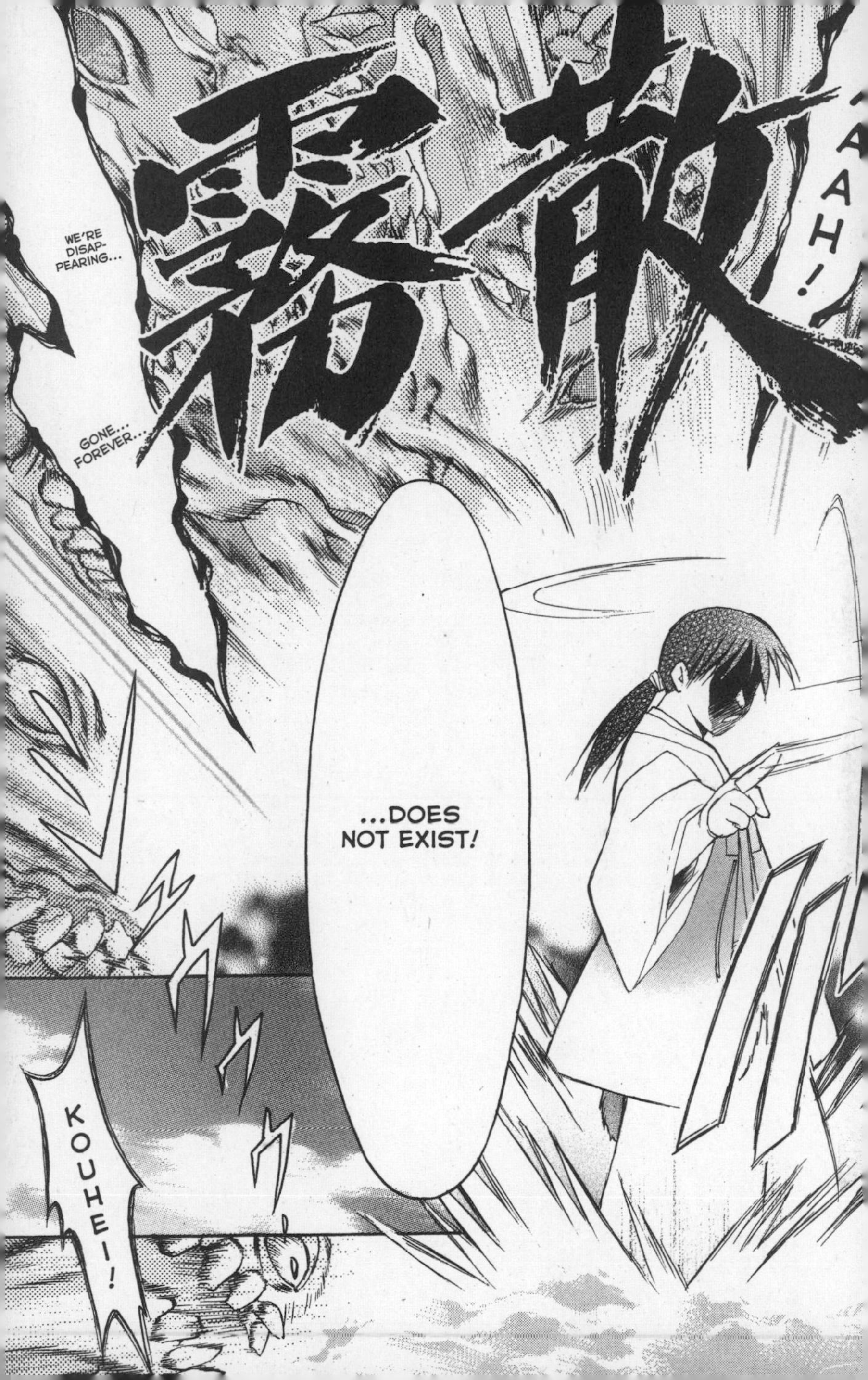
AAH!
霧散
WE'RE DISAPPEARING...
GONE... FOREVER...
...DOES NOT EXIST!
KOUHEI!

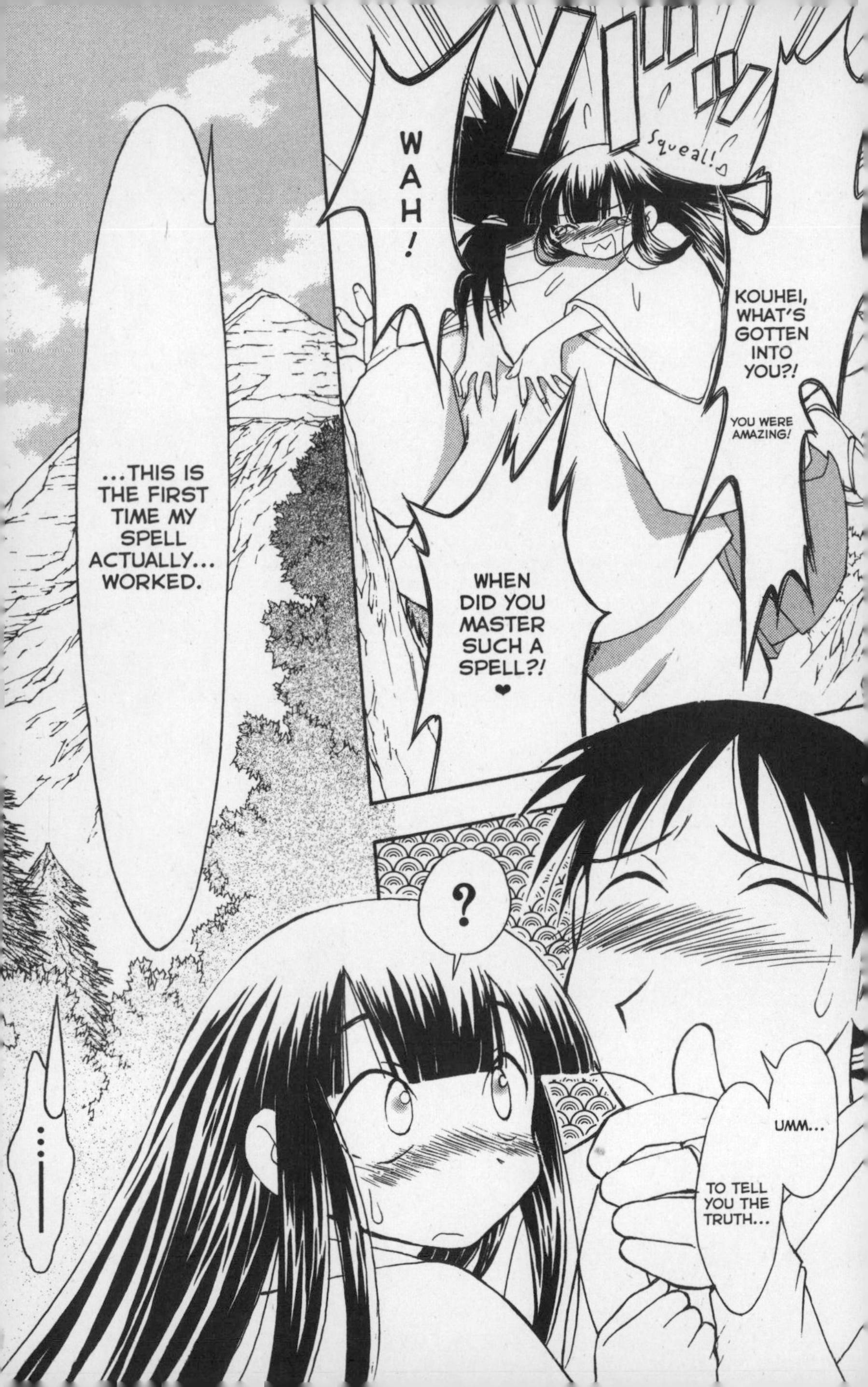

KOUHEI, WHAT'S GOTTEN INTO YOU?!
YOU WERE AMAZING!
Squeal!♡
WAH!
WHEN DID YOU MASTER SUCH A SPELL?! ❤
UMM...
TO TELL YOU THE TRUTH...
?
...THIS IS THE FIRST TIME MY SPELL ACTUALLY... WORKED.
...—

Moon 月詠 Phase

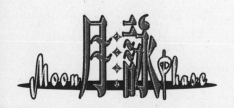

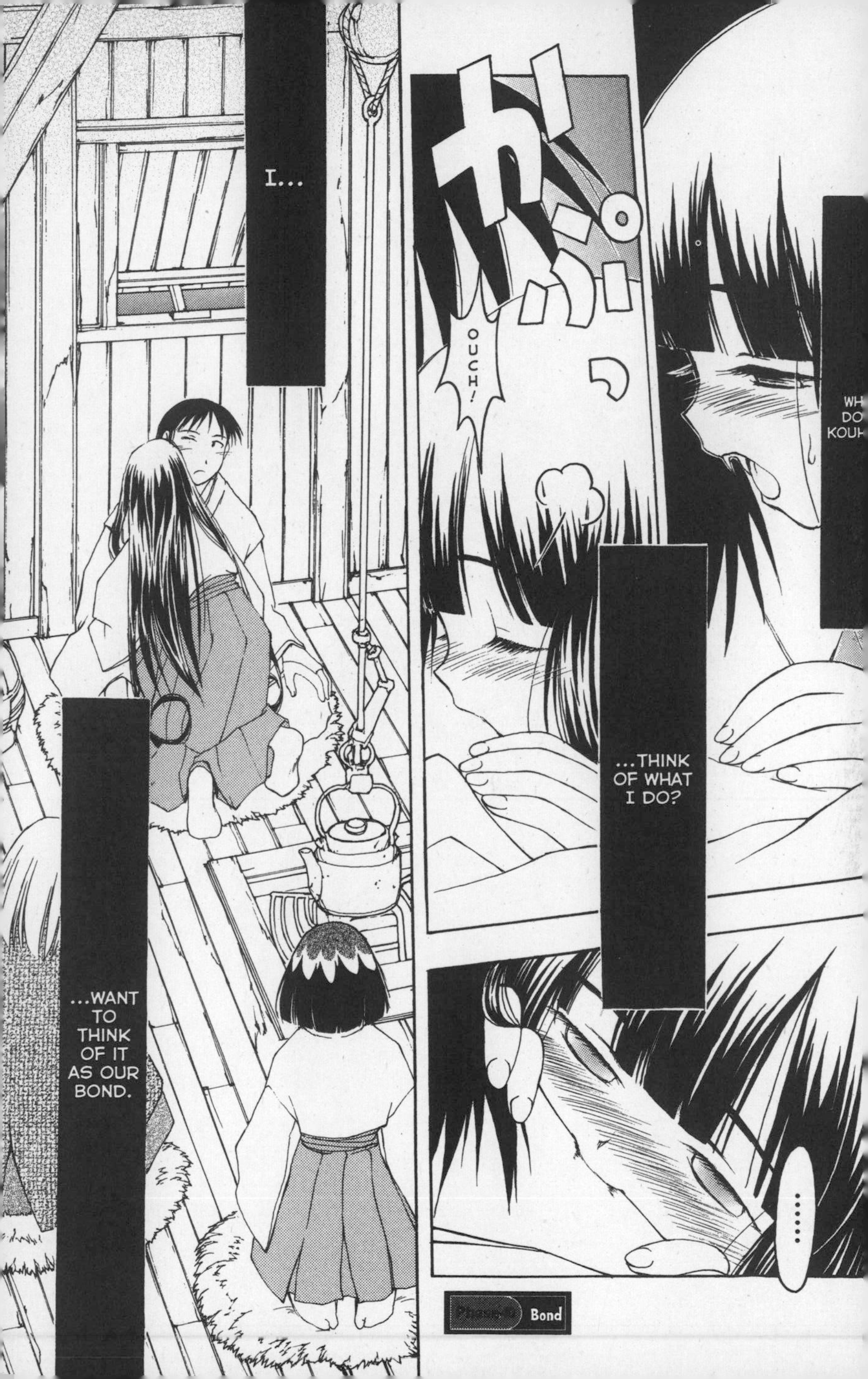
WH
DO
KOUH
OUCH!
...THINK OF WHAT I DO?
......
I...
...WANT TO THINK OF IT AS OUR BOND.
Bond

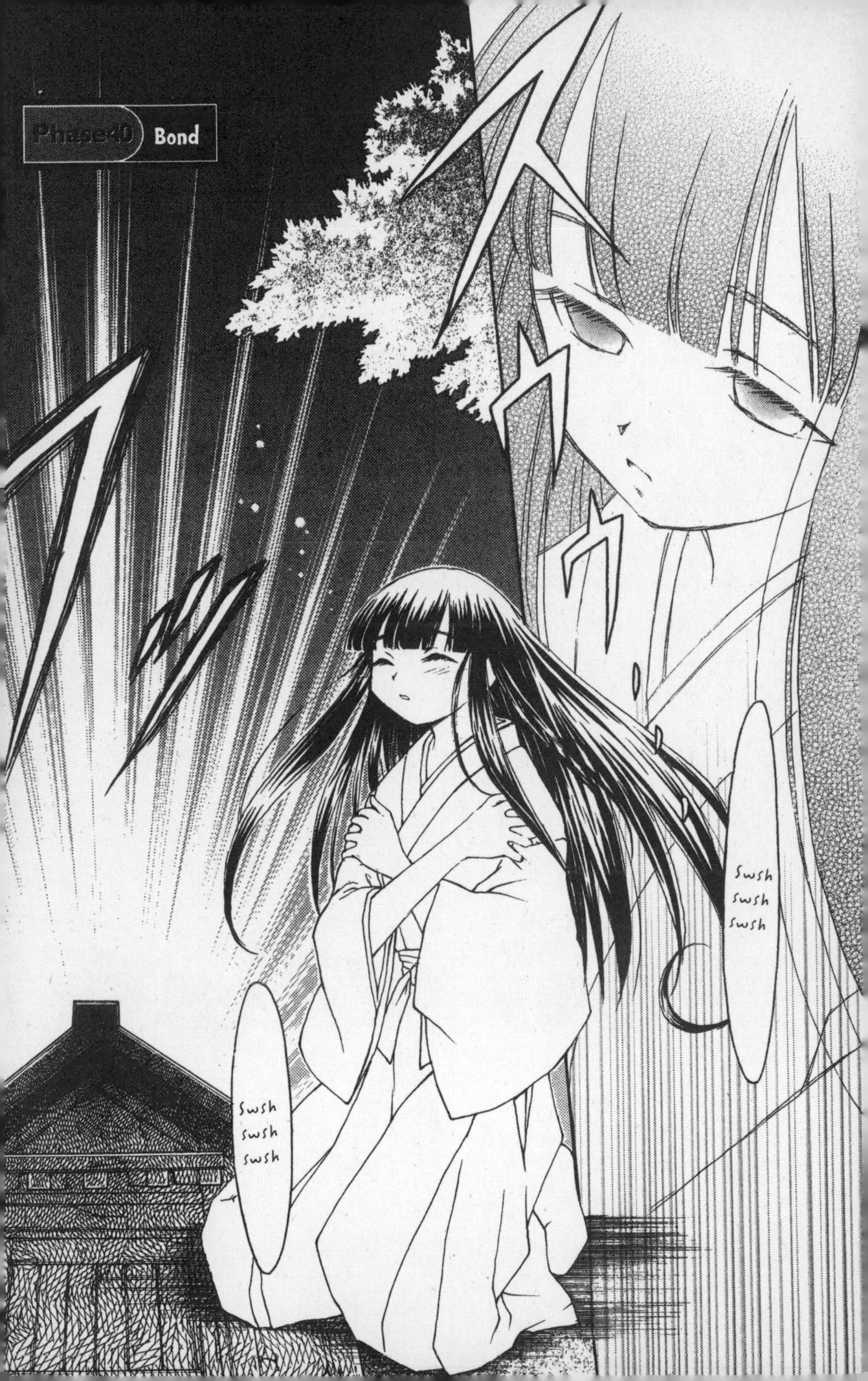
Phase40 Bond
Swsh swsh swsh
Swsh swsh swsh

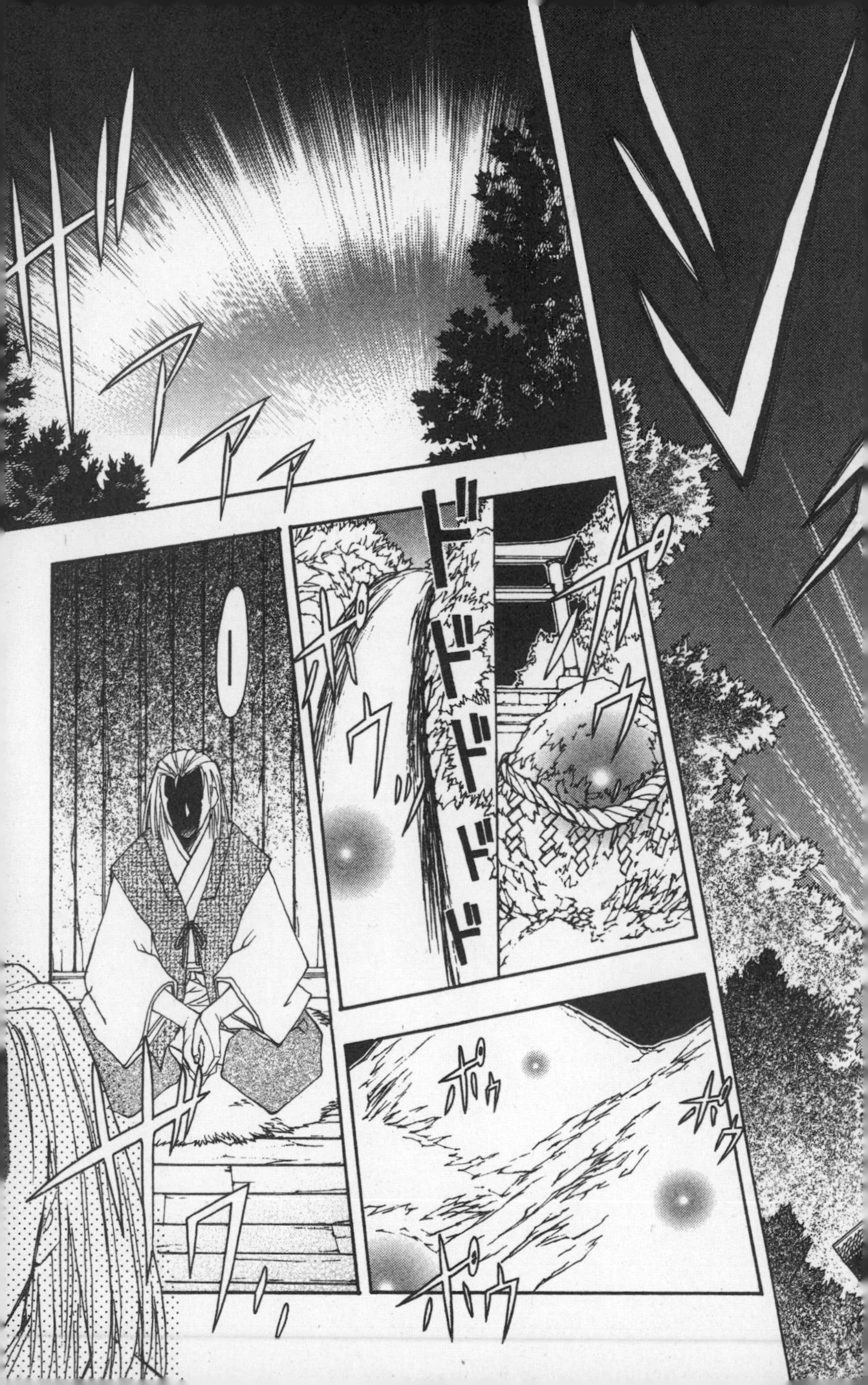

ザァァァ
ポゥ
ドドドドド
ポゥ
ポゥ
ポゥ
ポゥ

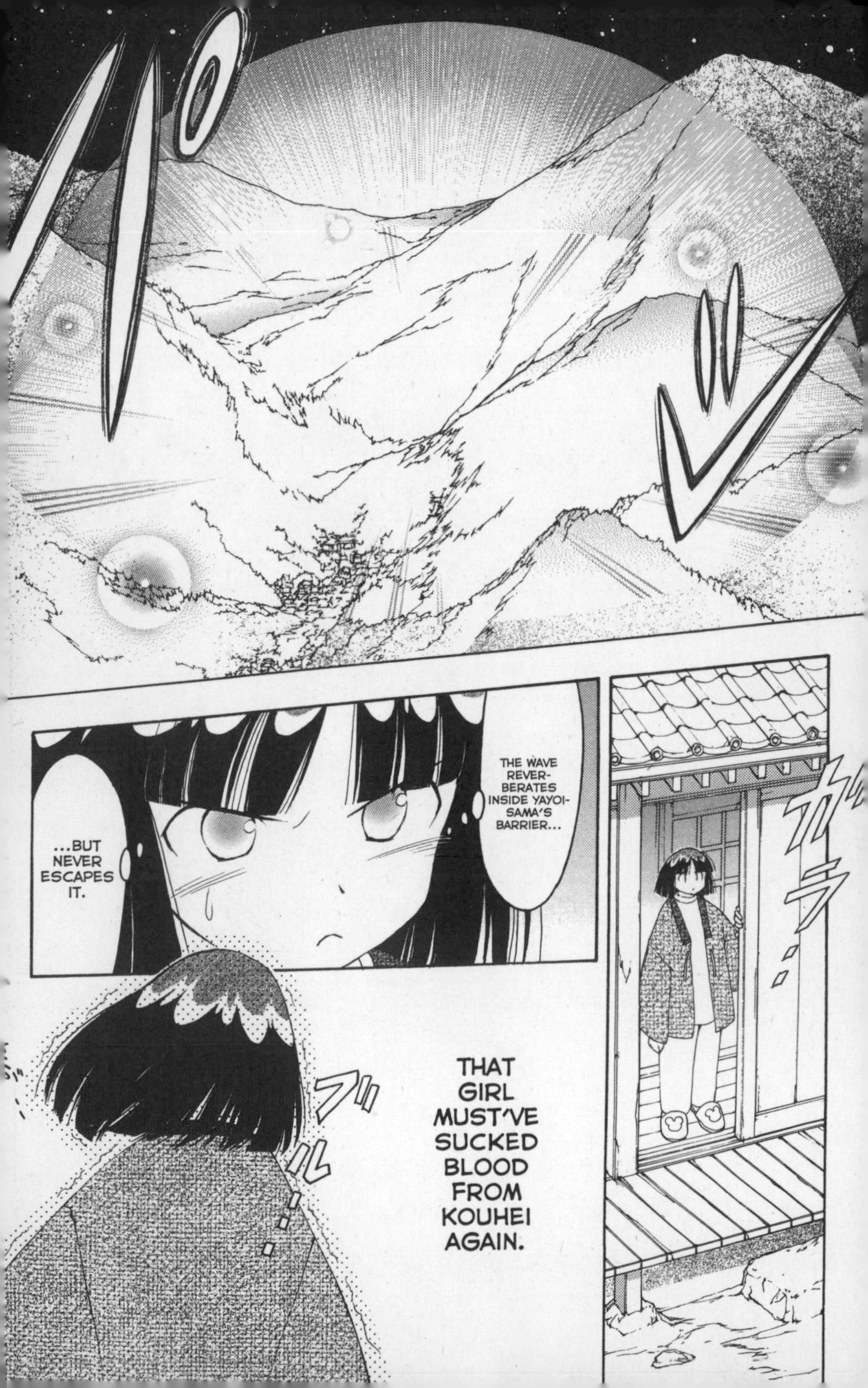
THE WAVE REVERBERATES INSIDE YAYOI-SAMA'S BARRIER...
...BUT NEVER ESCAPES IT.
THAT GIRL MUST'VE SUCKED BLOOD FROM KOUHEI AGAIN.

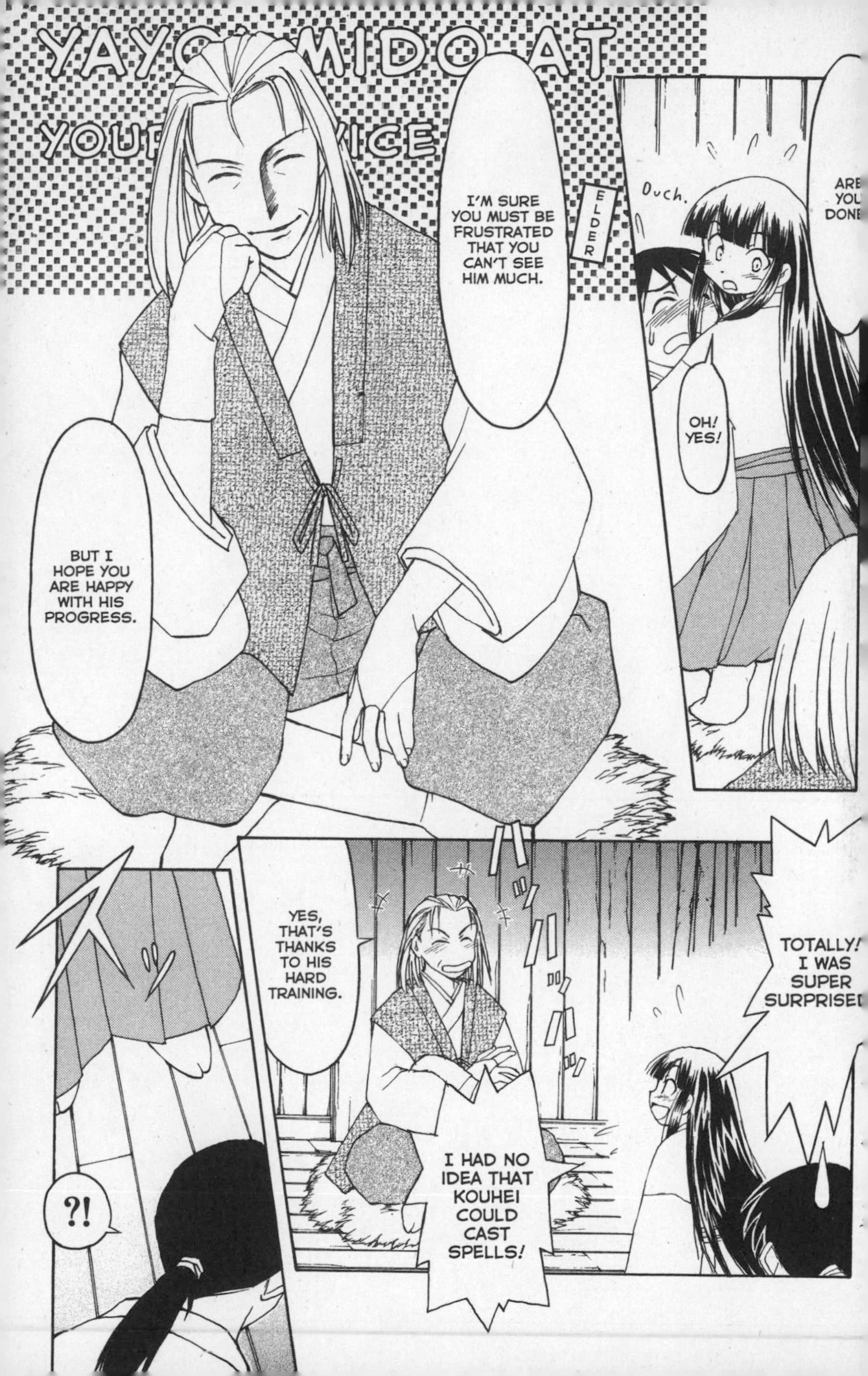
ARE YOU DONE
Ouch.
OH! YES!
YAYO MIDO AT YOU VICE
ELDER
I'M SURE YOU MUST BE FRUSTRATED THAT YOU CAN'T SEE HIM MUCH.
BUT I HOPE YOU ARE HAPPY WITH HIS PROGRESS.
TOTALLY! I WAS SUPER SURPRISED
I HAD NO IDEA THAT KOUHEI COULD CAST SPELLS!
YES, THAT'S THANKS TO HIS HARD TRAINING.
?!

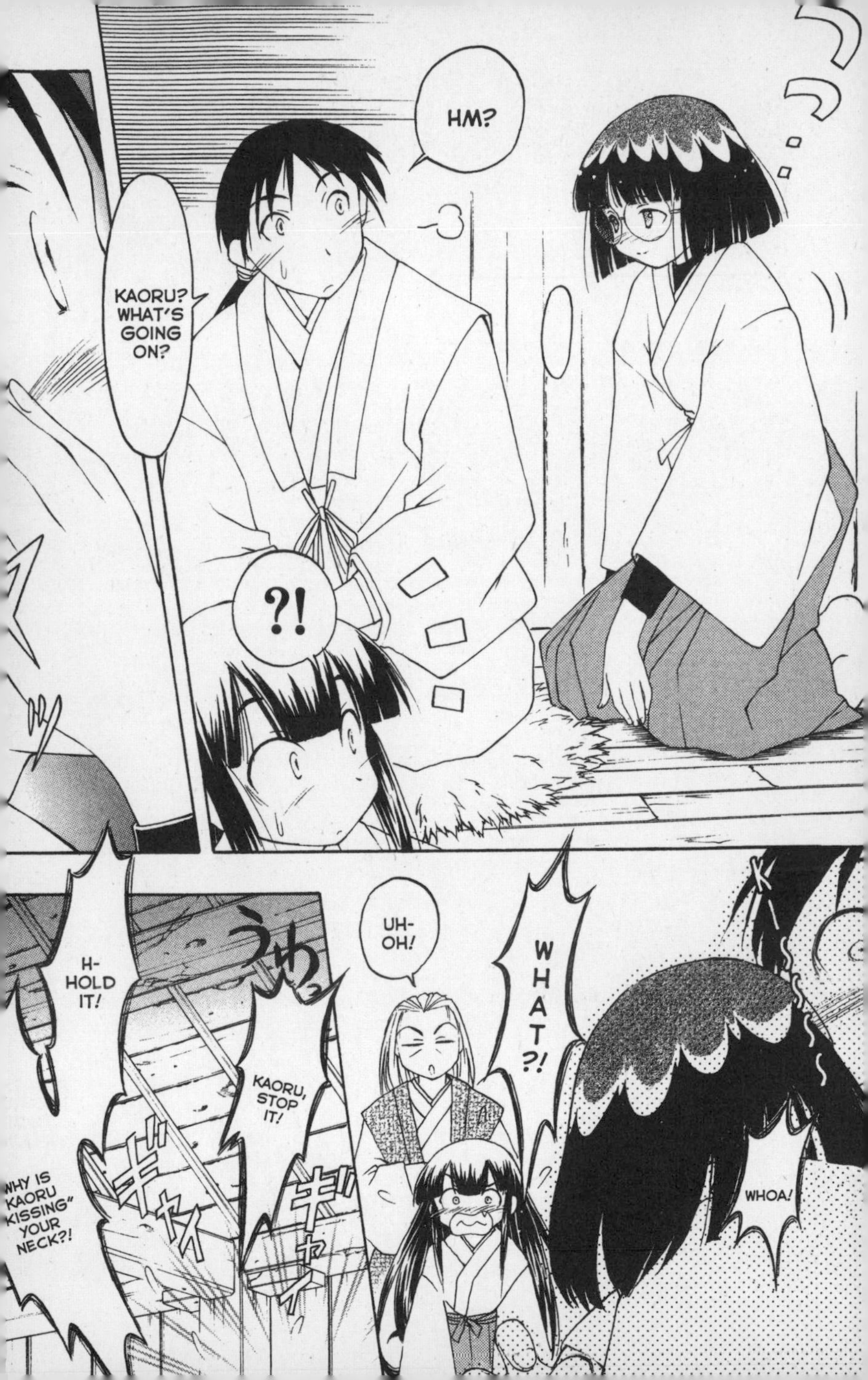
HM?
KAORU? WHAT'S GOING ON?
?!
WHOA!
WHAT?!
UH-OH!
KAORU, STOP IT!
うわっ
H-HOLD IT!
WHY IS KAORU "KISSING" YOUR NECK?!

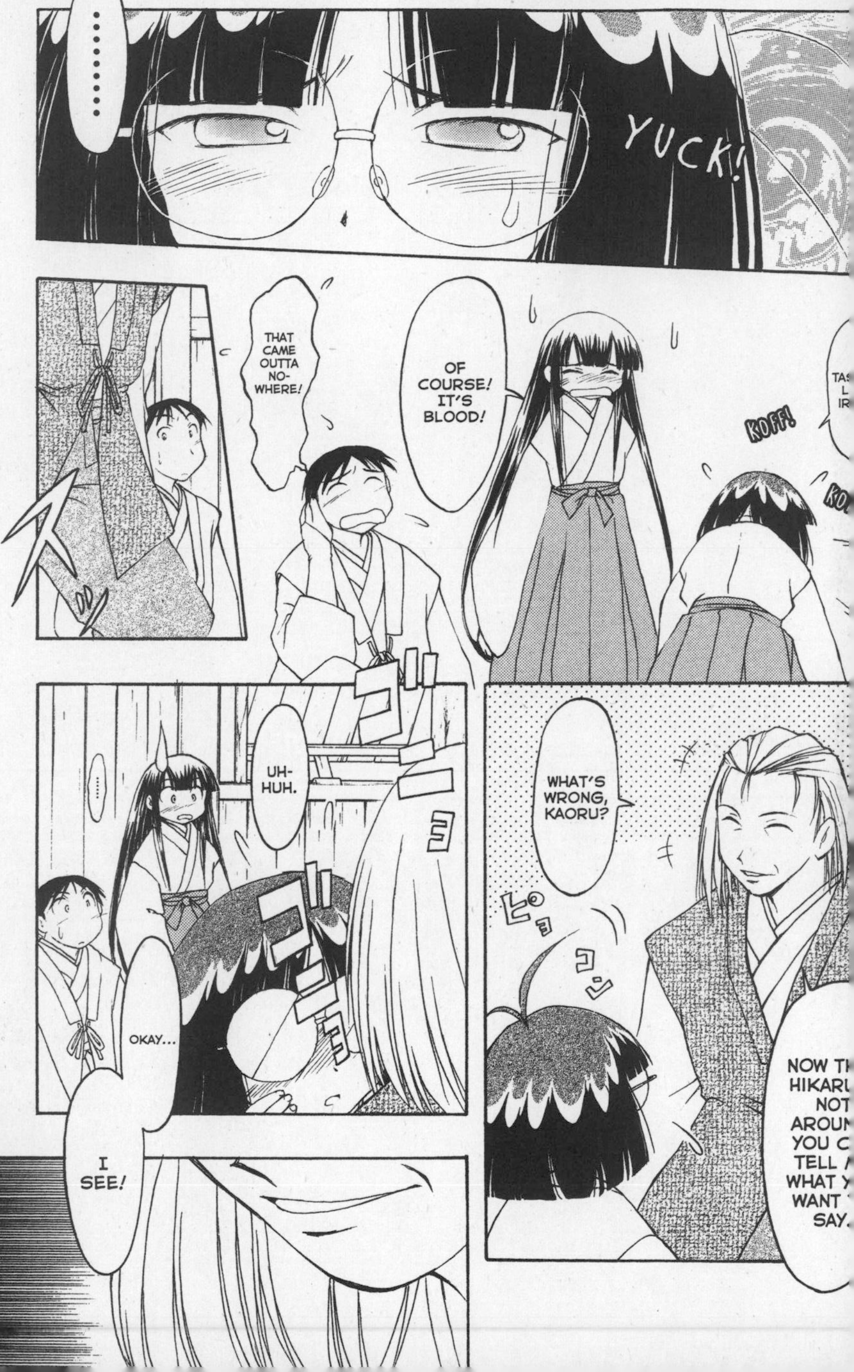
YUCK!
......
KOFF!
OF COURSE! IT'S BLOOD!
THAT CAME OUTTA NO-WHERE!
WHAT'S WRONG, KAORU?
UH-HUH.
......
OKAY...
I SEE!

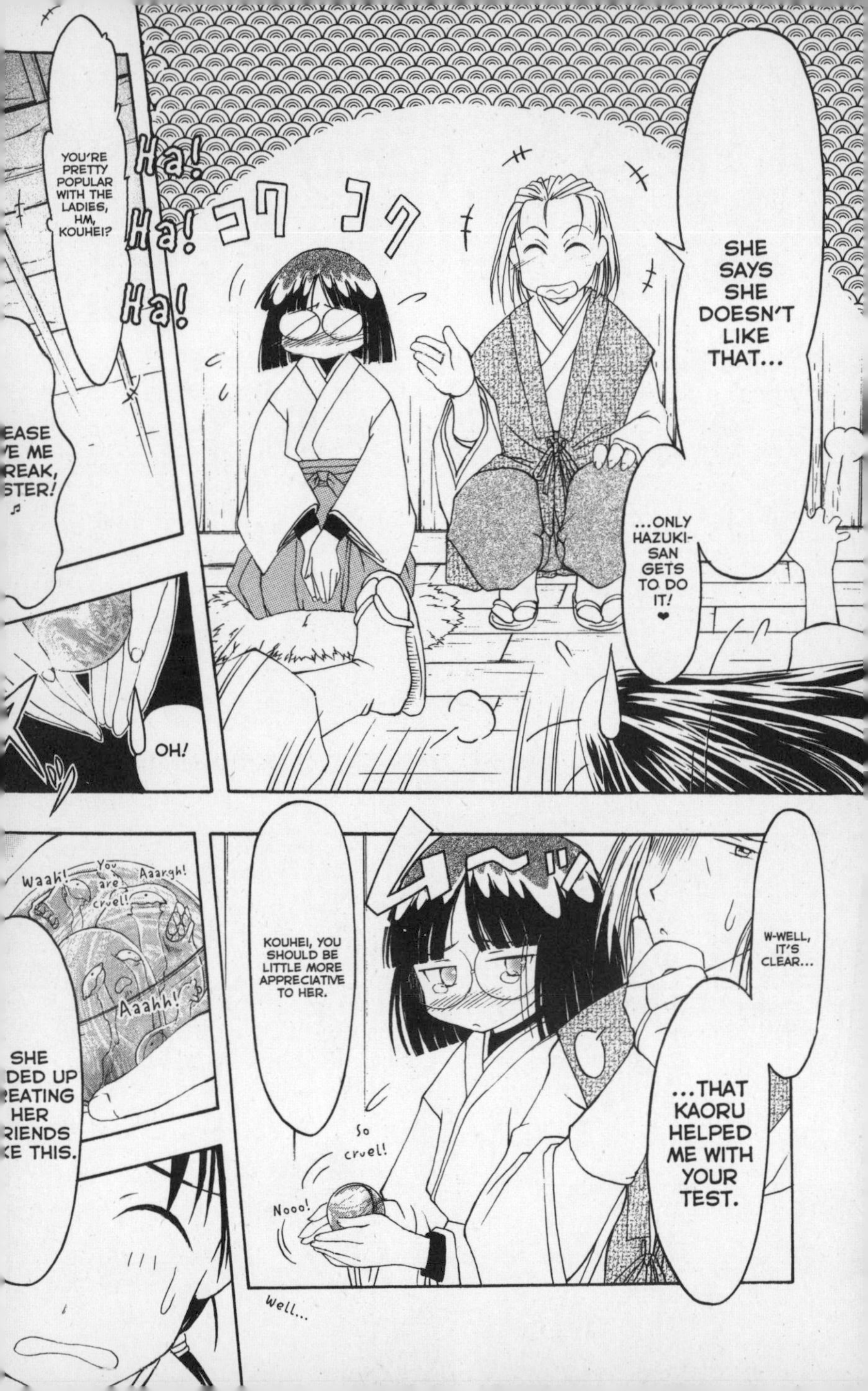
SHE SAYS SHE DOESN'T LIKE THAT...
...ONLY HAZUKI-SAN GETS TO DO IT! ❤
コク コク
Ha! Ha! Ha!
YOU'RE PRETTY POPULAR WITH THE LADIES, HM, KOUHEI?
EASE 'E ME REAK, STER! ♪
OH!
W-WELL, IT'S CLEAR...
...THAT KAORU HELPED ME WITH YOUR TEST.
KOUHEI, YOU SHOULD BE LITTLE MORE APPRECIATIVE TO HER.
So cruel!
Nooo!
Waah!
You are cruel!
Aaargh!
Aaahh!
SHE DED UP REATING HER RIENDS KE THIS.
Well...

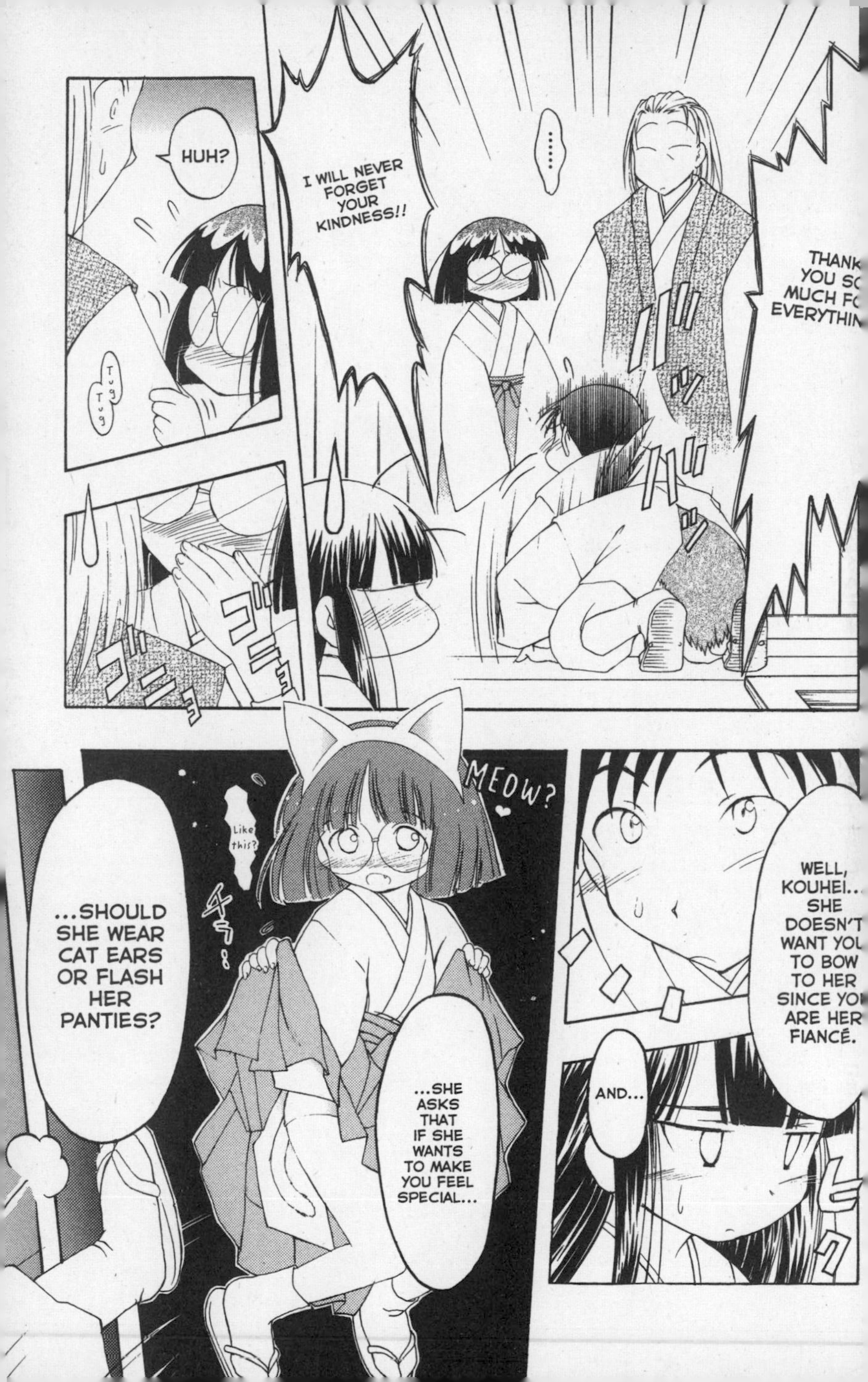

THANK YOU SO MUCH FO EVERYTHIN
I WILL NEVER FORGET YOUR KINDNESS!!
......
HUH?
Tug Tug
WELL, KOUHEI... SHE DOESN'T WANT YOU TO BOW TO HER SINCE YOU ARE HER FIANCÉ.
AND...
...SHE ASKS THAT IF SHE WANTS TO MAKE YOU FEEL SPECIAL...
...SHOULD SHE WEAR CAT EARS OR FLASH HER PANTIES?
MEOW?
Like this?

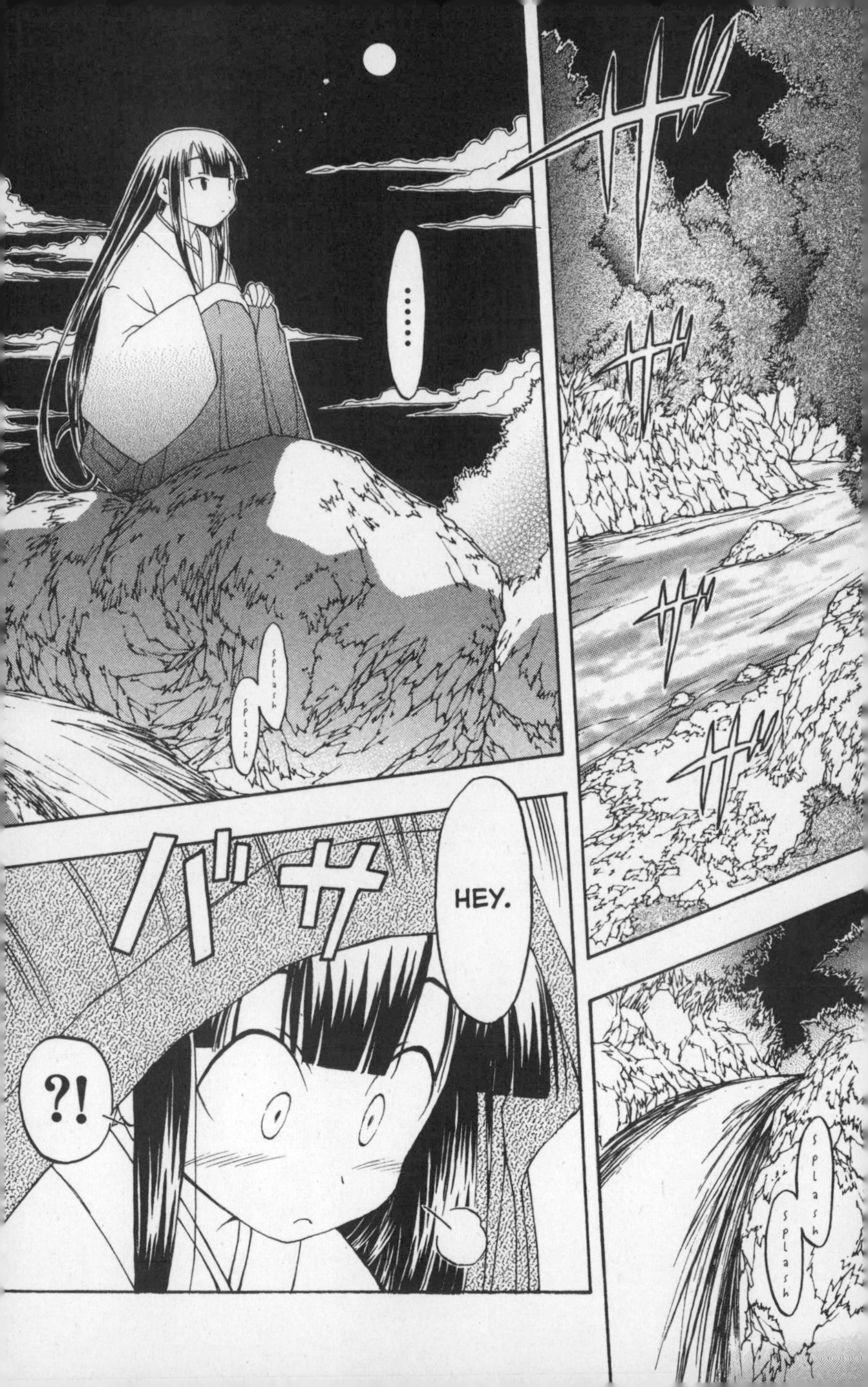
......
SPLASH
SPLASH
SPLASH
SPLASH
バサ
HEY.
?!

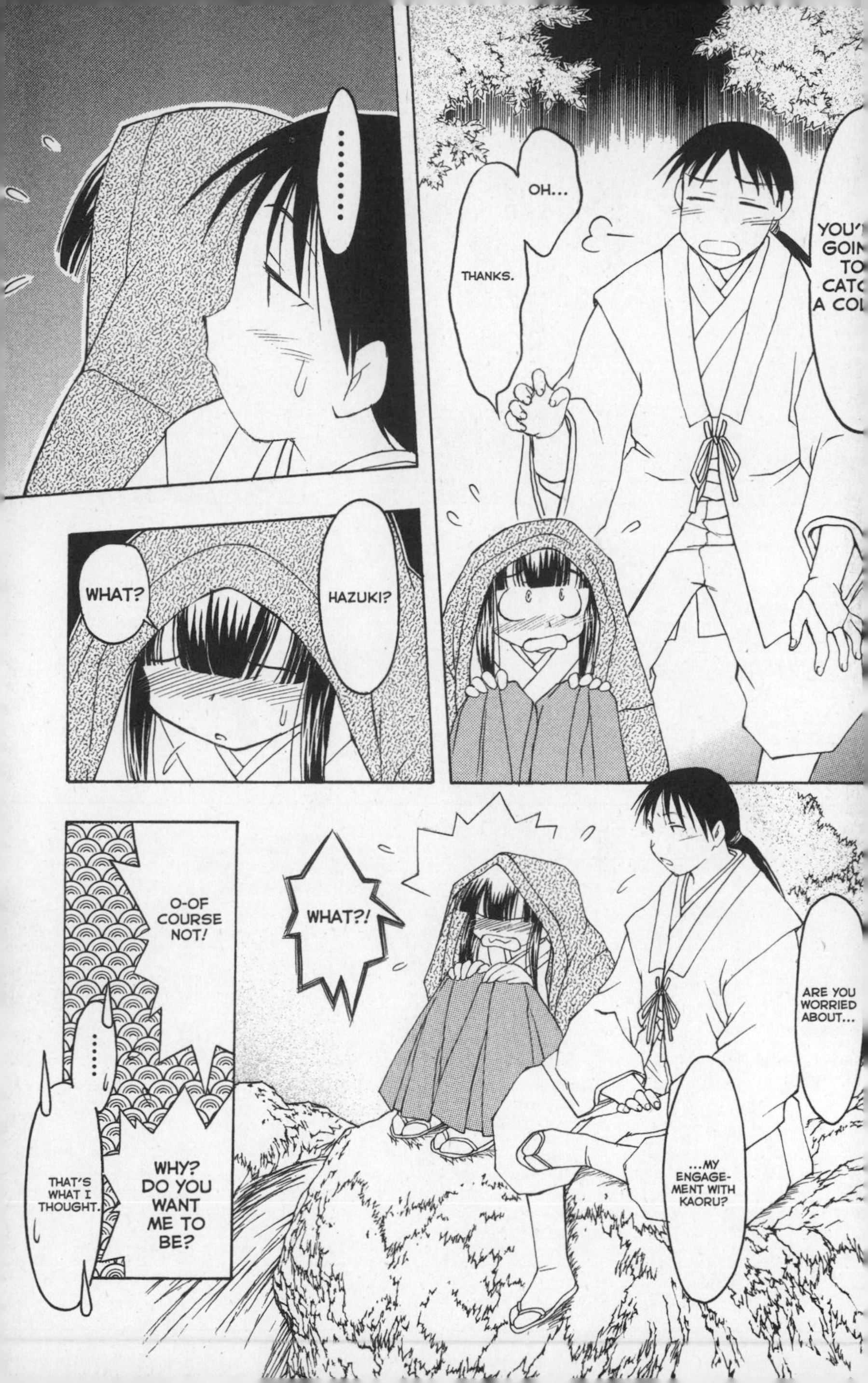
YOU' GOIN TO CATC A CO
OH...
THANKS.
....
HAZUKI?
WHAT?
ARE YOU WORRIED ABOUT...
...MY ENGAGEMENT WITH KAORU?
WHAT?!
O-OF COURSE NOT!
WHY? DO YOU WANT ME TO BE?
......
THAT'S WHAT I THOUGHT.

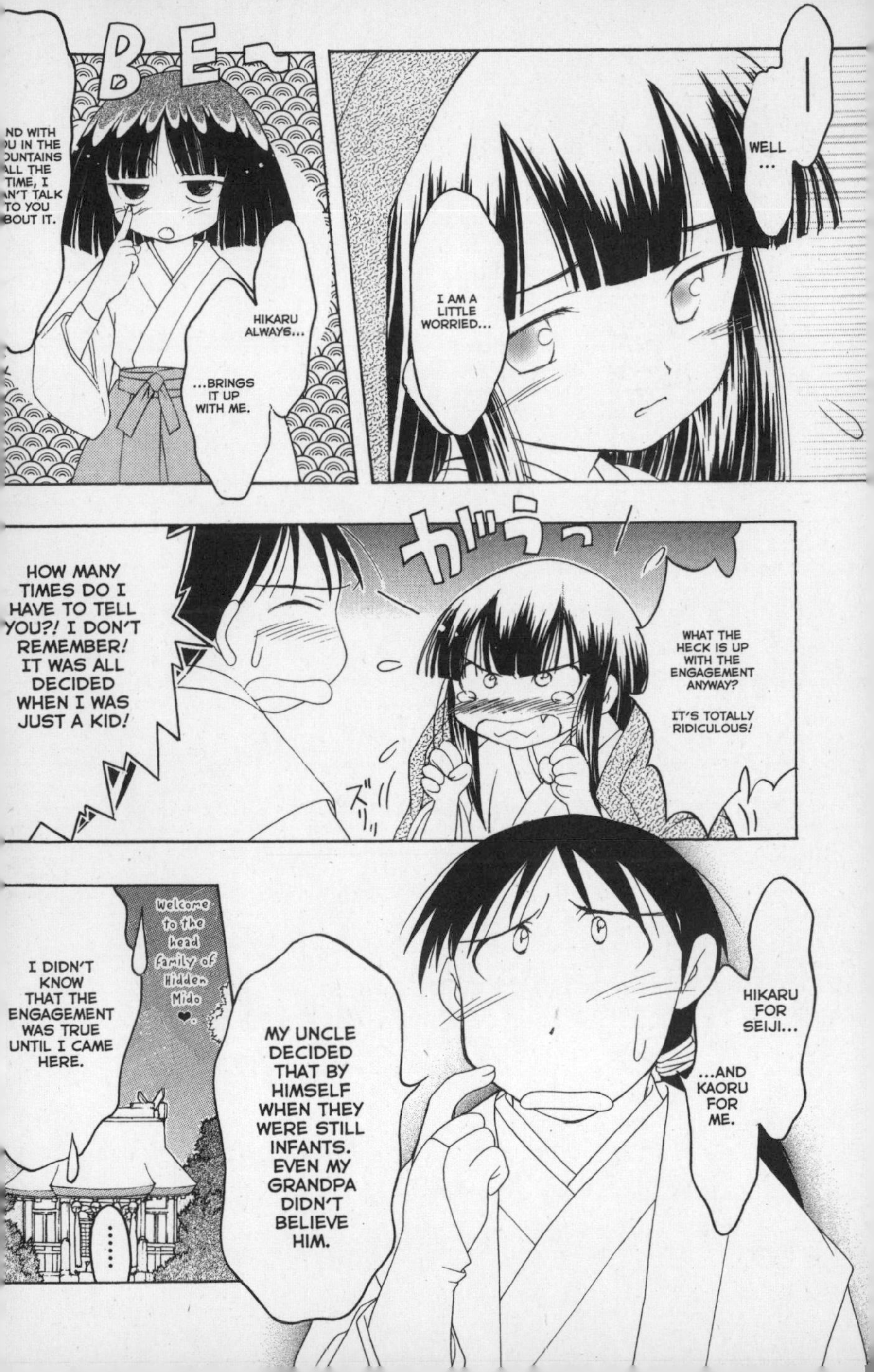
WELL ...
I AM A LITTLE WORRIED...
BE~
HIKARU ALWAYS...
...BRINGS IT UP WITH ME.
ND WITH OU IN THE OUNTAINS ALL THE TIME, I AN'T TALK TO YOU BOUT IT.
がうっ!
WHAT THE HECK IS UP WITH THE ENGAGEMENT ANYWAY?
IT'S TOTALLY RIDICULOUS!
HOW MANY TIMES DO I HAVE TO TELL YOU?! I DON'T REMEMBER! IT WAS ALL DECIDED WHEN I WAS JUST A KID!
HIKARU FOR SEIJI...
...AND KAORU FOR ME.
MY UNCLE DECIDED THAT BY HIMSELF WHEN THEY WERE STILL INFANTS. EVEN MY GRANDPA DIDN'T BELIEVE HIM.
I DIDN'T KNOW THAT THE ENGAGEMENT WAS TRUE UNTIL I CAME HERE.
Welcome to the head family of Hidden Mido ❤.
......

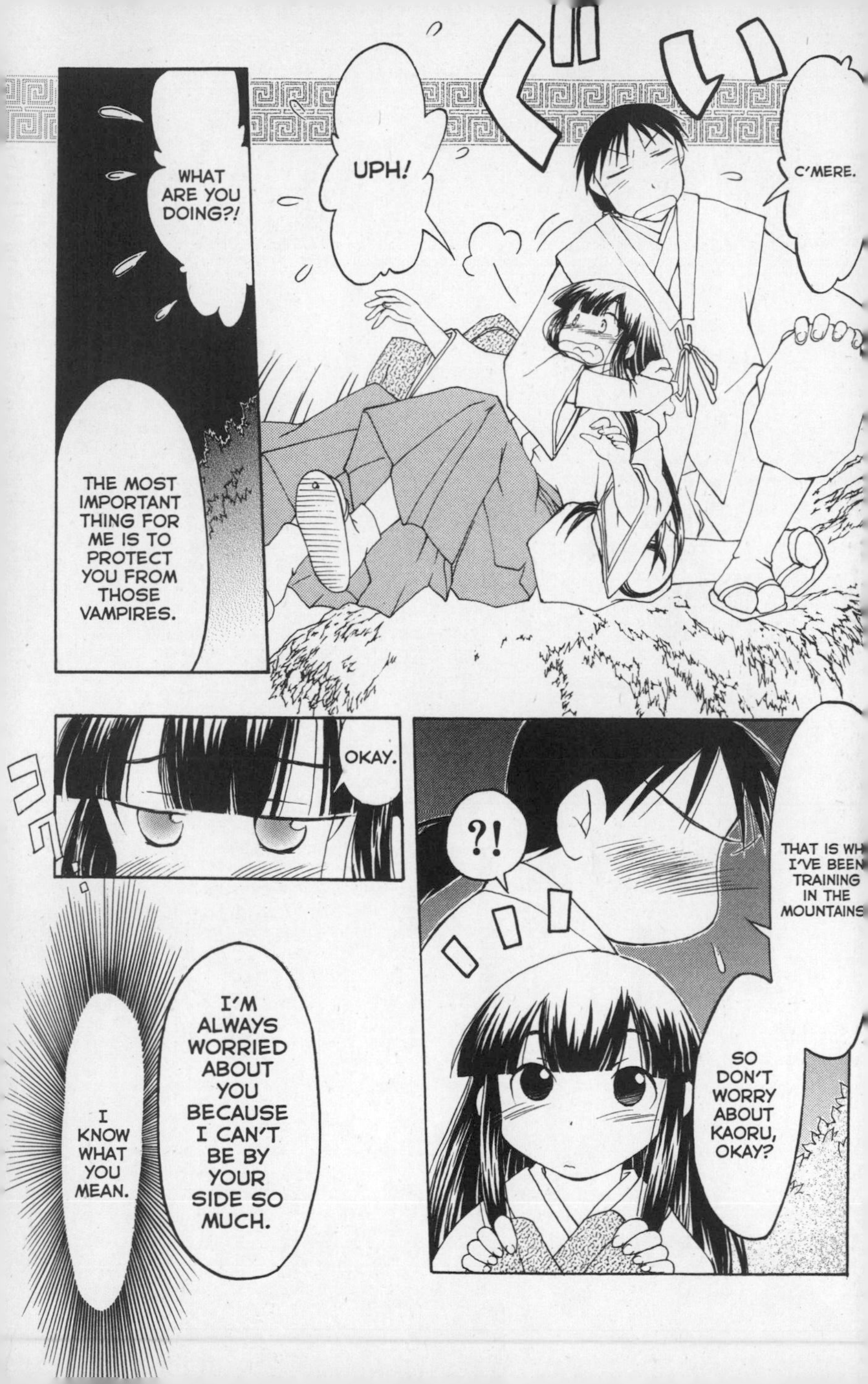
C'MERE.
UPH!
WHAT ARE YOU DOING?!
THE MOST IMPORTANT THING FOR ME IS TO PROTECT YOU FROM THOSE VAMPIRES.
THAT IS WH I'VE BEEN TRAINING IN THE MOUNTAINS
?!
SO DON'T WORRY ABOUT KAORU, OKAY?
OKAY.
I'M ALWAYS WORRIED ABOUT YOU BECAUSE I CAN'T BE BY YOUR SIDE SO MUCH.
I KNOW WHAT YOU MEAN.

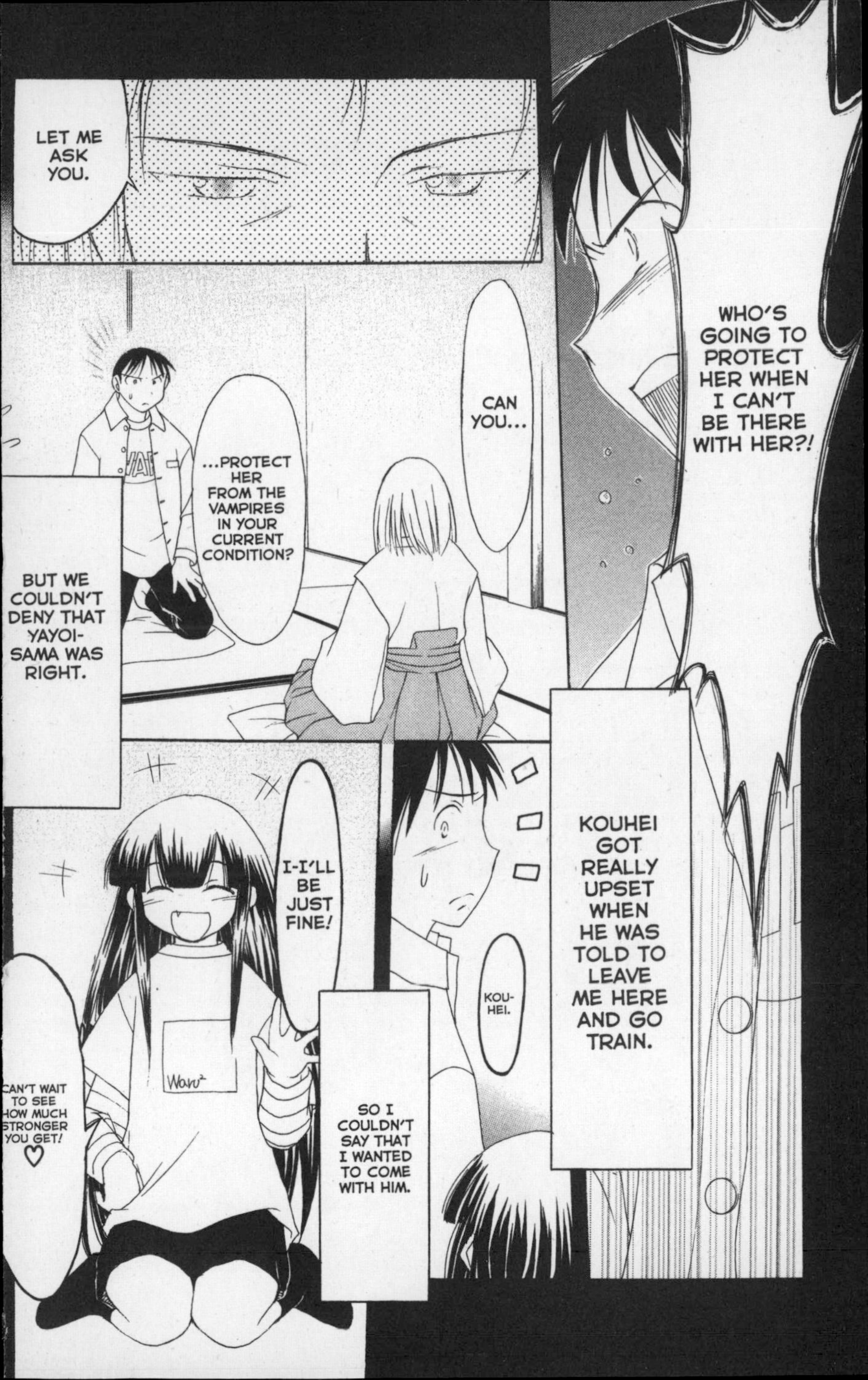
WHO'S GOING TO PROTECT HER WHEN I CAN'T BE THERE WITH HER?!
KOUHEI GOT REALLY UPSET WHEN HE WAS TOLD TO LEAVE ME HERE AND GO TRAIN.
LET ME ASK YOU.
CAN YOU...
...PROTECT HER FROM THE VAMPIRES IN YOUR CURRENT CONDITION?
BUT WE COULDN'T DENY THAT YAYOI-SAMA WAS RIGHT.
KOU-HEI.
I-I'LL BE JUST FINE!
CAN'T WAIT TO SEE HOW MUCH STRONGER YOU GET! ♡
SO I COULDN'T SAY THAT I WANTED TO COME WITH HIM.

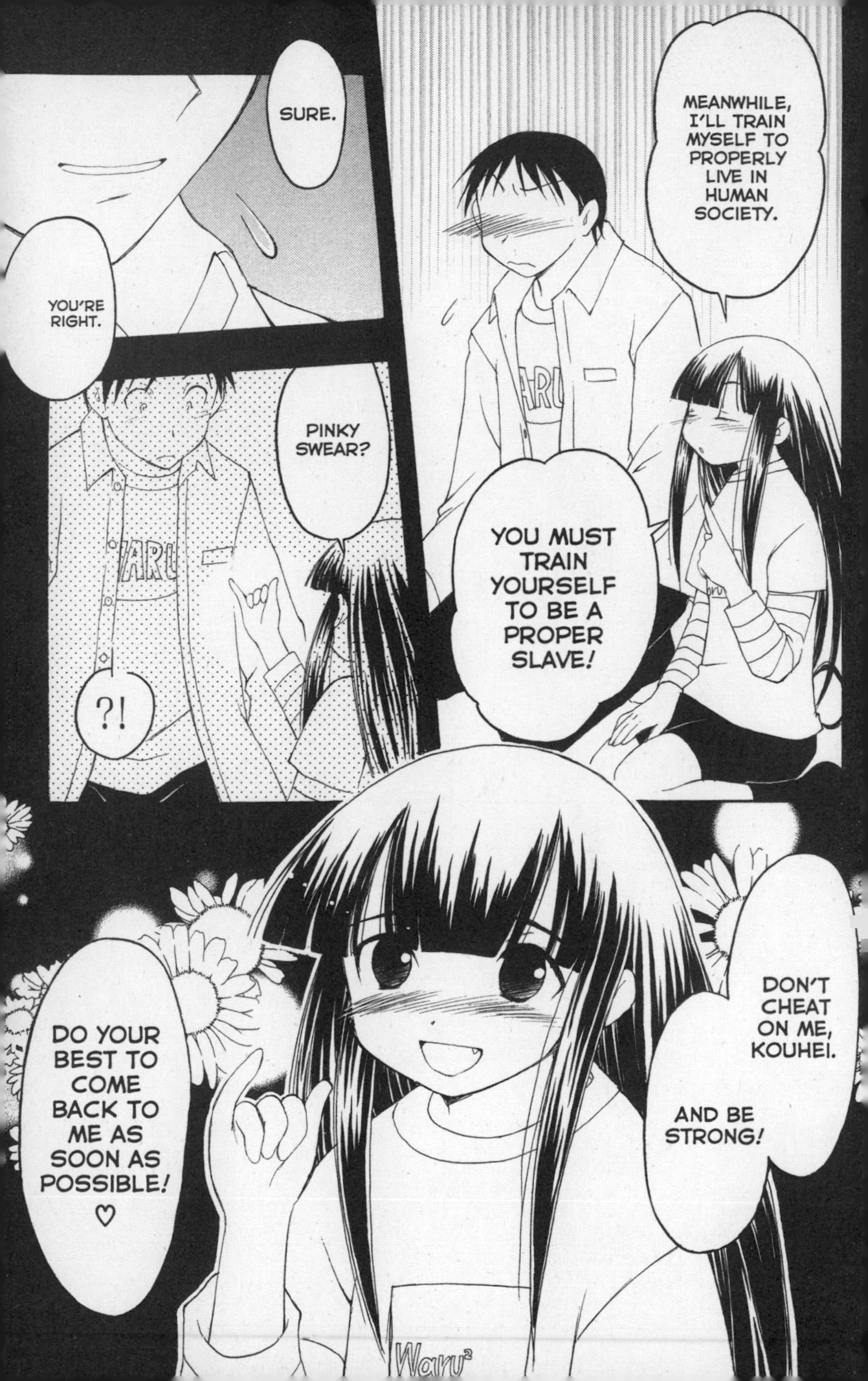
MEANWHILE, I'LL TRAIN MYSELF TO PROPERLY LIVE IN HUMAN SOCIETY.
YOU MUST TRAIN YOURSELF TO BE A PROPER SLAVE!
SURE.
YOU'RE RIGHT.
PINKY SWEAR?
?!
DON'T CHEAT ON ME, KOUHEI.
AND BE STRONG!
DO YOUR BEST TO COME BACK TO ME AS SOON AS POSSIBLE! ♡

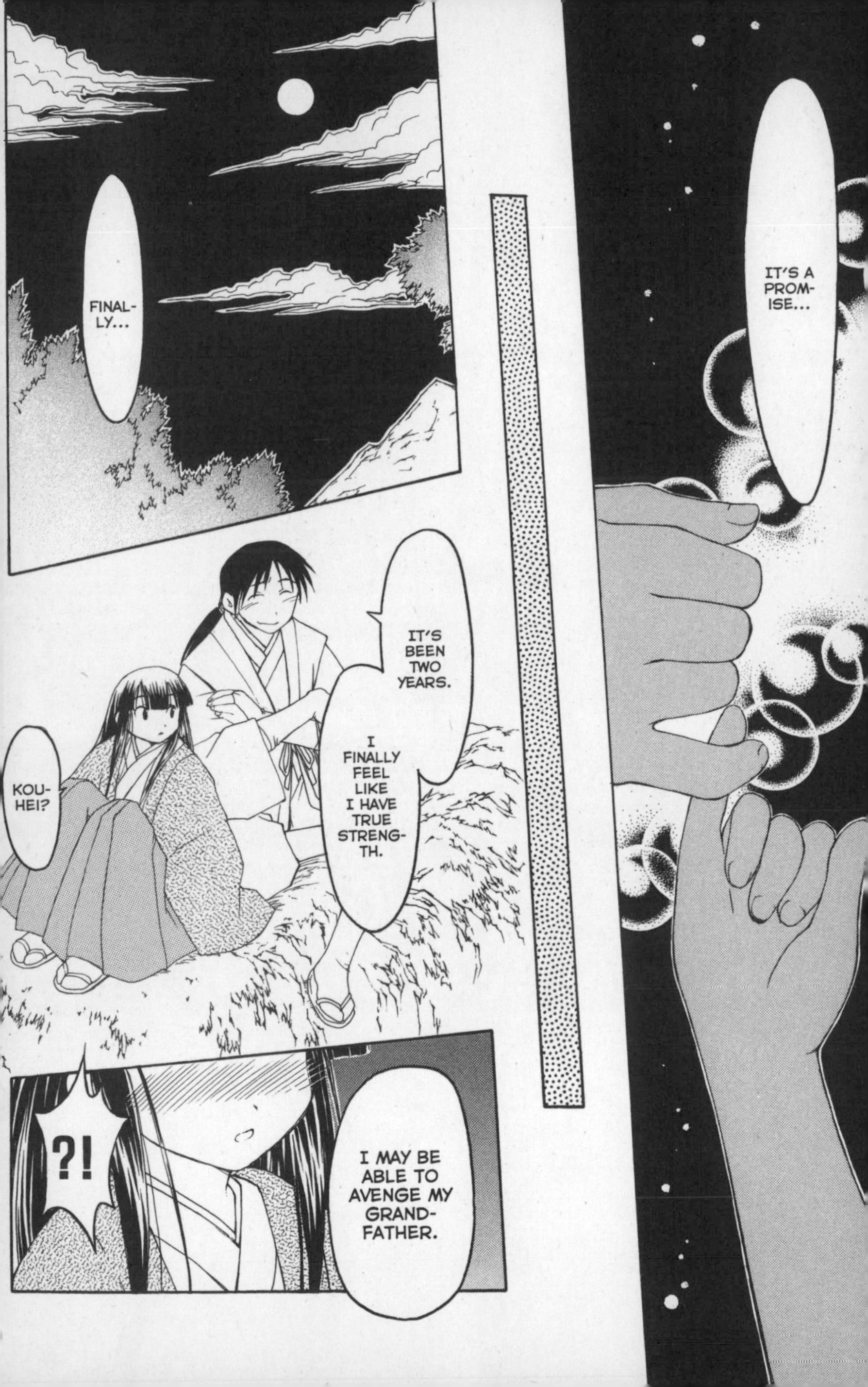
IT'S A PROMISE...
FINALLY...
IT'S BEEN TWO YEARS.
I FINALLY FEEL LIKE I HAVE TRUE STRENGTH.
KOUHEI?
I MAY BE ABLE TO AVENGE MY GRANDFATHER.
?!

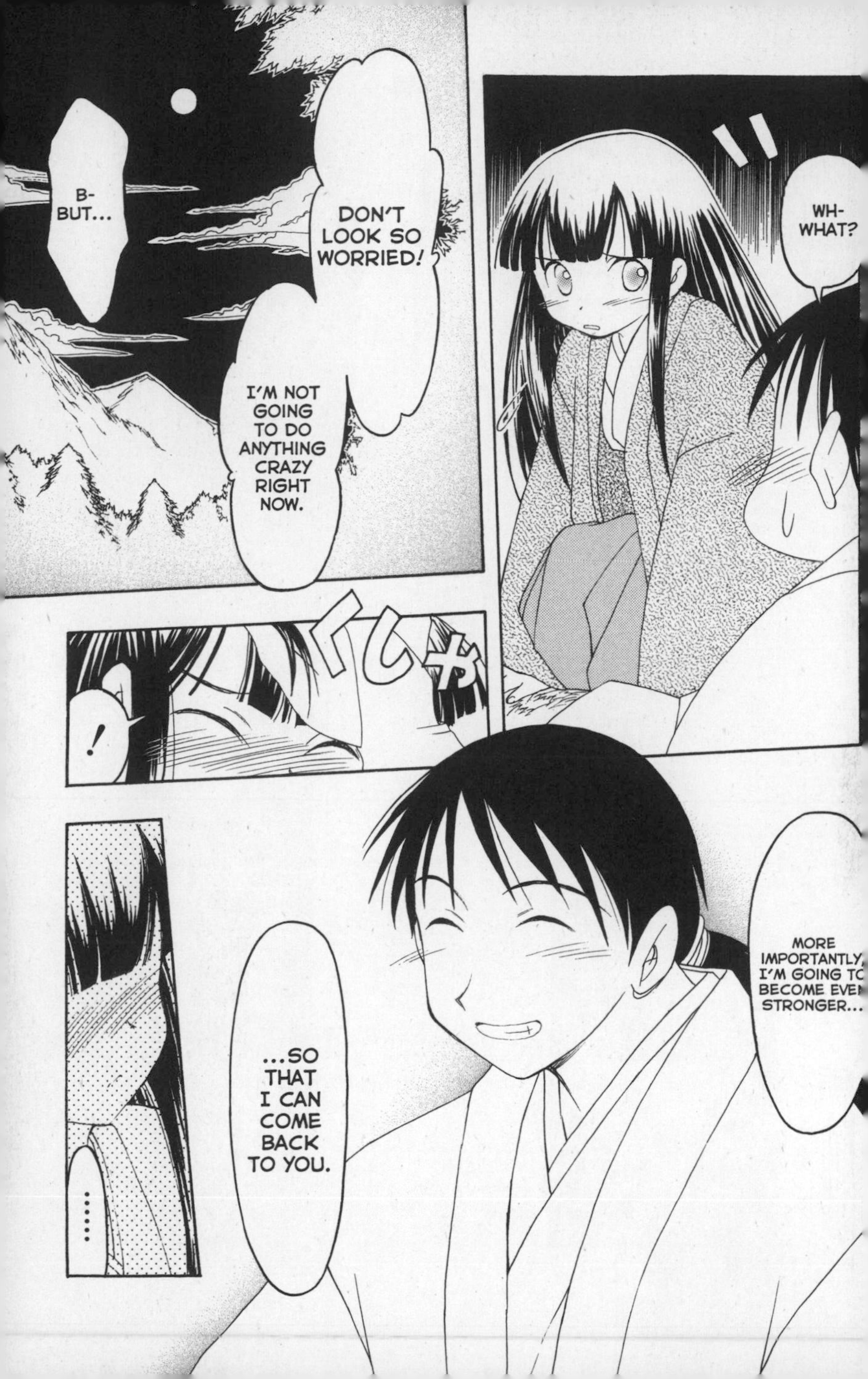
DON'T LOOK SO WORRIED!
I'M NOT GOING TO DO ANYTHING CRAZY RIGHT NOW.
B-BUT...
WH- WHAT?
くしゃ
!
MORE IMPORTANTLY, I'M GOING TO BECOME EVEN STRONGER...
...SO THAT I CAN COME BACK TO YOU.
......

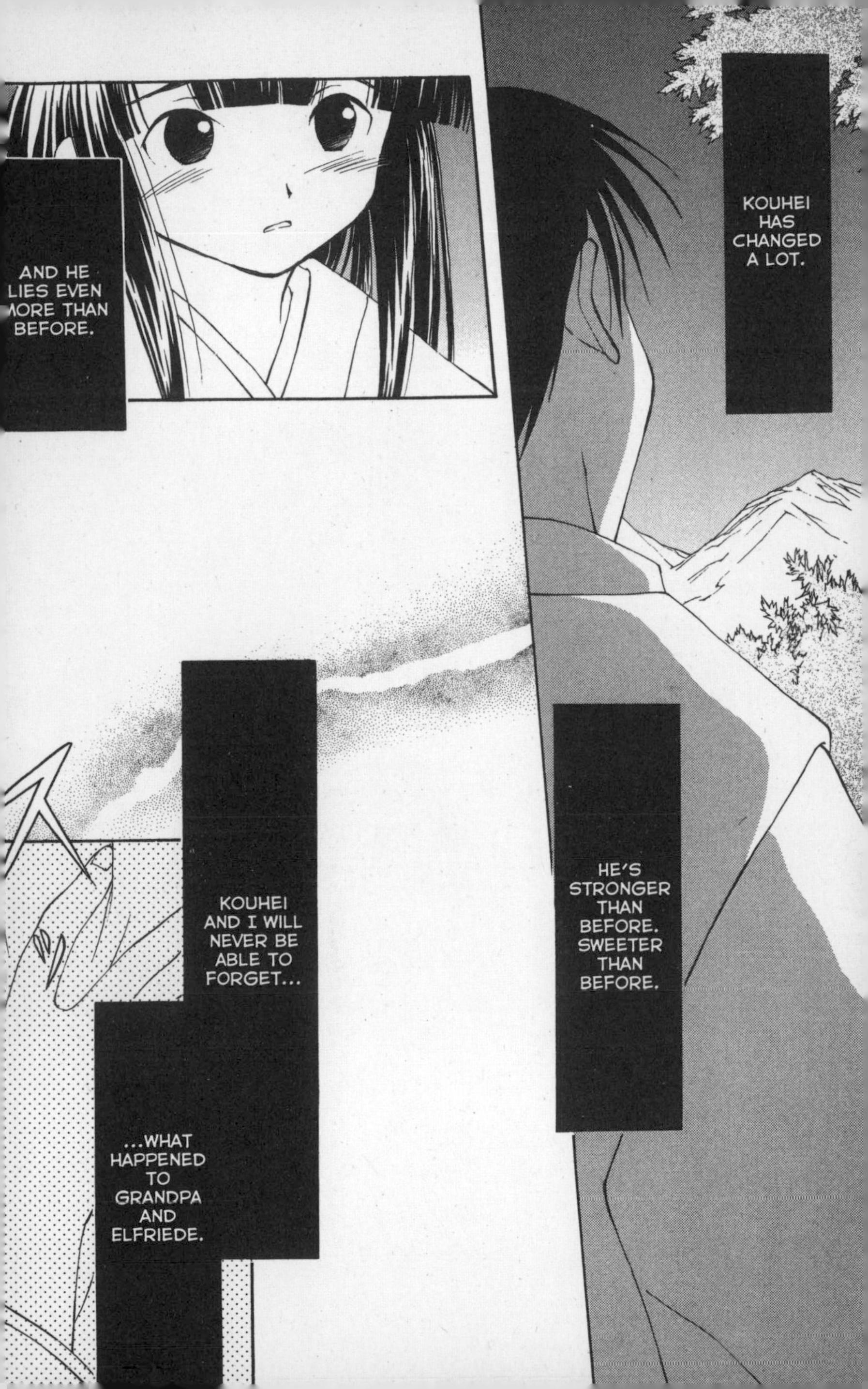
KOUHEI HAS CHANGED A LOT.
HE'S STRONGER THAN BEFORE. SWEETER THAN BEFORE.
AND HE LIES EVEN MORE THAN BEFORE.
KOUHEI AND I WILL NEVER BE ABLE TO FORGET...
...WHAT HAPPENED TO GRANDPA AND ELFRIEDE.

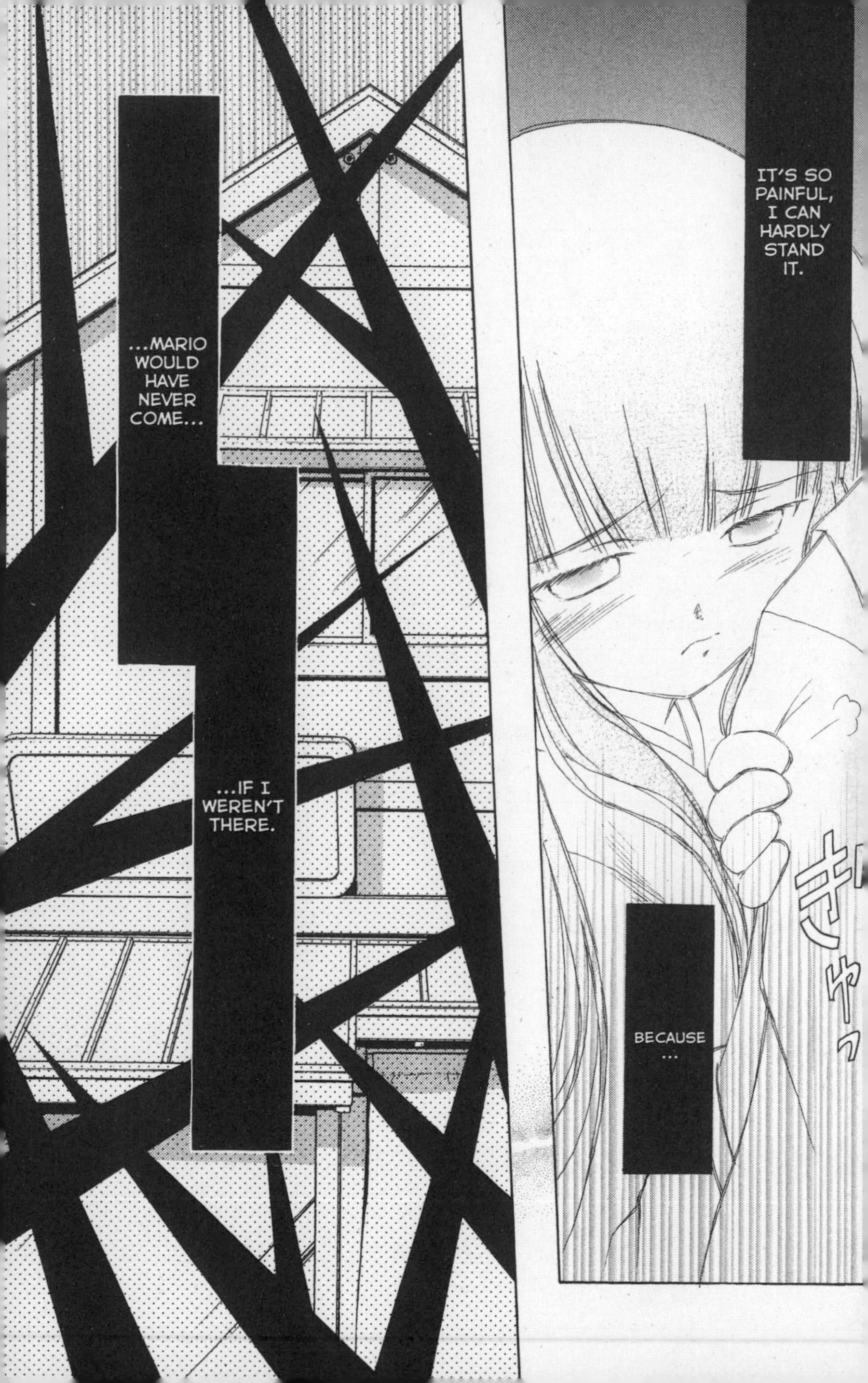
IT'S SO PAINFUL, I CAN HARDLY STAND IT.
きゅっ
BECAUSE ...
...MARIO WOULD HAVE NEVER COME...
...IF I WEREN'T THERE.

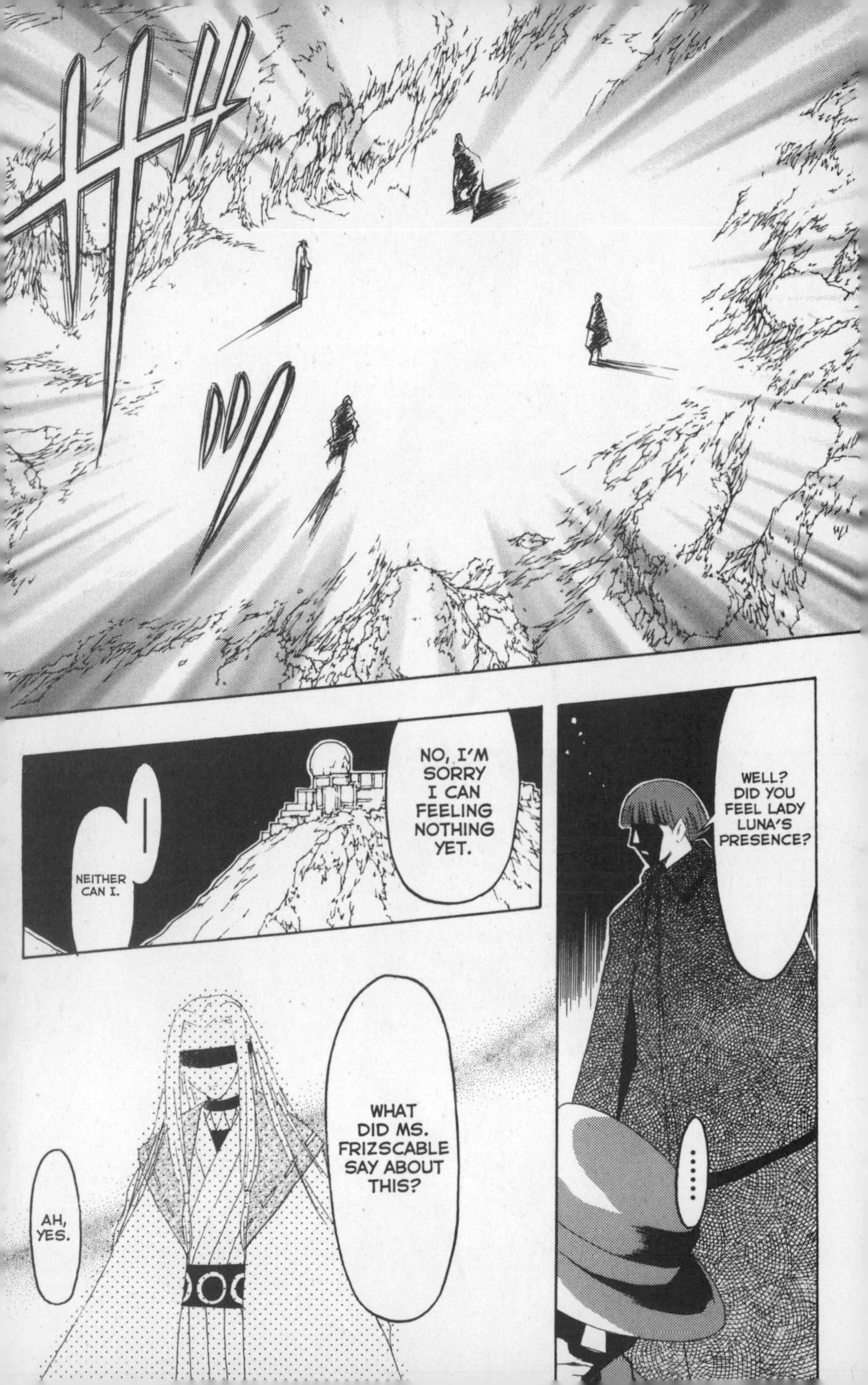
WELL? DID YOU FEEL LADY LUNA'S PRESENCE?
......
NO, I'M SORRY I CAN FEELING NOTHING YET.
NEITHER CAN I.
WHAT DID MS. FRIZSCABLE SAY ABOUT THIS?
AH, YES.

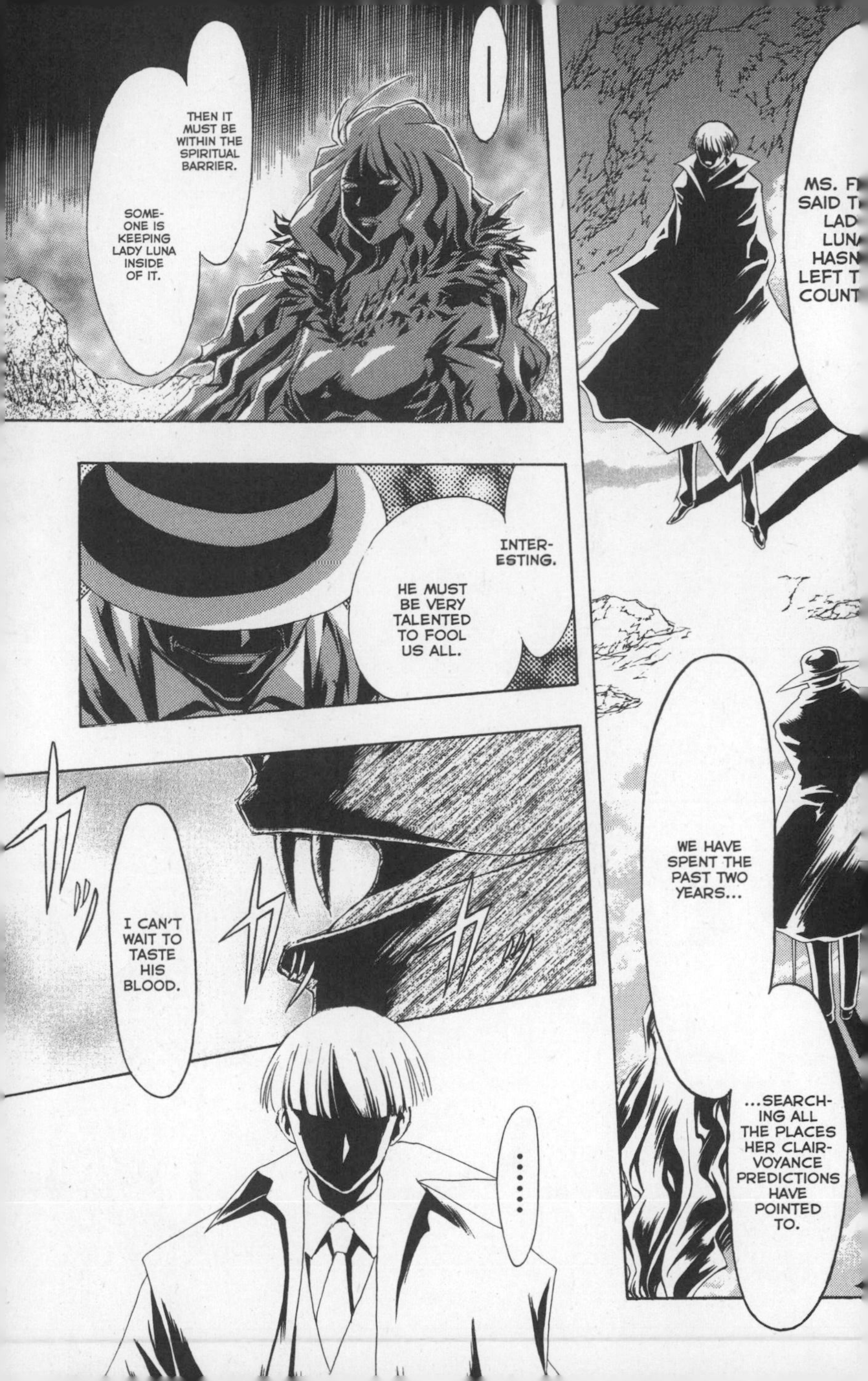

MS. F
SAID T
LAD
LUN
HASN
LEFT T
COUNT
WE HAVE SPENT THE PAST TWO YEARS...
...SEARCHING ALL THE PLACES HER CLAIRVOYANCE PREDICTIONS HAVE POINTED TO.
!
THEN IT MUST BE WITHIN THE SPIRITUAL BARRIER.
SOMEONE IS KEEPING LADY LUNA INSIDE OF IT.
INTERESTING.
HE MUST BE VERY TALENTED TO FOOL US ALL.
I CAN'T WAIT TO TASTE HIS BLOOD.
......

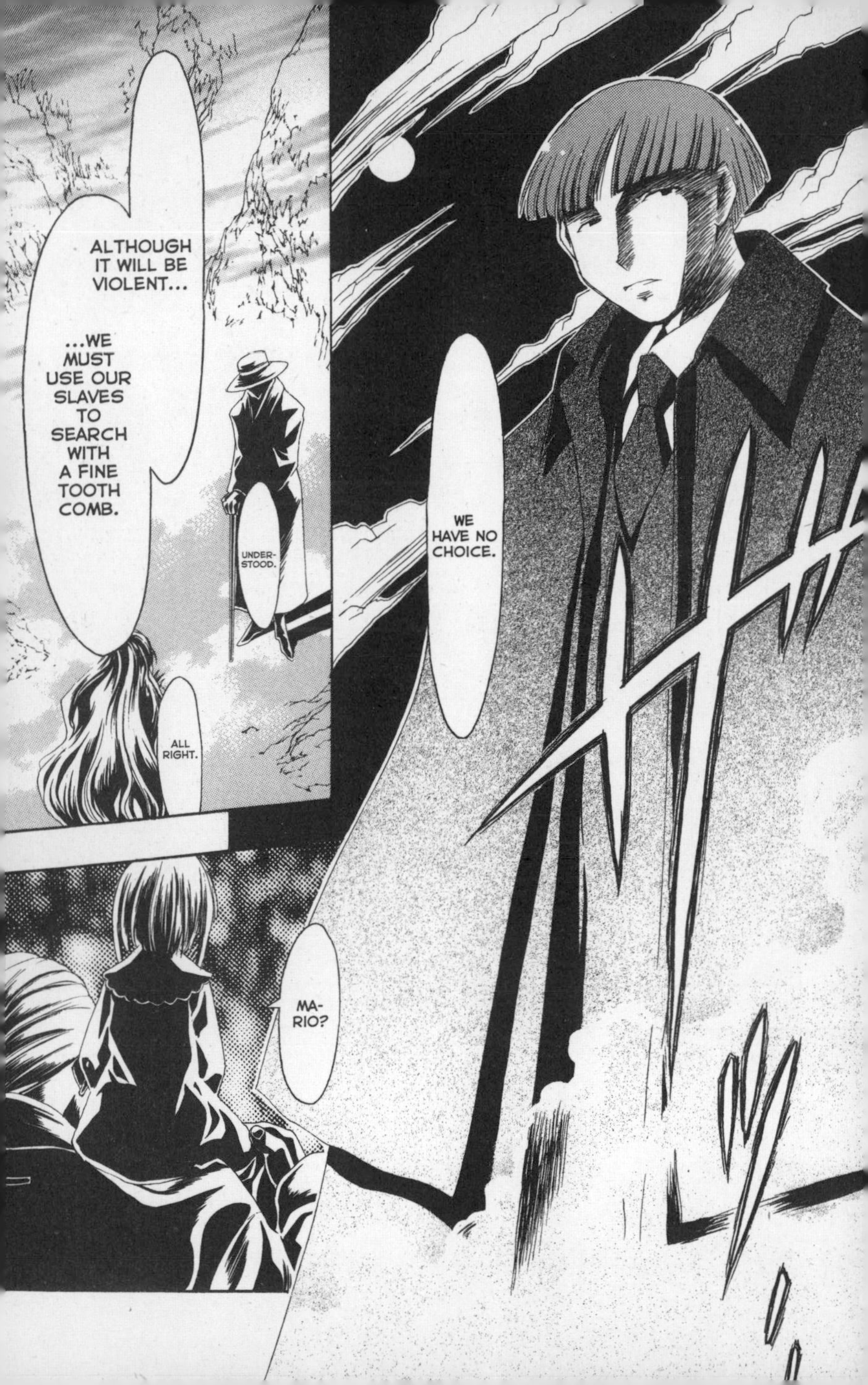
WE HAVE NO CHOICE.
ALTHOUGH IT WILL BE VIOLENT...
...WE MUST USE OUR SLAVES TO SEARCH WITH A FINE TOOTH COMB.
UNDER-STOOD.
ALL RIGHT.
MA-RIO?

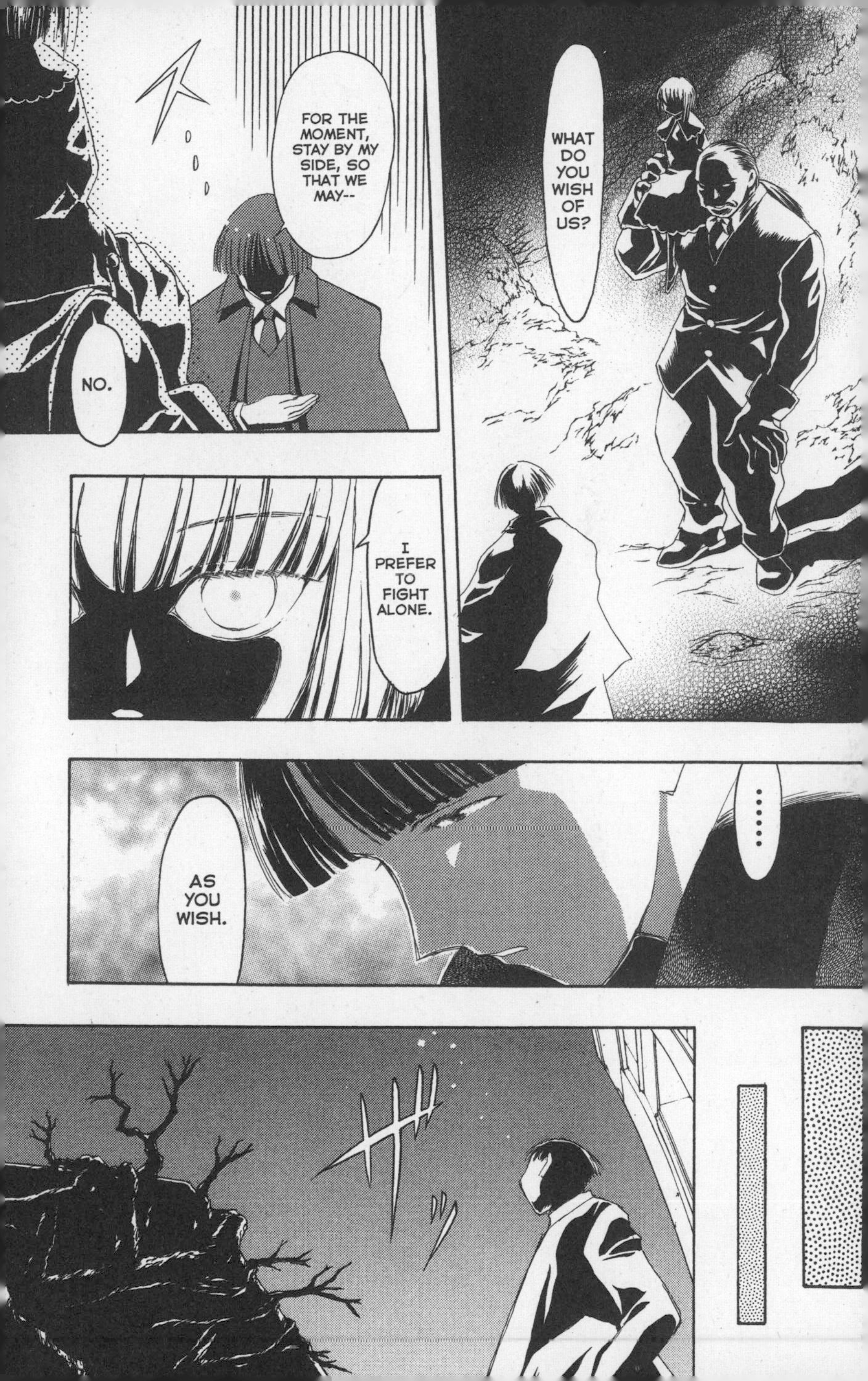
WHAT DO YOU WISH OF US?
FOR THE MOMENT, STAY BY MY SIDE, SO THAT WE MAY--
NO.
I PREFER TO FIGHT ALONE.
......
AS YOU WISH.

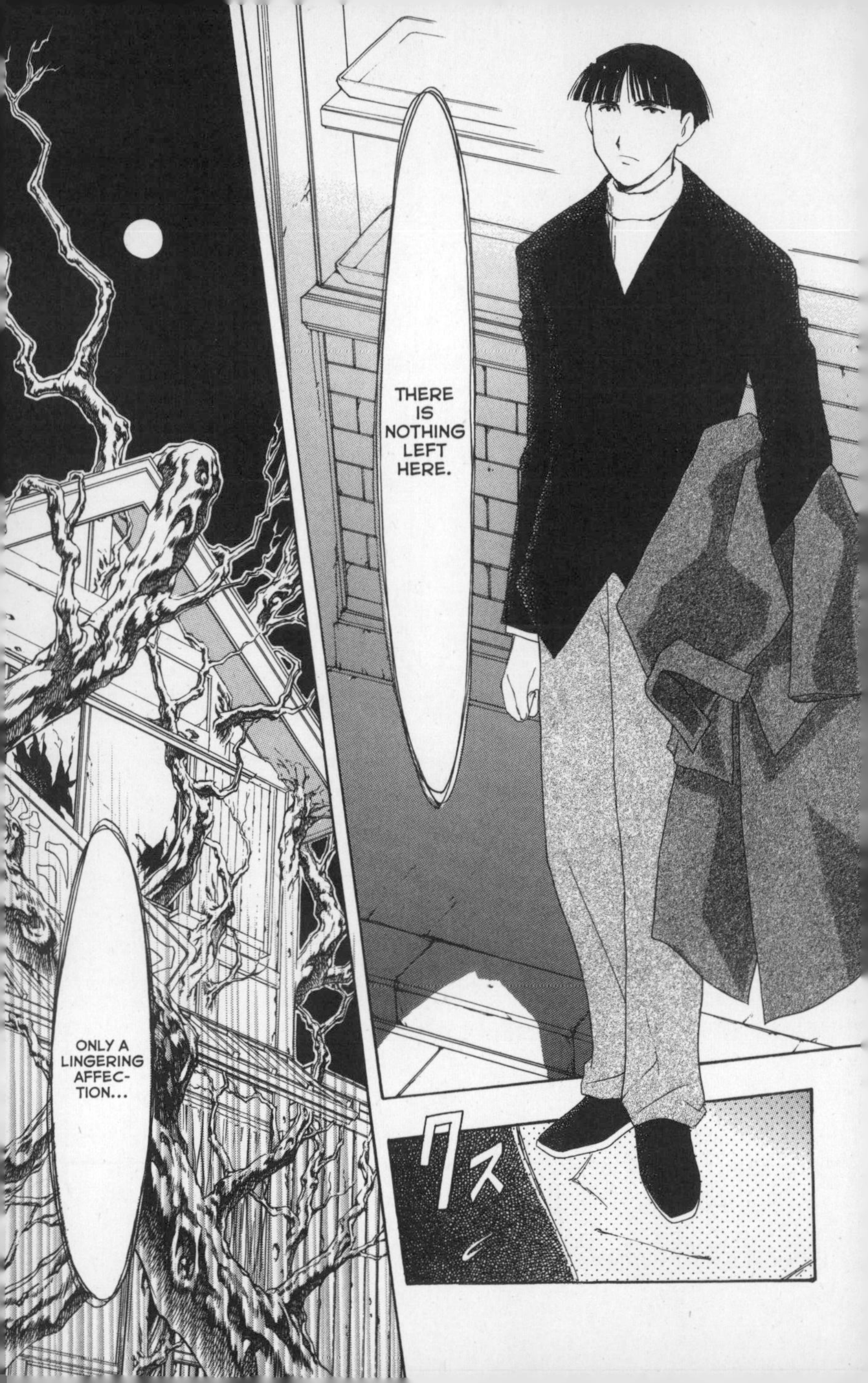
THERE IS NOTHING LEFT HERE.
クス
ONLY A LINGERING AFFEC-TION...

Moon 月詠 Phase

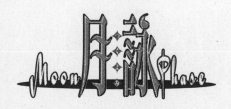

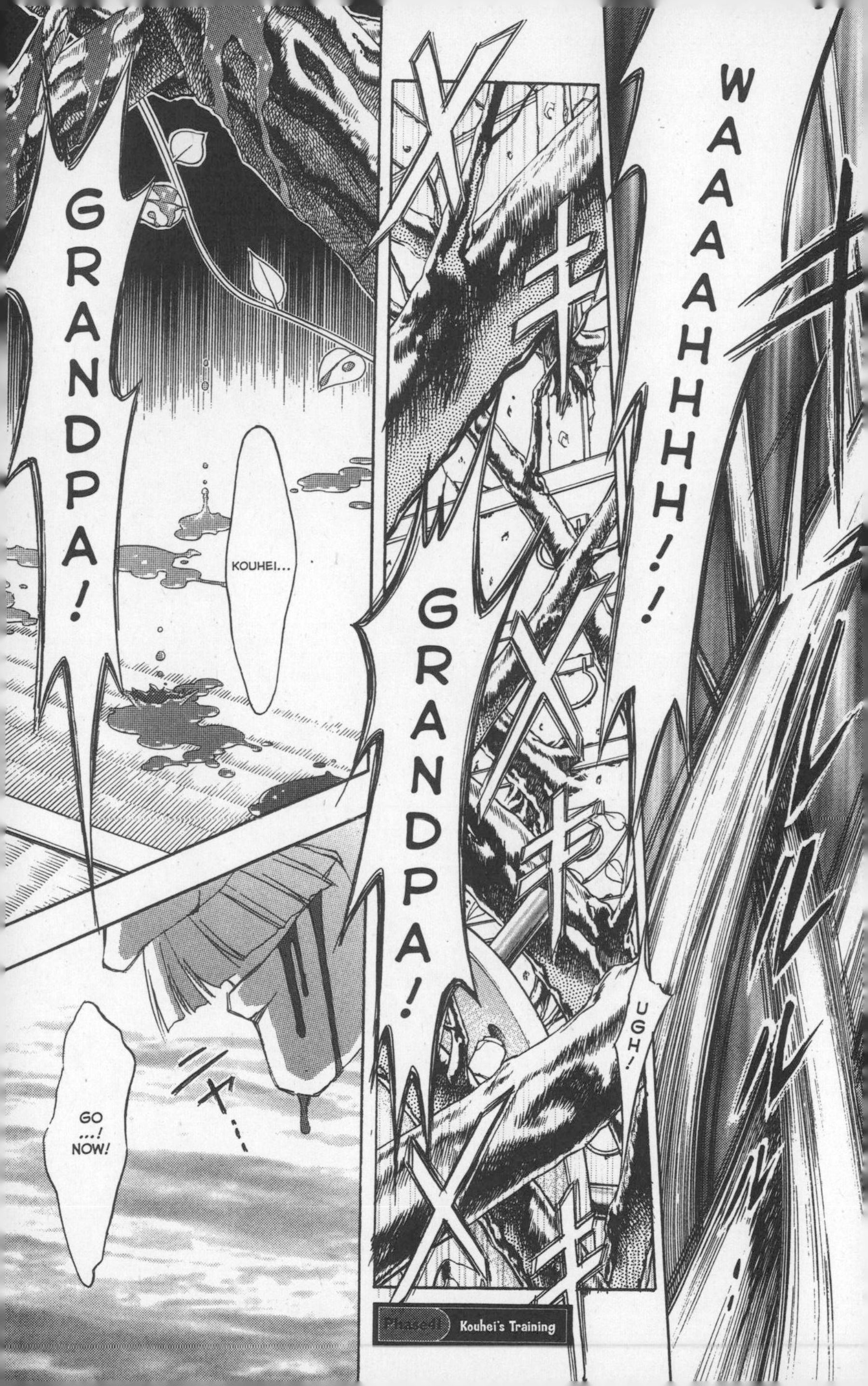

WAAAAHHHHH!!!
GRANDPA!
UGH!
Phase41 Kouhei's Training
GRANDPA!
KOUHEI...
GO...! NOW!

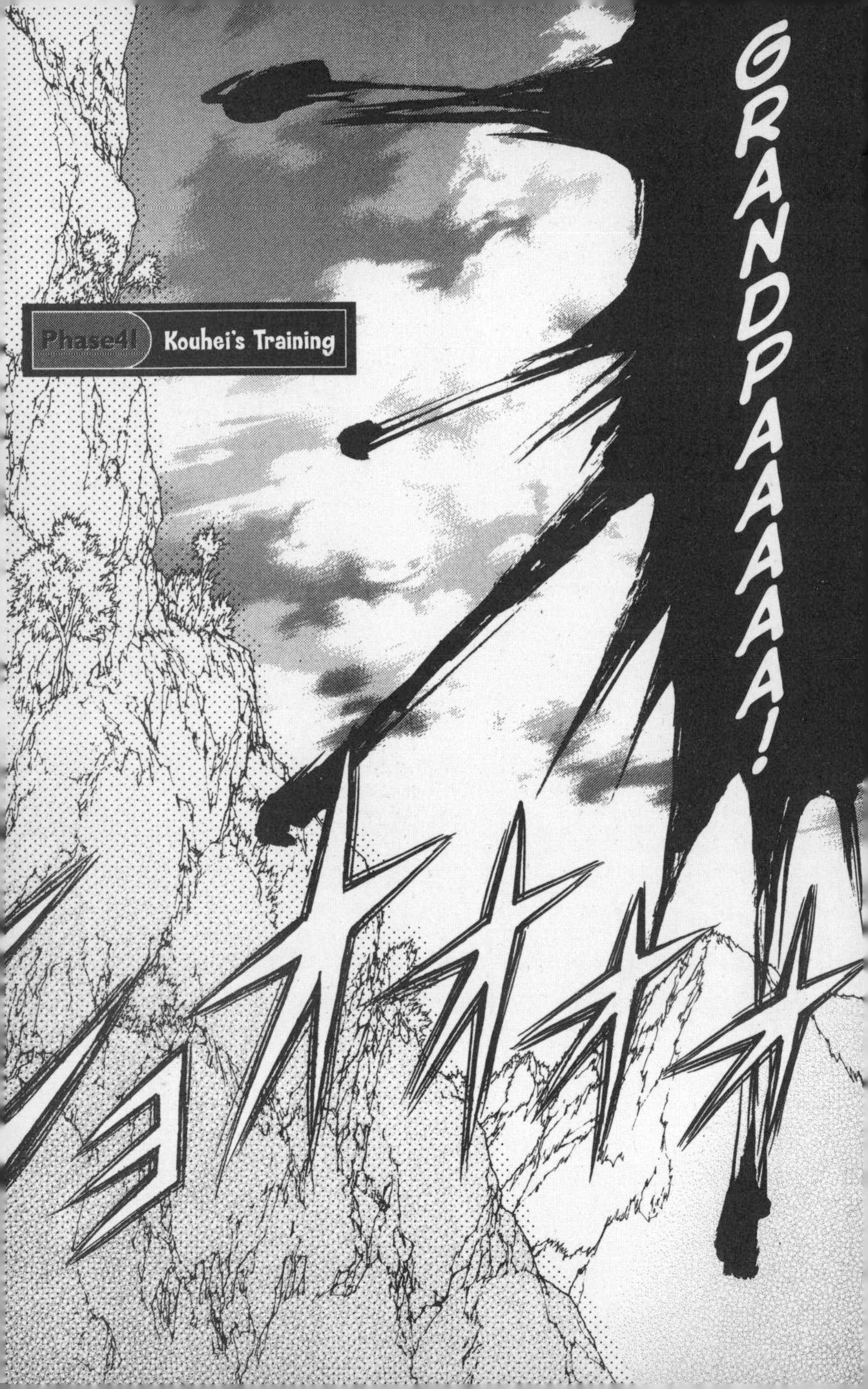
Phase41 Kouhei's Training
GRANDPAAAAA!

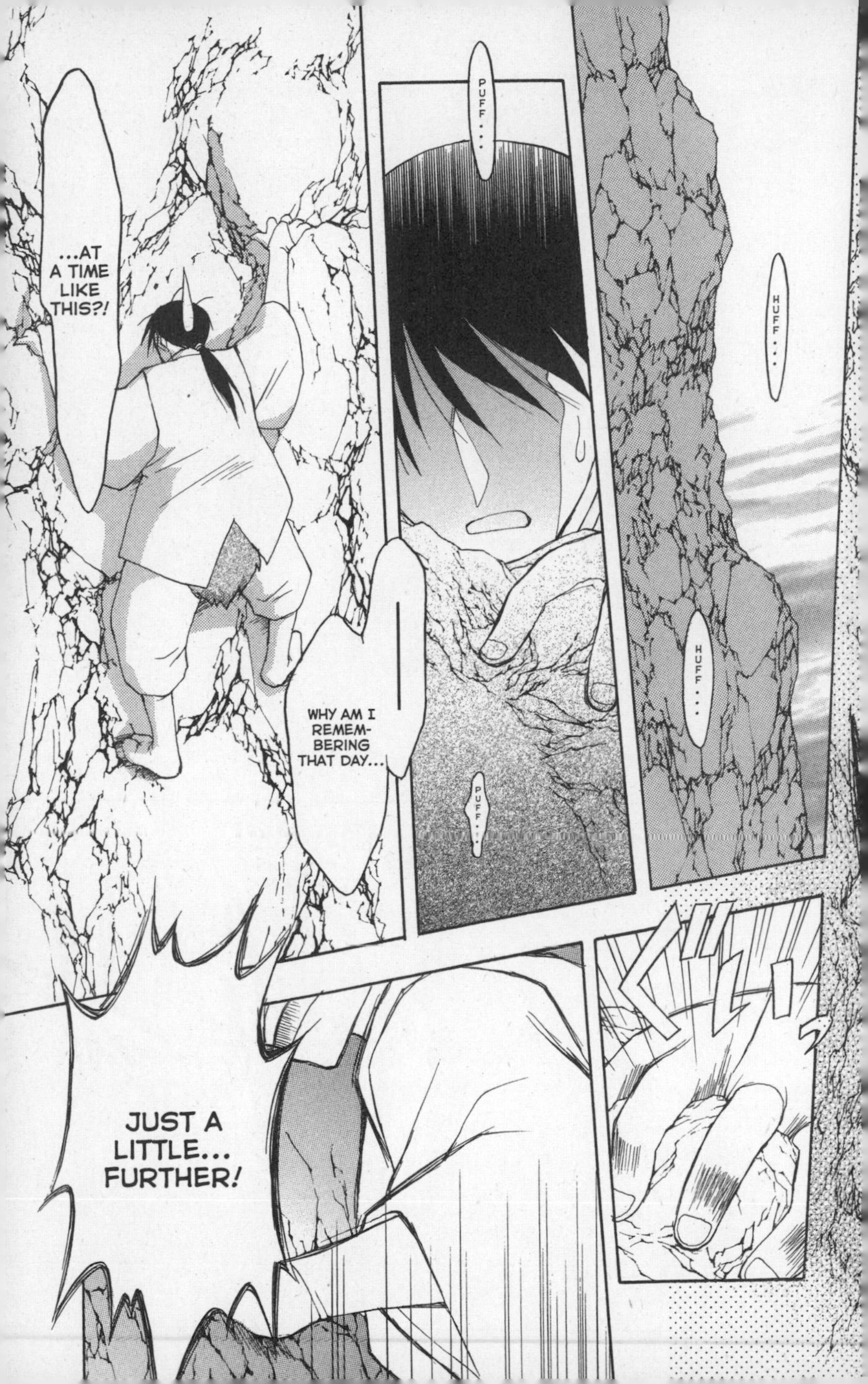
HUFF...
HUFF...
PUFF...
PUFF...
WHY AM I REMEM-BERING THAT DAY...
...AT A TIME LIKE THIS?!
JUST A LITTLE... FURTHER!

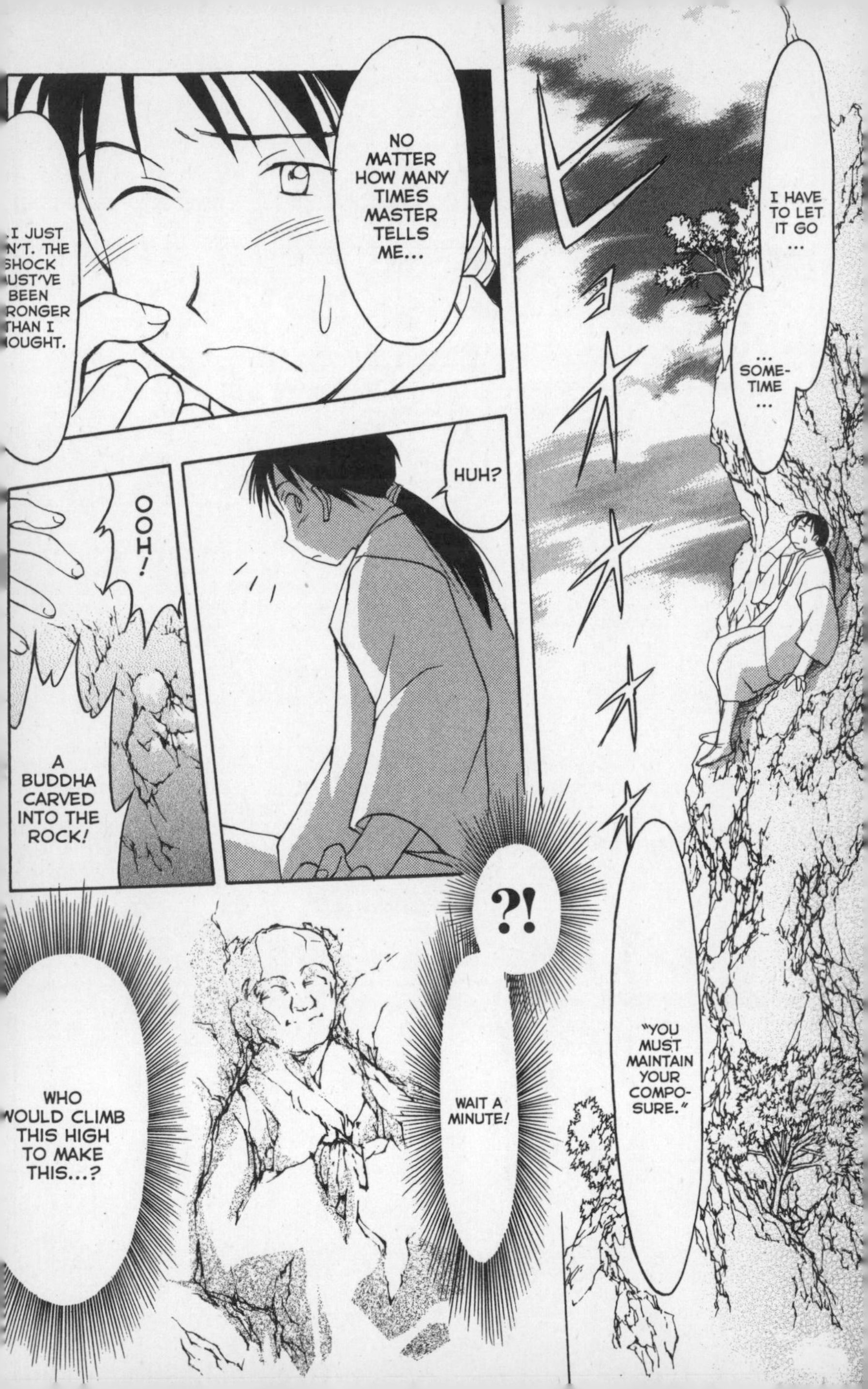
I HAVE TO LET IT GO ...
... SOMETIME ...
"YOU MUST MAINTAIN YOUR COMPOSURE."
NO MATTER HOW MANY TIMES MASTER TELLS ME...
.I JUST N'T. THE SHOCK UST'VE BEEN RONGER THAN I OUGHT.
HUH?
OOH!
A BUDDHA CARVED INTO THE ROCK!
?!
WAIT A MINUTE!
WHO WOULD CLIMB THIS HIGH TO MAKE THIS...?

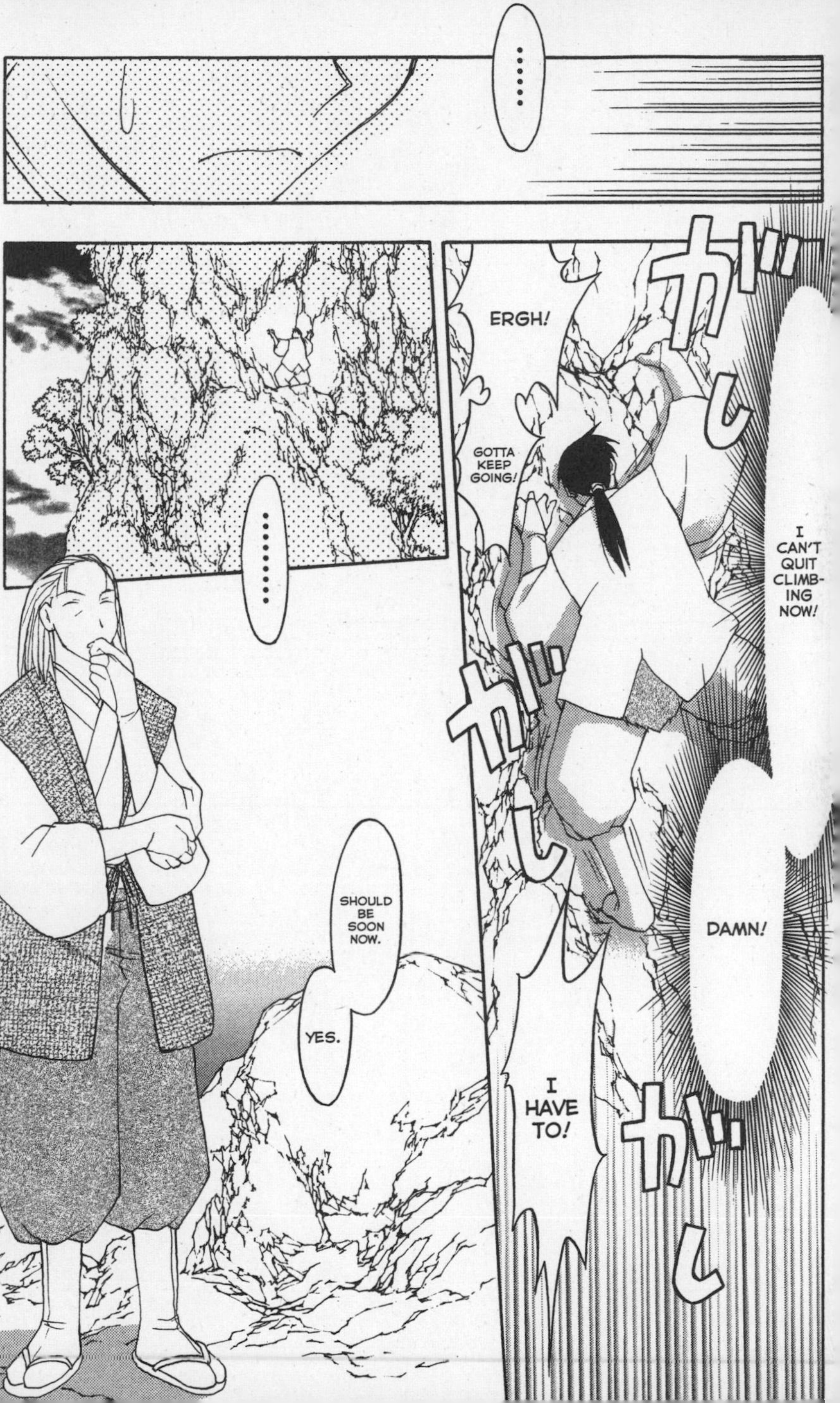
......
がし
I CAN'T QUIT CLIMBING NOW!
ERGH!
GOTTA KEEP GOING!
がし
DAMN!
がし
I HAVE TO!
......
SHOULD BE SOON NOW.
YES.

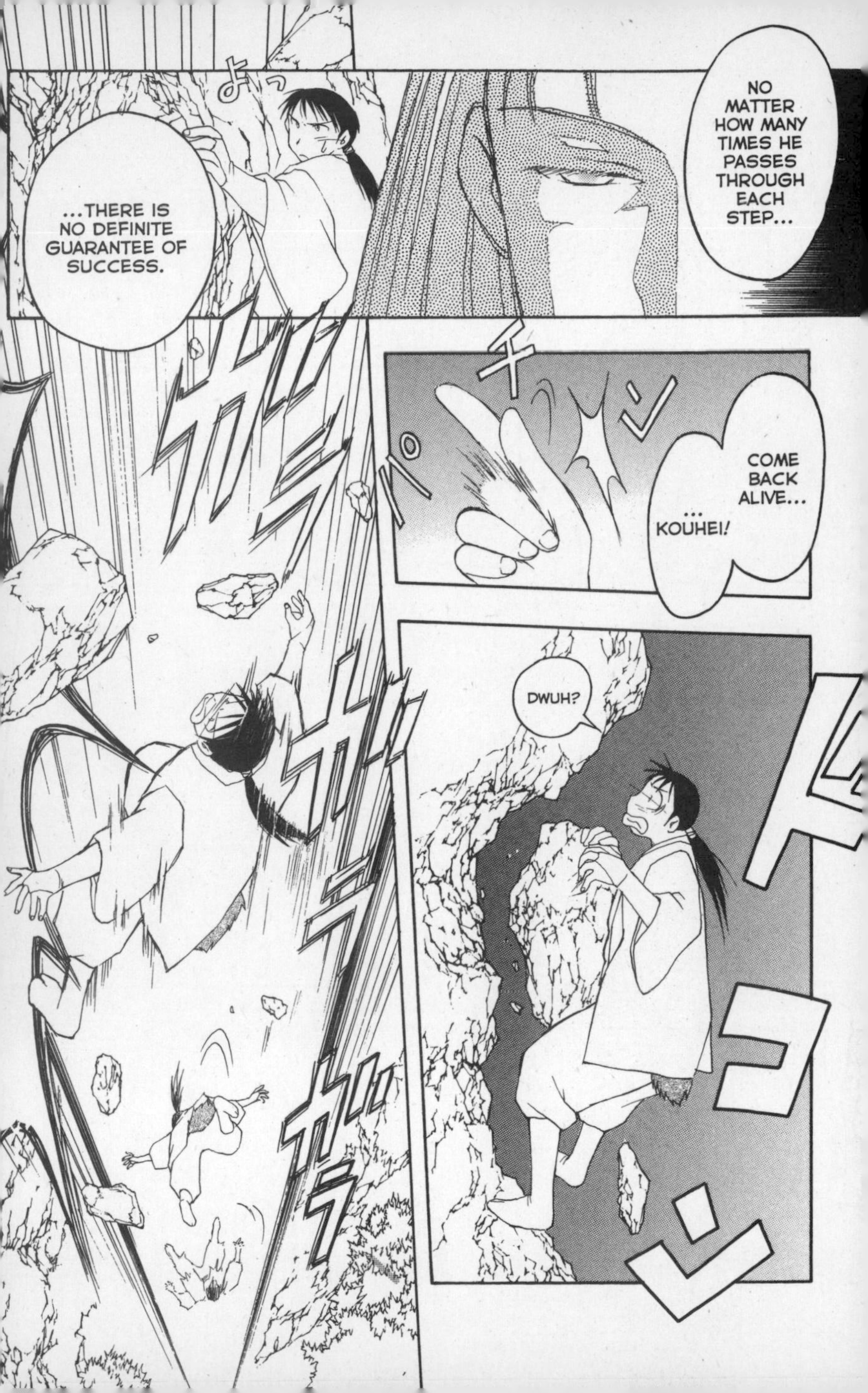
NO MATTER HOW MANY TIMES HE PASSES THROUGH EACH STEP...
よっ
...THERE IS NO DEFINITE GUARANTEE OF SUCCESS.
COME BACK ALIVE...
...KOUHEI!
DWUH?

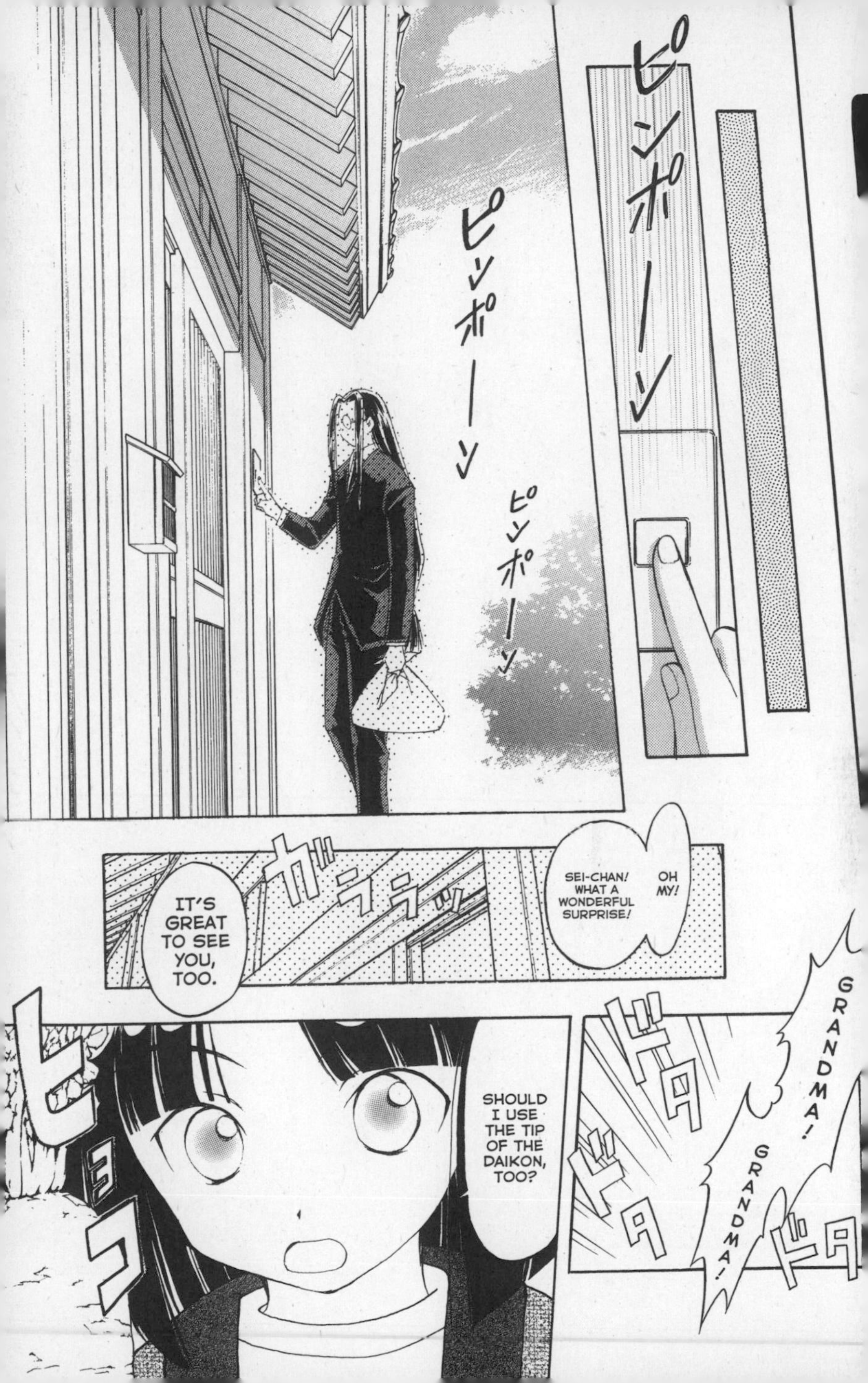
ピンポーン
ピンポーン
ピンポーン
OH MY!
SEI-CHAN! WHAT A WONDERFUL SURPRISE!
ガラッ
IT'S GREAT TO SEE YOU, TOO.
GRANDMA!
GRANDMA!
ドタ
ドタ
ドタ
ドタ
SHOULD I USE THE TIP OF THE DAIKON, TOO?
ヒョコ

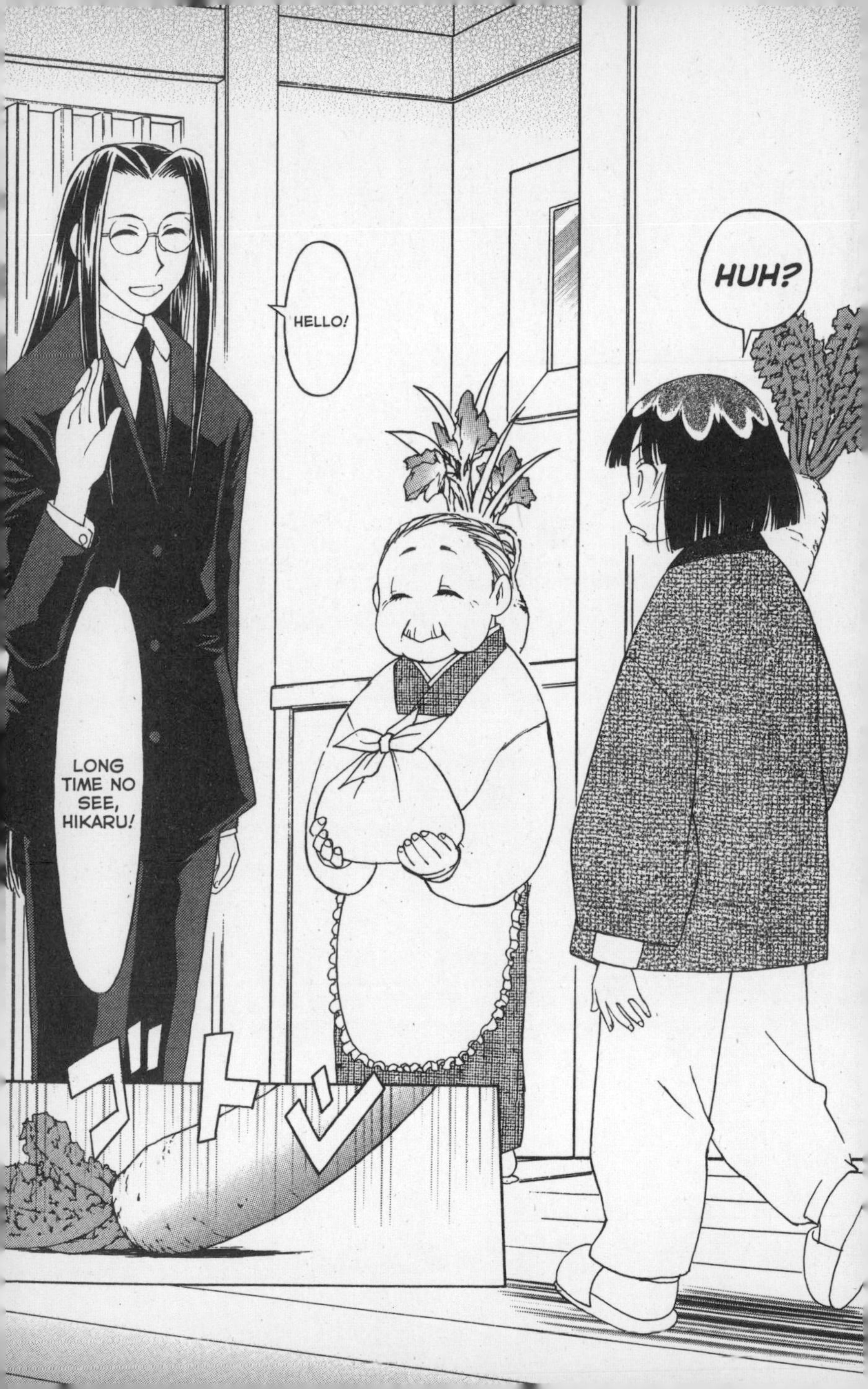
HUH?
HELLO!
LONG TIME NO SEE, HIKARU!
ゴトッ

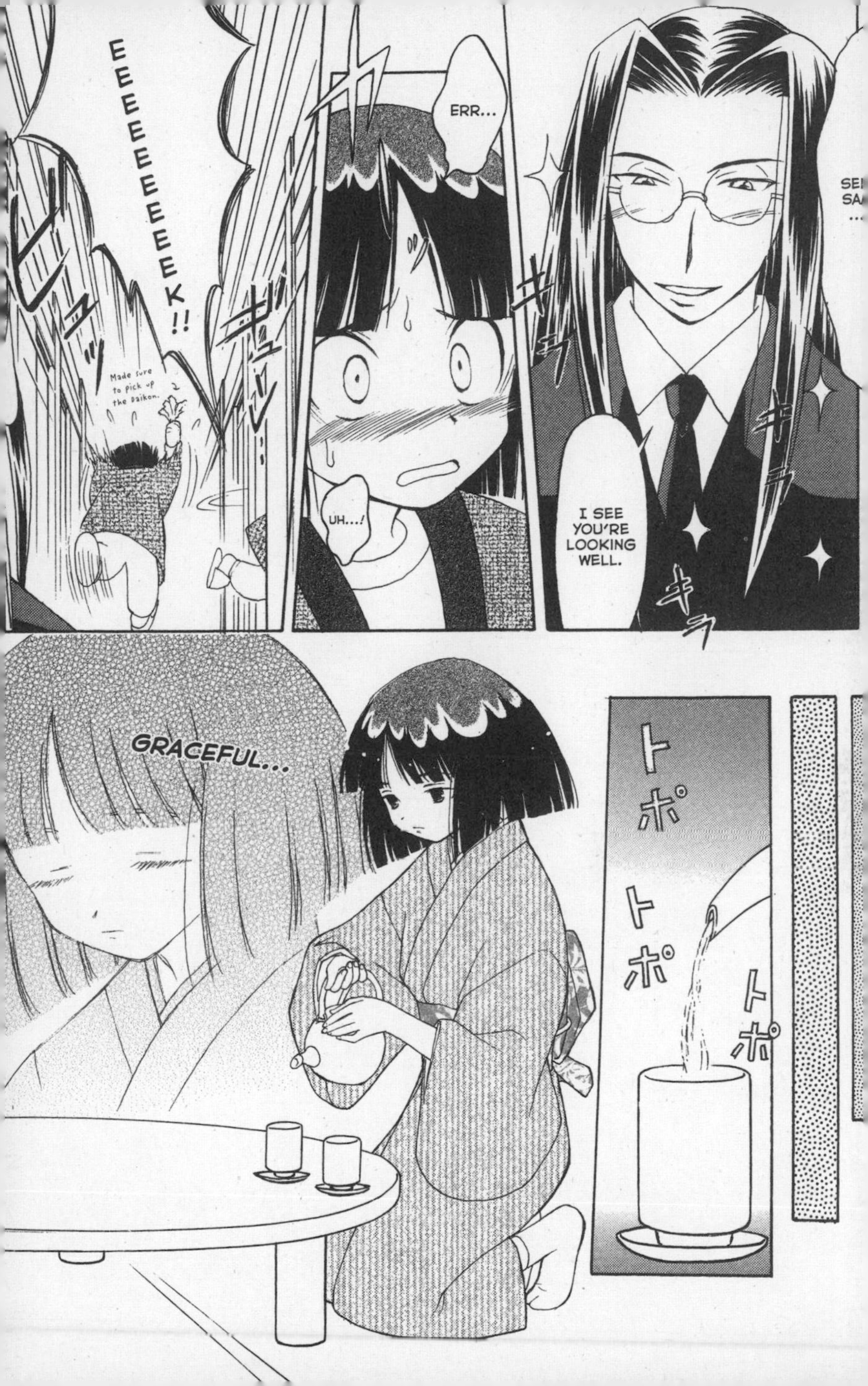

I SEE YOU'RE LOOKING WELL.
ERR...
UH...!
EEEEEEEEEEEK!!
Made sure to pick up the Daikon.
トポ
トポ
トポ
GRACEFUL...

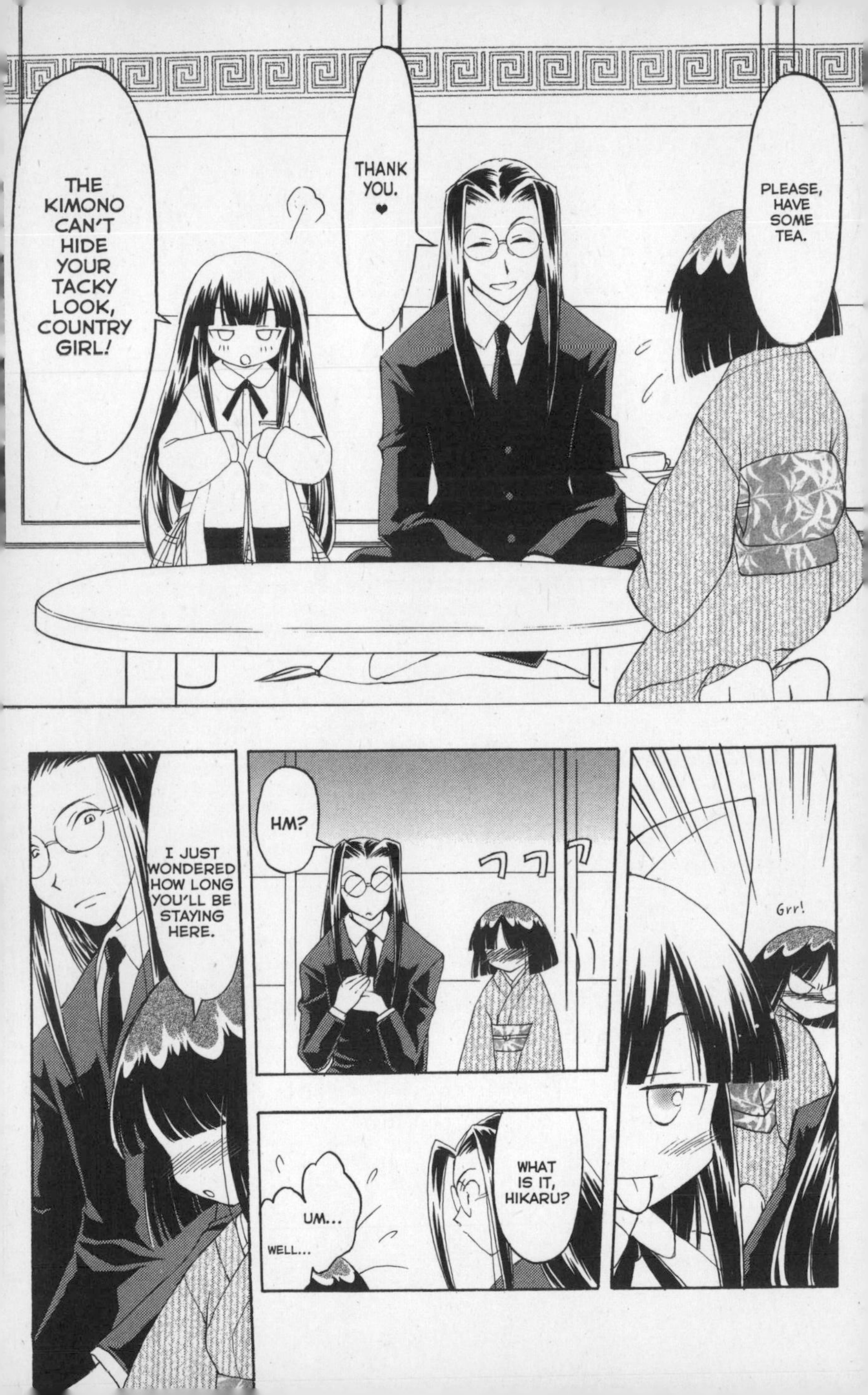
PLEASE, HAVE SOME TEA.
THANK YOU. ❤
THE KIMONO CAN'T HIDE YOUR TACKY LOOK, COUNTRY GIRL!
Grr!
HM?
WHAT IS IT, HIKARU?
UM...
WELL...
I JUST WONDERED HOW LONG YOU'LL BE STAYING HERE.

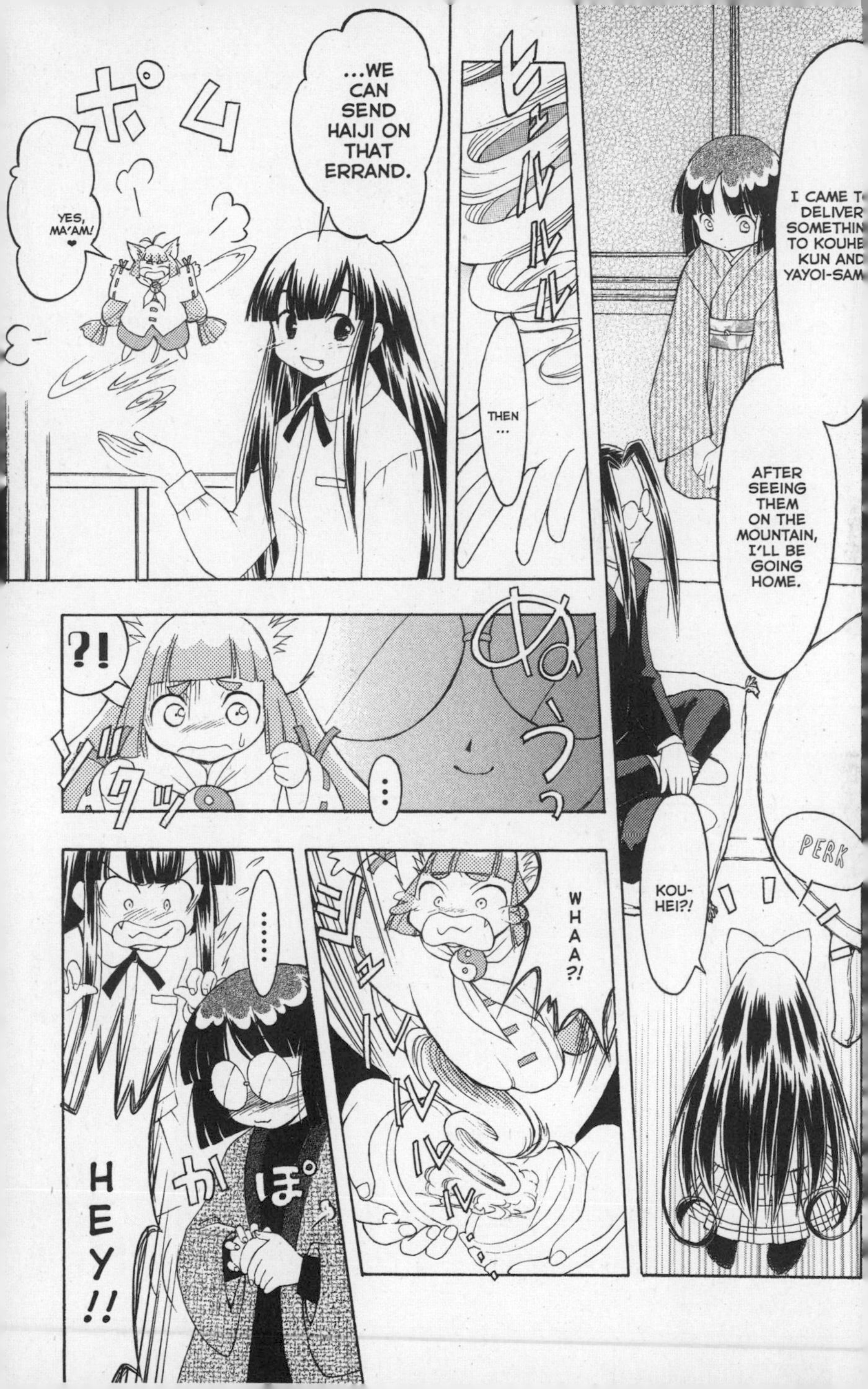
I CAME T DELIVER SOMETHIN TO KOUHE KUN AND YAYOI-SAM
AFTER SEEING THEM ON THE MOUNTAIN, I'LL BE GOING HOME.
ヒュルルル
THEN ...
...WE CAN SEND HAIJI ON THAT ERRAND.
ポム
YES, MA'AM! ❤
ぬうっ
...
?!
ゾクッ
PERK
KOU-HEI?!
WHAA?!
......
かぽ
HEY!!

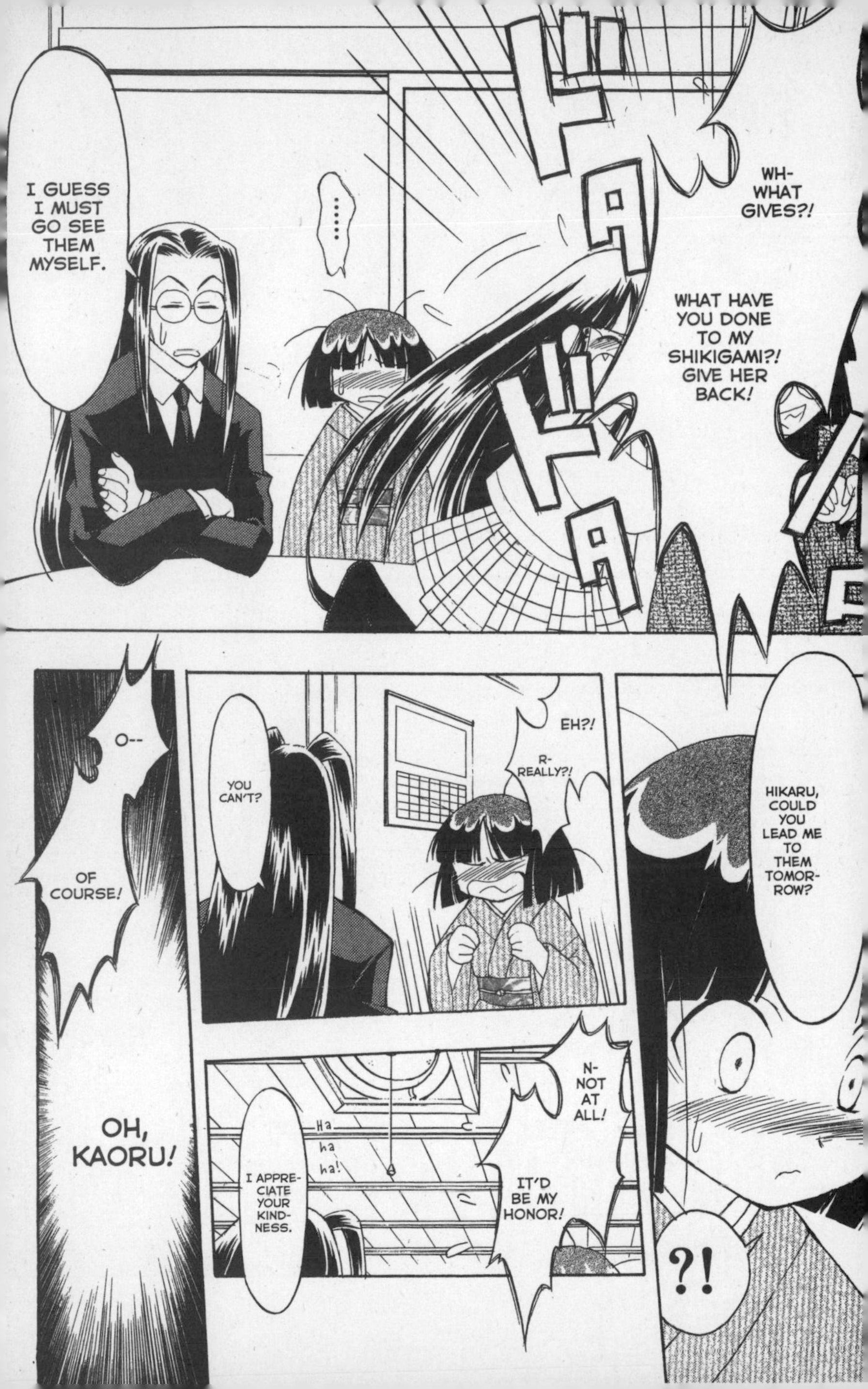
WH- WHAT GIVES?!
WHAT HAVE YOU DONE TO MY SHIKIGAMI?! GIVE HER BACK!
......
I GUESS I MUST GO SEE THEM MYSELF.
HIKARU, COULD YOU LEAD ME TO THEM TOMORROW?
?!
EH?!
R-REALLY?!
YOU CAN'T?
N-NOT AT ALL!
IT'D BE MY HONOR!
Ha ha ha!
I APPRECIATE YOUR KINDNESS.
O--
OF COURSE!
OH, KAORU!

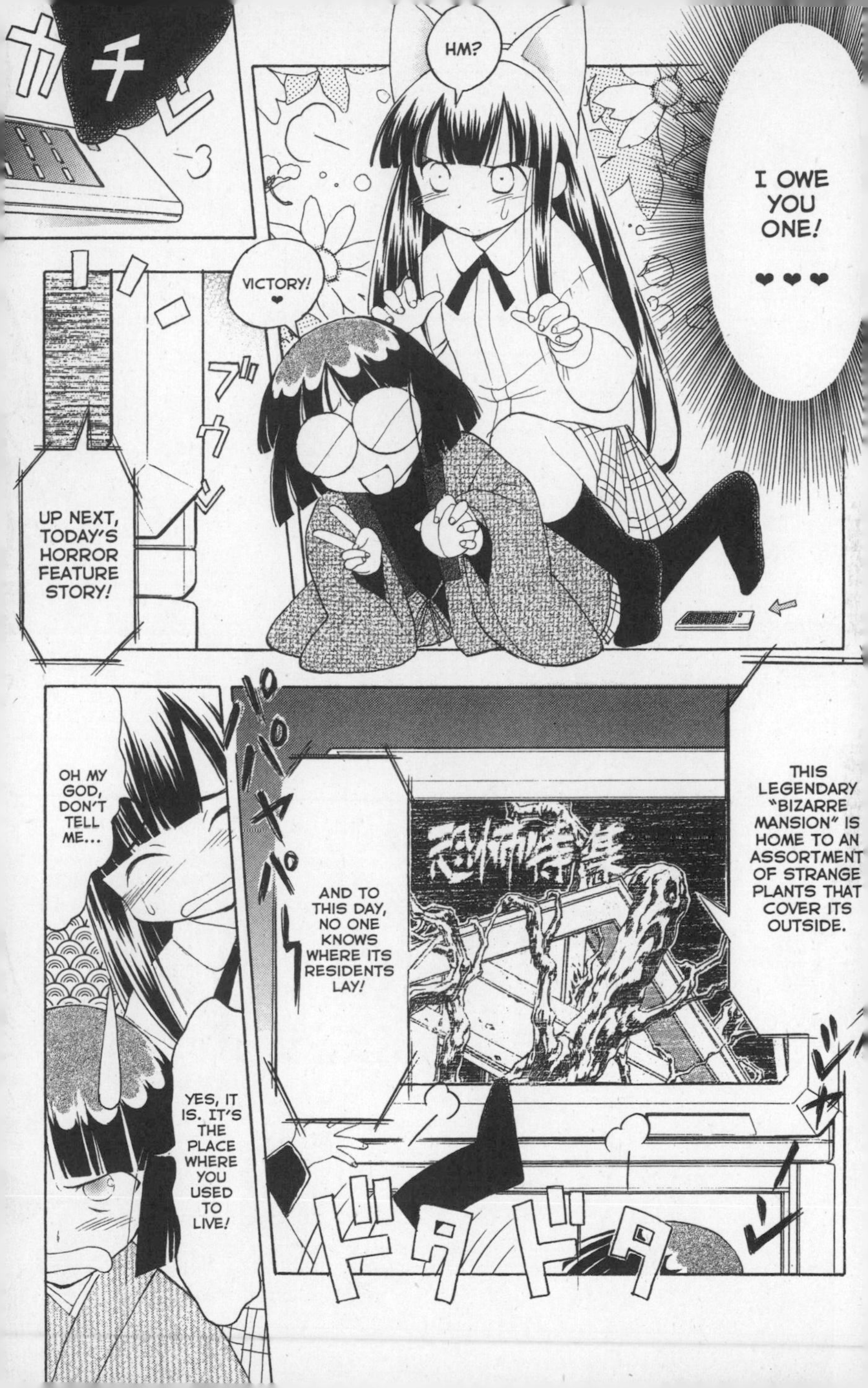
I OWE YOU ONE! ❤❤❤
HM?
VICTORY! ❤
UP NEXT, TODAY'S HORROR FEATURE STORY!
THIS LEGENDARY "BIZARRE MANSION" IS HOME TO AN ASSORTMENT OF STRANGE PLANTS THAT COVER ITS OUTSIDE.
AND TO THIS DAY, NO ONE KNOWS WHERE ITS RESIDENTS LAY!
ドタドタ
OH MY GOD, DON'T TELL ME...
YES, IT IS. IT'S THE PLACE WHERE YOU USED TO LIVE!

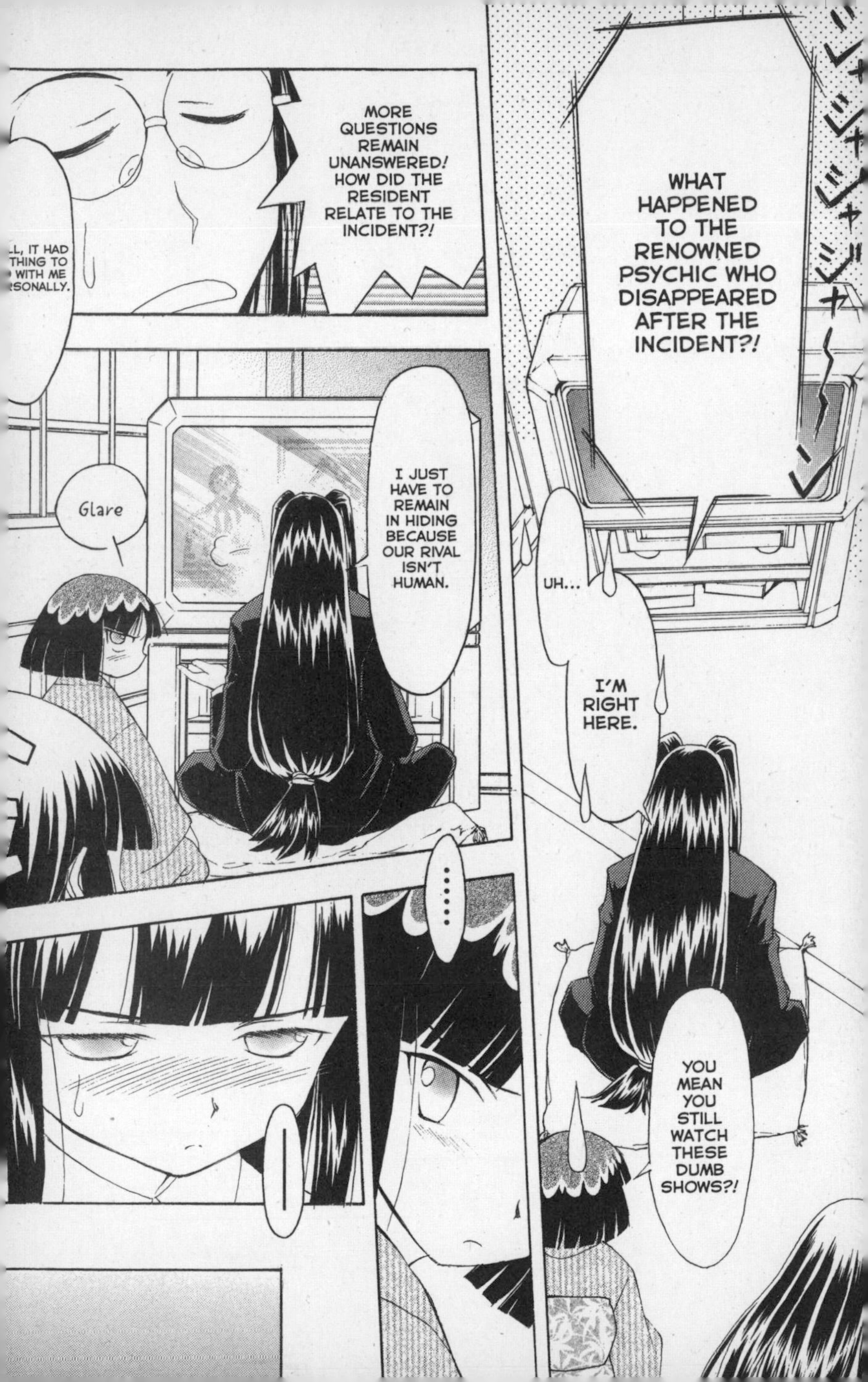
WHAT HAPPENED TO THE RENOWNED PSYCHIC WHO DISAPPEARED AFTER THE INCIDENT?!
MORE QUESTIONS REMAIN UNANSWERED! HOW DID THE RESIDENT RELATE TO THE INCIDENT?!
LL, IT HAD THING TO WITH ME RSONALLY.
I JUST HAVE TO REMAIN IN HIDING BECAUSE OUR RIVAL ISN'T HUMAN.
Glare
UH...
I'M RIGHT HERE.
......
!
YOU MEAN YOU STILL WATCH THESE DUMB SHOWS?!

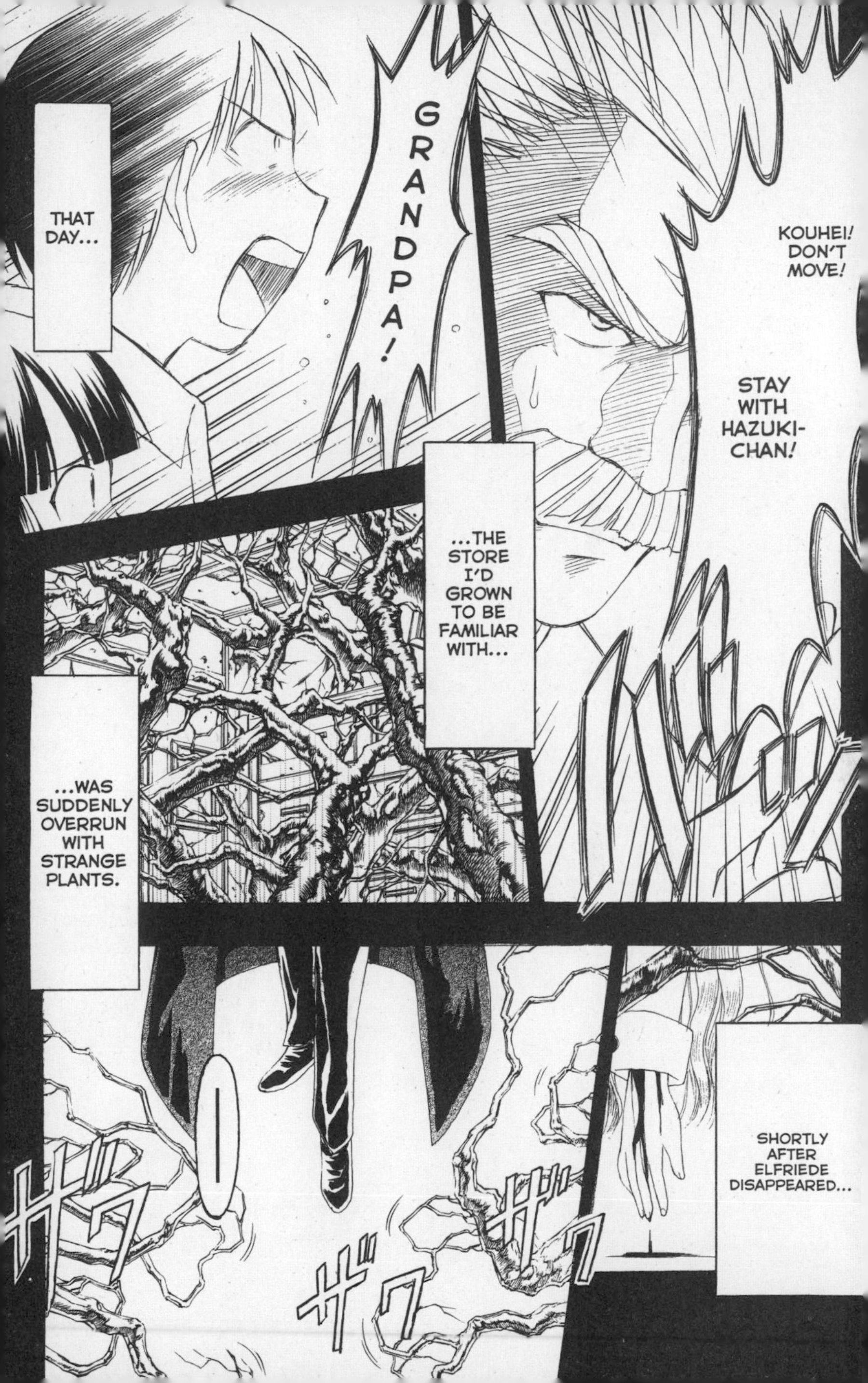
KOUHEI! DON'T MOVE!
STAY WITH HAZUKI-CHAN!
GRANDPA!
THAT DAY...
...THE STORE I'D GROWN TO BE FAMILIAR WITH...
...WAS SUDDENLY OVERRUN WITH STRANGE PLANTS.
SHORTLY AFTER ELFRIEDE DISAPPEARED...

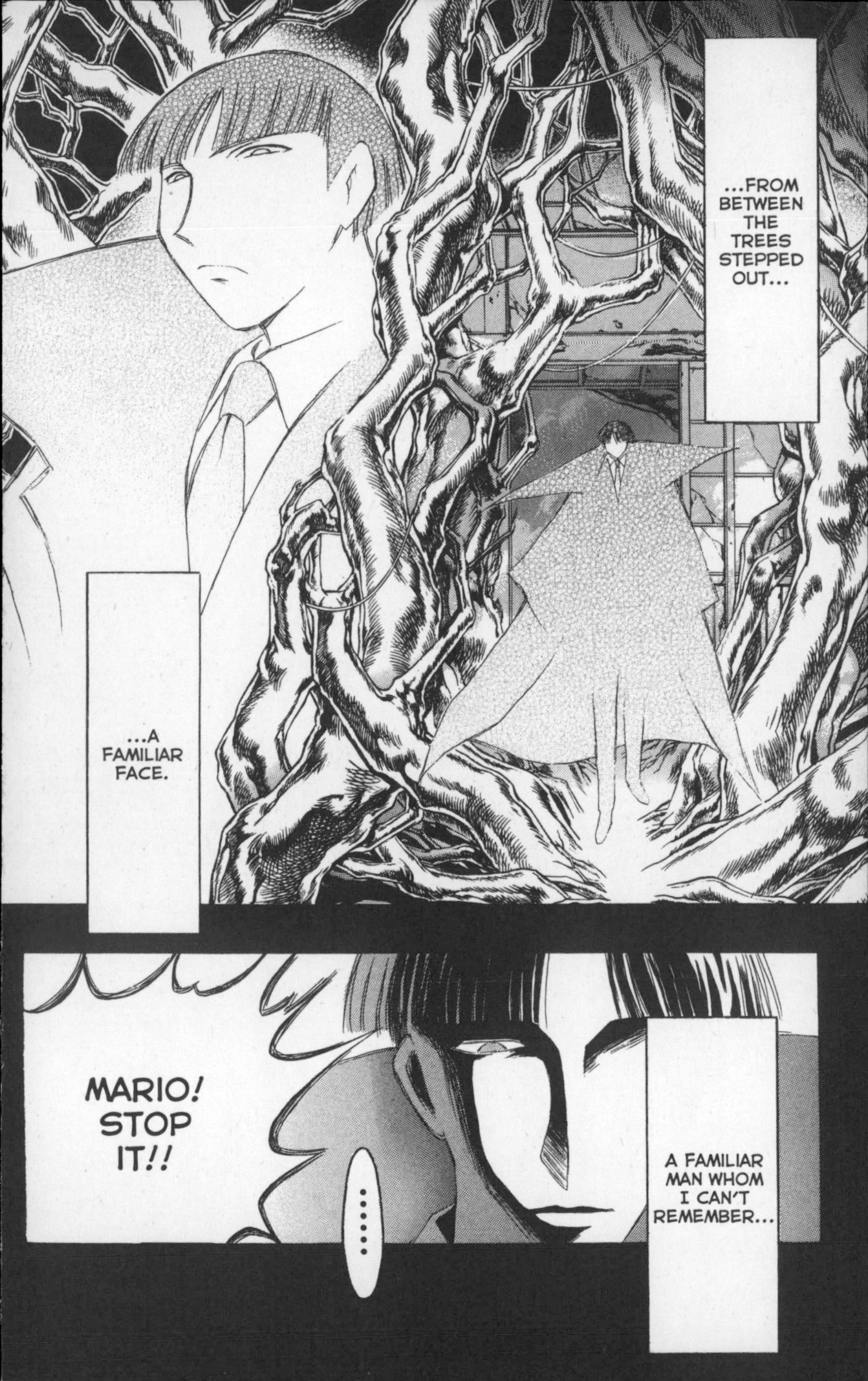
...FROM BETWEEN THE TREES STEPPED OUT...
...A FAMILIAR FACE.
A FAMILIAR MAN WHOM I CAN'T REMEMBER...
......
MARIO! STOP IT!!

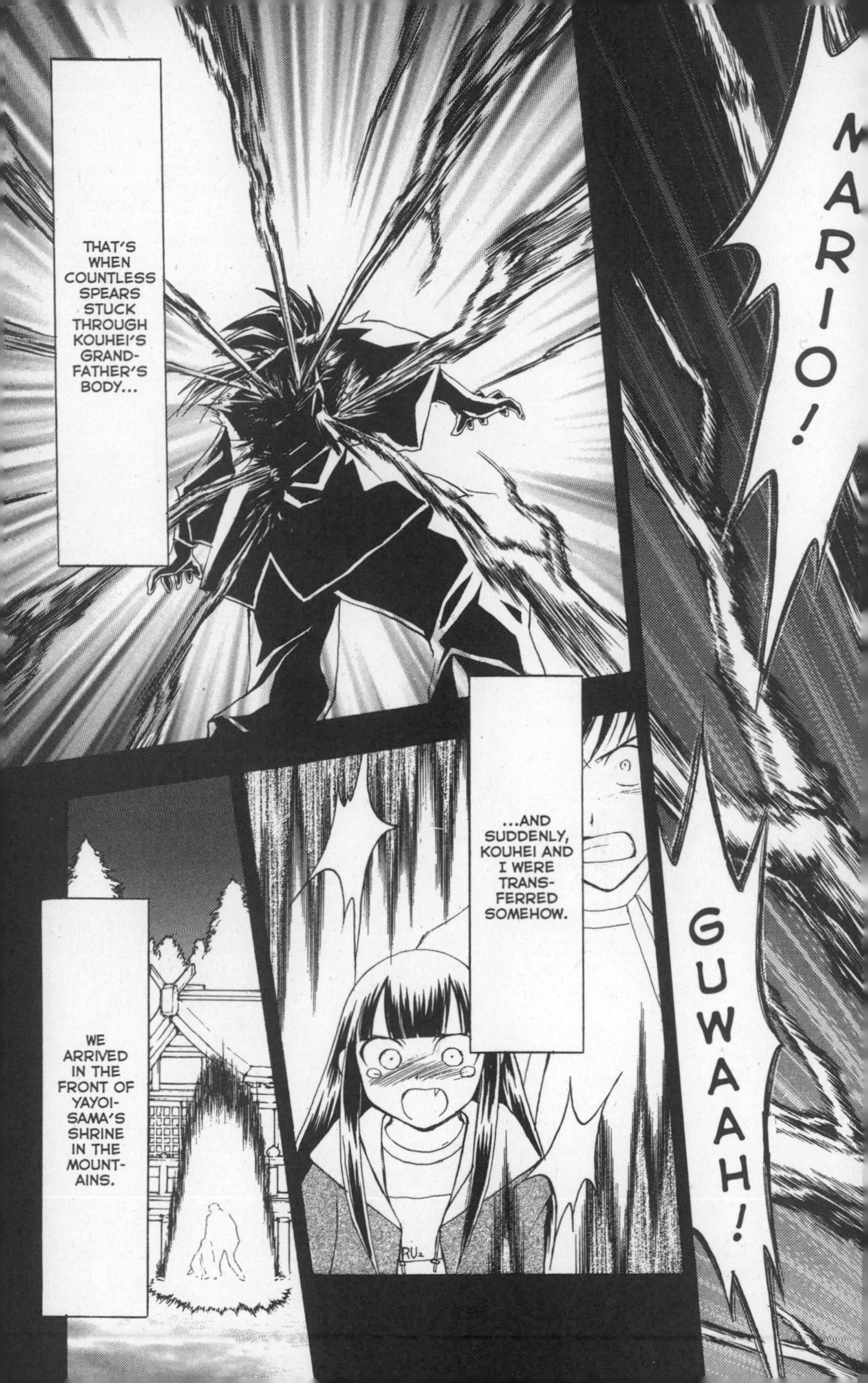
NARIO!
GUWAAH!
THAT'S WHEN COUNTLESS SPEARS STUCK THROUGH KOUHEI'S GRAND-FATHER'S BODY...
...AND SUDDENLY, KOUHEI AND I WERE TRANS-FERRED SOMEHOW.
WE ARRIVED IN THE FRONT OF YAYOI-SAMA'S SHRINE IN THE MOUNT-AINS.

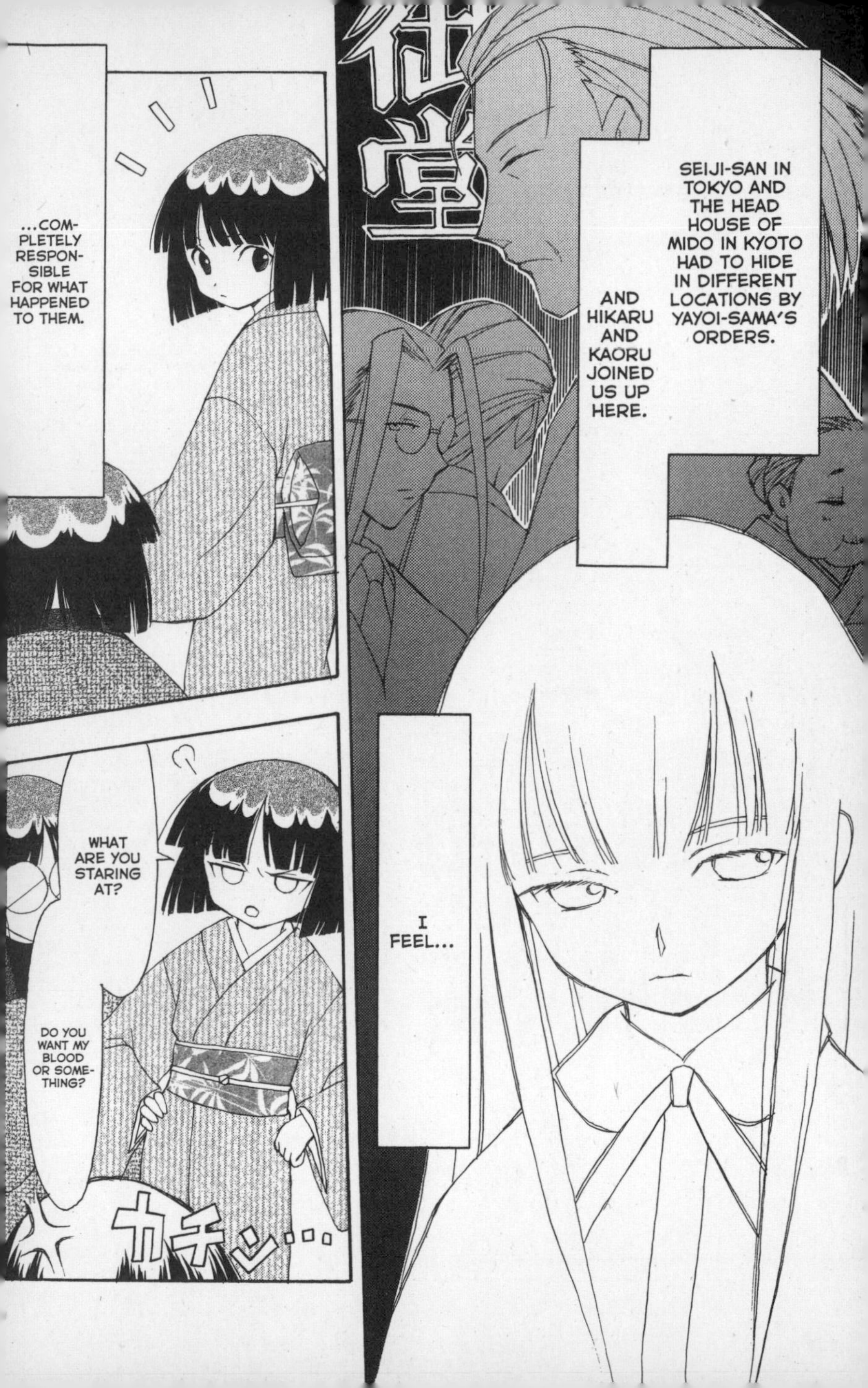
SEIJI-SAN IN TOKYO AND THE HEAD HOUSE OF MIDO IN KYOTO HAD TO HIDE IN DIFFERENT LOCATIONS BY YAYOI-SAMA'S ORDERS.
AND HIKARU AND KAORU JOINED US UP HERE.
I FEEL...
...COMPLETELY RESPONSIBLE FOR WHAT HAPPENED TO THEM.
WHAT ARE YOU STARING AT?
DO YOU WANT MY BLOOD OR SOMETHING?
カチン...

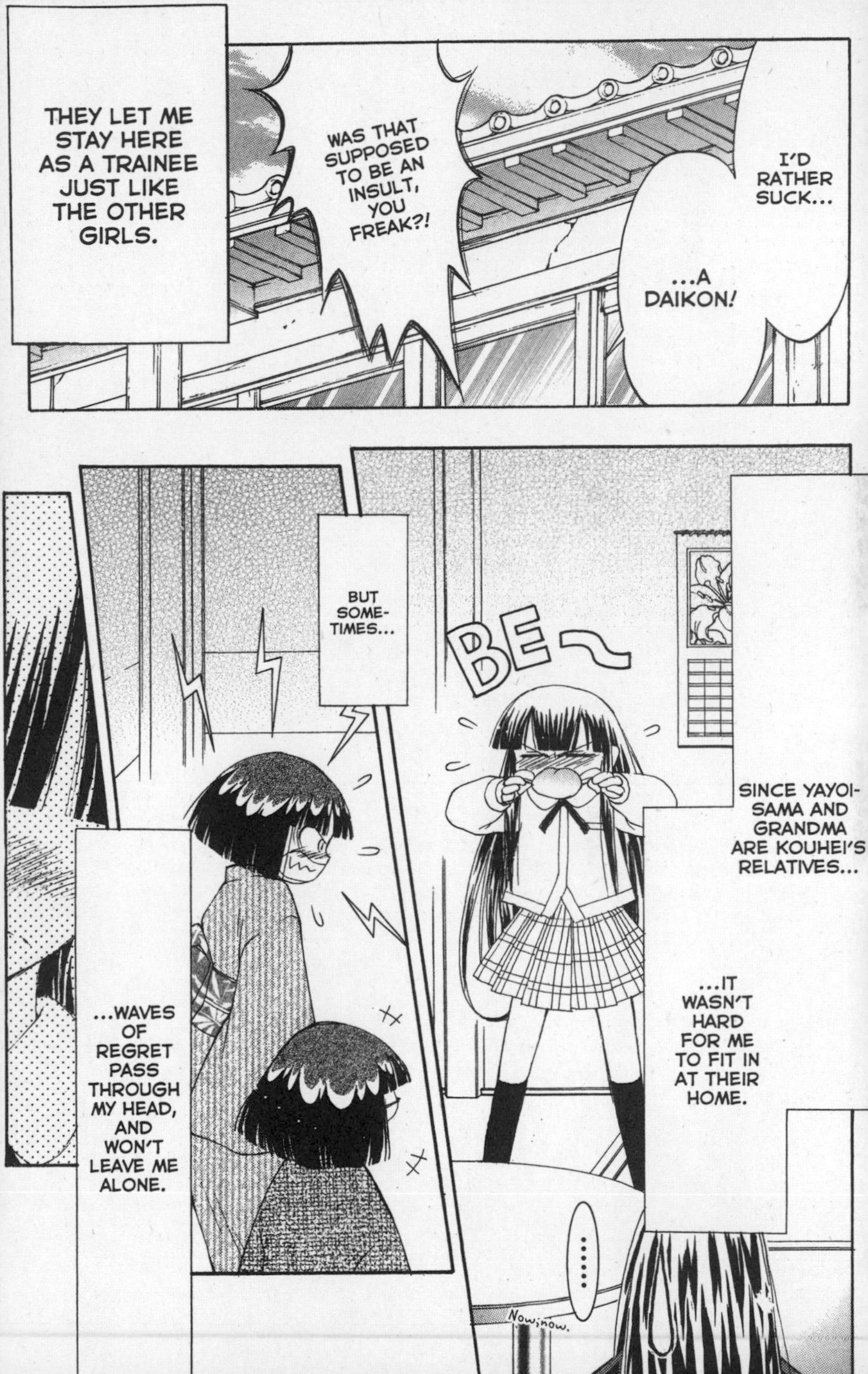
I'D RATHER SUCK...
...A DAIKON!
WAS THAT SUPPOSED TO BE AN INSULT, YOU FREAK?!
THEY LET ME STAY HERE AS A TRAINEE JUST LIKE THE OTHER GIRLS.
SINCE YAYOI-SAMA AND GRANDMA ARE KOUHEI'S RELATIVES...
...IT WASN'T HARD FOR ME TO FIT IN AT THEIR HOME.
BE~
BUT SOMETIMES...
......
Now, now.
...WAVES OF REGRET PASS THROUGH MY HEAD, AND WON'T LEAVE ME ALONE.

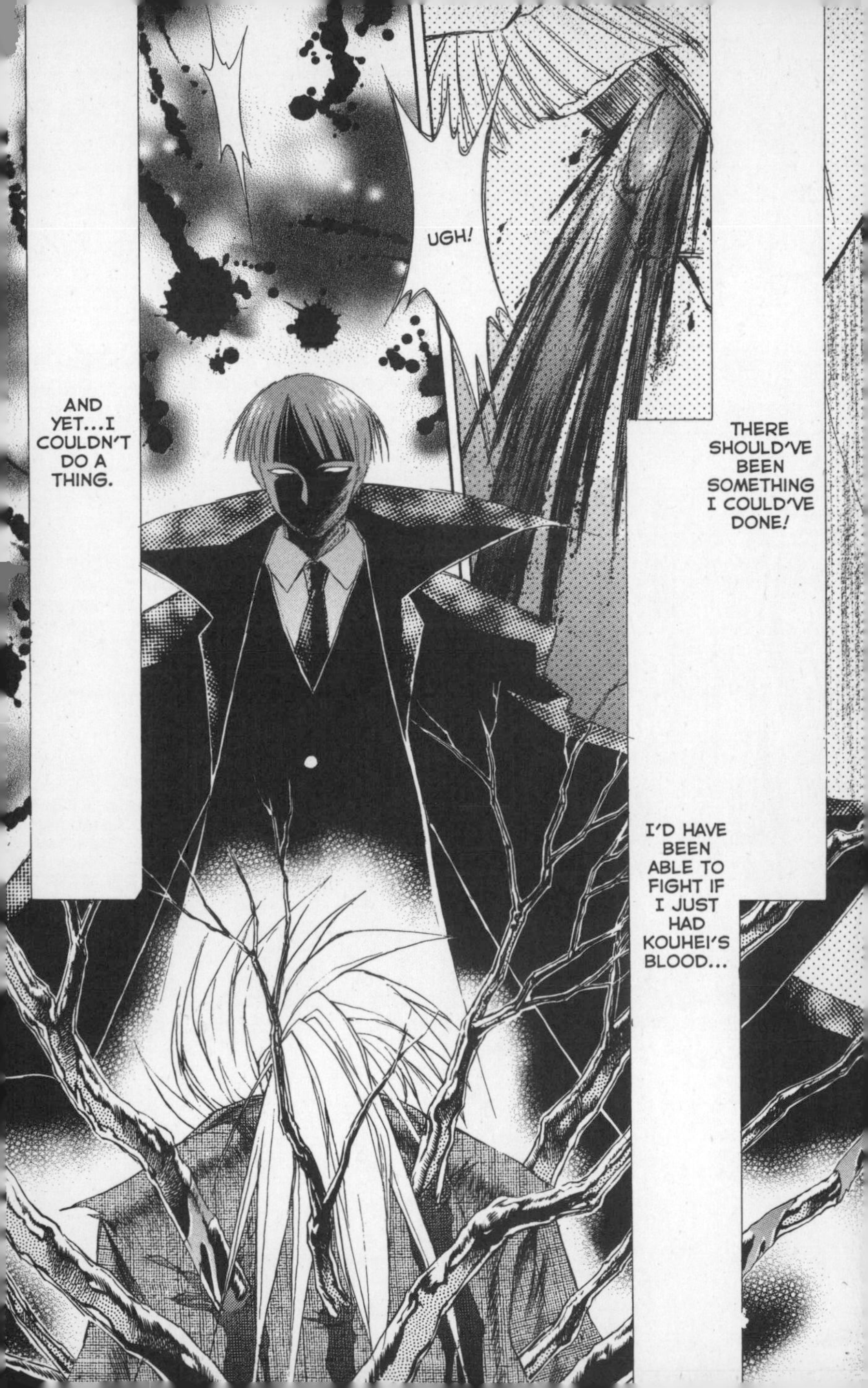
UGH!
THERE SHOULD'VE BEEN SOMETHING I COULD'VE DONE!
I'D HAVE BEEN ABLE TO FIGHT IF I JUST HAD KOUHEI'S BLOOD...
AND YET...I COULDN'T DO A THING.

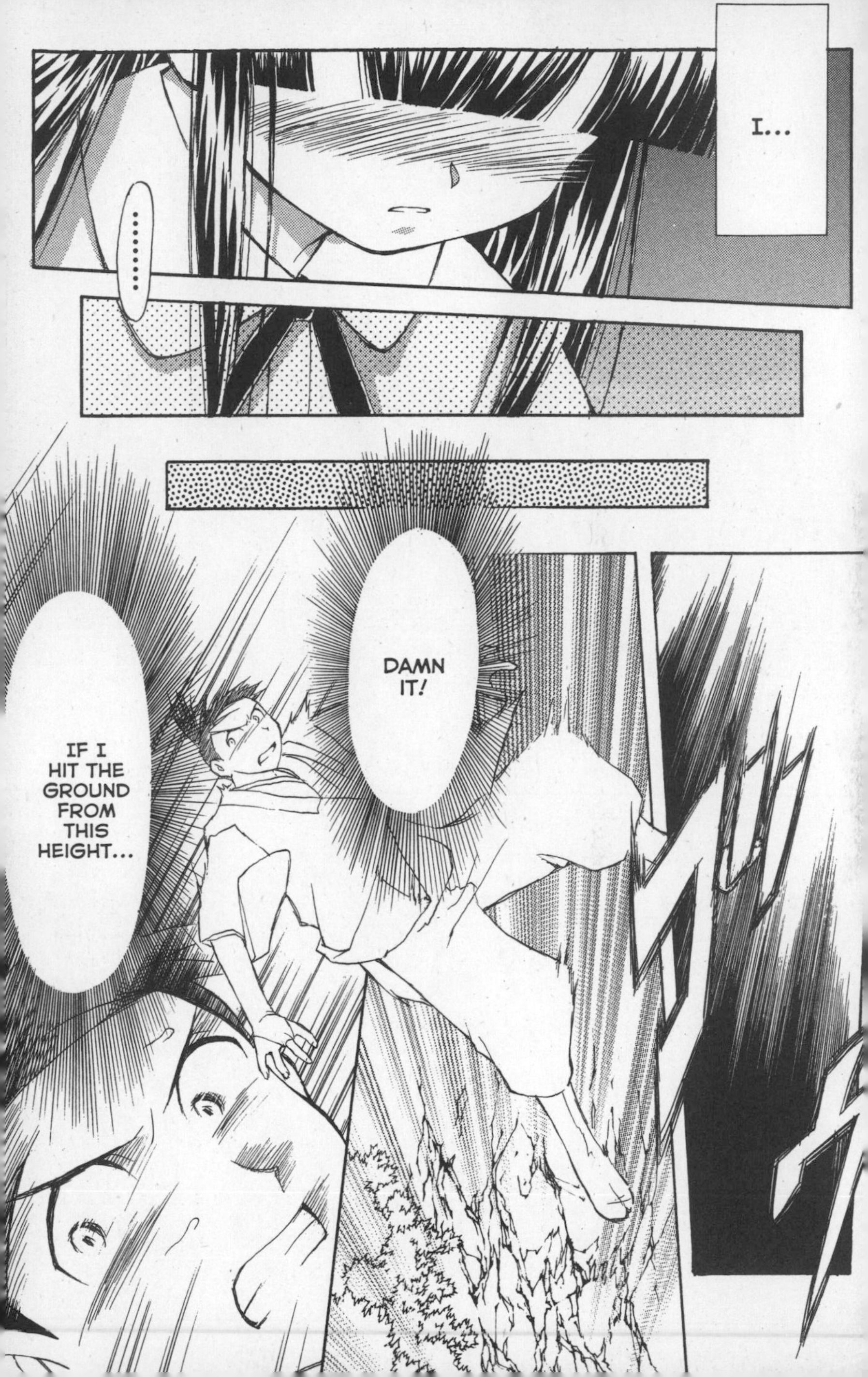
I...
......
DAMN IT!
IF I HIT THE GROUND FROM THIS HEIGHT...

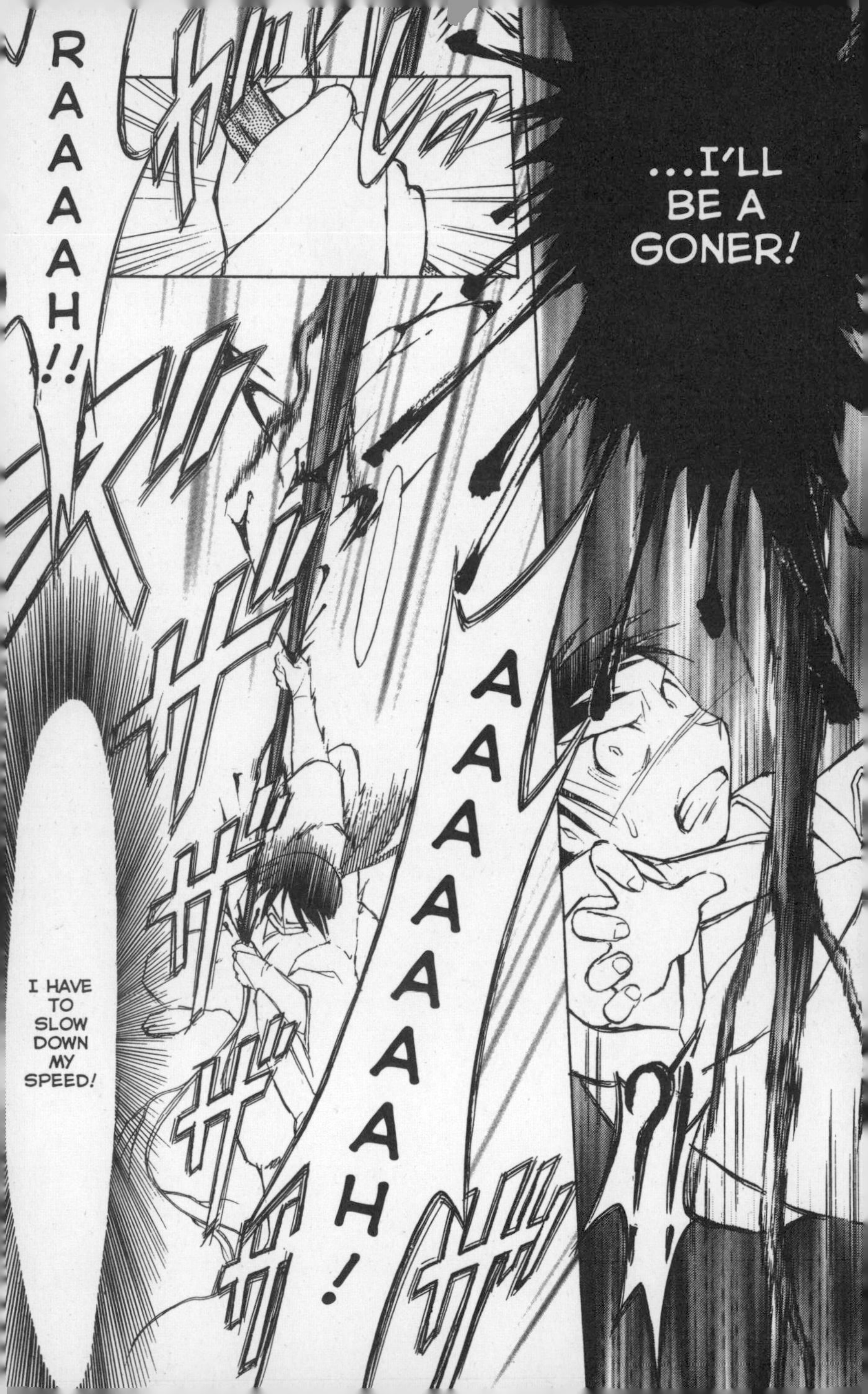
...I'LL BE A GONER!
RAAAAAH!!
AAAAAAAAH!
I HAVE TO SLOW DOWN MY SPEED!

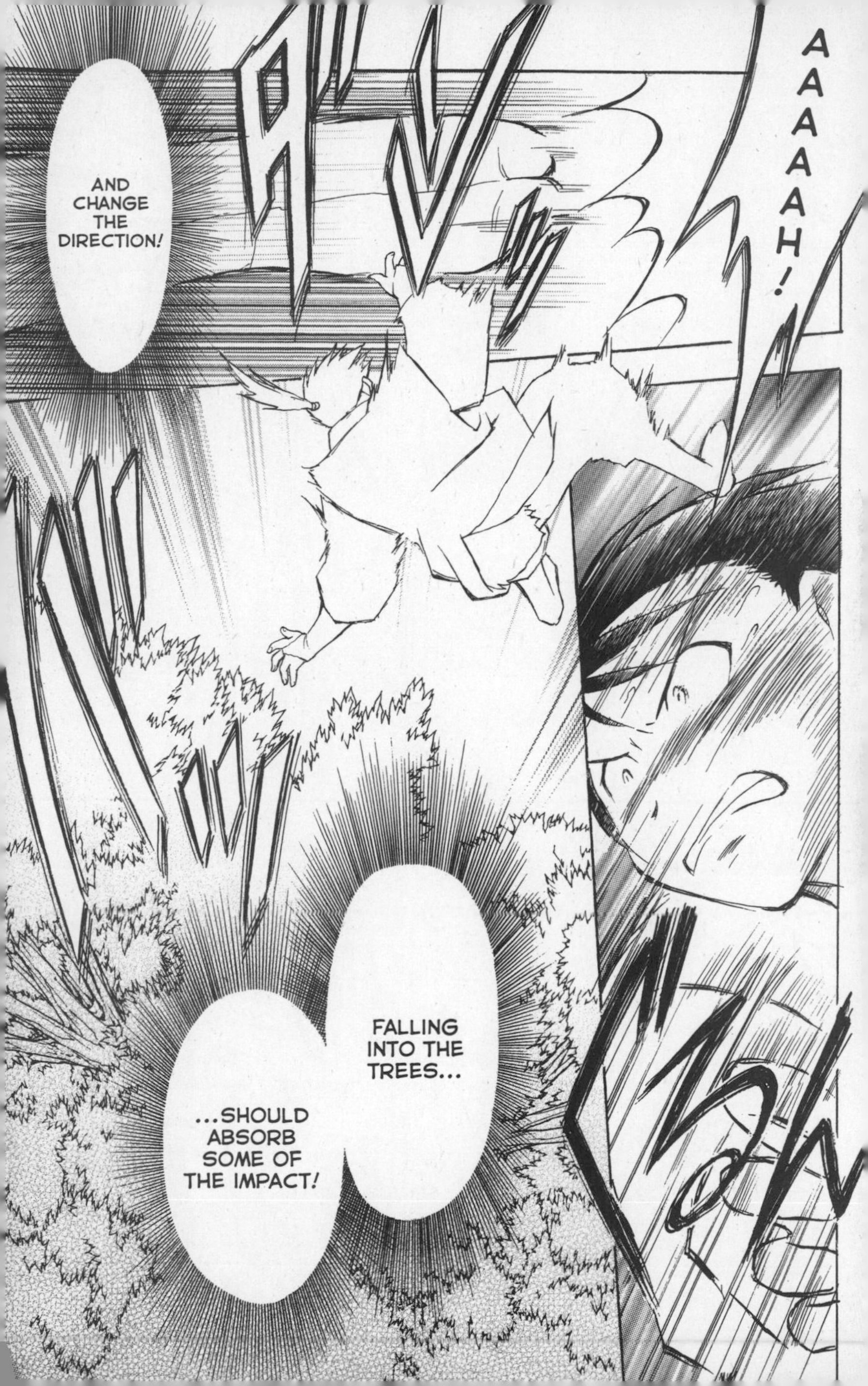
AAAAAH!
AND CHANGE THE DIRECTION!
FALLING INTO THE TREES...
...SHOULD ABSORB SOME OF THE IMPACT!

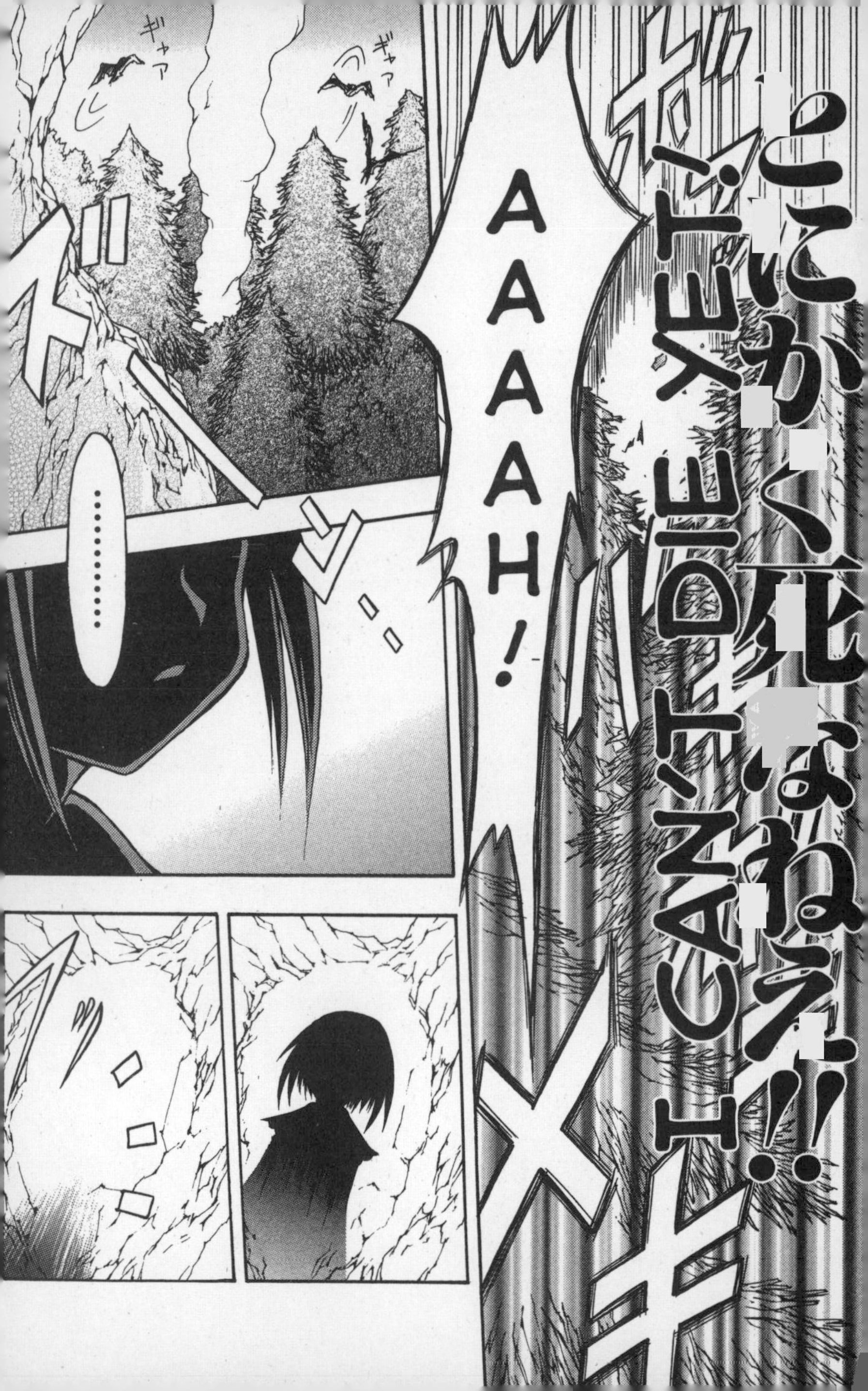
I CAN'T DIE YET!!
AAAAH!
ギャア
ギャア
…………

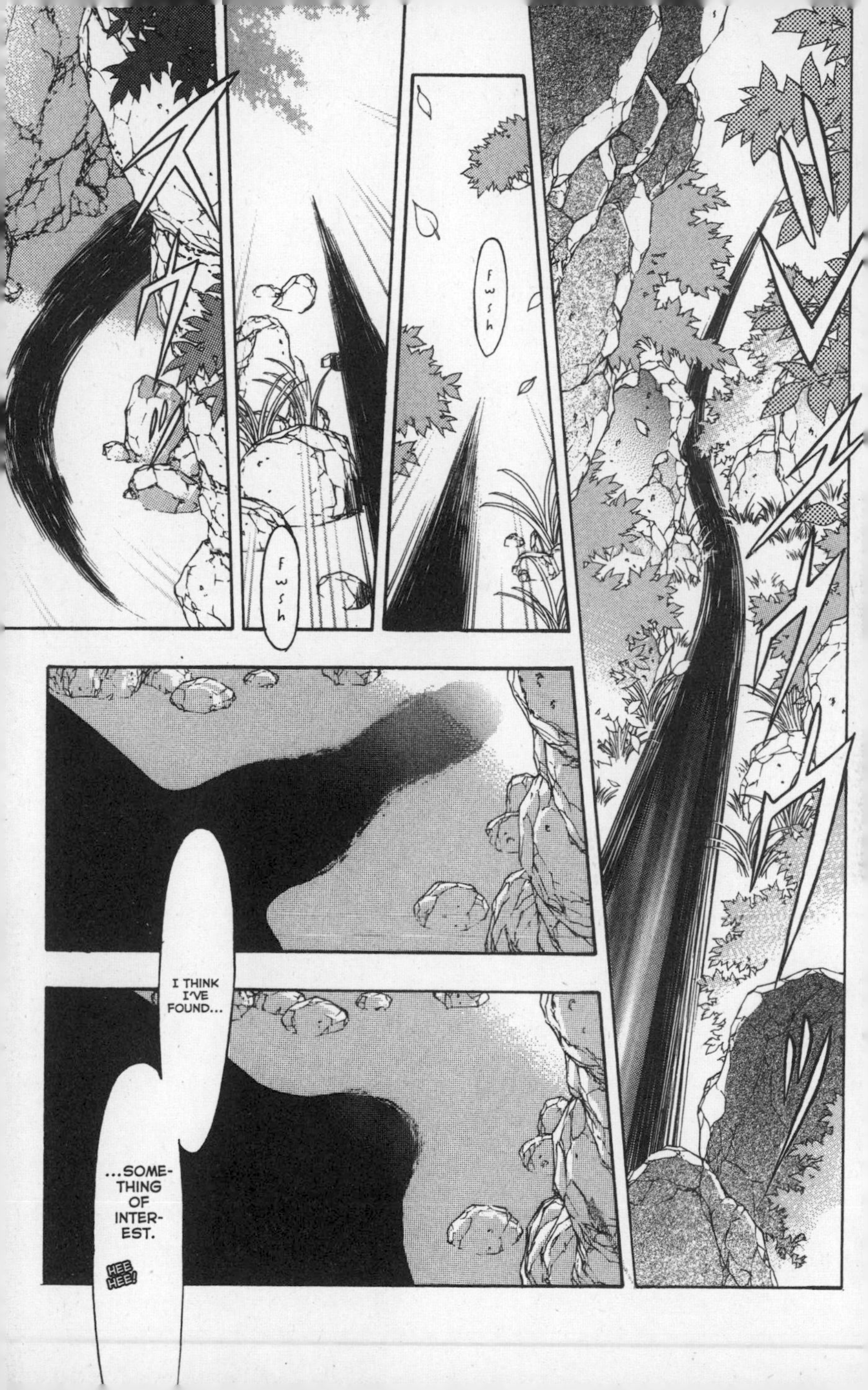

Fwsh
Fwsh
I THINK I'VE FOUND...
...SOME-THING OF INTER-EST.
HEE HEE!

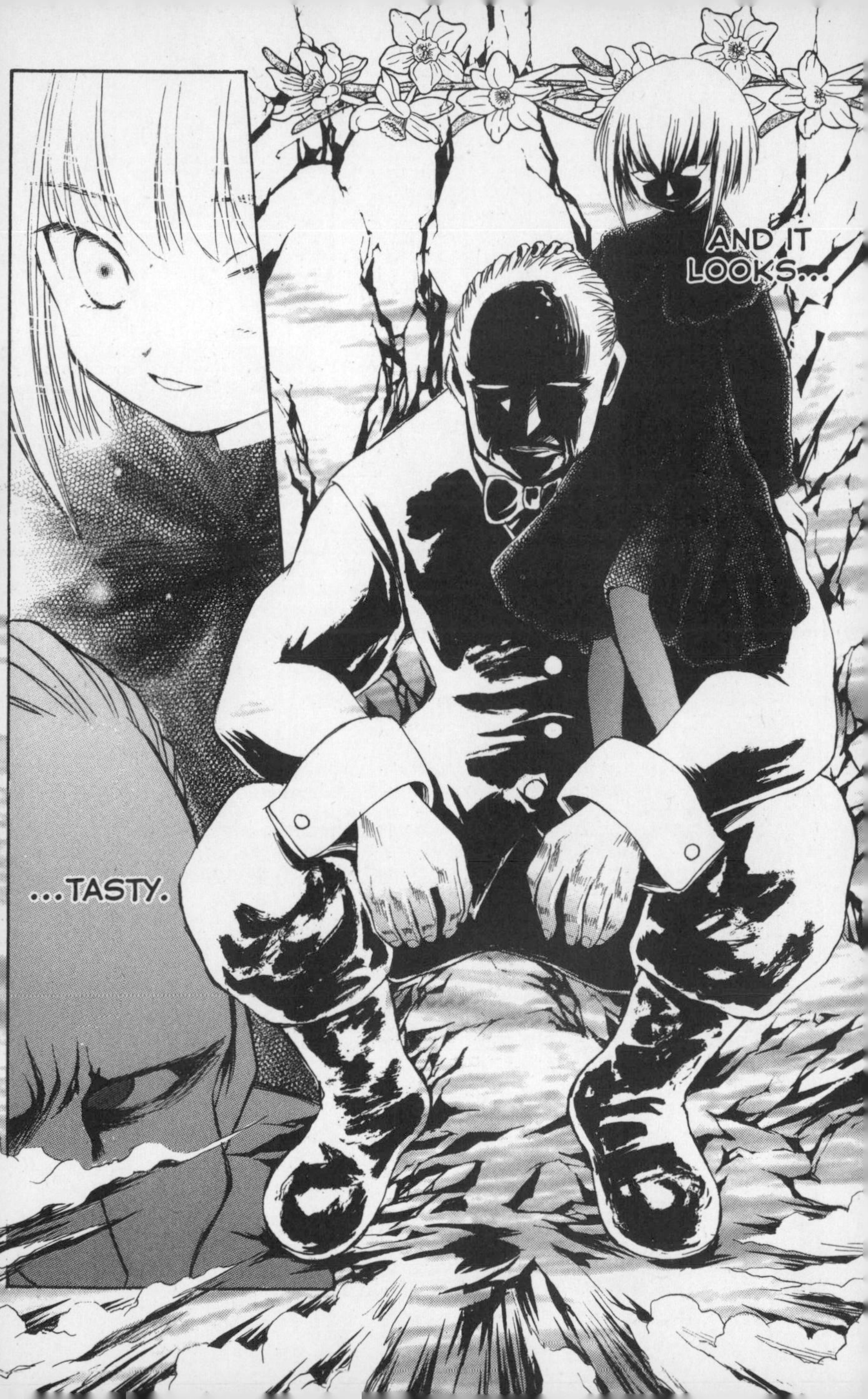
AND IT LOOKS...
...TASTY.

Moon 月詠 Phase

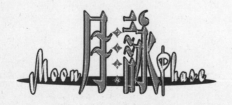

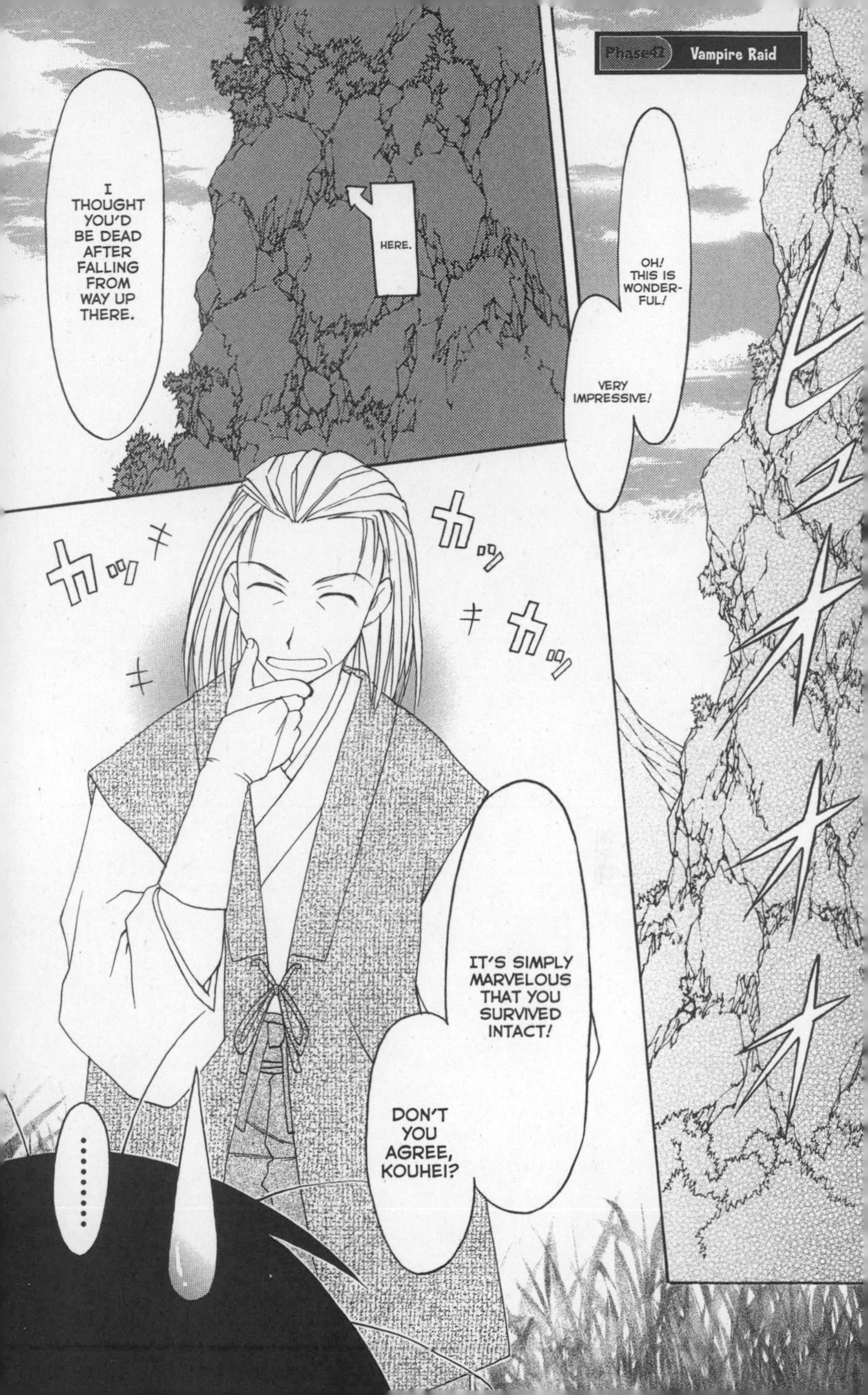
OH! THIS IS WONDERFUL!
VERY IMPRESSIVE!
ヒュオオオ
HERE.
I THOUGHT YOU'D BE DEAD AFTER FALLING FROM WAY UP THERE.
カッ
キ カッ
カッ キ
キ
IT'S SIMPLY MARVELOUS THAT YOU SURVIVED INTACT!
DON'T YOU AGREE, KOUHEI?
....

Phase42 Vampire Raid

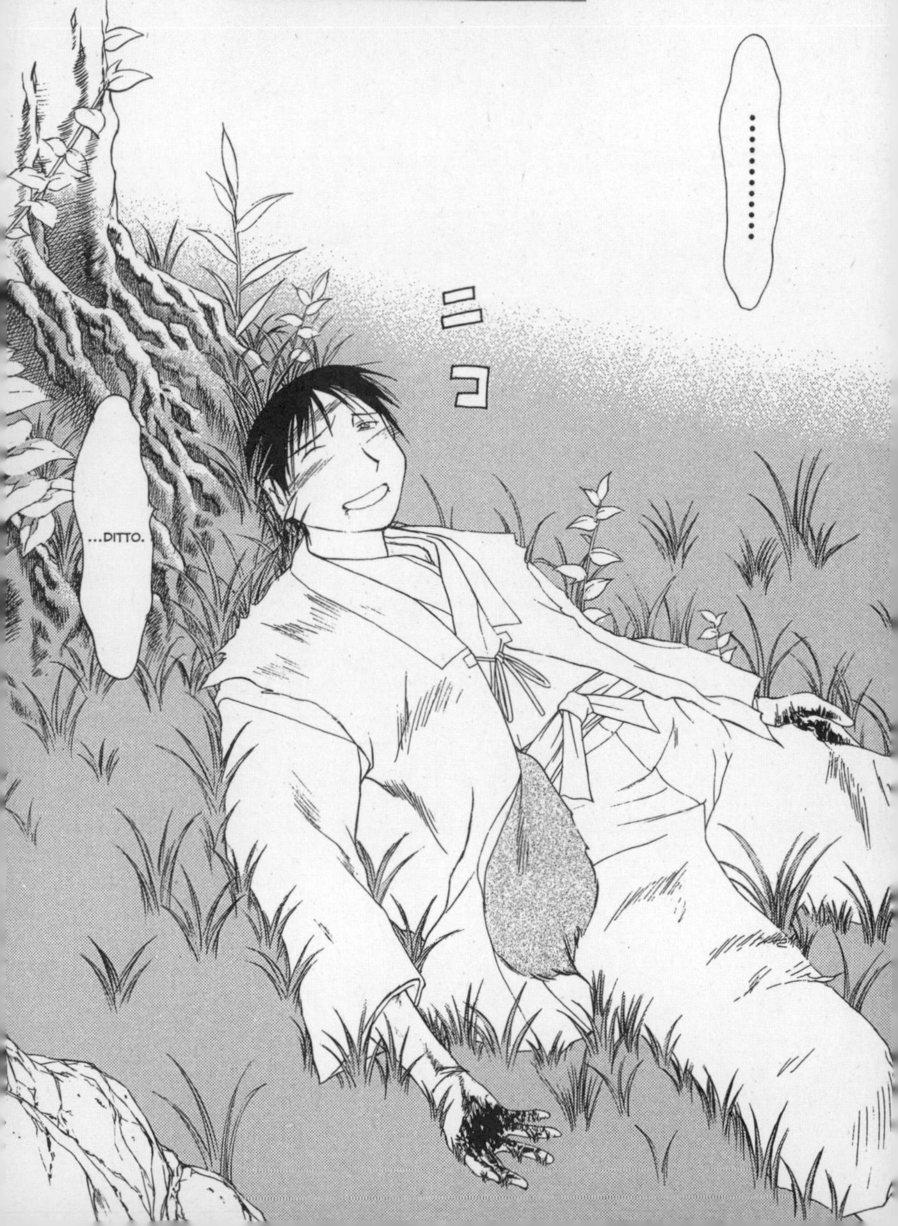
......
ニコ
...DITTO.

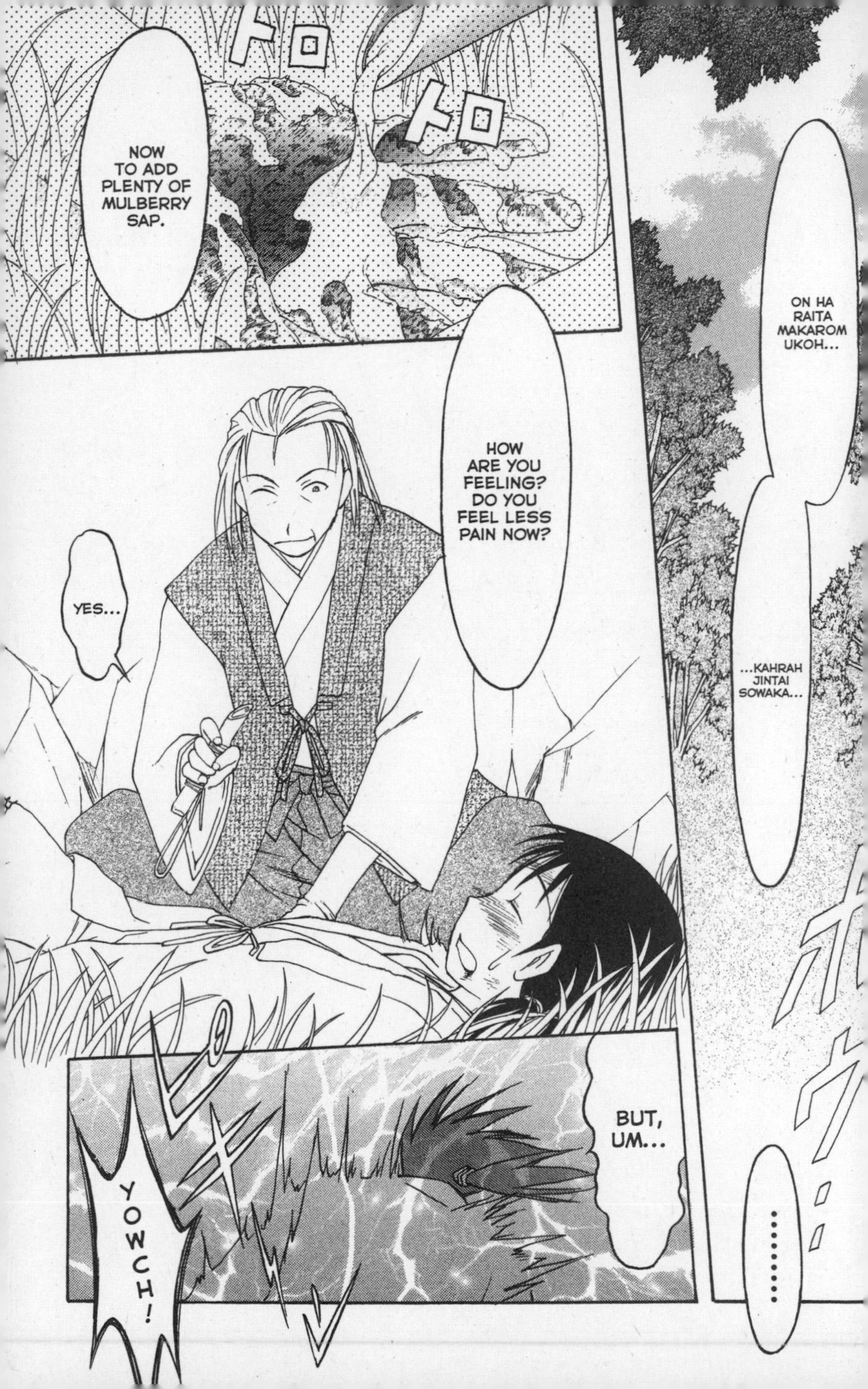
ON HA RAITA MAKAROM UKOH...
...KAHRAH JINTAI SOWAKA...
......
トロ
トロ
NOW TO ADD PLENTY OF MULBERRY SAP.
HOW ARE YOU FEELING? DO YOU FEEL LESS PAIN NOW?
YES...
BUT, UM...
YOWCH!

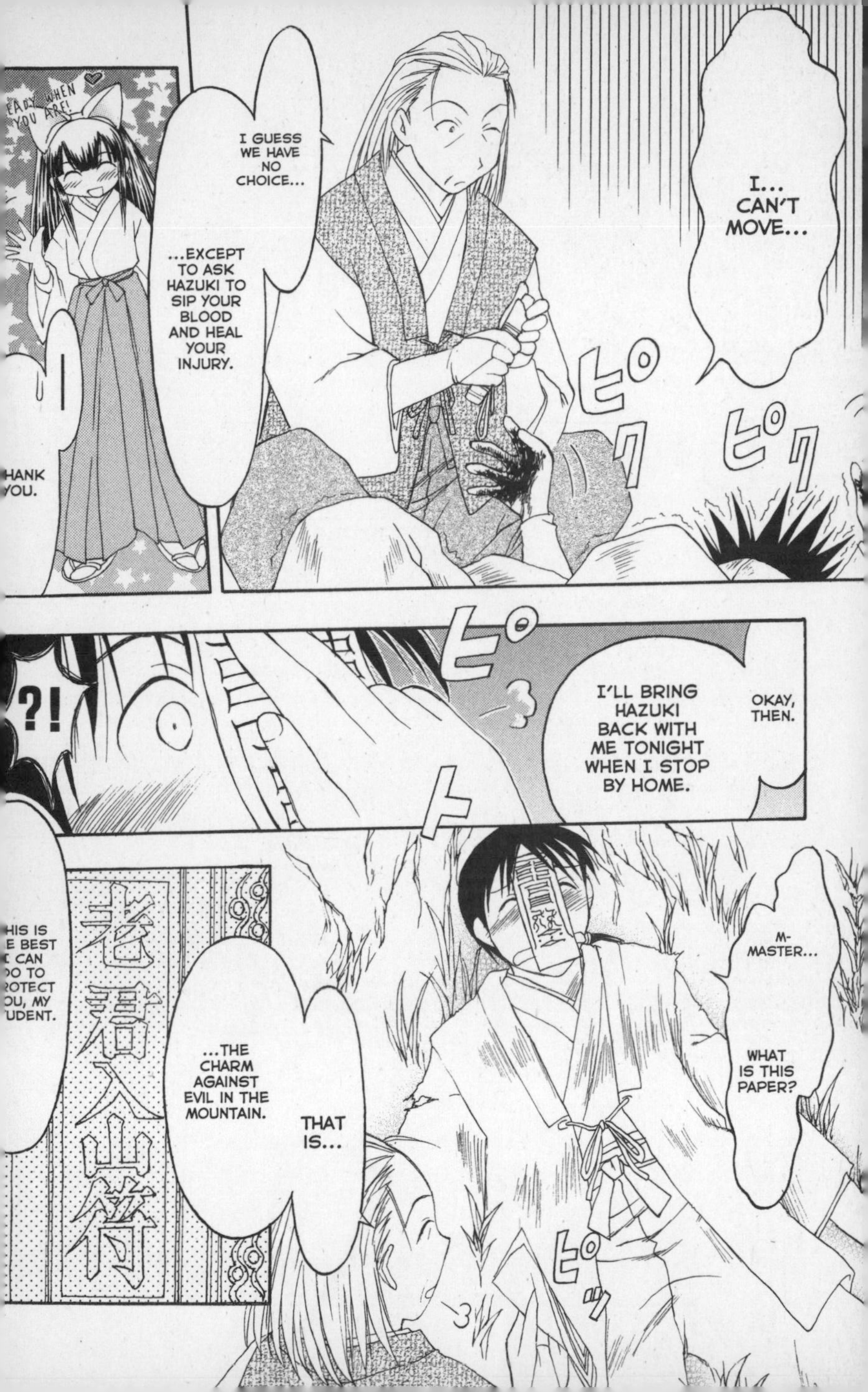
I... CAN'T MOVE...
ピク
ピク
I GUESS WE HAVE NO CHOICE...
...EXCEPT TO ASK HAZUKI TO SIP YOUR BLOOD AND HEAL YOUR INJURY.
READY WHEN YOU ARE!
HANK YOU.
OKAY, THEN.
I'LL BRING HAZUKI BACK WITH ME TONIGHT WHEN I STOP BY HOME.
ピト
?!
M-MASTER...
WHAT IS THIS PAPER?
ピッ
THAT IS...
...THE CHARM AGAINST EVIL IN THE MOUNTAIN.
老君入山符
HIS IS E BEST CAN DO TO ROTECT OU, MY UDENT.

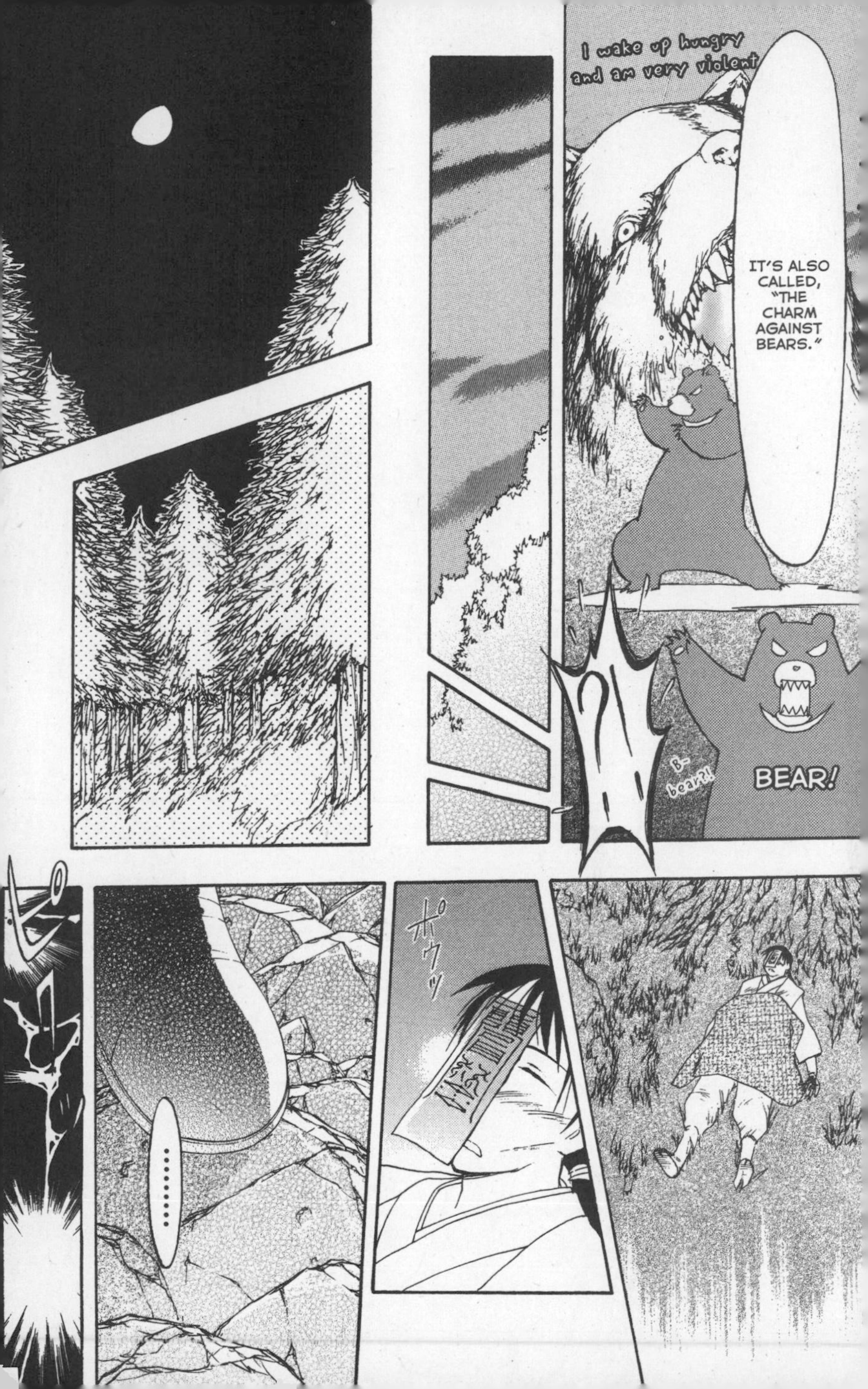

I wake up hungry and am very violent
IT'S ALSO CALLED, "THE CHARM AGAINST BEARS."
BEAR!
B- bear?!
ポウッ
……

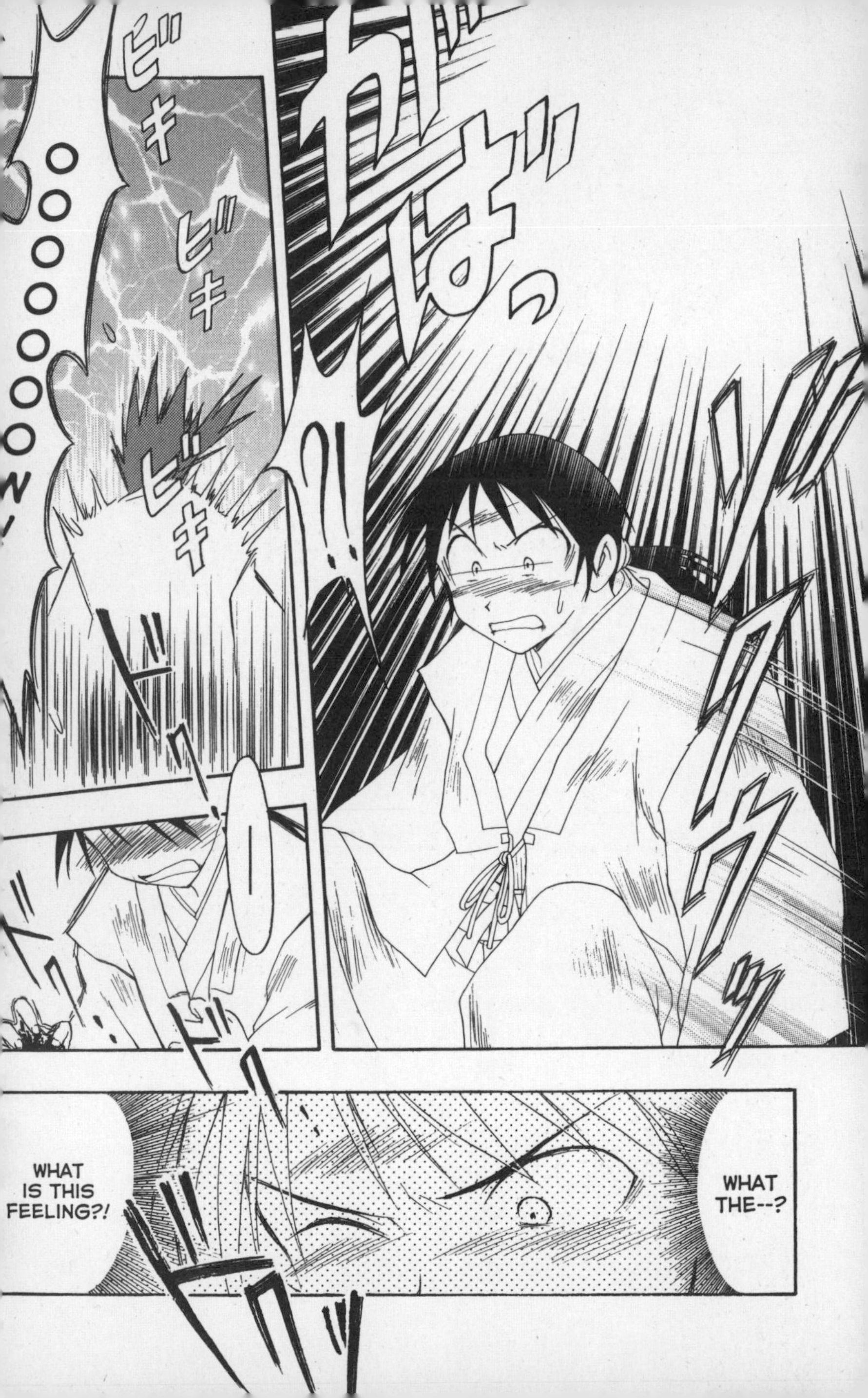
?!
ばっ
ビキ
ビキ
ビキ
OOOOOOOON!
WHAT THE--?
WHAT IS THIS FEELING?!

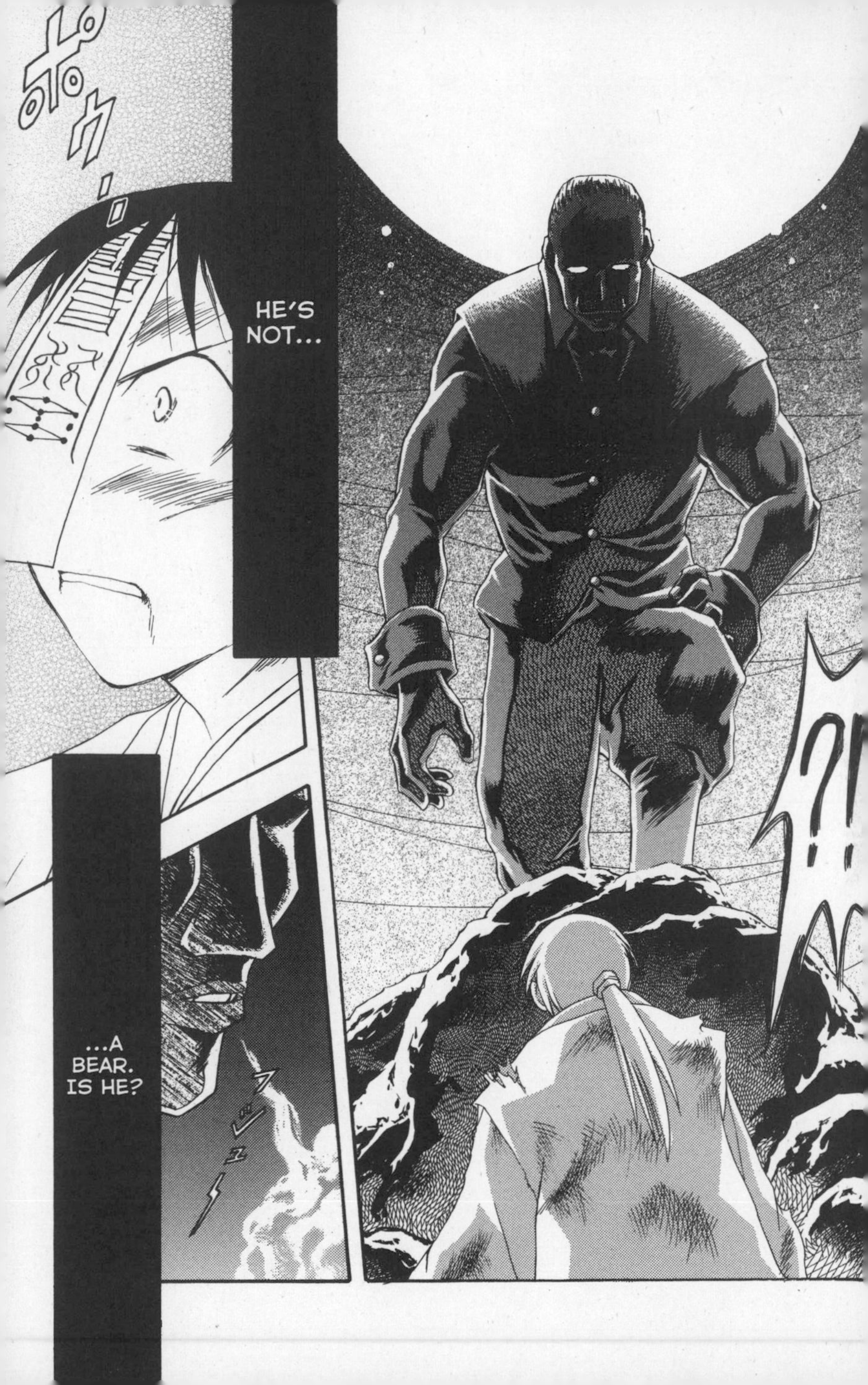
?!
HE'S NOT...
...A BEAR. IS HE?

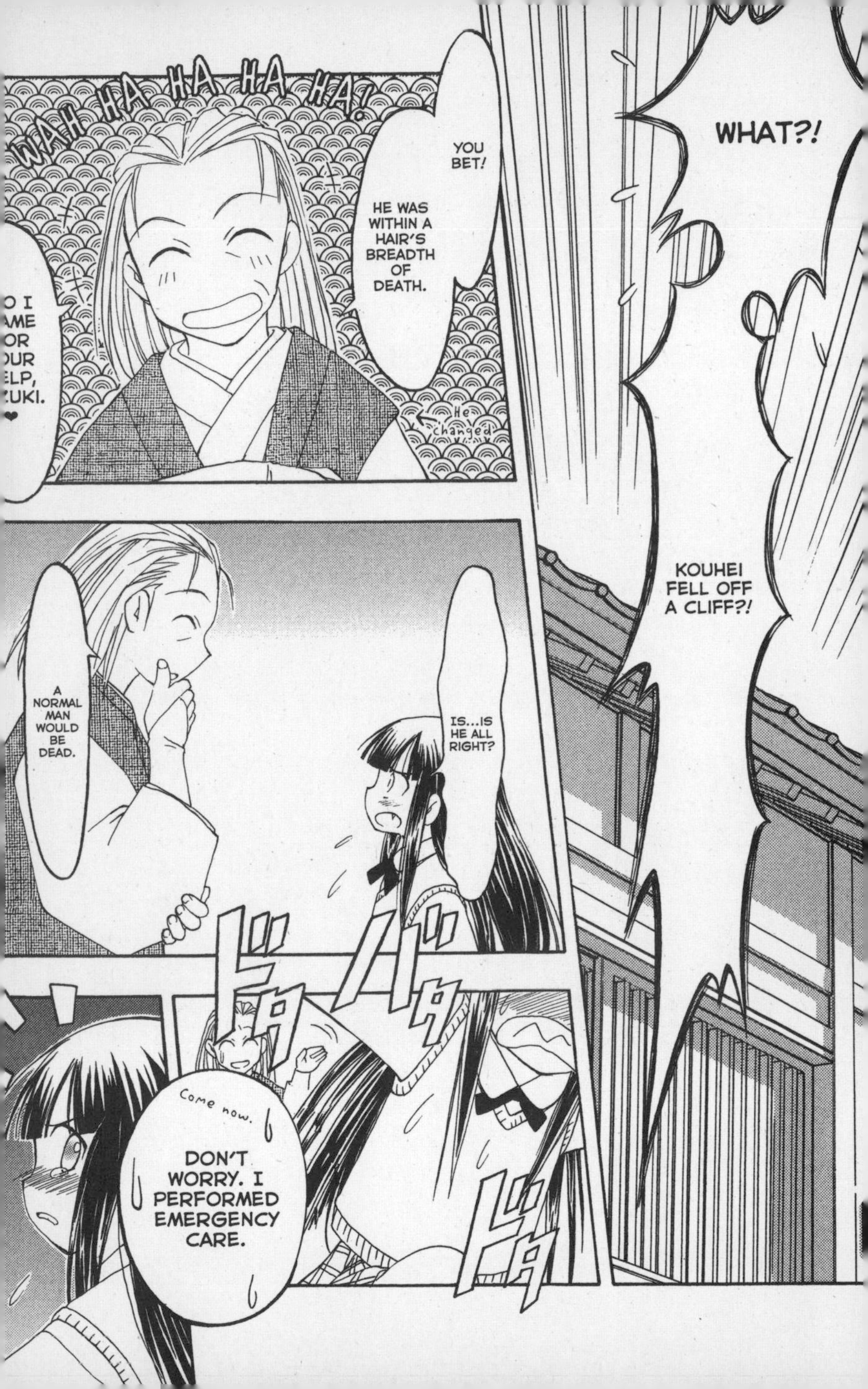
WHAT?!
KOUHEI FELL OFF A CLIFF?!
YOU BET! HE WAS WITHIN A HAIR'S BREADTH OF DEATH.
WAH HA HA HA HA!
He changed
O I AME OR OUR ELP, ZUKI. ❤
IS...IS HE ALL RIGHT?
A NORMAL MAN WOULD BE DEAD.
Come now.
DON'T WORRY. I PERFORMED EMERGENCY CARE.

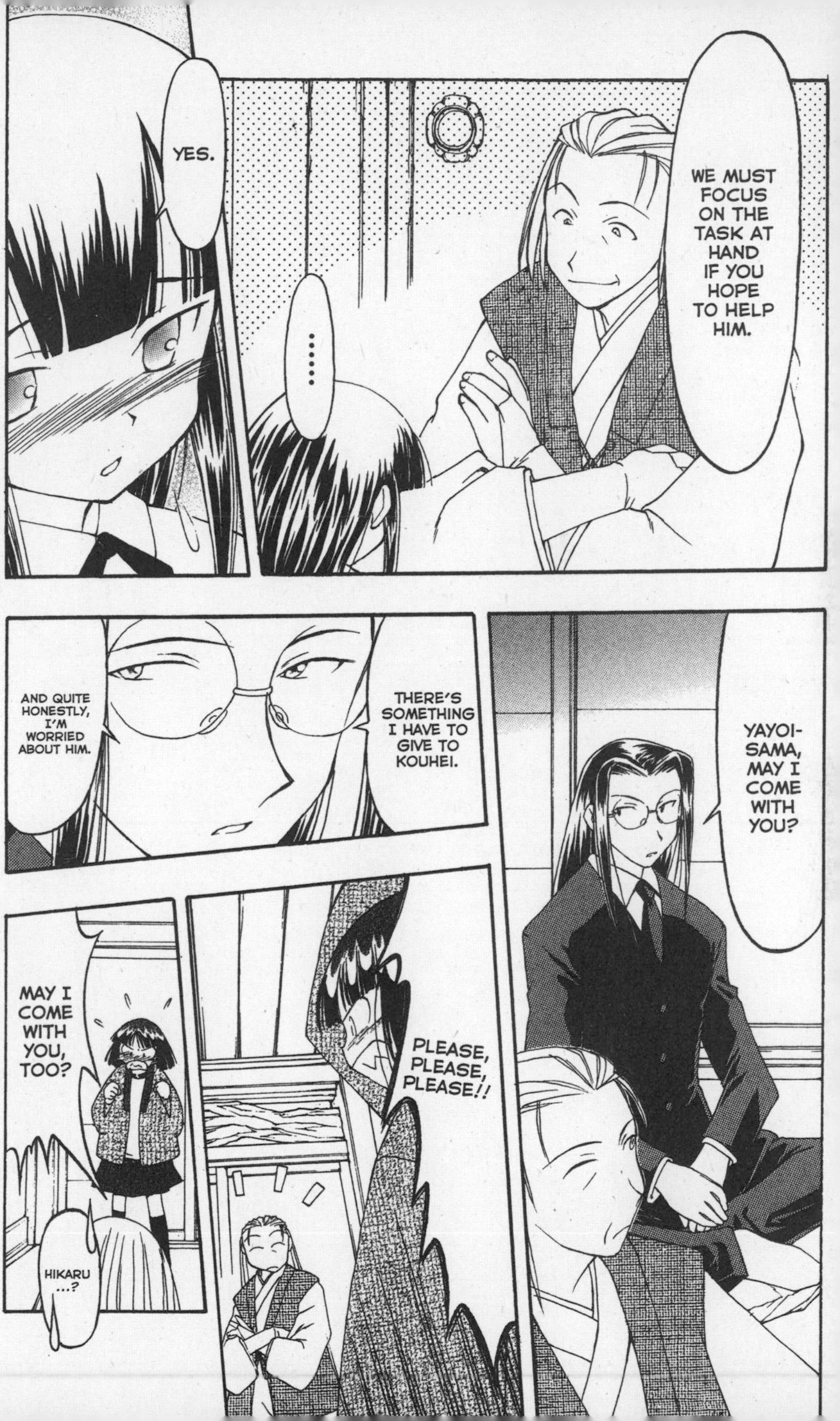
WE MUST FOCUS ON THE TASK AT HAND IF YOU HOPE TO HELP HIM.
......
YES.
YAYOI-SAMA, MAY I COME WITH YOU?
THERE'S SOMETHING I HAVE TO GIVE TO KOUHEI.
AND QUITE HONESTLY, I'M WORRIED ABOUT HIM.
PLEASE, PLEASE, PLEASE!!
MAY I COME WITH YOU, TOO?
HIKARU ...?

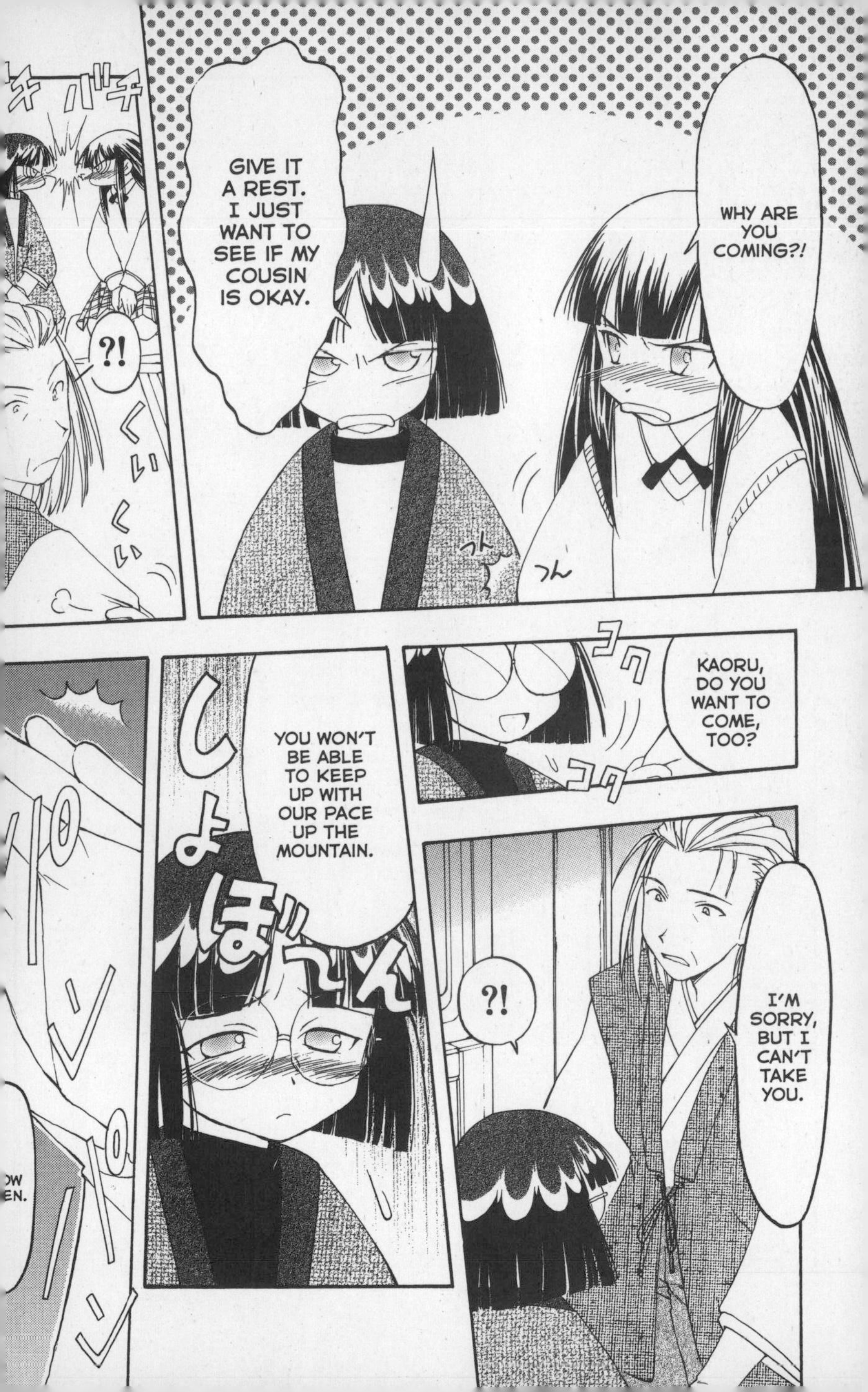
WHY ARE YOU COMING?!
GIVE IT A REST. I JUST WANT TO SEE IF MY COUSIN IS OKAY.
つん
つん
バチ
?!
くい
くい
KAORU, DO YOU WANT TO COME, TOO?
コク
コク
I'M SORRY, BUT I CAN'T TAKE YOU.
?!
YOU WON'T BE ABLE TO KEEP UP WITH OUR PACE UP THE MOUNTAIN.
しょぼーん

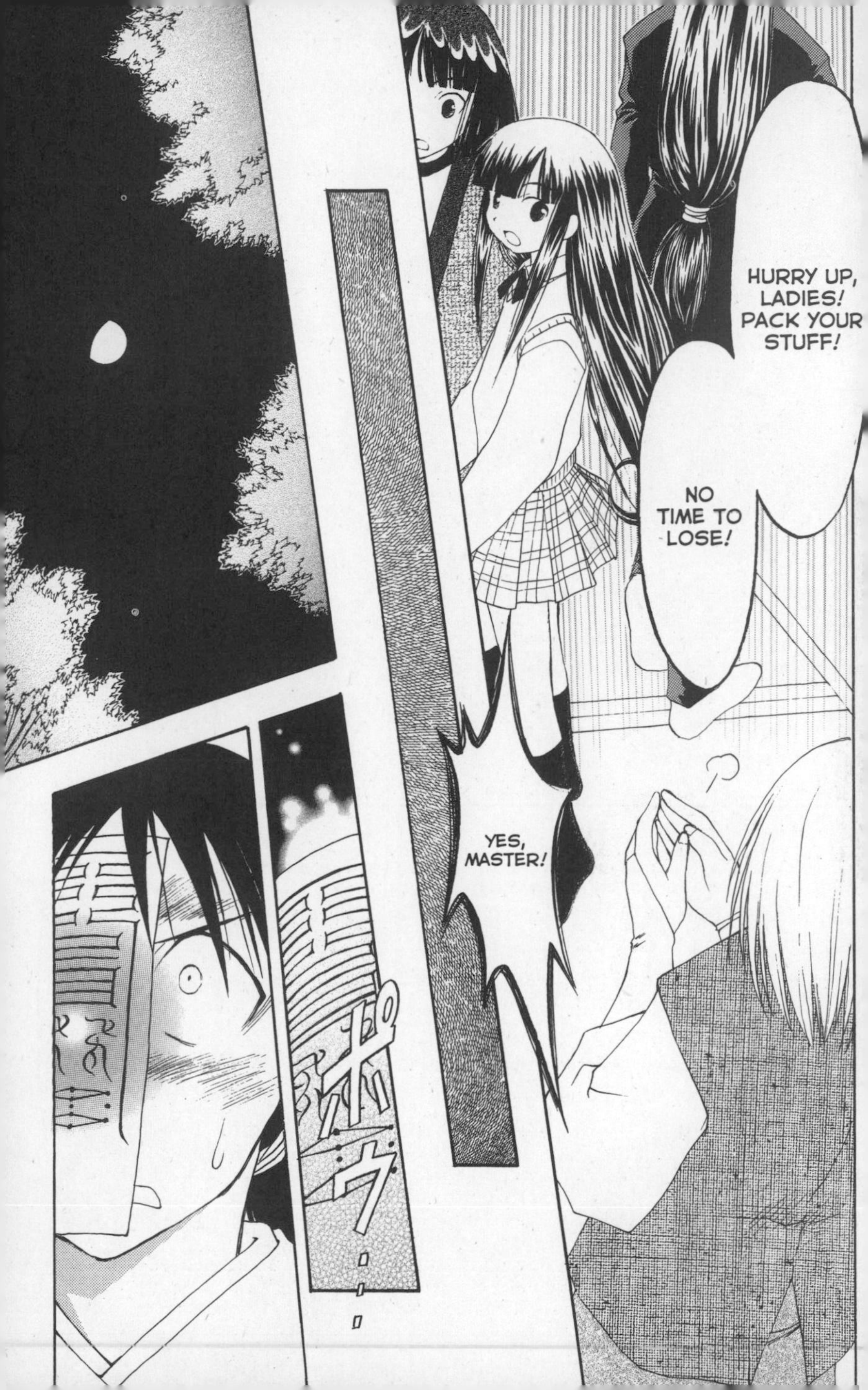
HURRY UP, LADIES! PACK YOUR STUFF!
NO TIME TO LOSE!
YES, MASTER!

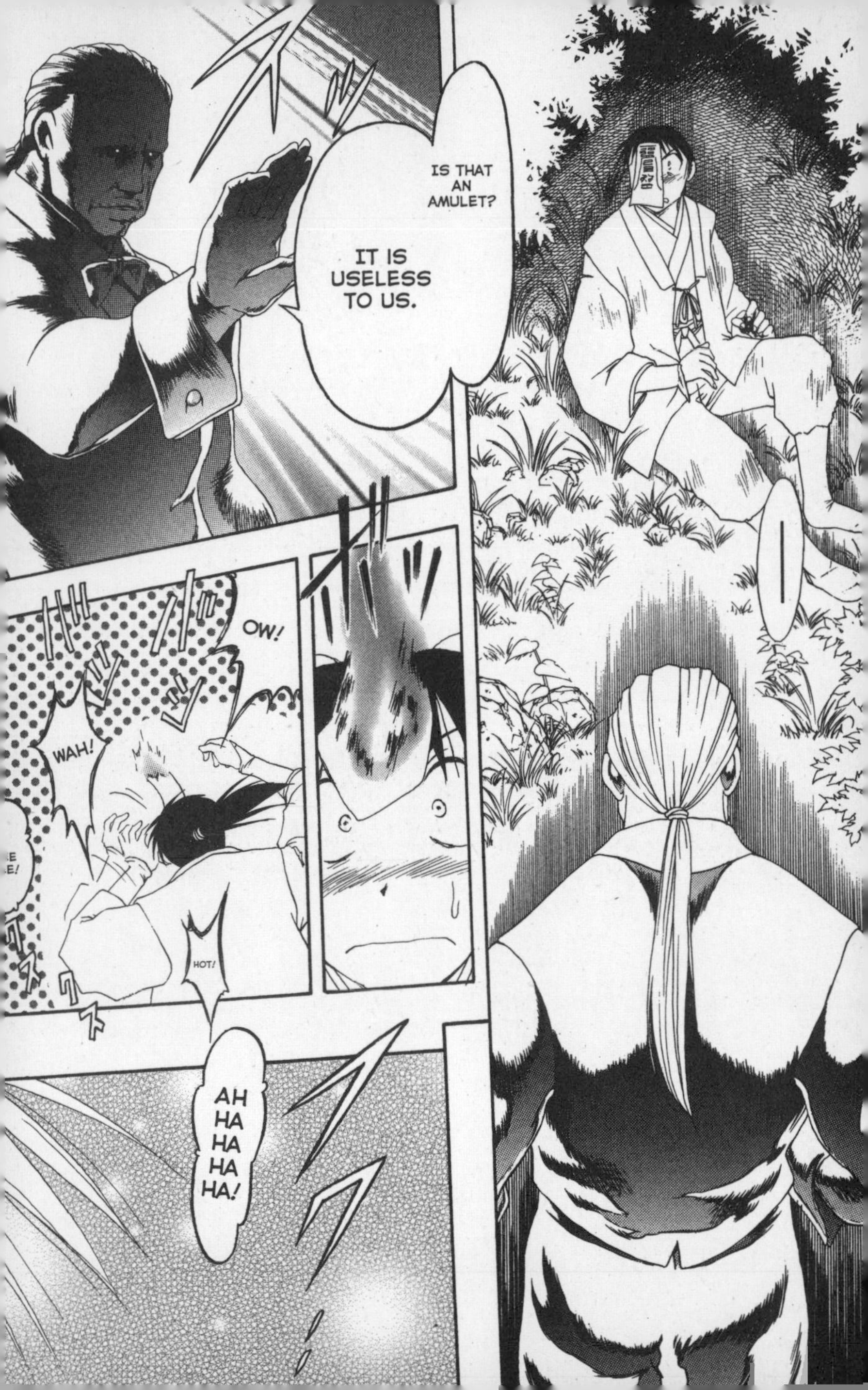
IS THAT AN AMULET?
IT IS USELESS TO US.
OW!
WAH!
HOT!
AH HA HA HA HA HA!

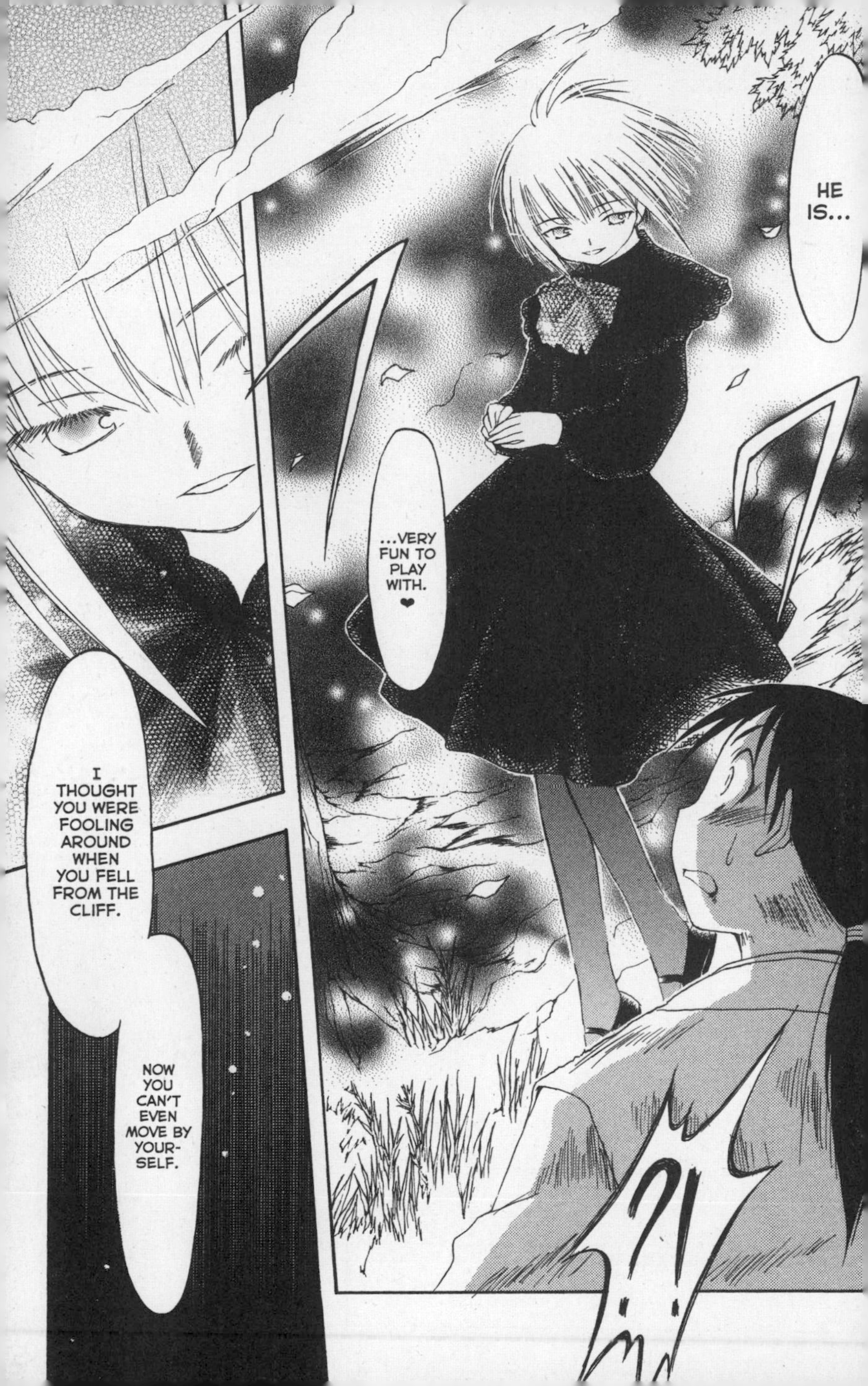
HE IS...
...VERY FUN TO PLAY WITH. ❤
?!
I THOUGHT YOU WERE FOOLING AROUND WHEN YOU FELL FROM THE CLIFF.
NOW YOU CAN'T EVEN MOVE BY YOUR-SELF.

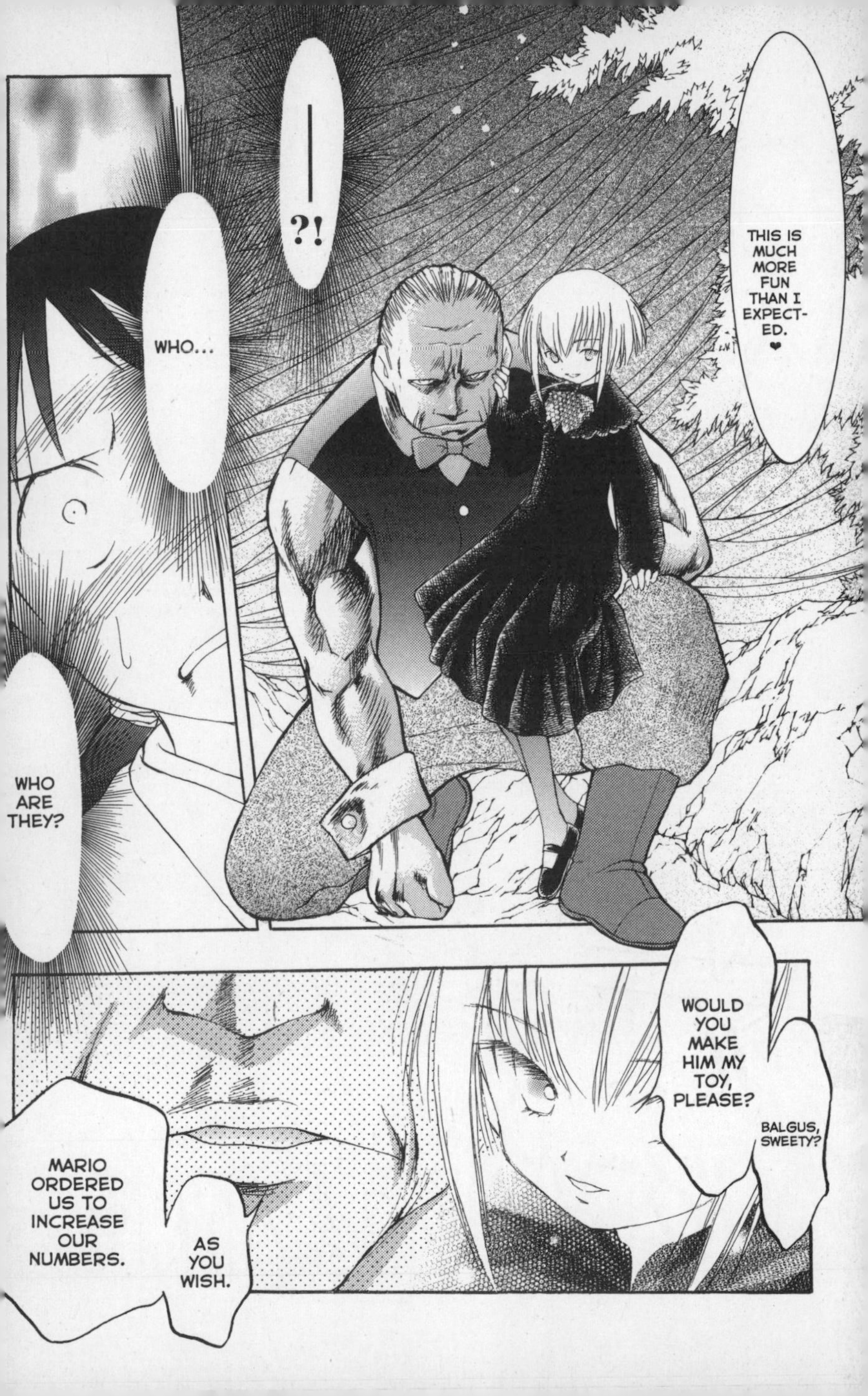
THIS IS MUCH MORE FUN THAN I EXPECTED. ❤
—?!
WHO...
WHO ARE THEY?
WOULD YOU MAKE HIM MY TOY, PLEASE?
BALGUS, SWEETY?
MARIO ORDERED US TO INCREASE OUR NUMBERS.
AS YOU WISH.

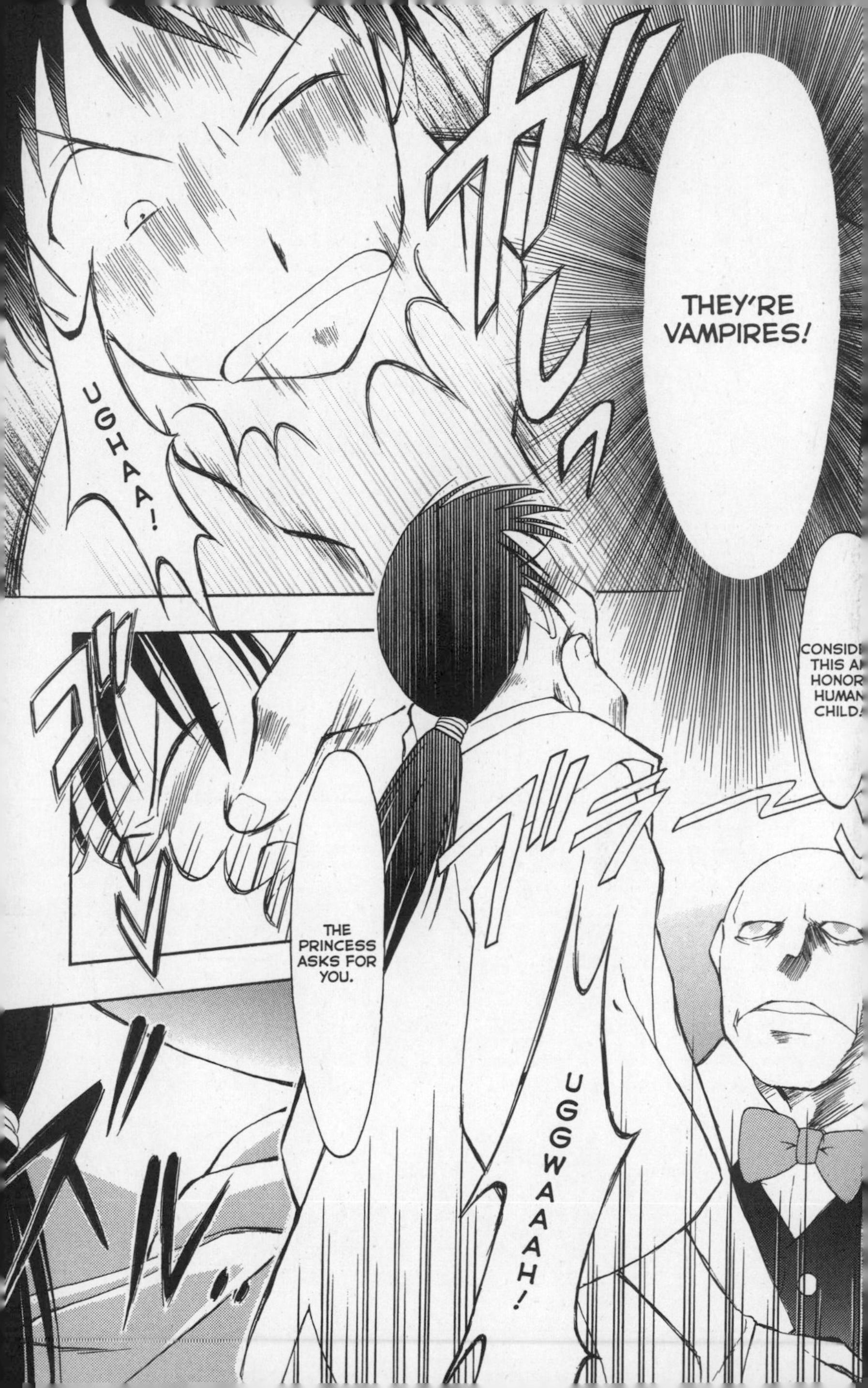
THEY'RE VAMPIRES!
UGHAA!
CONSIDE THIS A HONOR HUMAN CHILD.
THE PRINCESS ASKS FOR YOU.
UGGWAAAAH!

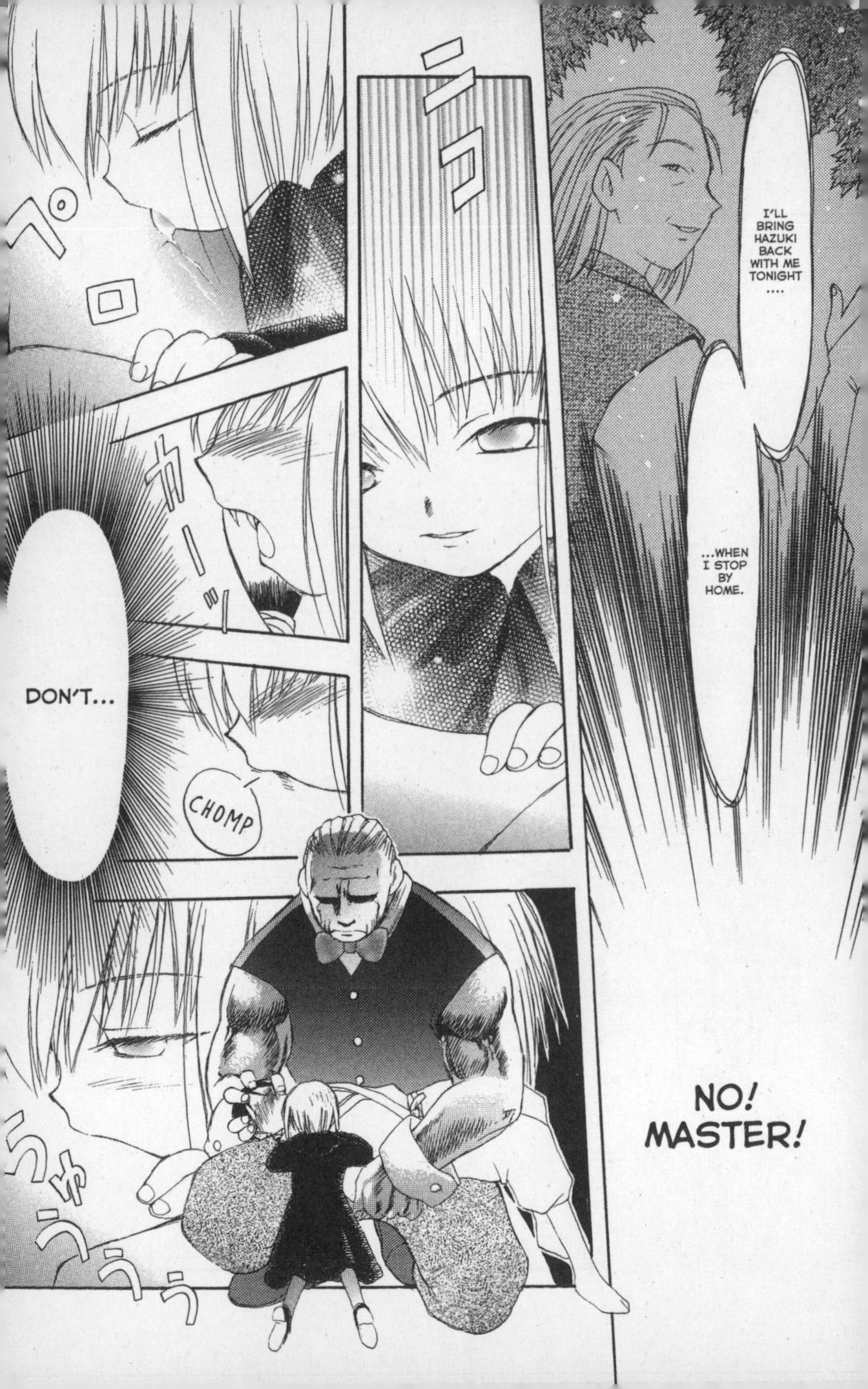
I'LL BRING HAZUKI BACK WITH ME TONIGHT ....
...WHEN I STOP BY HOME.
DON'T...
CHOMP
NO! MASTER!

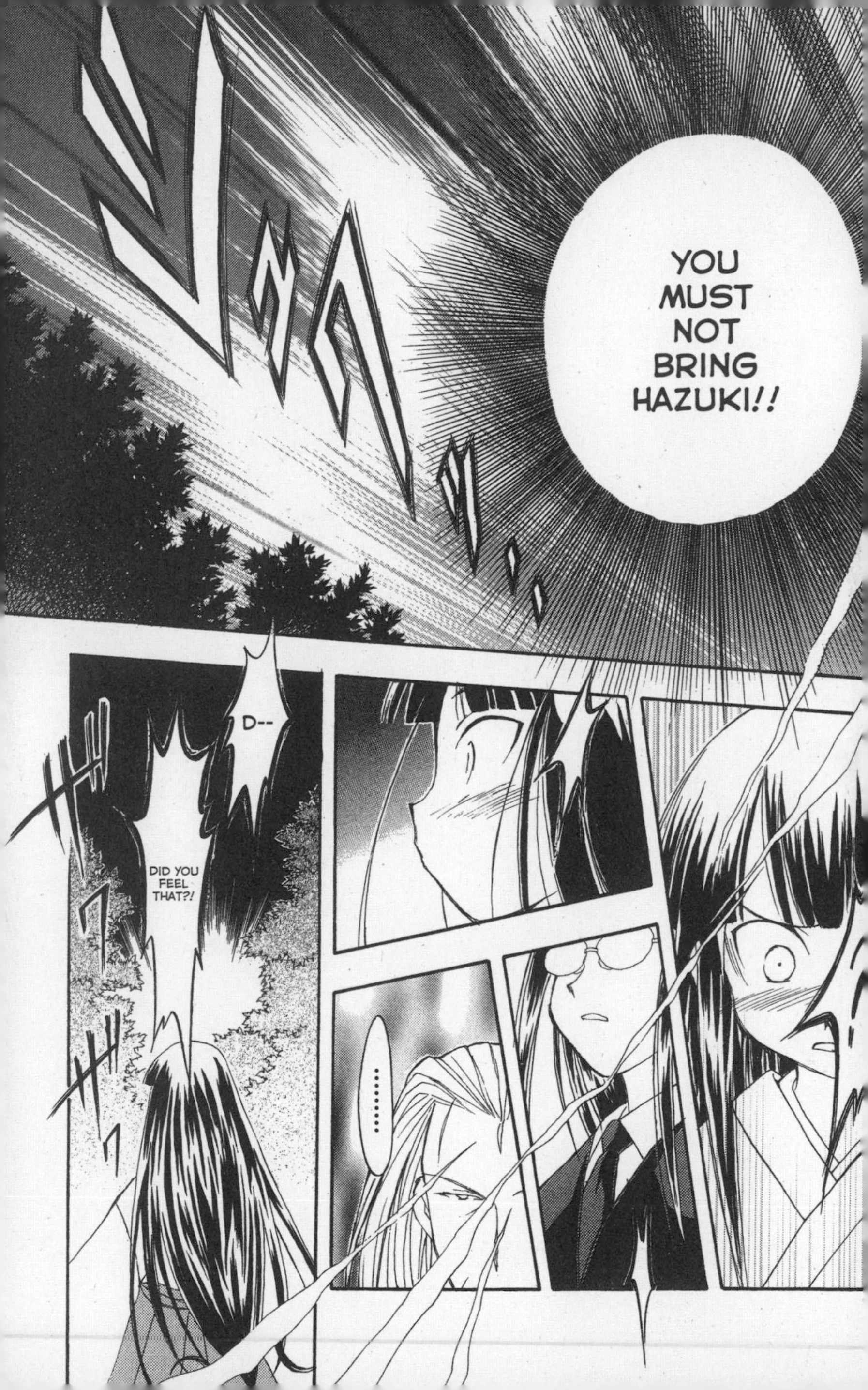
YOU MUST NOT BRING HAZUKI!!
......
D--
DID YOU FEEL THAT?!

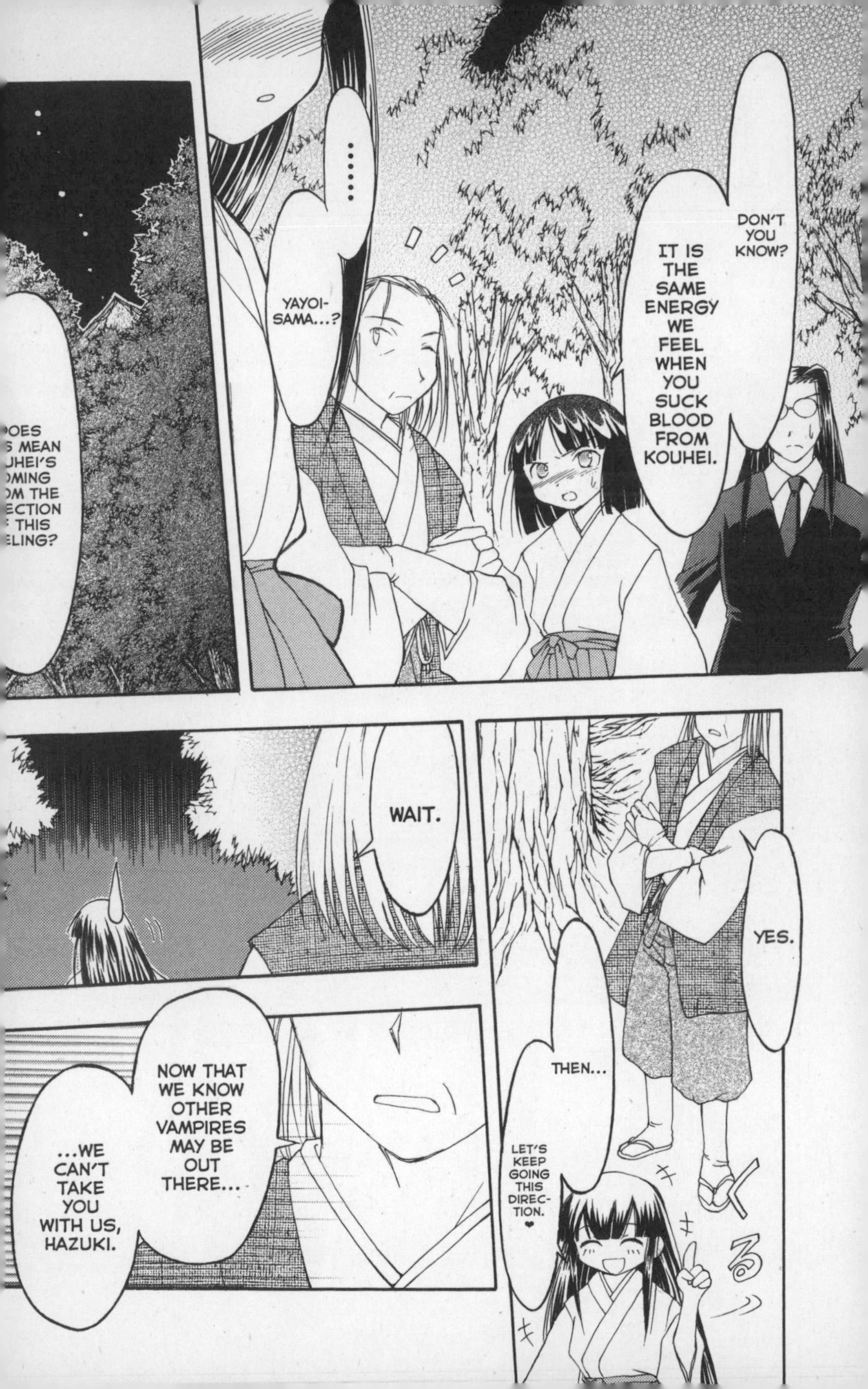
......
DON'T YOU KNOW?
IT IS THE SAME ENERGY WE FEEL WHEN YOU SUCK BLOOD FROM KOUHEI.
YAYOI-SAMA...?
POES S MEAN UHEI'S OMING OM THE ECTION F THIS ELING?
YES.
THEN...
LET'S KEEP GOING THIS DIREC-TION. ❤
WAIT.
NOW THAT WE KNOW OTHER VAMPIRES MAY BE OUT THERE...
...WE CAN'T TAKE YOU WITH US, HAZUKI.

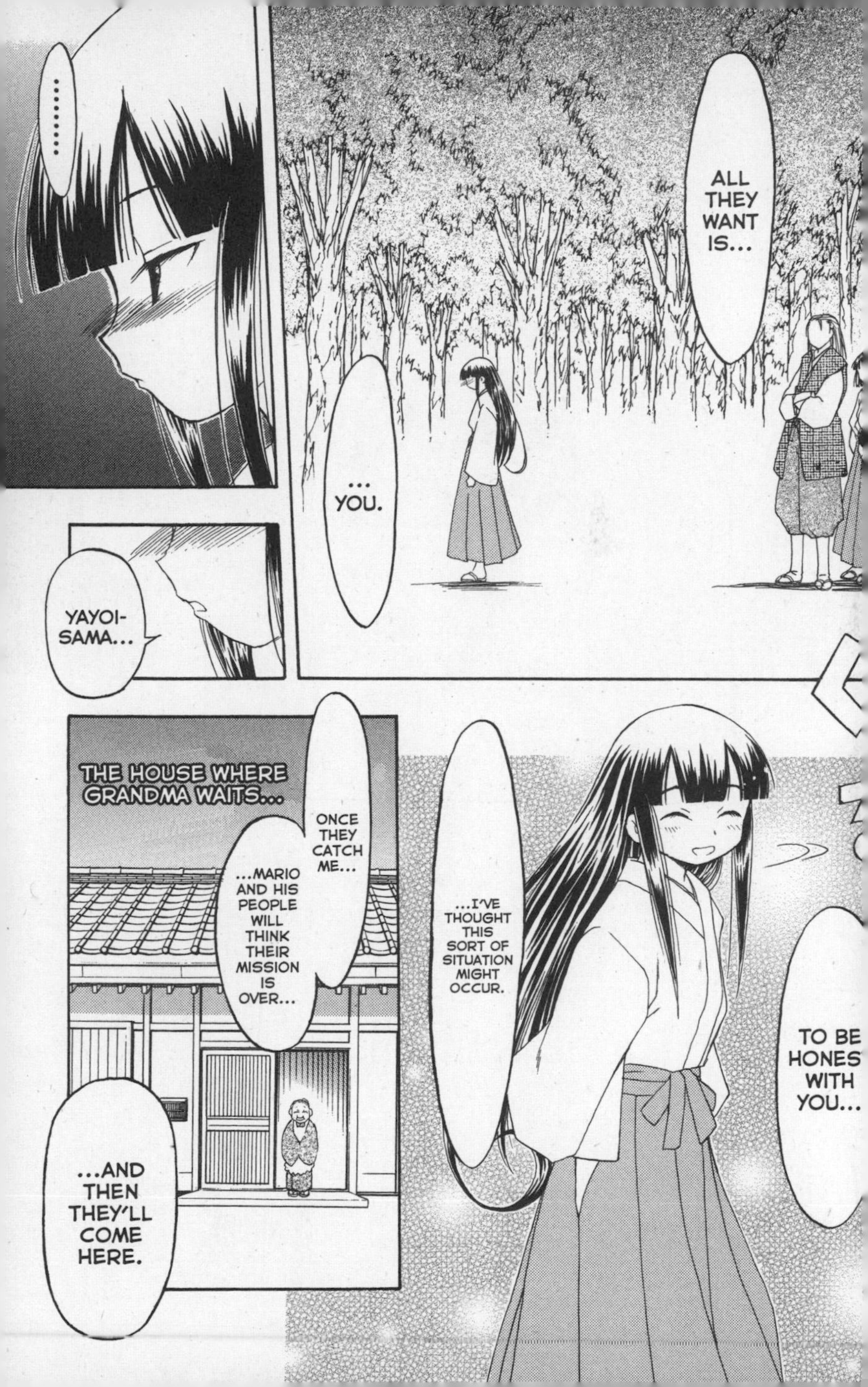
ALL THEY WANT IS...
...YOU.
......
YAYOI-SAMA...
TO BE HONES WITH YOU...
...I'VE THOUGHT THIS SORT OF SITUATION MIGHT OCCUR.
THE HOUSE WHERE GRANDMA WAITS...
ONCE THEY CATCH ME...
...MARIO AND HIS PEOPLE WILL THINK THEIR MISSION IS OVER...
...AND THEN THEY'LL COME HERE.

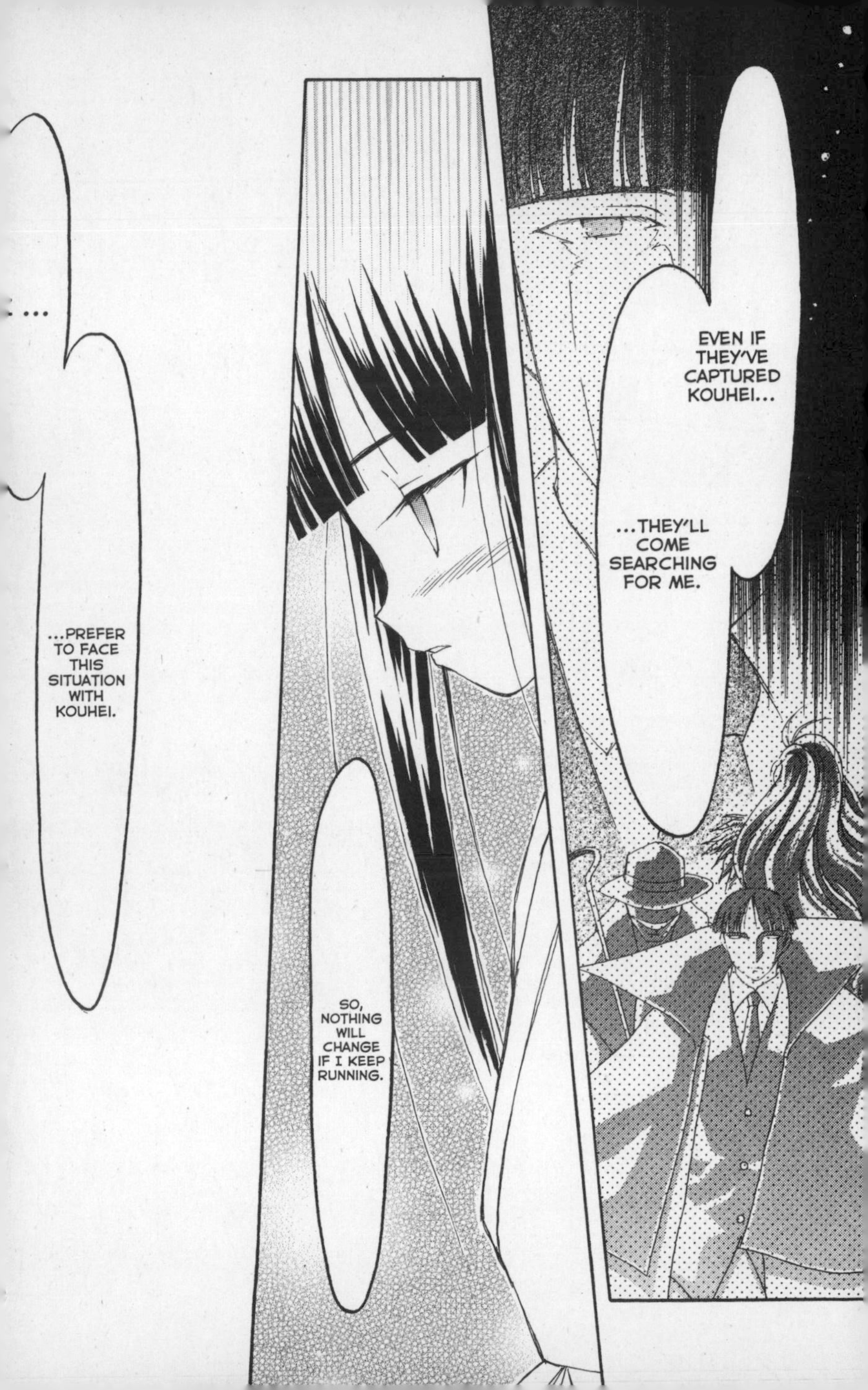
EVEN IF THEY'VE CAPTURED KOUHEI...
...THEY'LL COME SEARCHING FOR ME.
SO, NOTHING WILL CHANGE IF I KEEP RUNNING.
...
...PREFER TO FACE THIS SITUATION WITH KOUHEI.

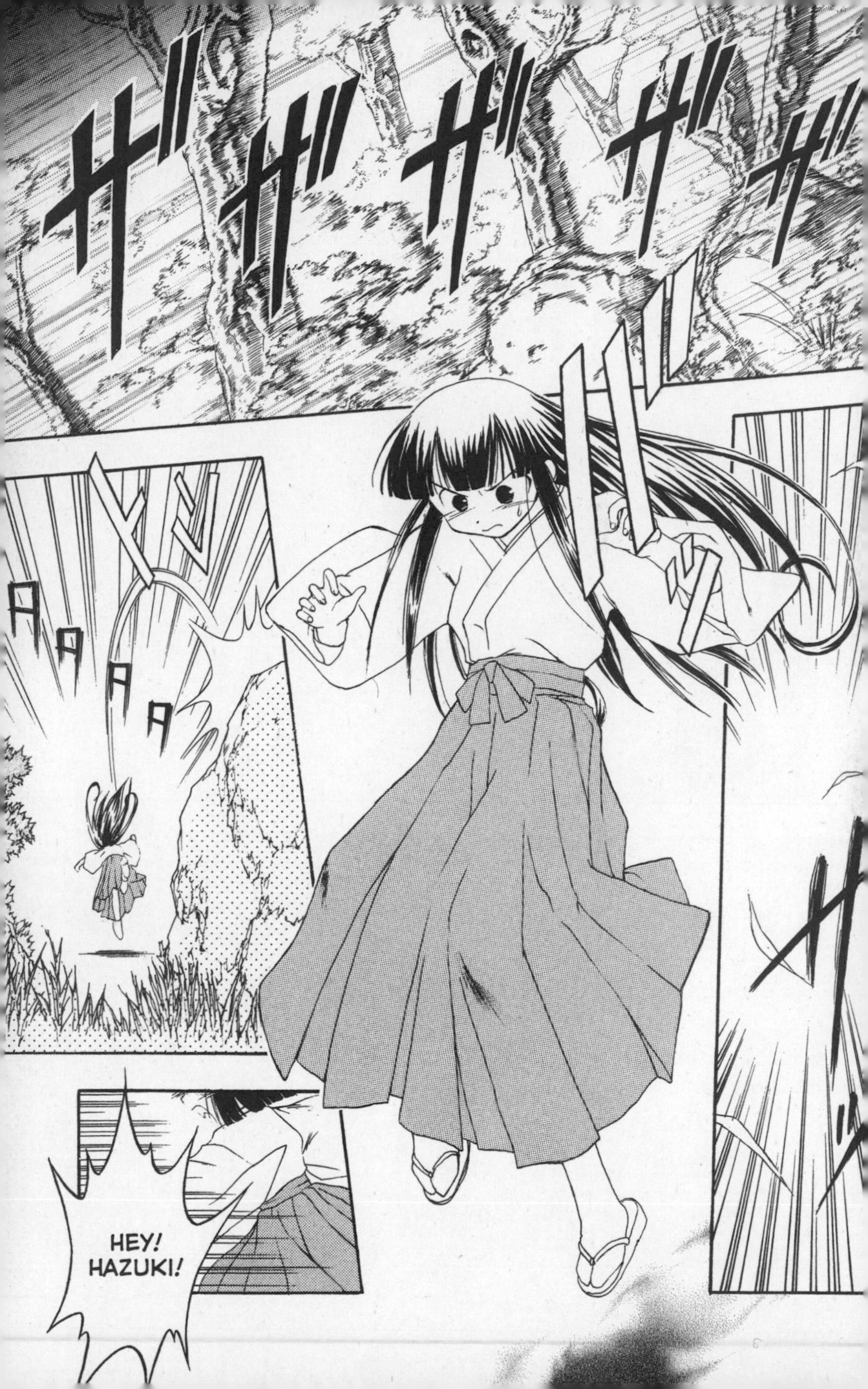
HEY! HAZUKI!

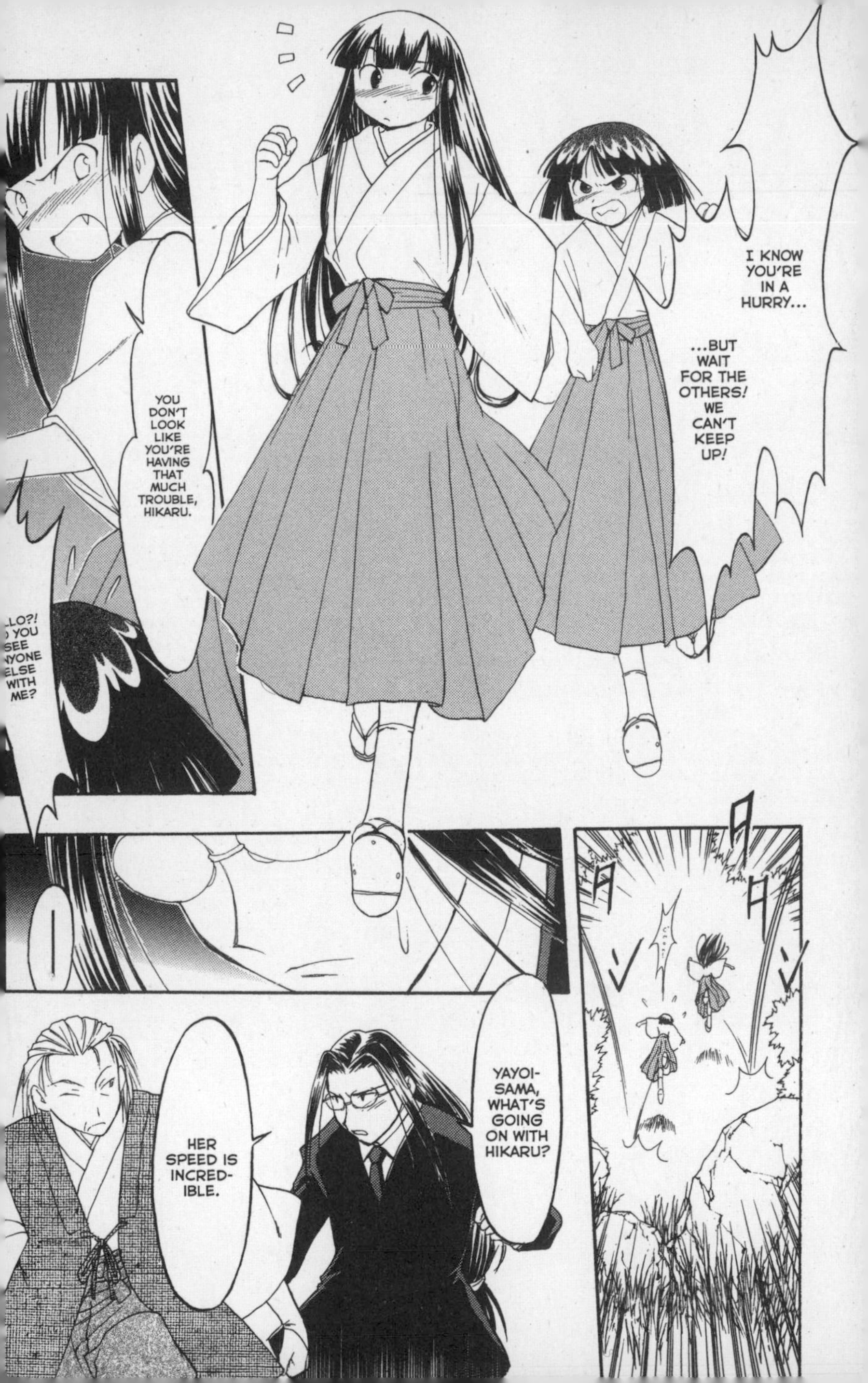
I KNOW YOU'RE IN A HURRY...
...BUT WAIT FOR THE OTHERS! WE CAN'T KEEP UP!
YOU DON'T LOOK LIKE YOU'RE HAVING THAT MUCH TROUBLE, HIKARU.
LLO?! D YOU SEE NYONE ELSE WITH ME?
YAYOI-SAMA, WHAT'S GOING ON WITH HIKARU?
HER SPEED IS INCRED-IBLE.

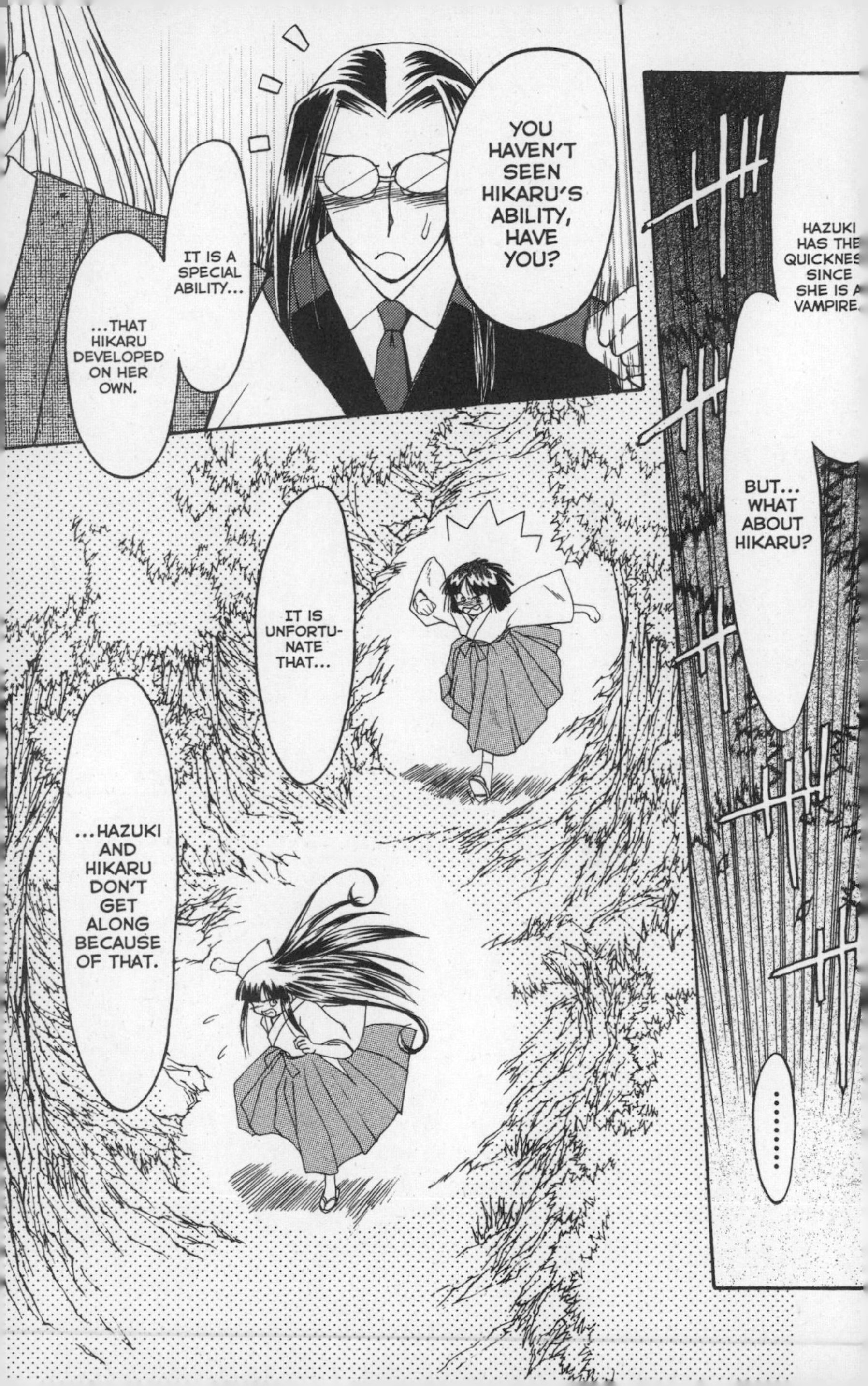
HAZUKI HAS THE QUICKNES SINCE SHE IS A VAMPIRE.
BUT... WHAT ABOUT HIKARU?
......
YOU HAVEN'T SEEN HIKARU'S ABILITY, HAVE YOU?
IT IS A SPECIAL ABILITY...
...THAT HIKARU DEVELOPED ON HER OWN.
IT IS UNFORTU-NATE THAT...
...HAZUKI AND HIKARU DON'T GET ALONG BECAUSE OF THAT.

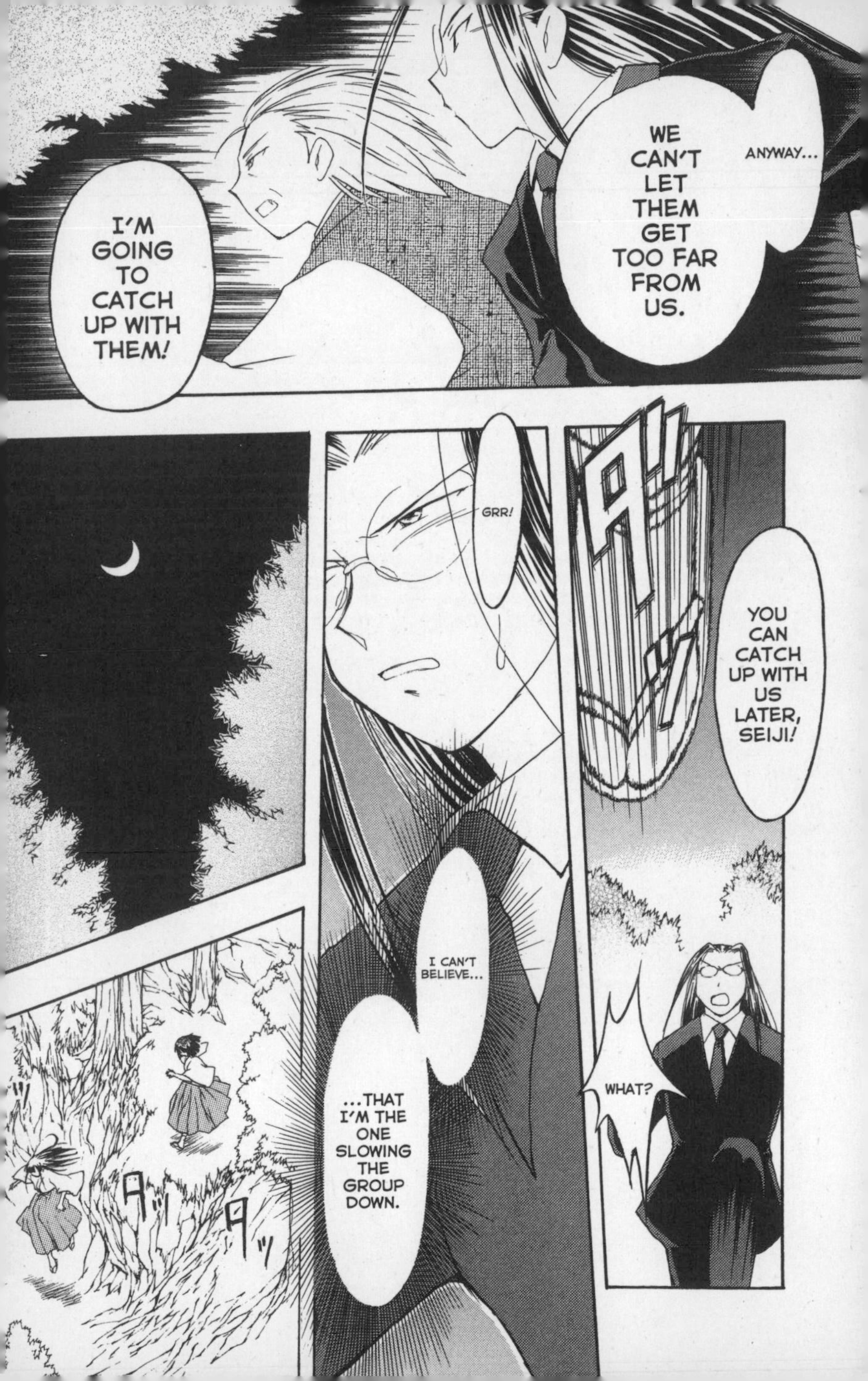
ANYWAY...
WE CAN'T LET THEM GET TOO FAR FROM US.
I'M GOING TO CATCH UP WITH THEM!
YOU CAN CATCH UP WITH US LATER, SEIJI!
WHAT?
GRR!
I CAN'T BELIEVE...
...THAT I'M THE ONE SLOWING THE GROUP DOWN.
タッ
タッ

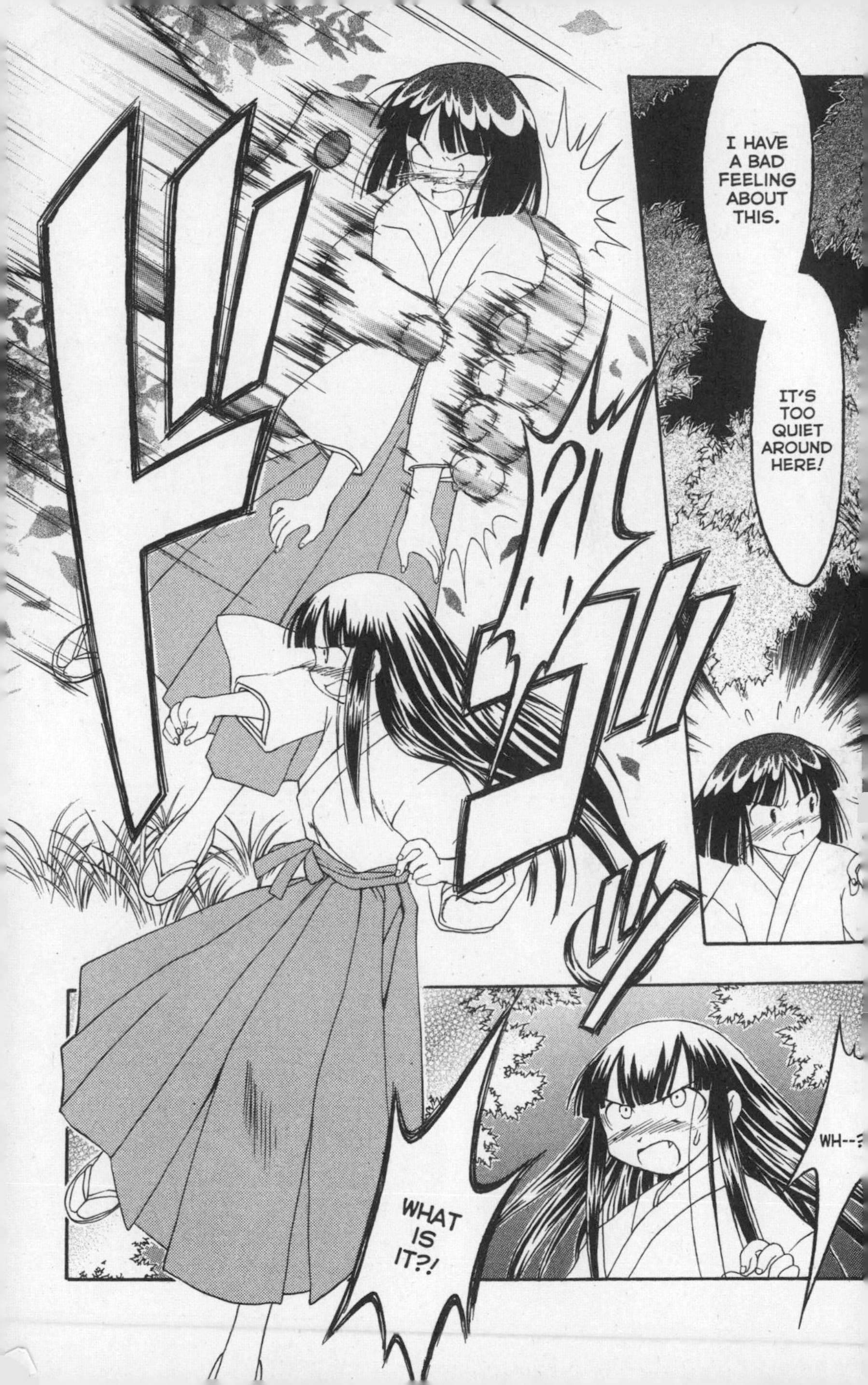
I HAVE A BAD FEELING ABOUT THIS.
IT'S TOO QUIET AROUND HERE!
WH--?
WHAT IS IT?!

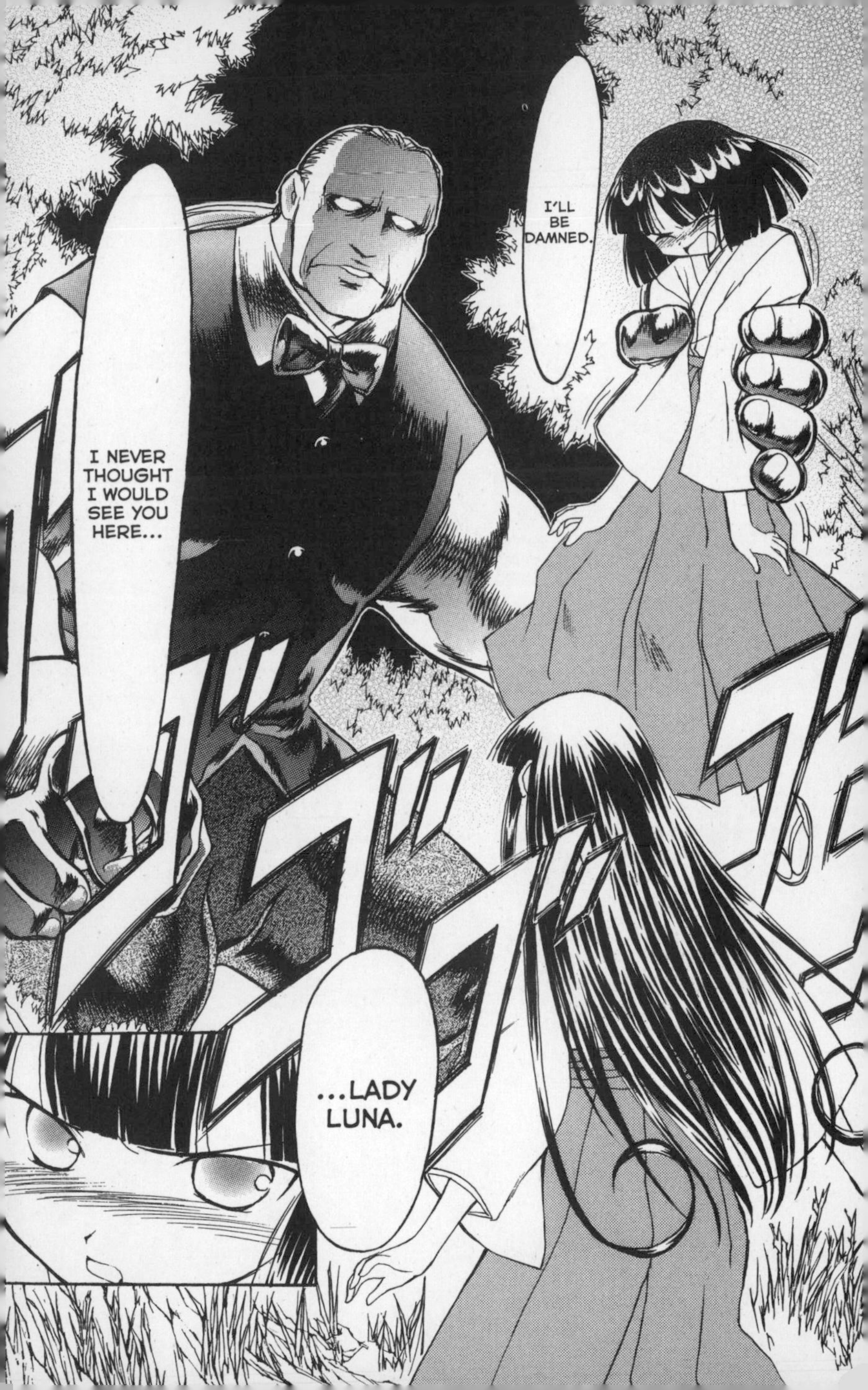
I'LL BE DAMNED.
I NEVER THOUGHT I WOULD SEE YOU HERE...
...LADY LUNA.

Moon 月詠 Phase

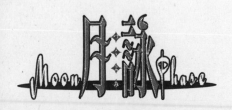

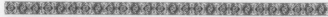

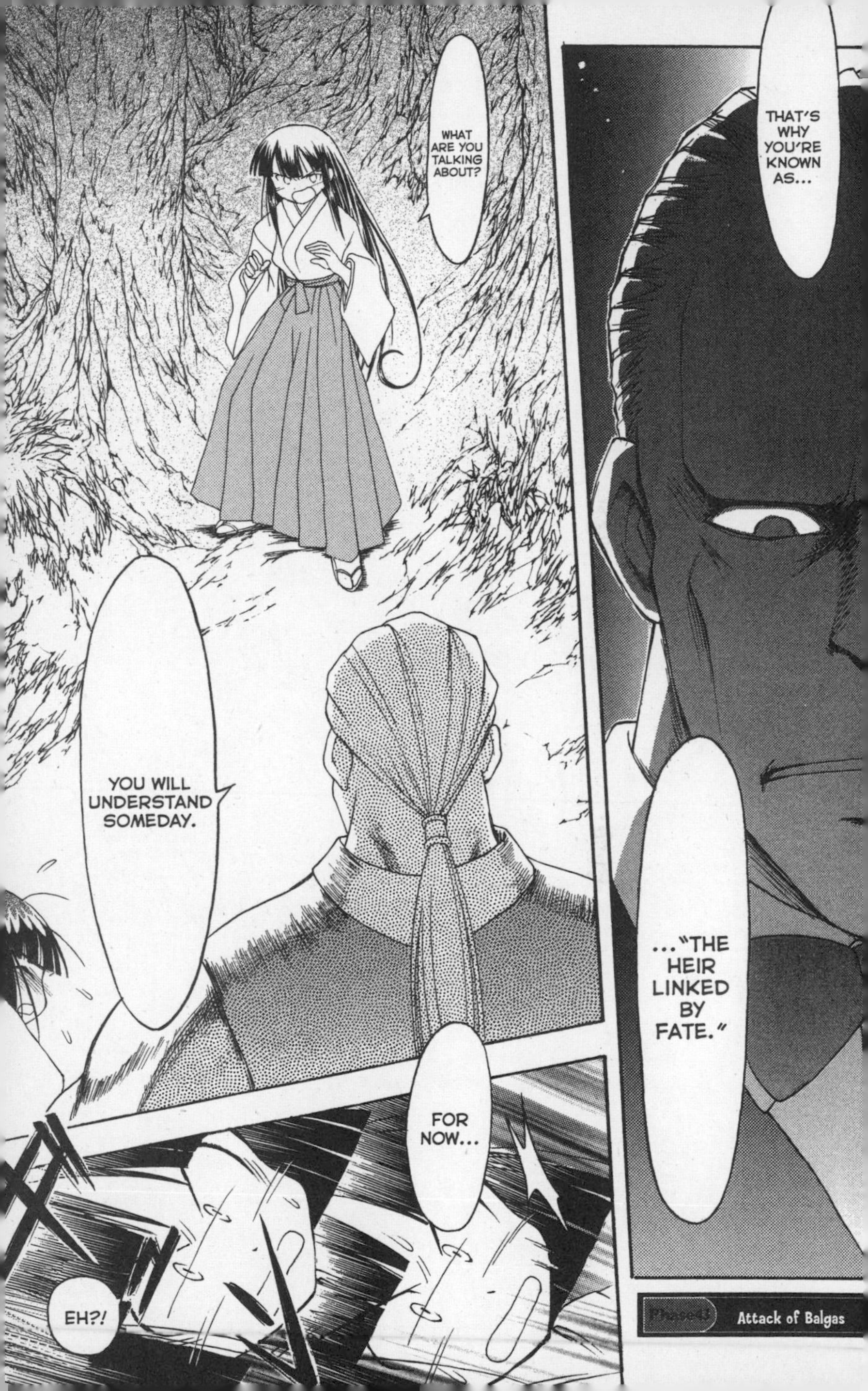
THAT'S WHY YOU'RE KNOWN AS...
..."THE HEIR LINKED BY FATE."
WHAT ARE YOU TALKING ABOUT?
YOU WILL UNDERSTAND SOMEDAY.
FOR NOW...
EH?!
Phase43 Attack of Balgas

Phase43 Attack of Balgus

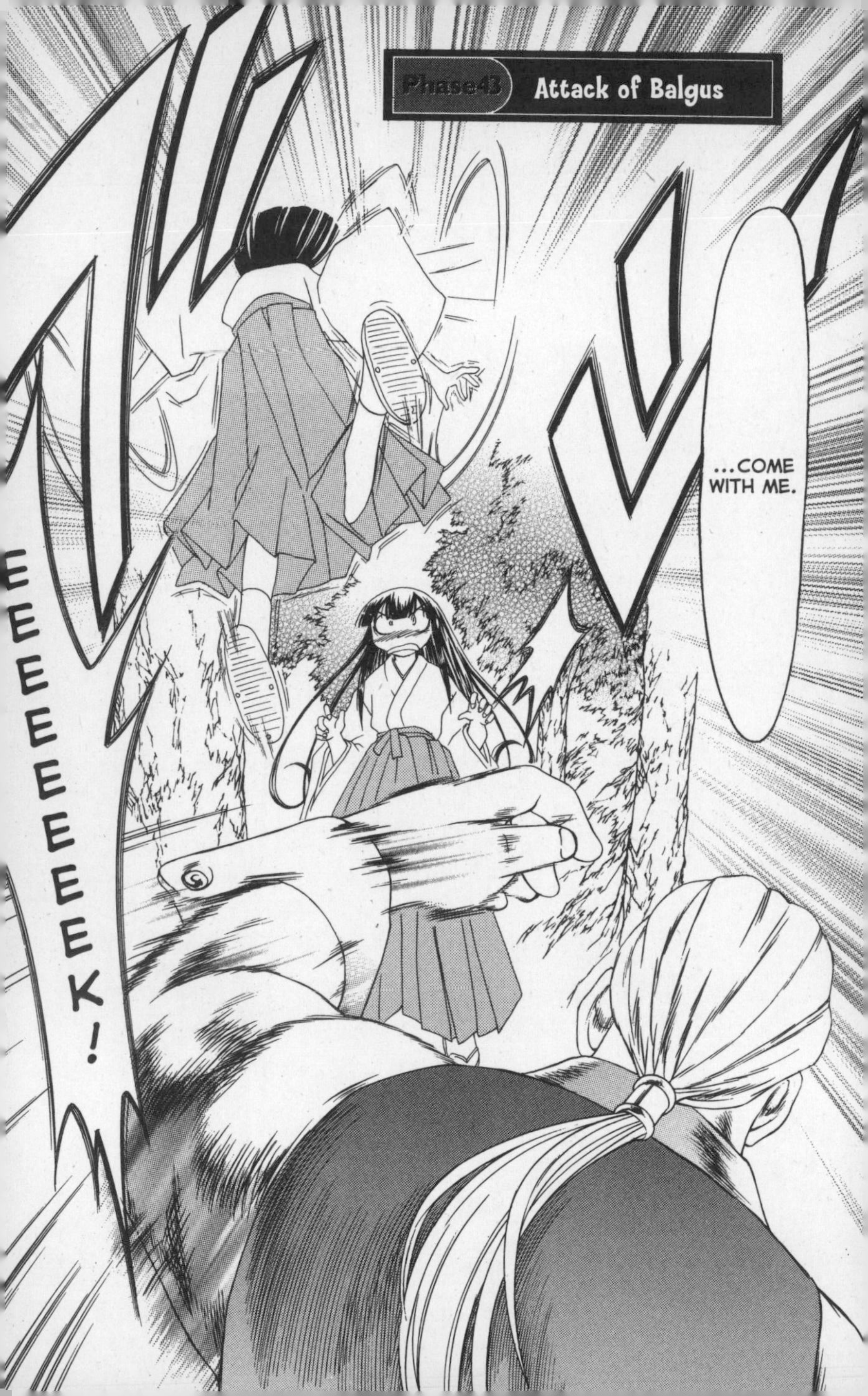
...COME WITH ME.
EEEEEEEEEK!

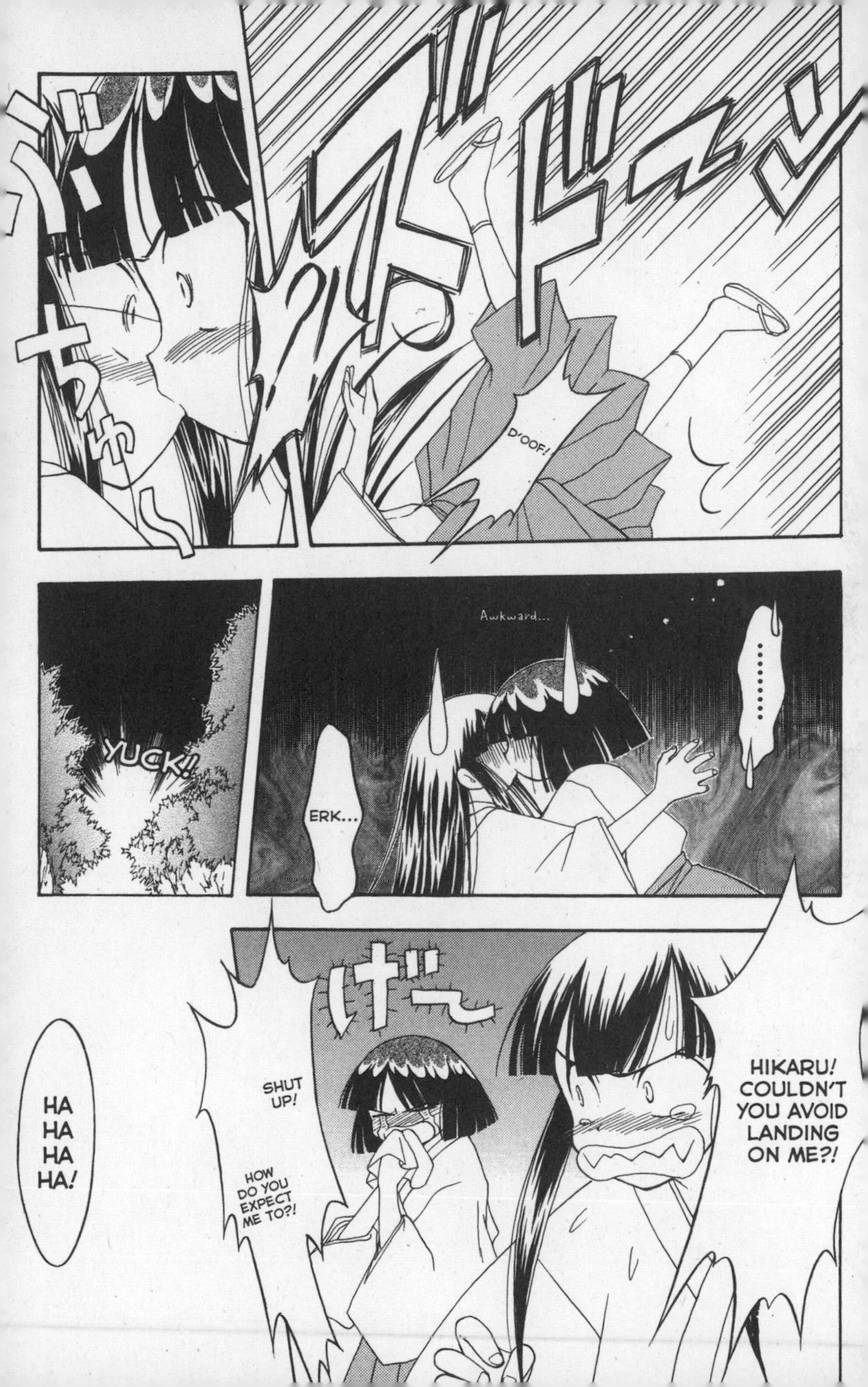

D'OOF!
ちゅ〜
Awkward...
......
ERK...
YUCK!
HIKARU! COULDN'T YOU AVOID LANDING ON ME?!
げ〜
SHUT UP!
HOW DO YOU EXPECT ME TO?!
HA HA HA HA!

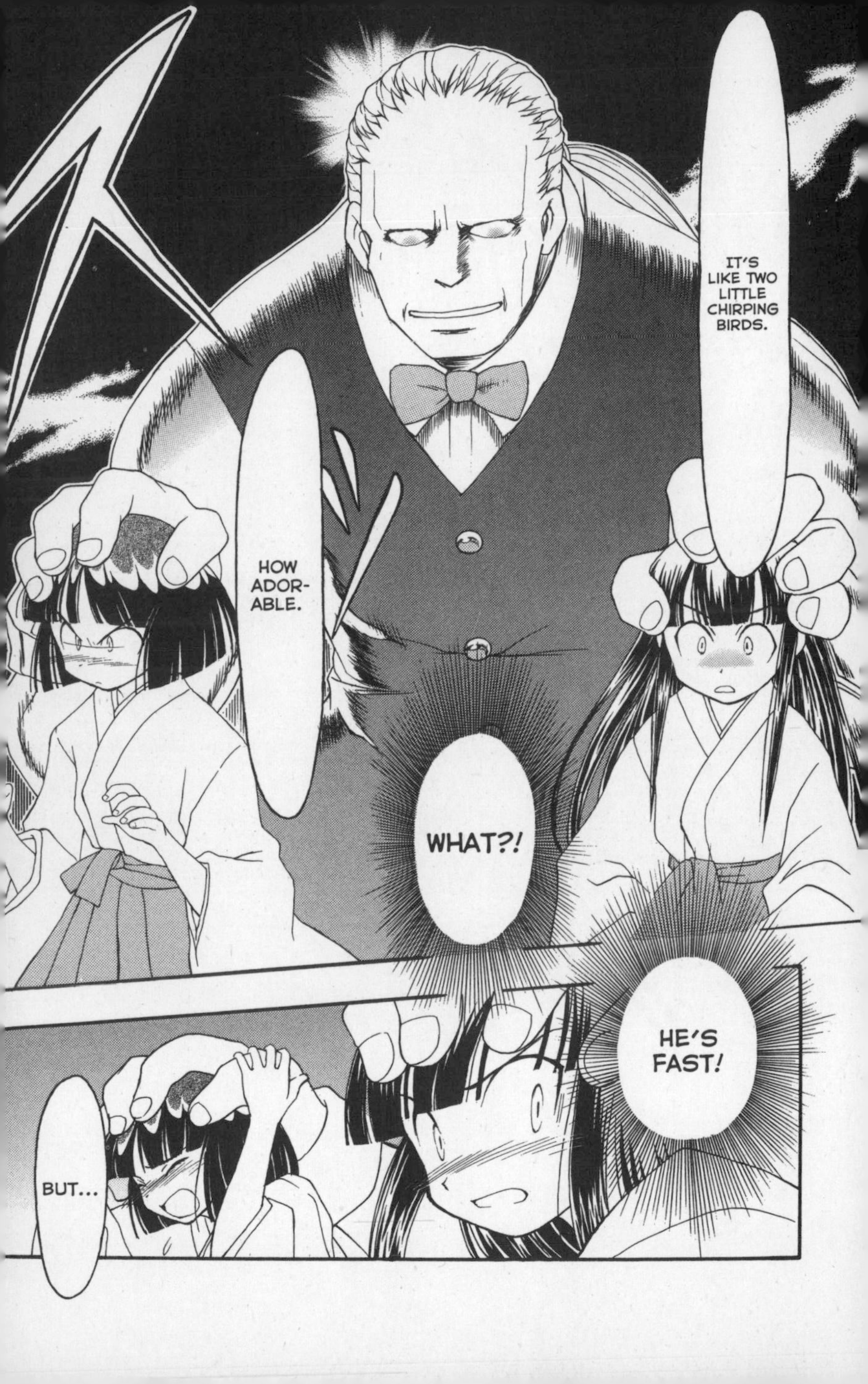
IT'S LIKE TWO LITTLE CHIRPING BIRDS.
HOW ADORABLE.
WHAT?!
HE'S FAST!
BUT...

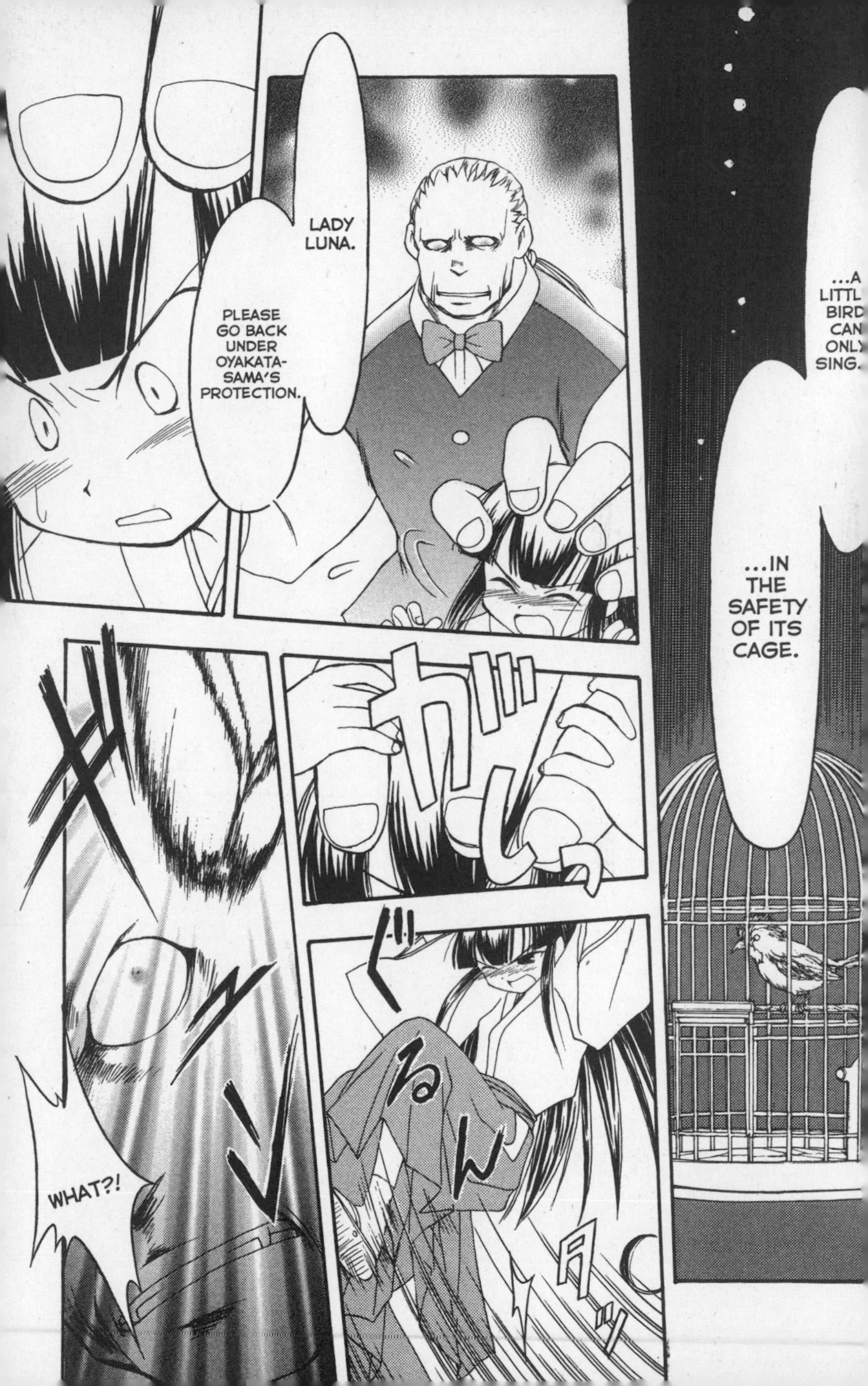
...A LITTL BIRD CAN ONLY SING.
...IN THE SAFETY OF ITS CAGE.
LADY LUNA.
PLEASE GO BACK UNDER OYAKATA-SAMA'S PROTECTION.
WHAT?!

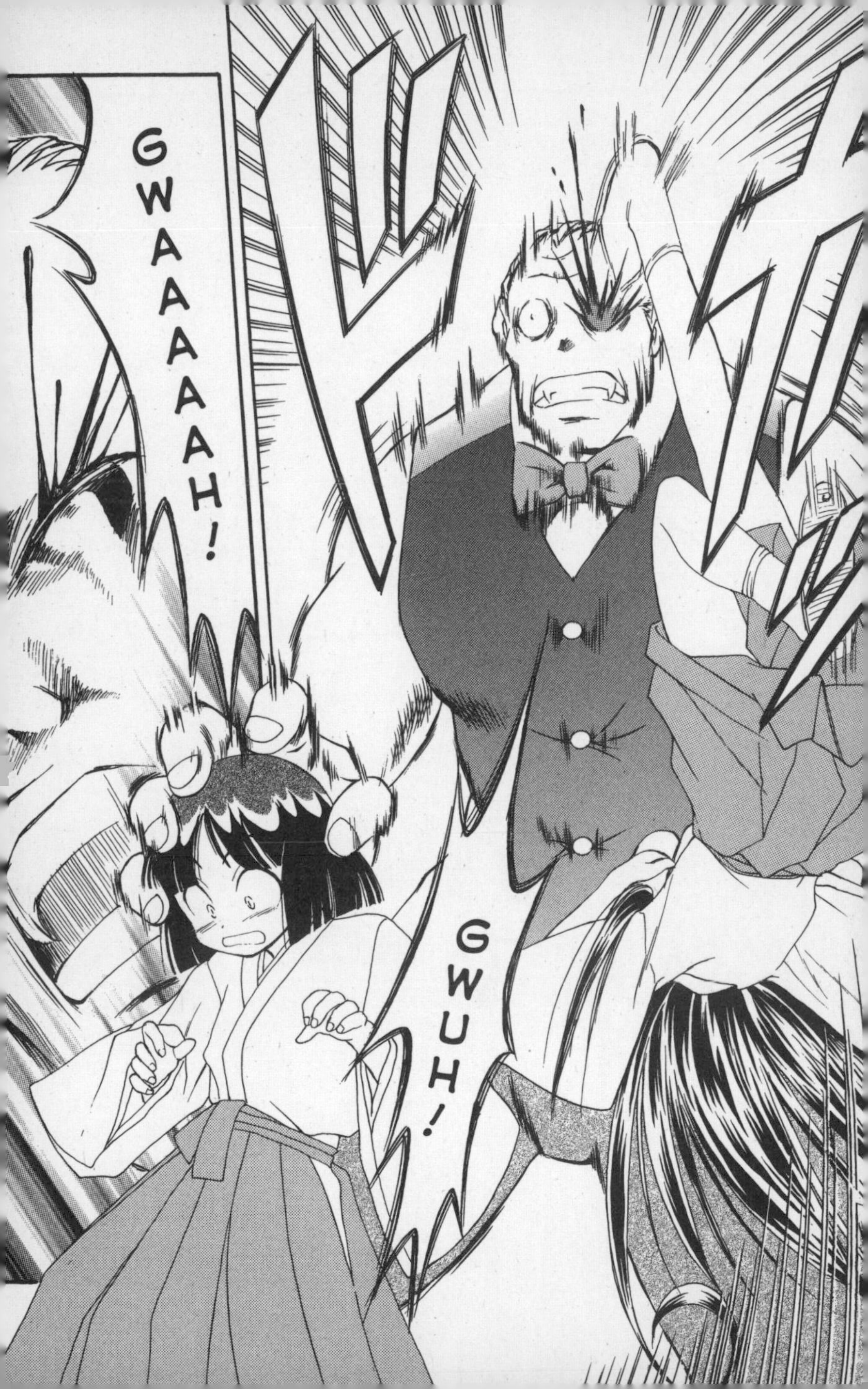
GWAAAAAAH!
GWUH!

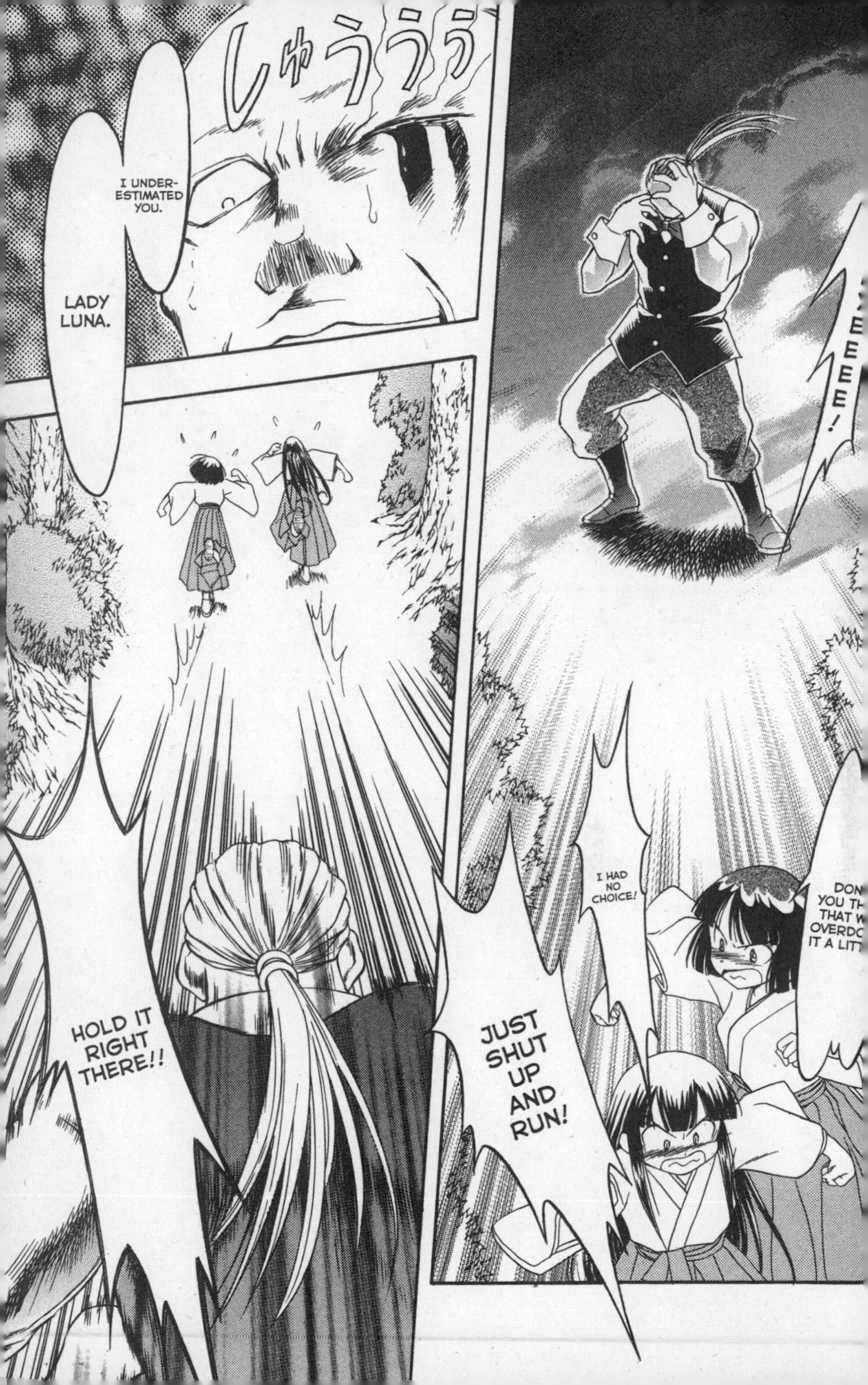
EEEEE!
DON YOU TH THAT W OVERDO IT A LITT
I HAD NO CHOICE!
JUST SHUT UP AND RUN!
しゅううう
I UNDER-ESTIMATED YOU.
LADY LUNA.
HOLD IT RIGHT THERE!!

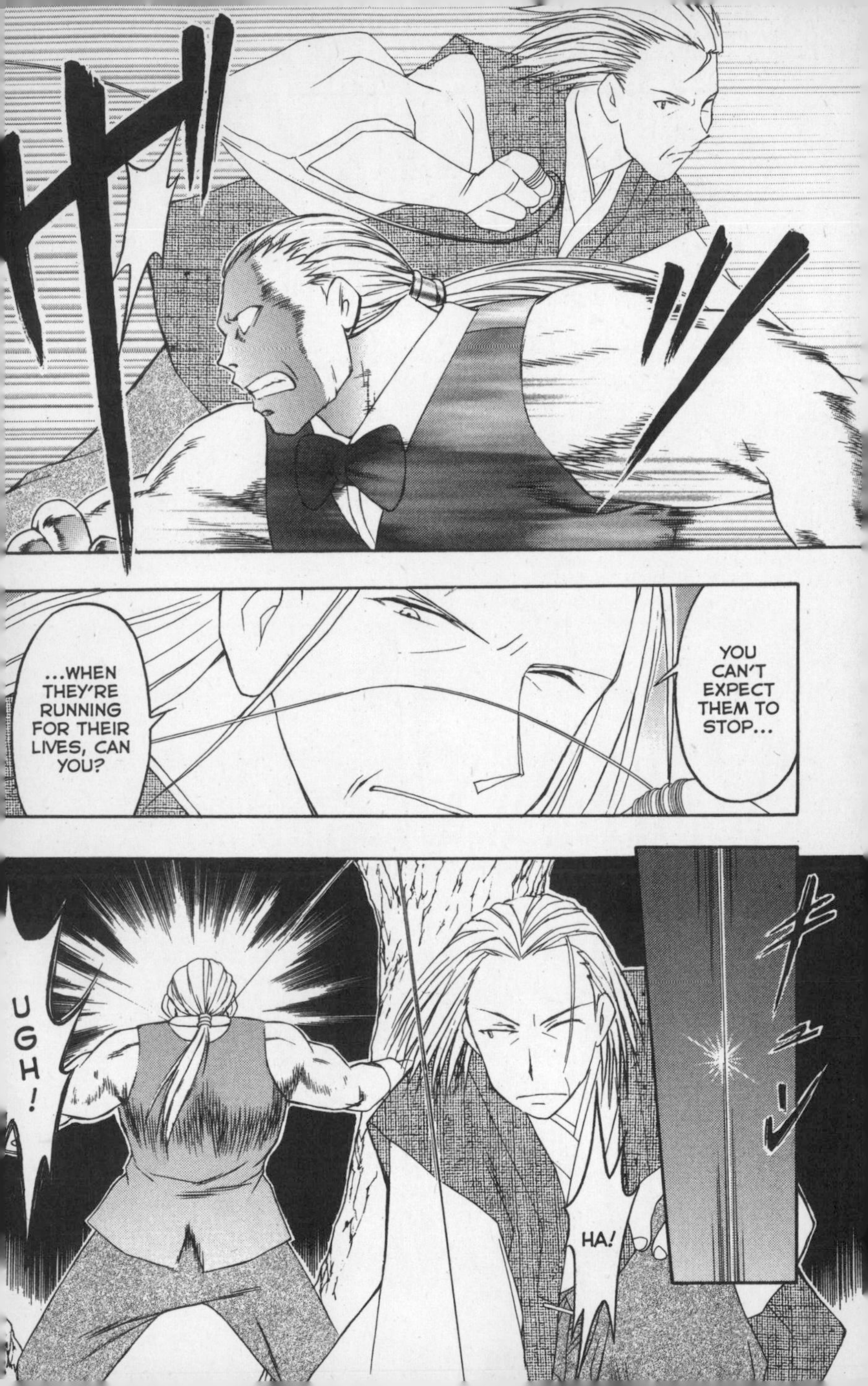
YOU CAN'T EXPECT THEM TO STOP...
...WHEN THEY'RE RUNNING FOR THEIR LIVES, CAN YOU?
HA!
UGH!

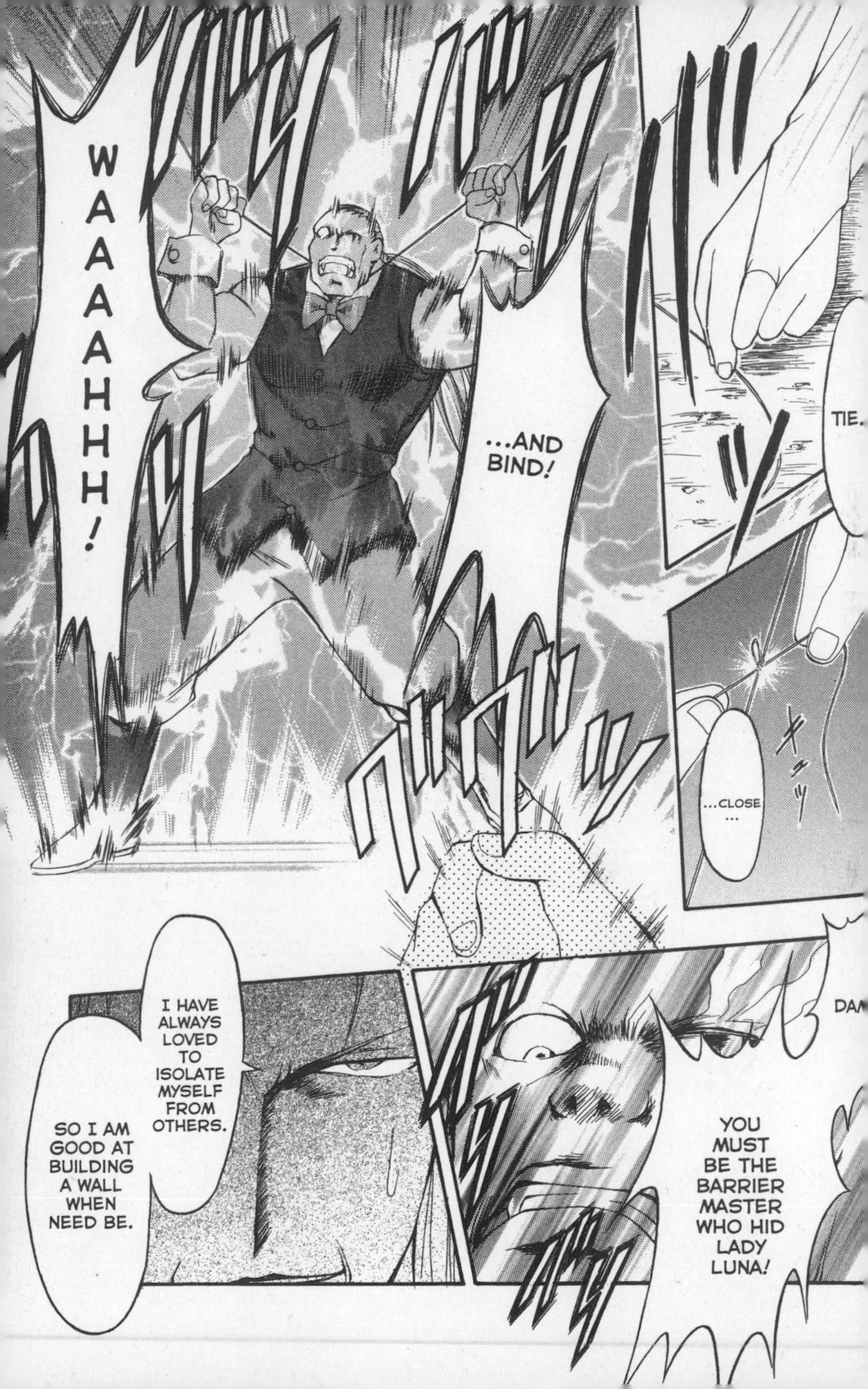
TIE.
...CLOSE...
キュッ
...AND BIND!
WAAAAAHHH!
DAM
YOU MUST BE THE BARRIER MASTER WHO HID LADY LUNA!
I HAVE ALWAYS LOVED TO ISOLATE MYSELF FROM OTHERS.
SO I AM GOOD AT BUILDING A WALL WHEN NEED BE.

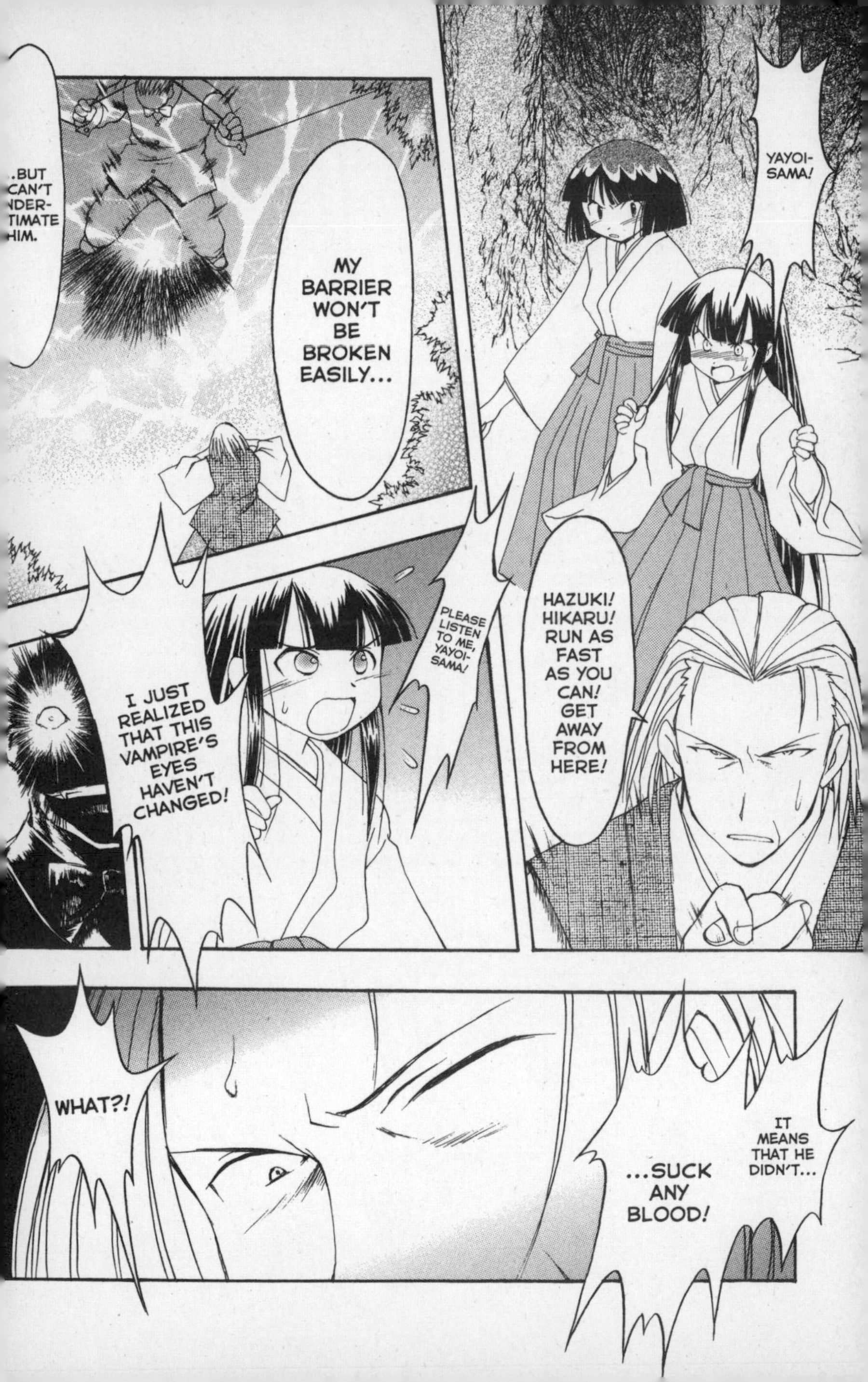
YAYOI-SAMA!
MY BARRIER WON'T BE BROKEN EASILY...
...BUT I CAN'T UNDER-ESTIMATE HIM.
HAZUKI! HIKARU! RUN AS FAST AS YOU CAN! GET AWAY FROM HERE!
PLEASE LISTEN TO ME, YAYOI-SAMA!
I JUST REALIZED THAT THIS VAMPIRE'S EYES HAVEN'T CHANGED!
IT MEANS THAT HE DIDN'T...
...SUCK ANY BLOOD!
WHAT?!

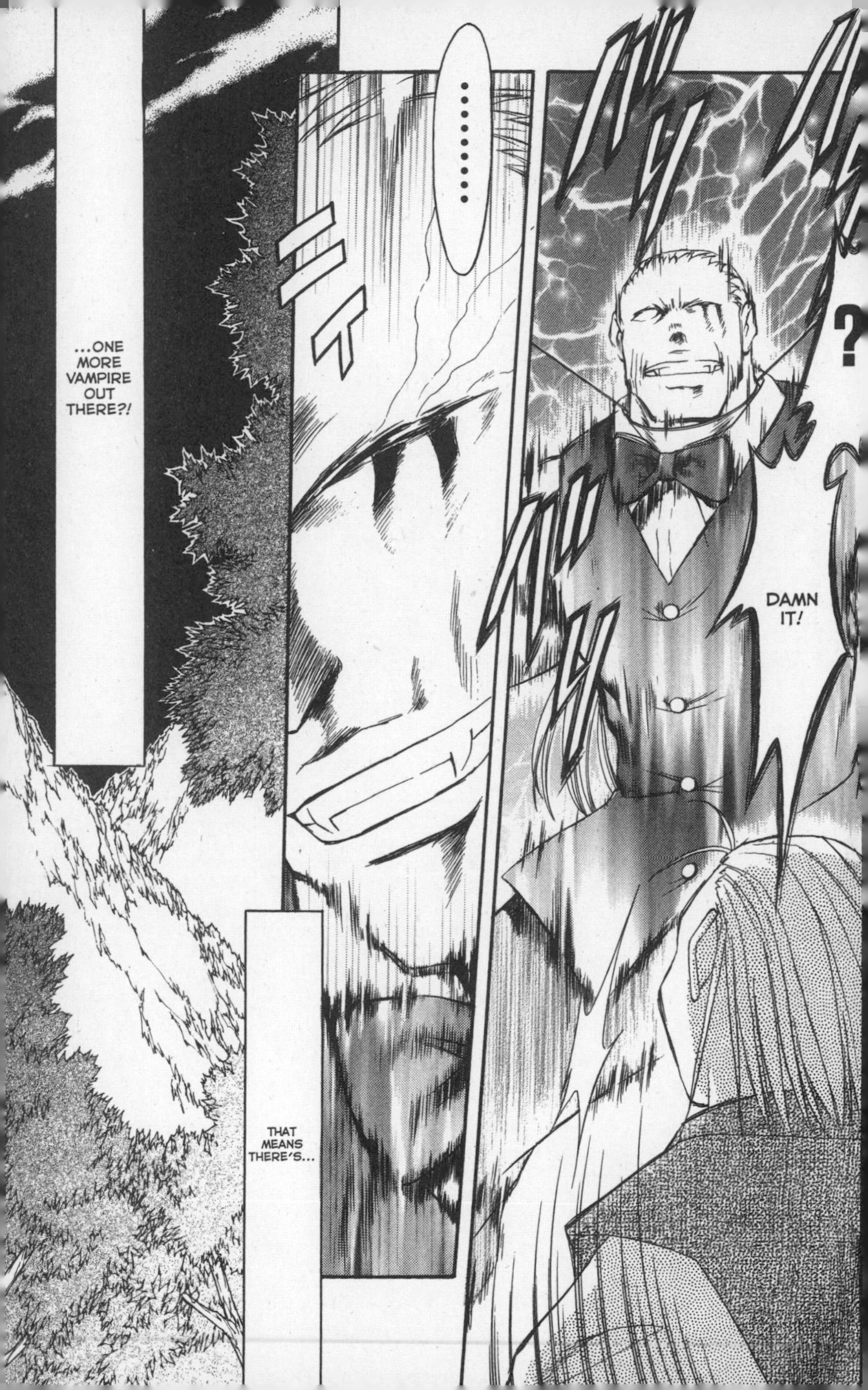
?
DAMN IT!
......
THAT MEANS THERE'S...
...ONE MORE VAMPIRE OUT THERE?!

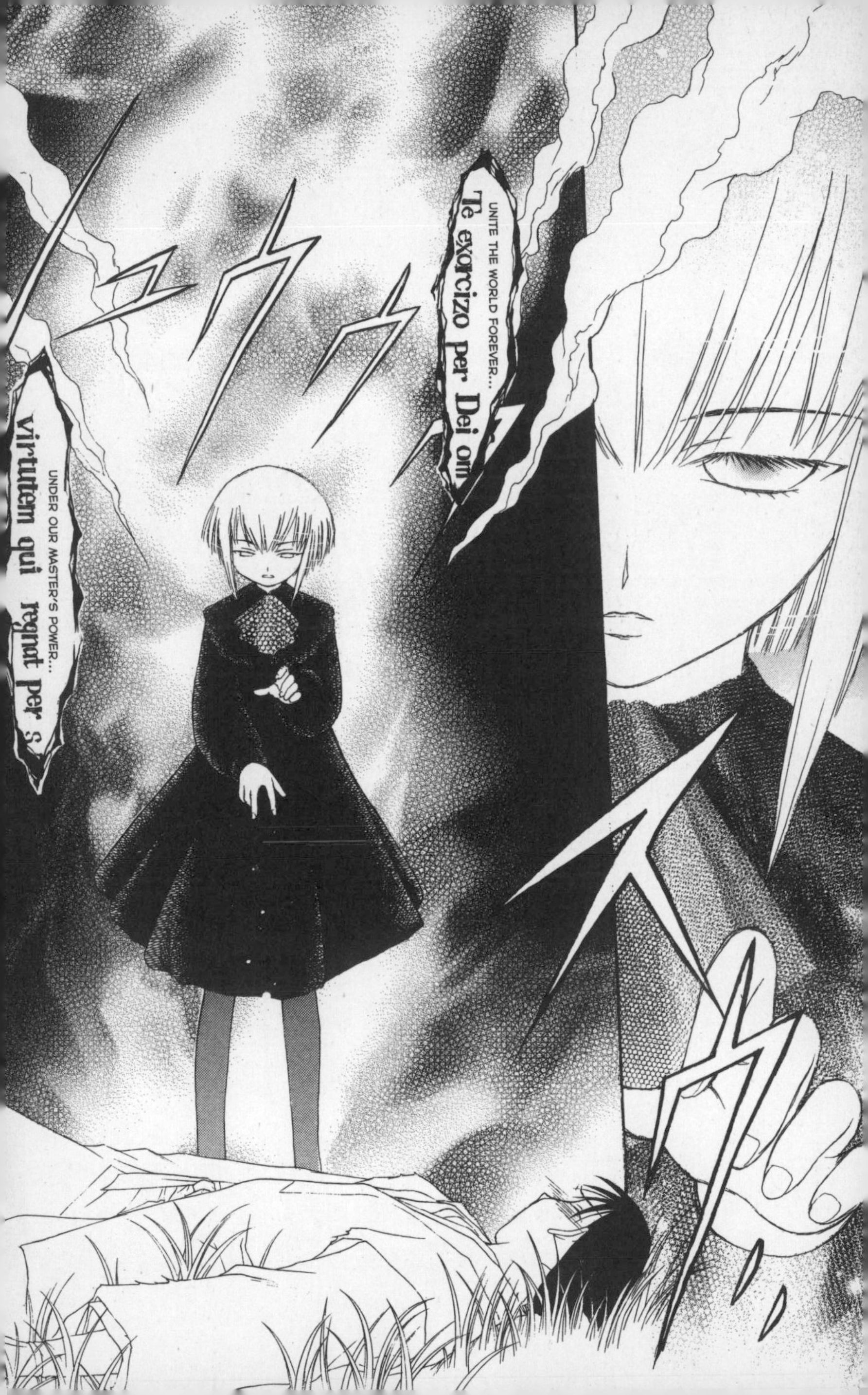
UNITE THE WORLD FOREVER...
Te exorcizo per Dei om
UNDER OUR MASTER'S POWER...
virtutem qui regnat per s

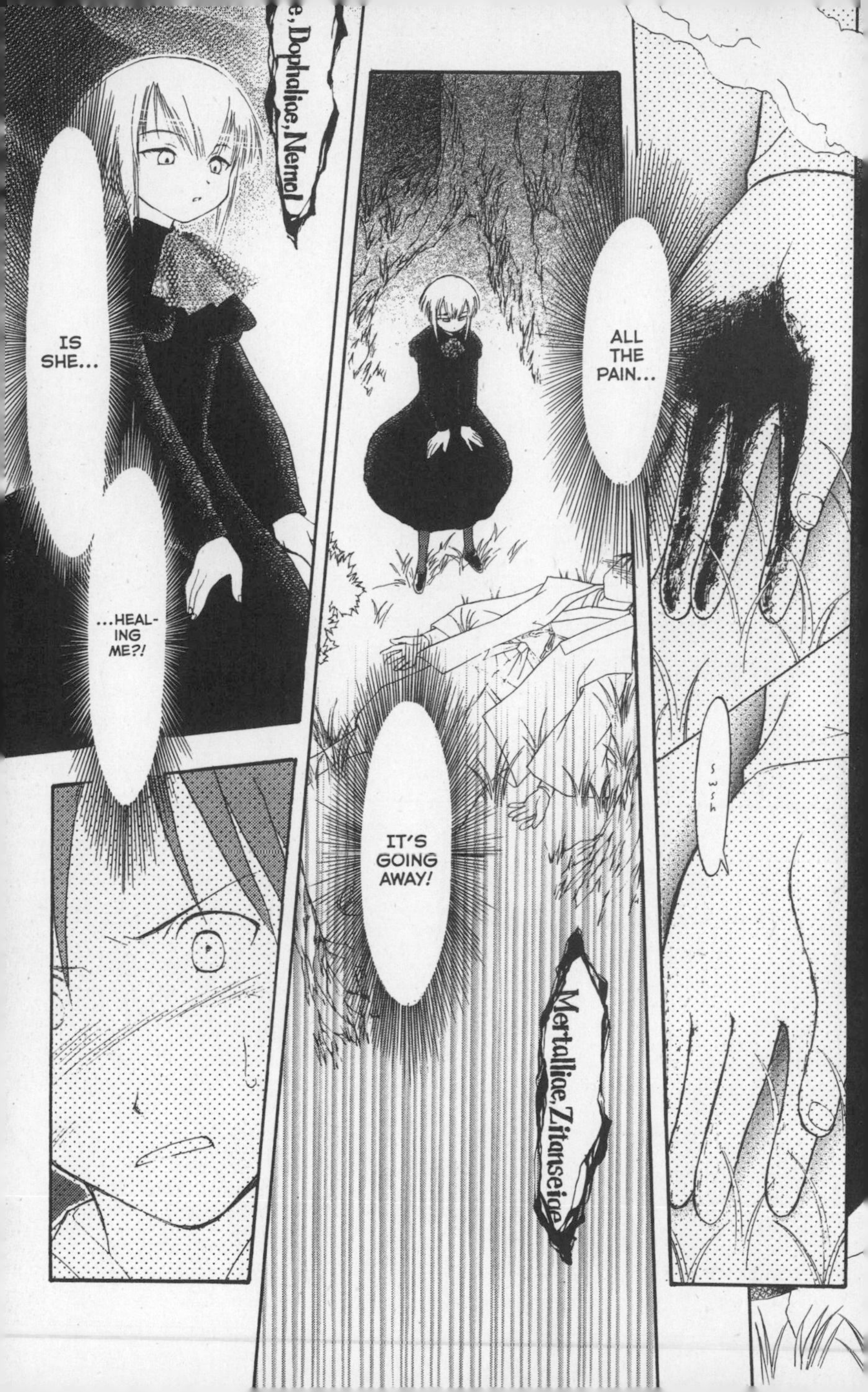

ALL THE PAIN...
swsh
IT'S GOING AWAY!
Mertalliae, Zitanseiae
e, Dophaliae, Nemo!
IS SHE...
...HEAL-ING ME?!

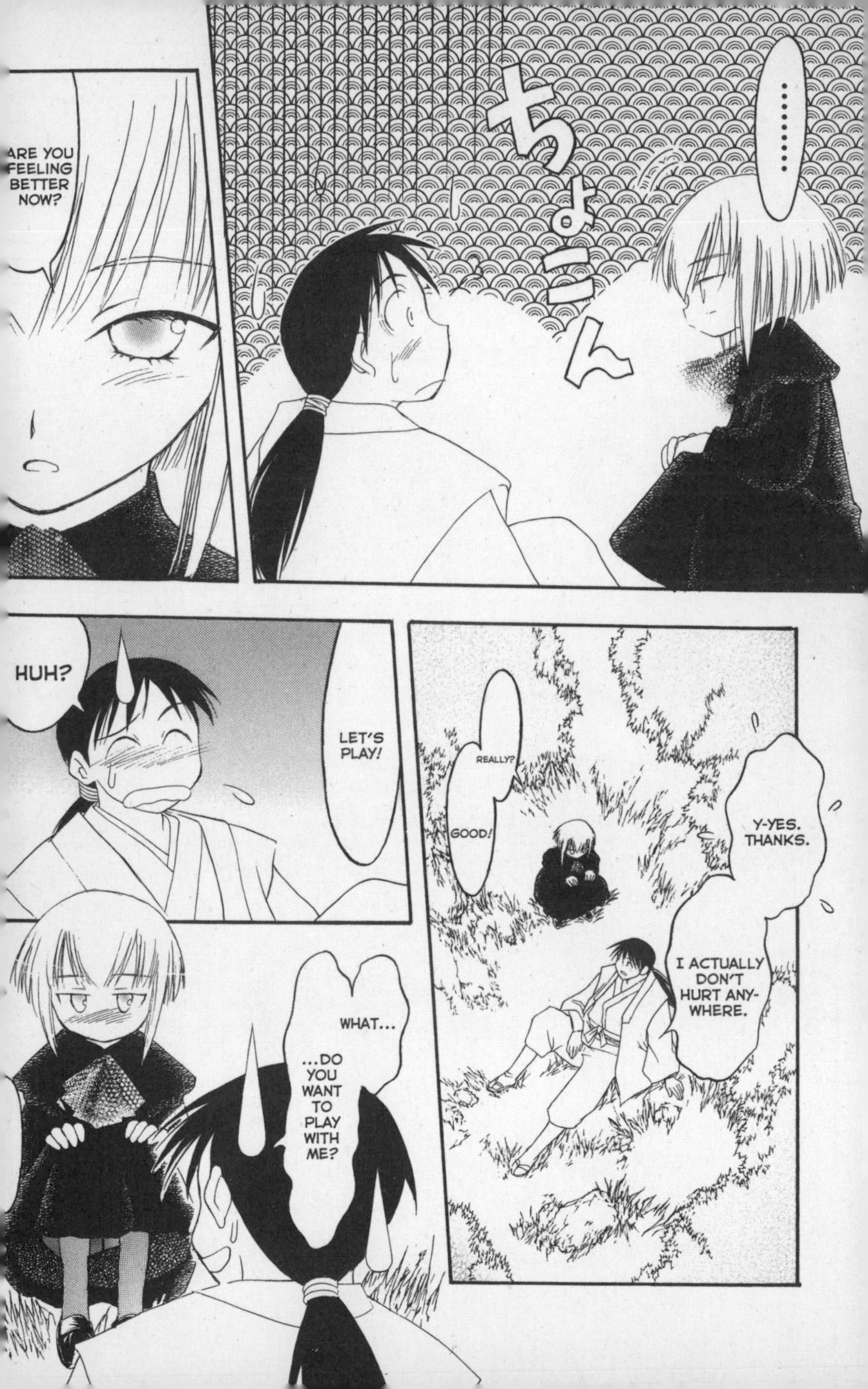
......
ちょこん
ARE YOU FEELING BETTER NOW?
Y-YES. THANKS.
I ACTUALLY DON'T HURT ANY-WHERE.
REALLY?
GOOD!
LET'S PLAY!
HUH?
WHAT...
...DO YOU WANT TO PLAY WITH ME?

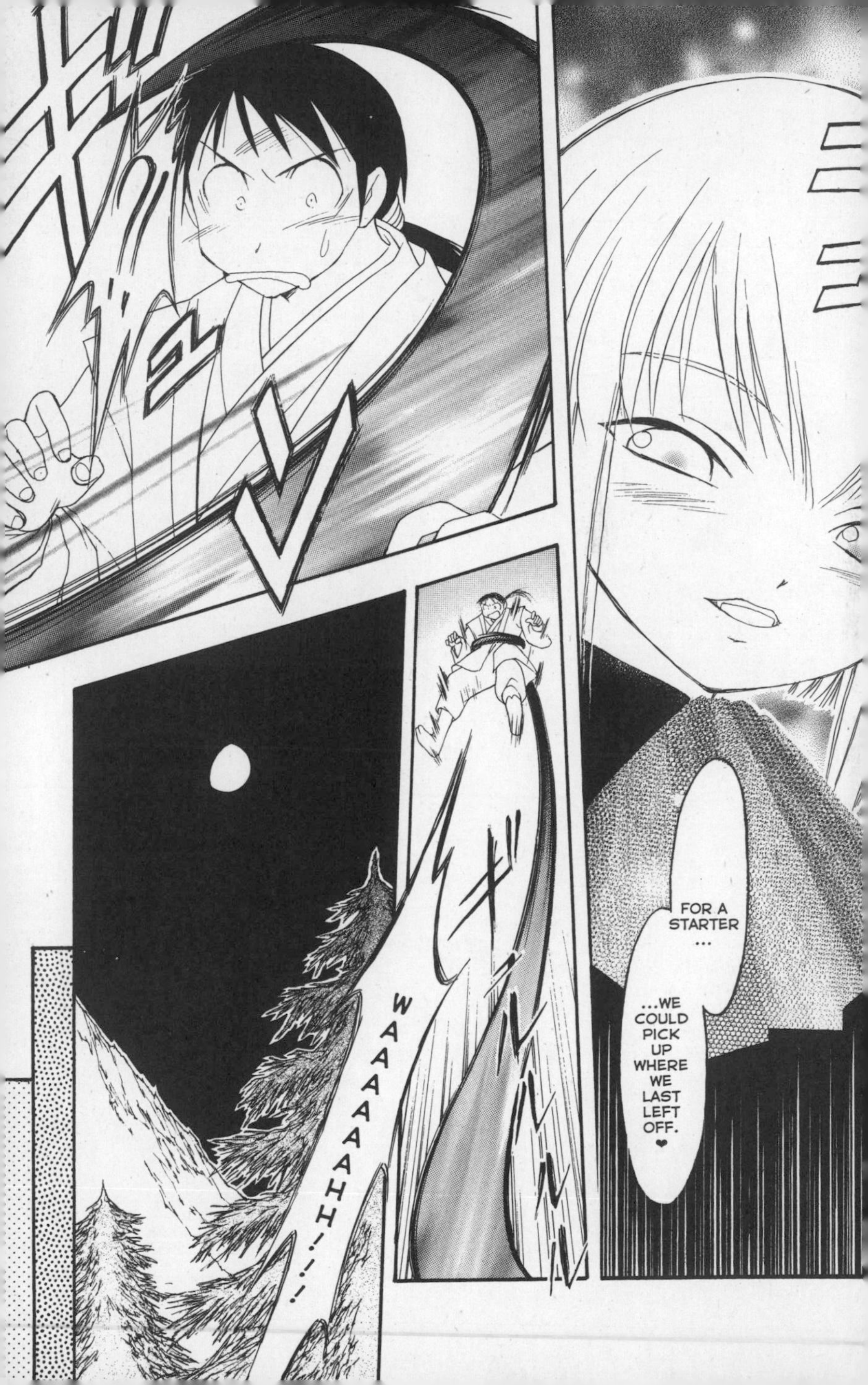
FOR A STARTER ...
...WE COULD PICK UP WHERE WE LAST LEFT OFF. ❤
WAAAAAAAHH!!!

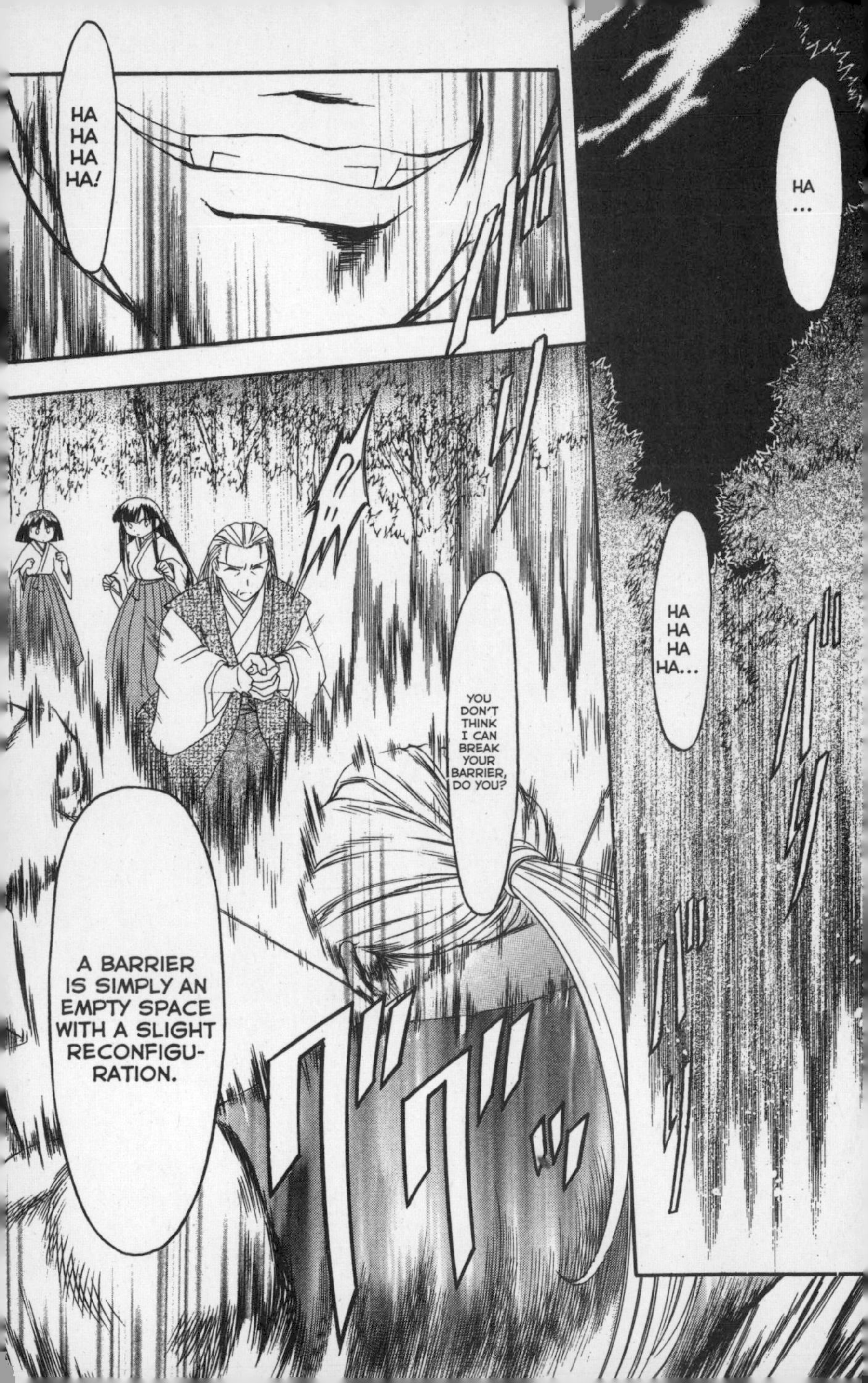
HA ...
HA HA HA HA...
HA HA HA HA!
YOU DON'T THINK I CAN BREAK YOUR BARRIER, DO YOU?
A BARRIER IS SIMPLY AN EMPTY SPACE WITH A SLIGHT RECONFIGU-RATION.

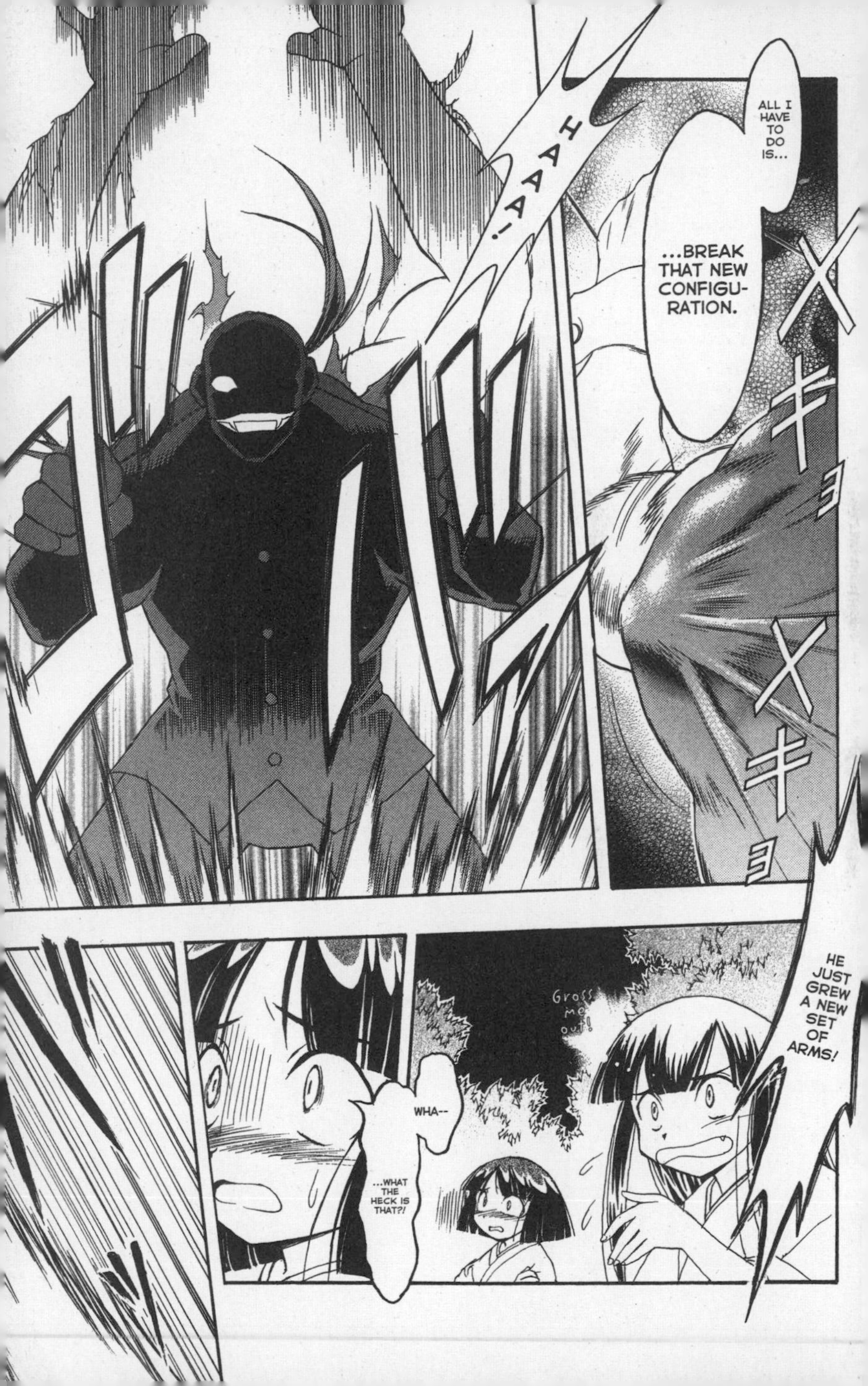
ALL I HAVE TO DO IS...
...BREAK THAT NEW CONFIGU-RATION.
メキョメキョ
HAAAA!
HE JUST GREW A NEW SET OF ARMS!
Gross me out!
WHA--
...WHAT THE HECK IS THAT?!

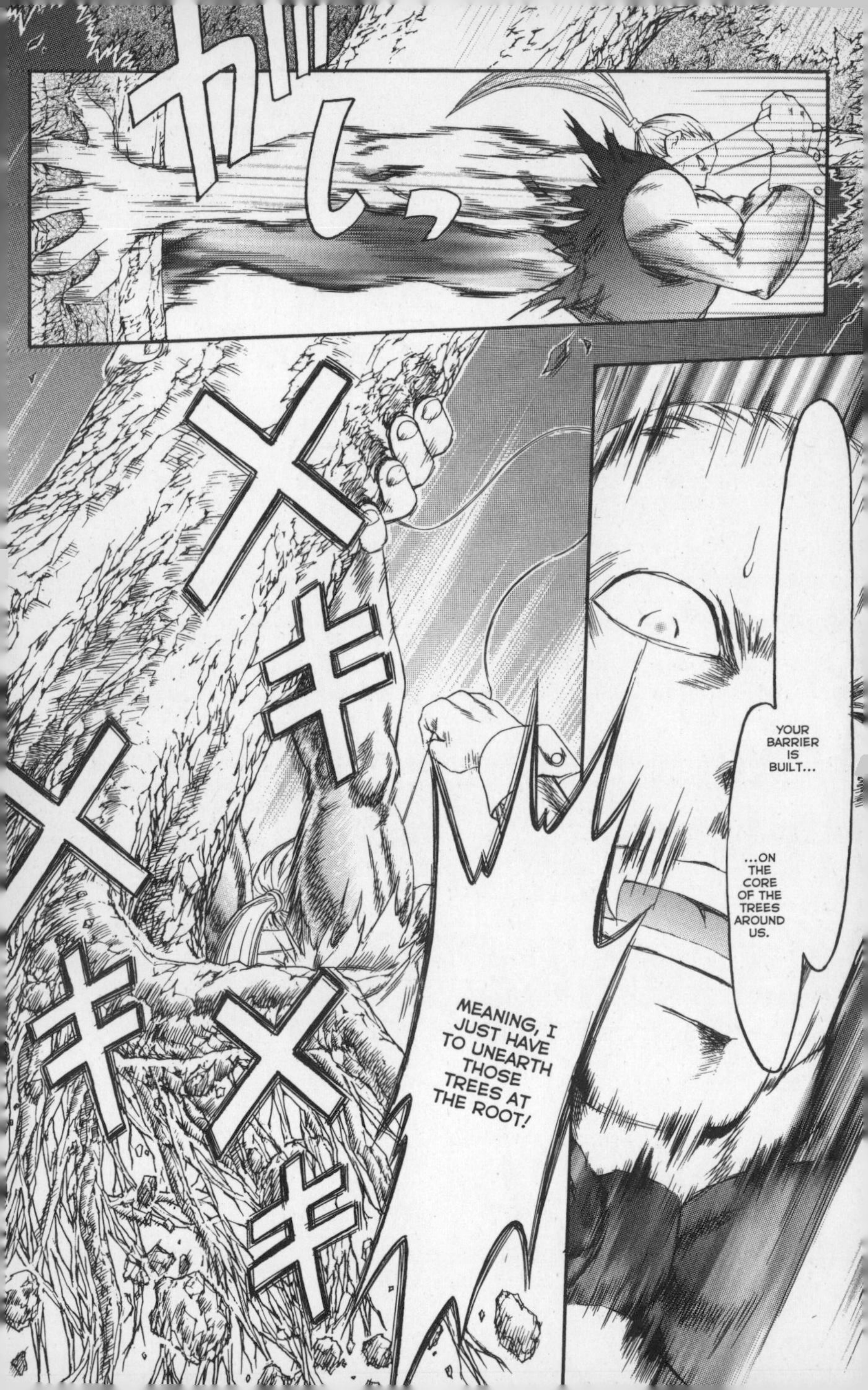
YOUR BARRIER IS BUILT...
...ON THE CORE OF THE TREES AROUND US.
MEANING, I JUST HAVE TO UNEARTH THOSE TREES AT THE ROOT!

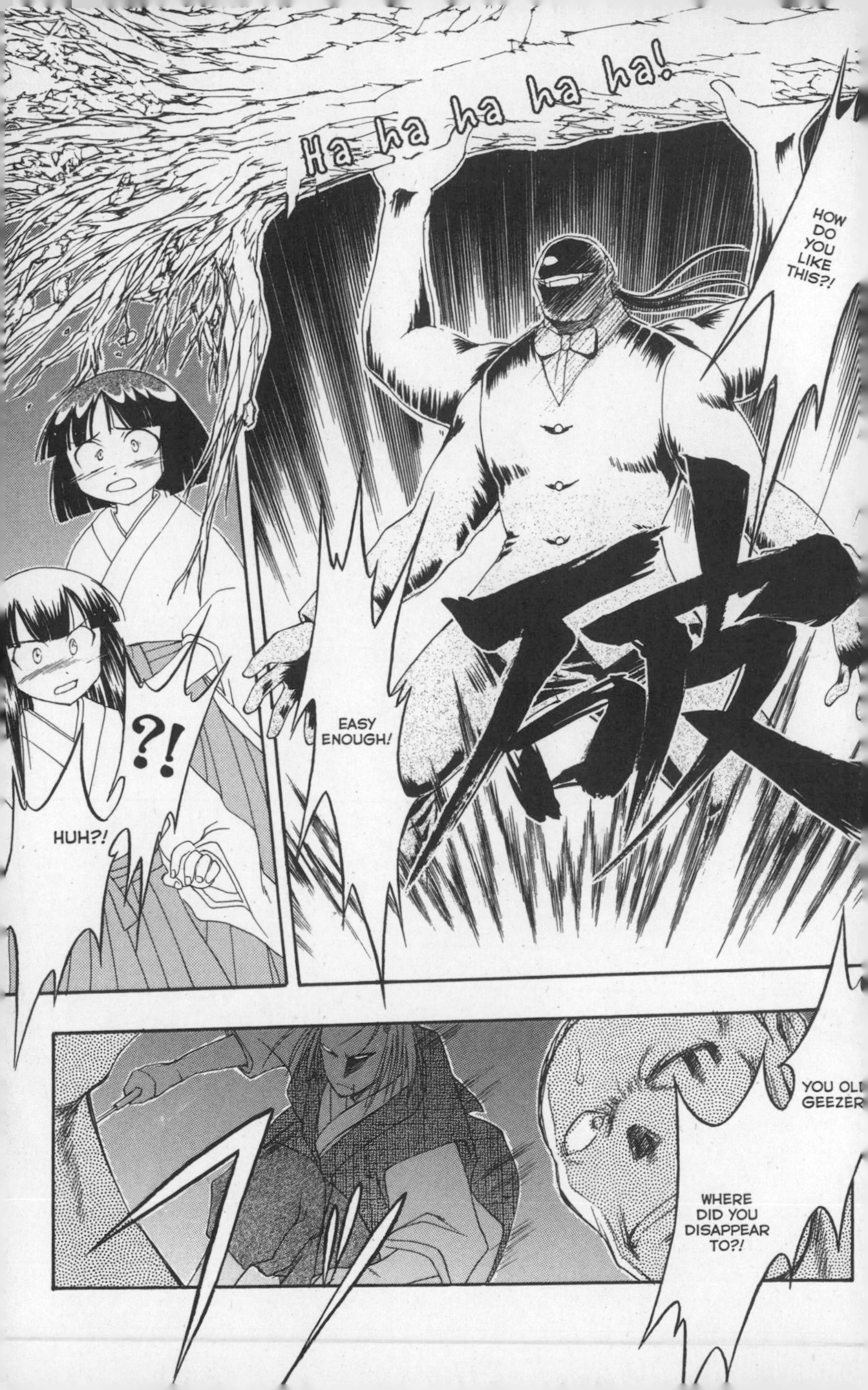
Ha ha ha ha ha ha!
HOW DO YOU LIKE THIS?!
EASY ENOUGH!
?!
HUH?!
YOU OL
GEEZER
WHERE DID YOU DISAPPEAR TO?!

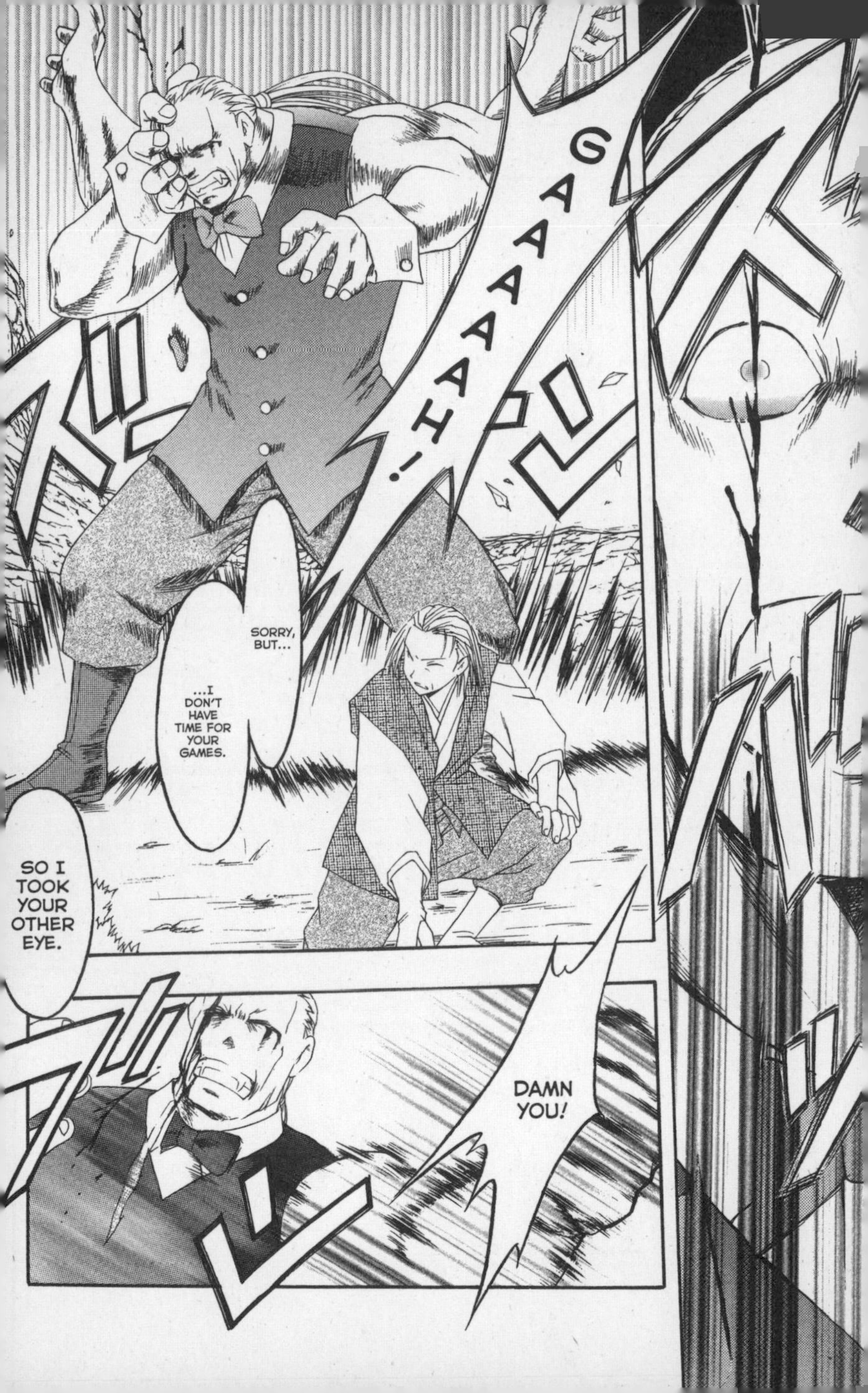
GAAAAAH!
SORRY, BUT...
...I DON'T HAVE TIME FOR YOUR GAMES.
SO I TOOK YOUR OTHER EYE.
DAMN YOU!

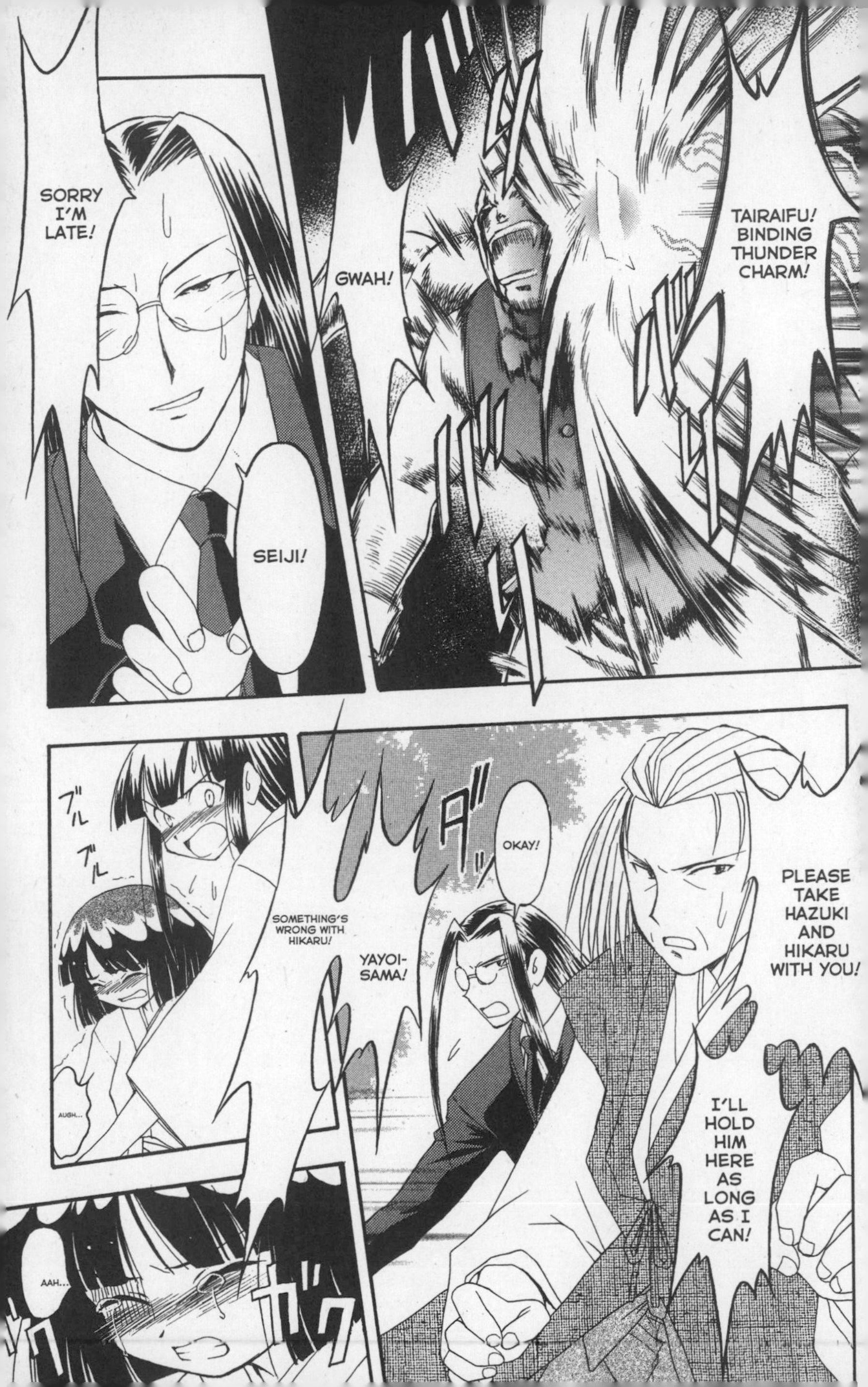
TAIRAIFU! BINDING THUNDER CHARM!
GWAH!
SORRY I'M LATE!
SEIJI!
PLEASE TAKE HAZUKI AND HIKARU WITH YOU!
I'LL HOLD HIM HERE AS LONG AS I CAN!
OKAY!
YAYOI-SAMA!
SOMETHING'S WRONG WITH HIKARU!
ブル ブル
AUGH...
AAH...

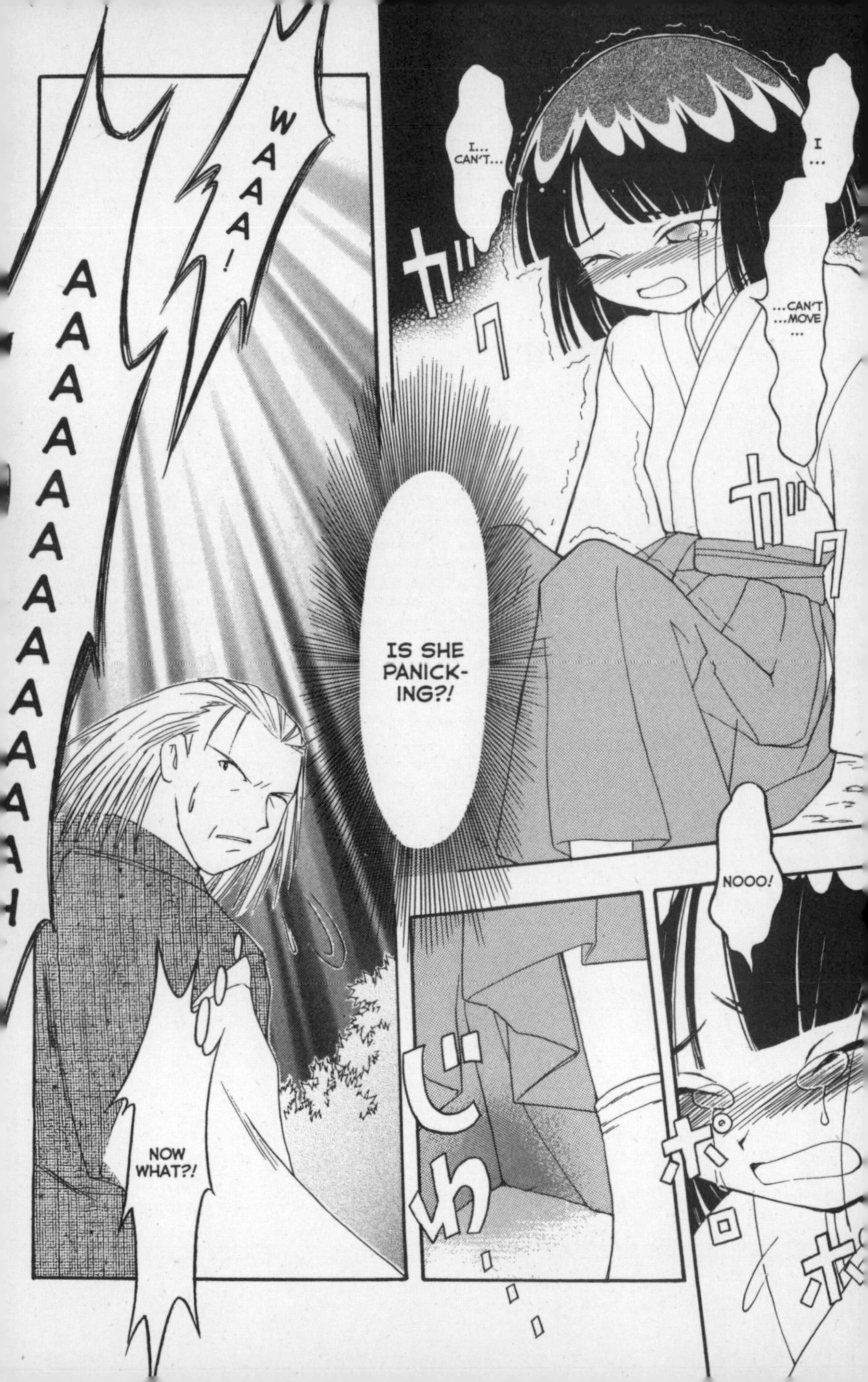
I
...
I...
CAN'T...
...CAN'T
...MOVE
...
ガク
ガク
NOOO!
じわ
ポロ
ポロ
WAAA!
AAAAAAAAAAAAH
IS SHE PANICK-
ING?!
NOW WHAT?!

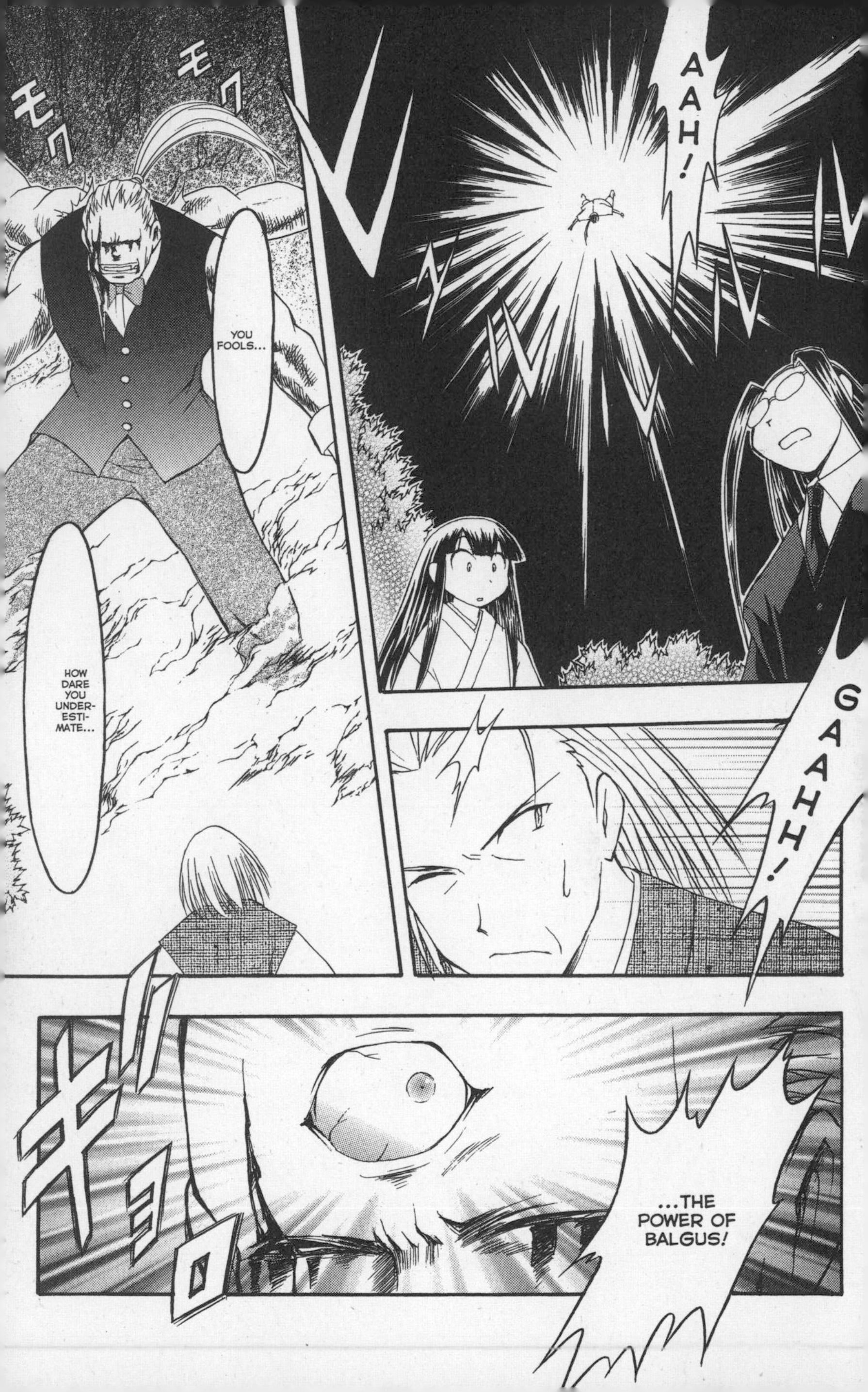
AAH!
GAAHH!
YOU FOOLS...
HOW DARE YOU UNDER-ESTIMATE...
モク モク
ギョロ
...THE POWER OF BALGUS!

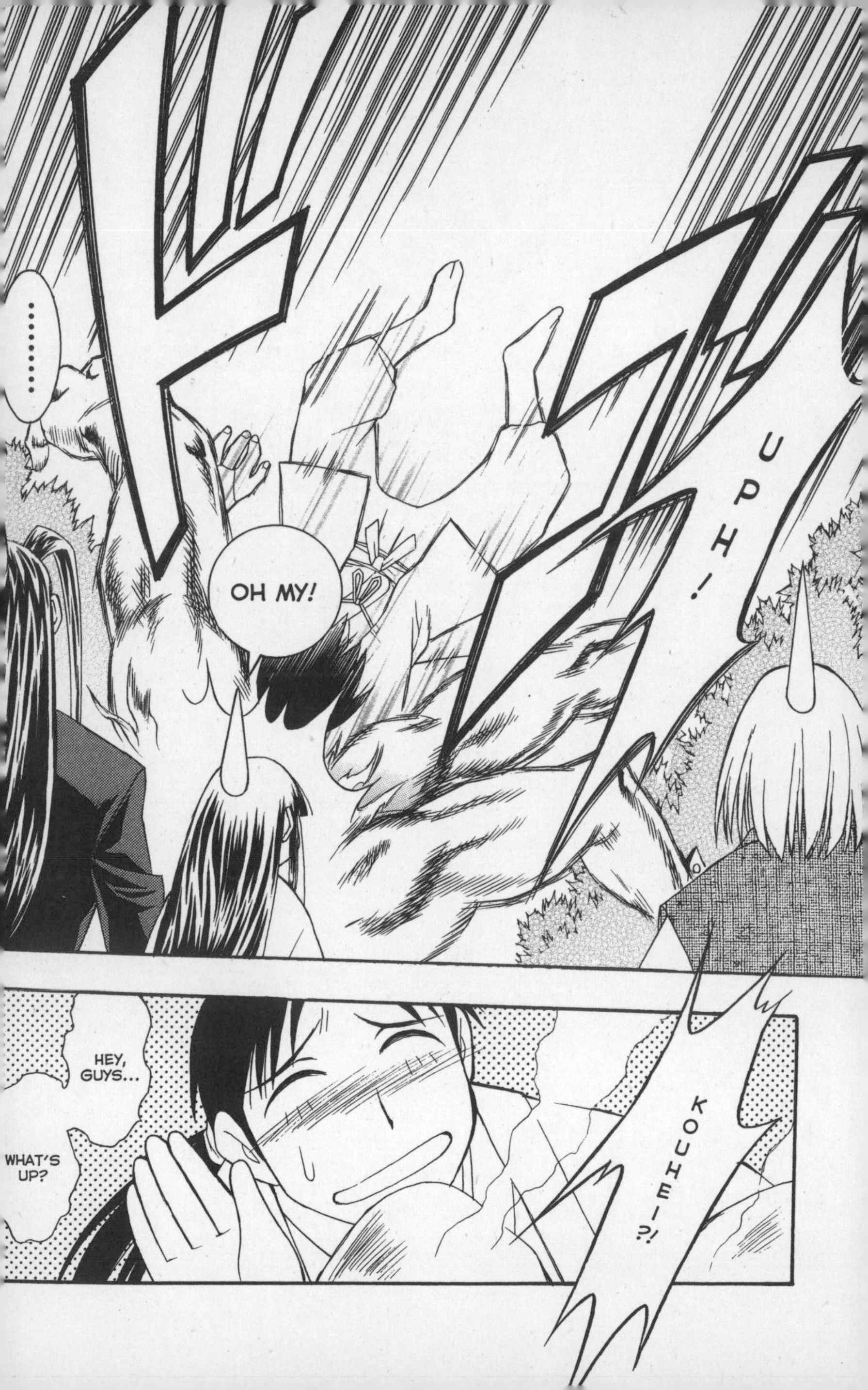
UPH!
OH MY!
......
KOUHEI!?!
HEY, GUYS...
WHAT'S UP?

Moon 月詠 Phase

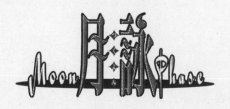

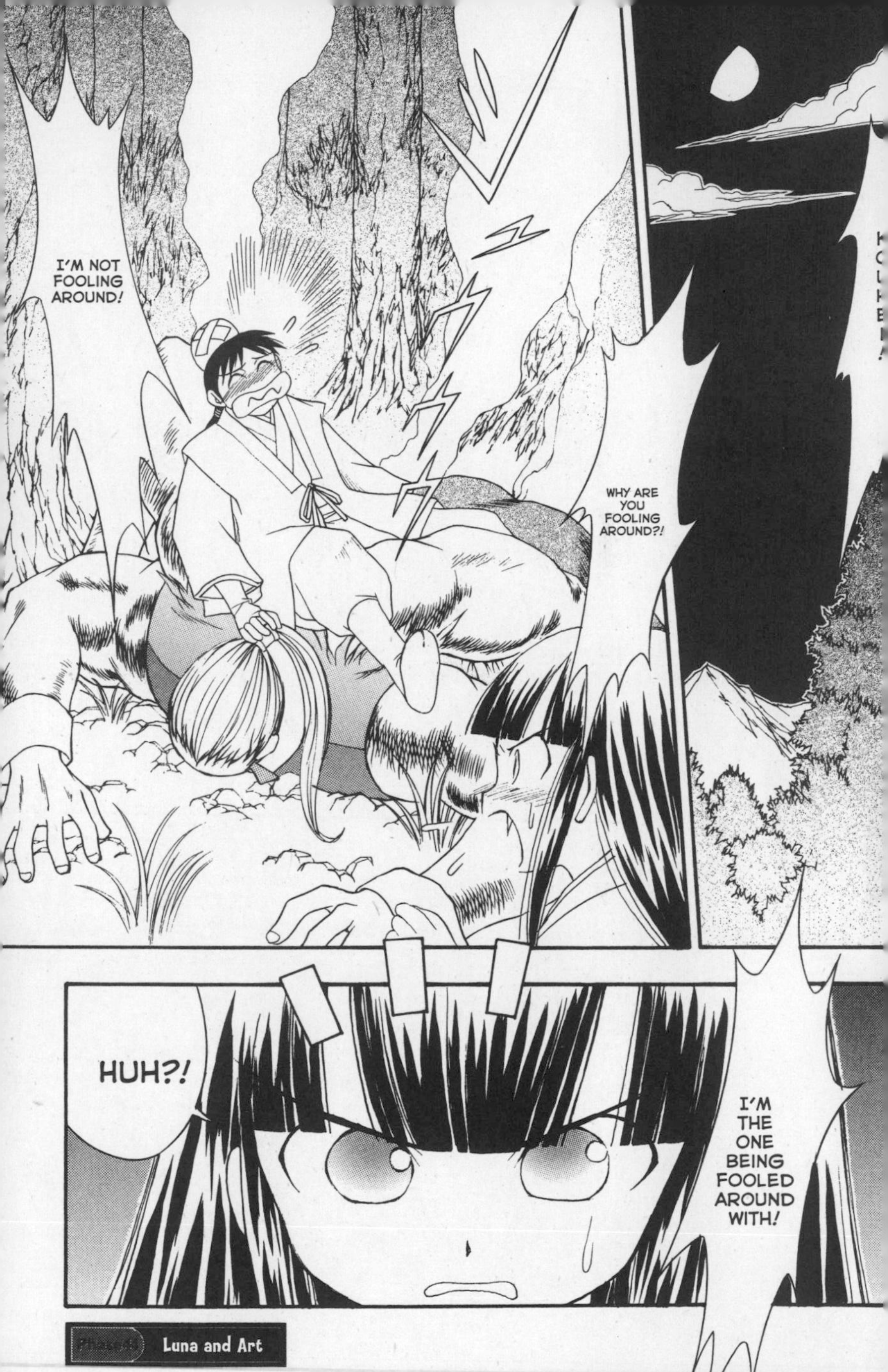
KOUHEI!
WHY ARE YOU FOOLING AROUND?!
I'M NOT FOOLING AROUND!
I'M THE ONE BEING FOOLED AROUND WITH!
HUH?!

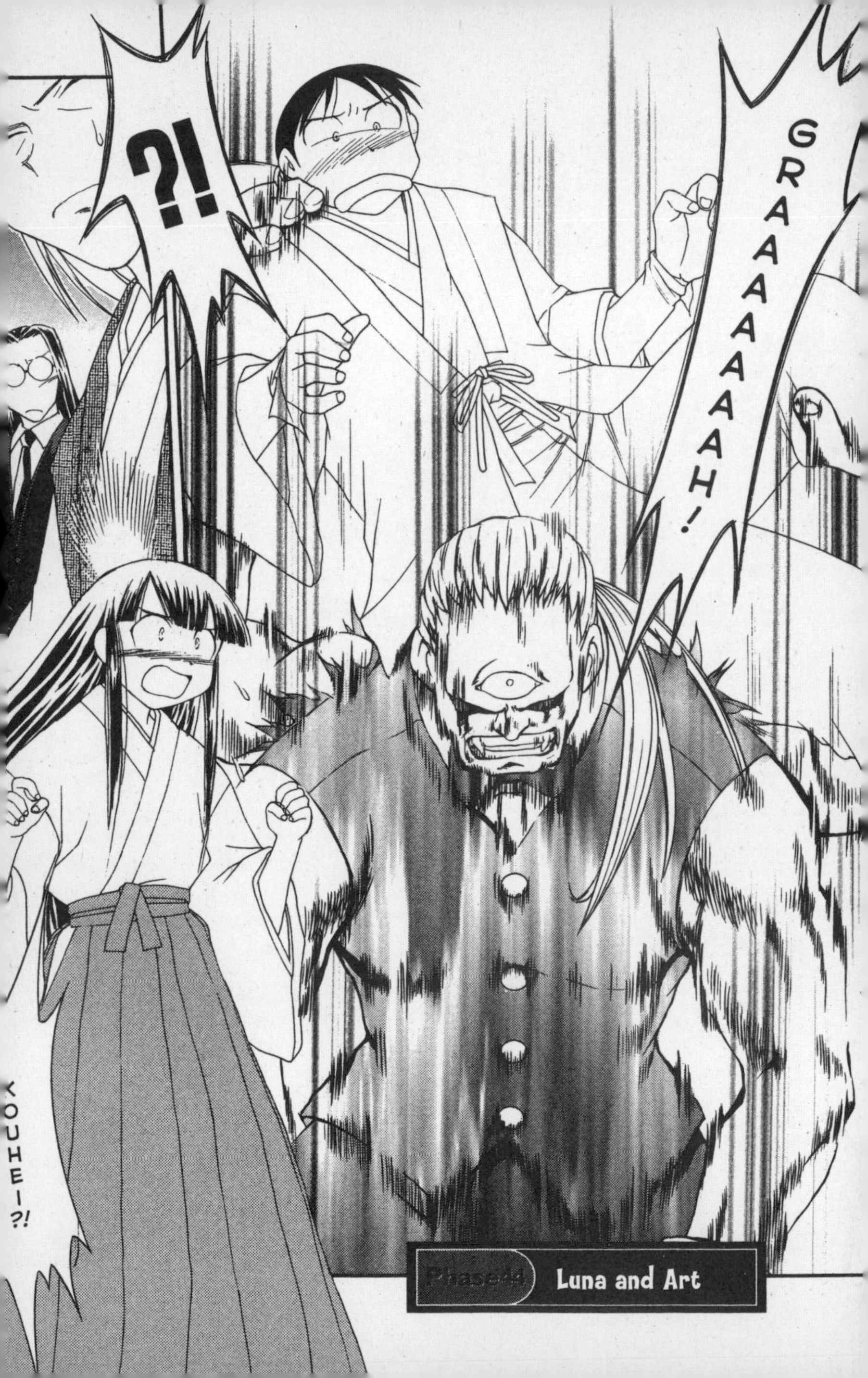
GRAAAAAAAH!
?!
KOUHEI?!
Phase44
Luna and Art

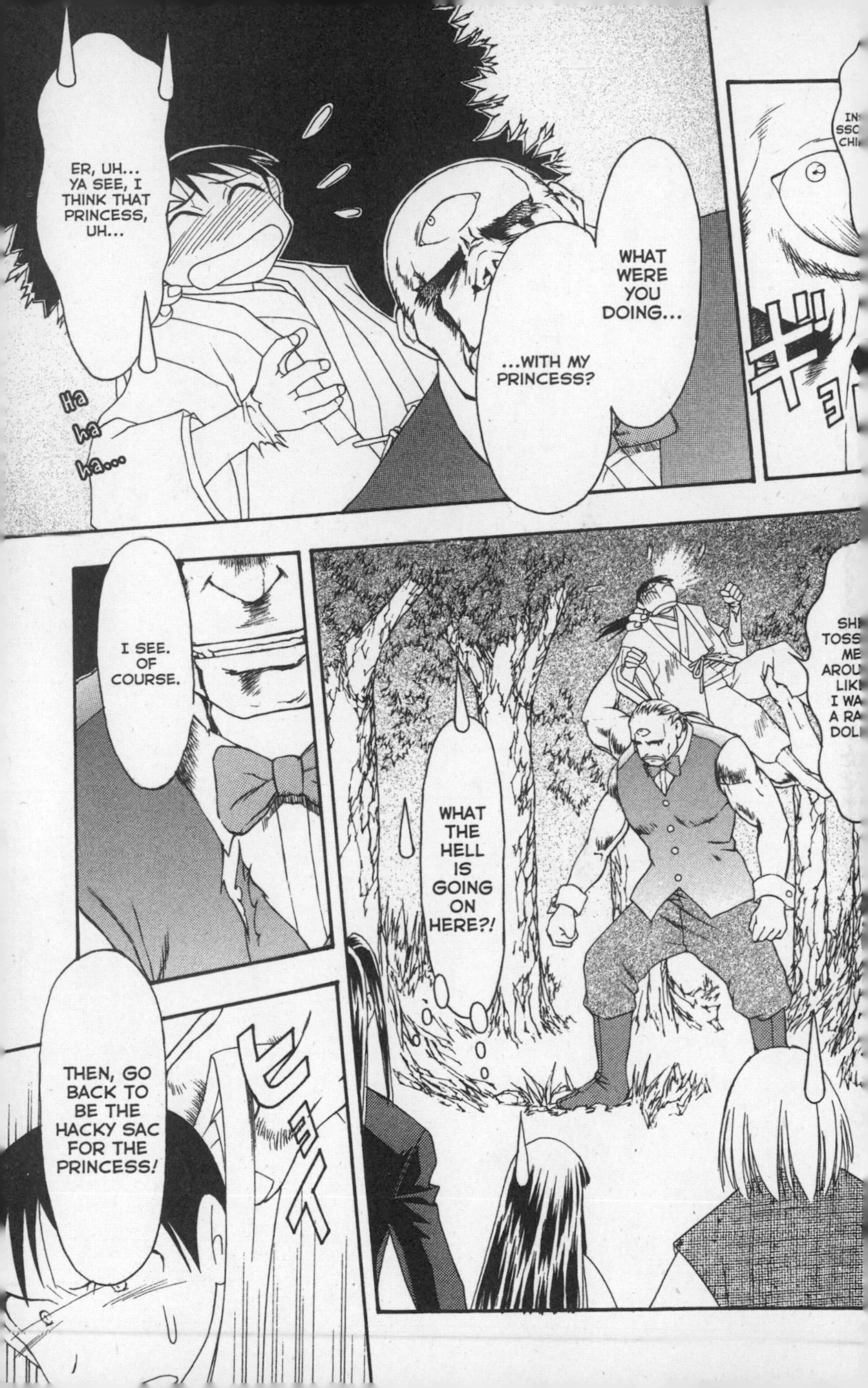
WHAT WERE YOU DOING...
...WITH MY PRINCESS?
ER, UH... YA SEE, I THINK THAT PRINCESS, UH...
Ha ha ha...
WHAT THE HELL IS GOING ON HERE?!
I SEE. OF COURSE.
THEN, GO BACK TO BE THE HACKY SAC FOR THE PRINCESS!
ヒョイ

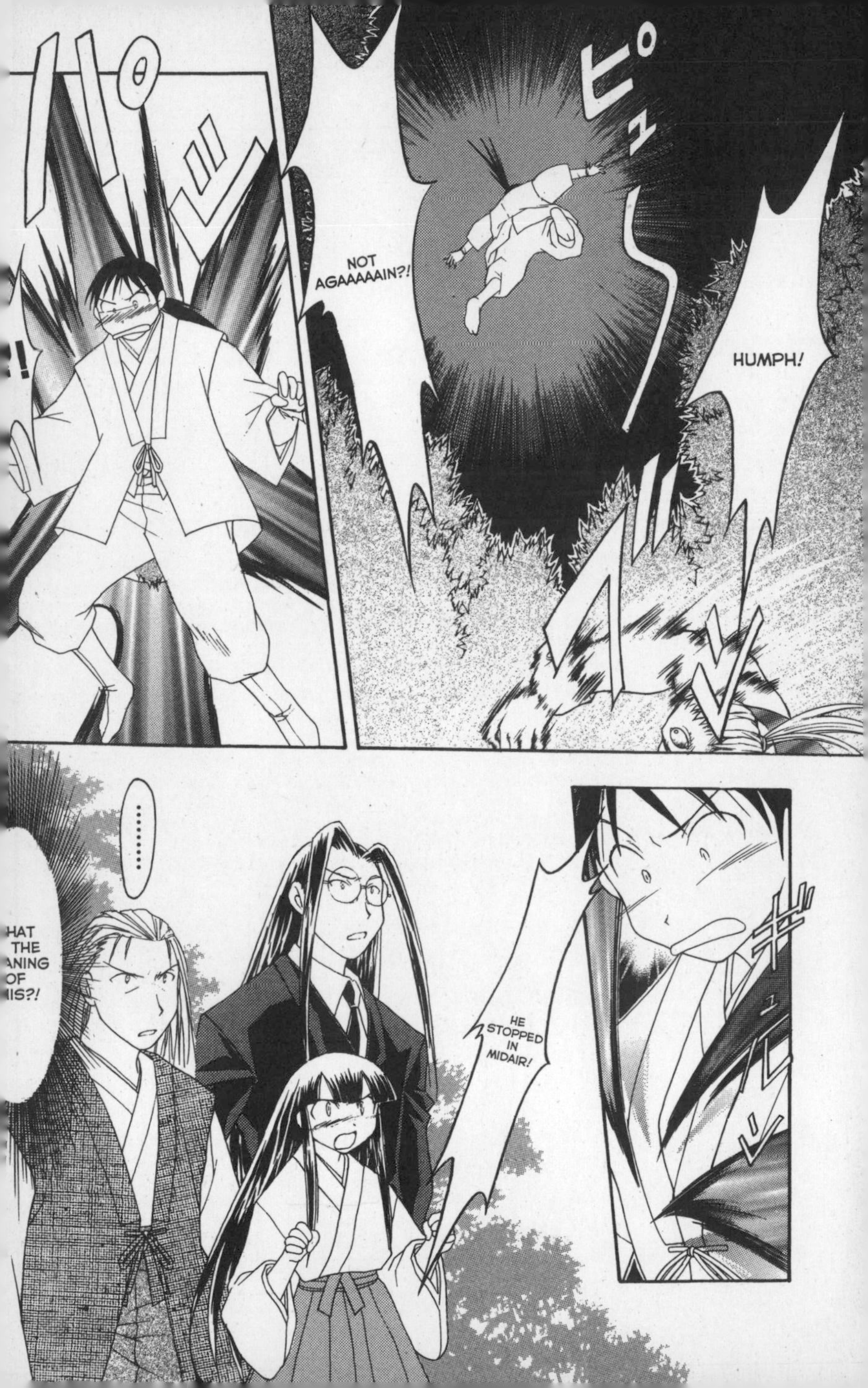
HUMPH!
NOT AGAAAAAIN?!
HE STOPPED IN MIDAIR!
......
HAT THE ANING OF IS?!

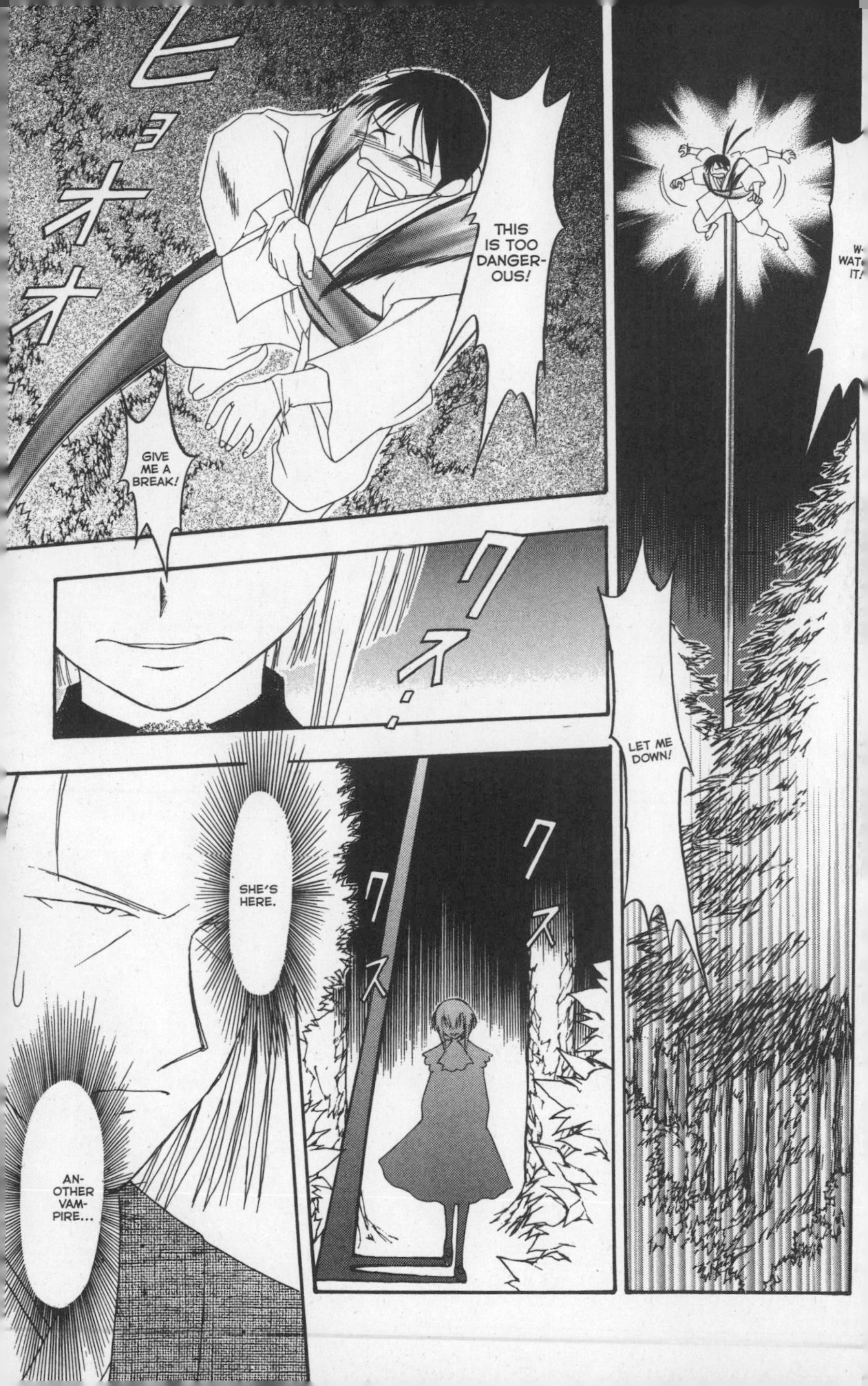
W-
WAT
IT!
LET ME DOWN!
ヒョオオオ
THIS IS TOO DANGER-OUS!
GIVE ME A BREAK!
クイ..
クスクス
SHE'S HERE.
AN-OTHER VAM-PIRE...

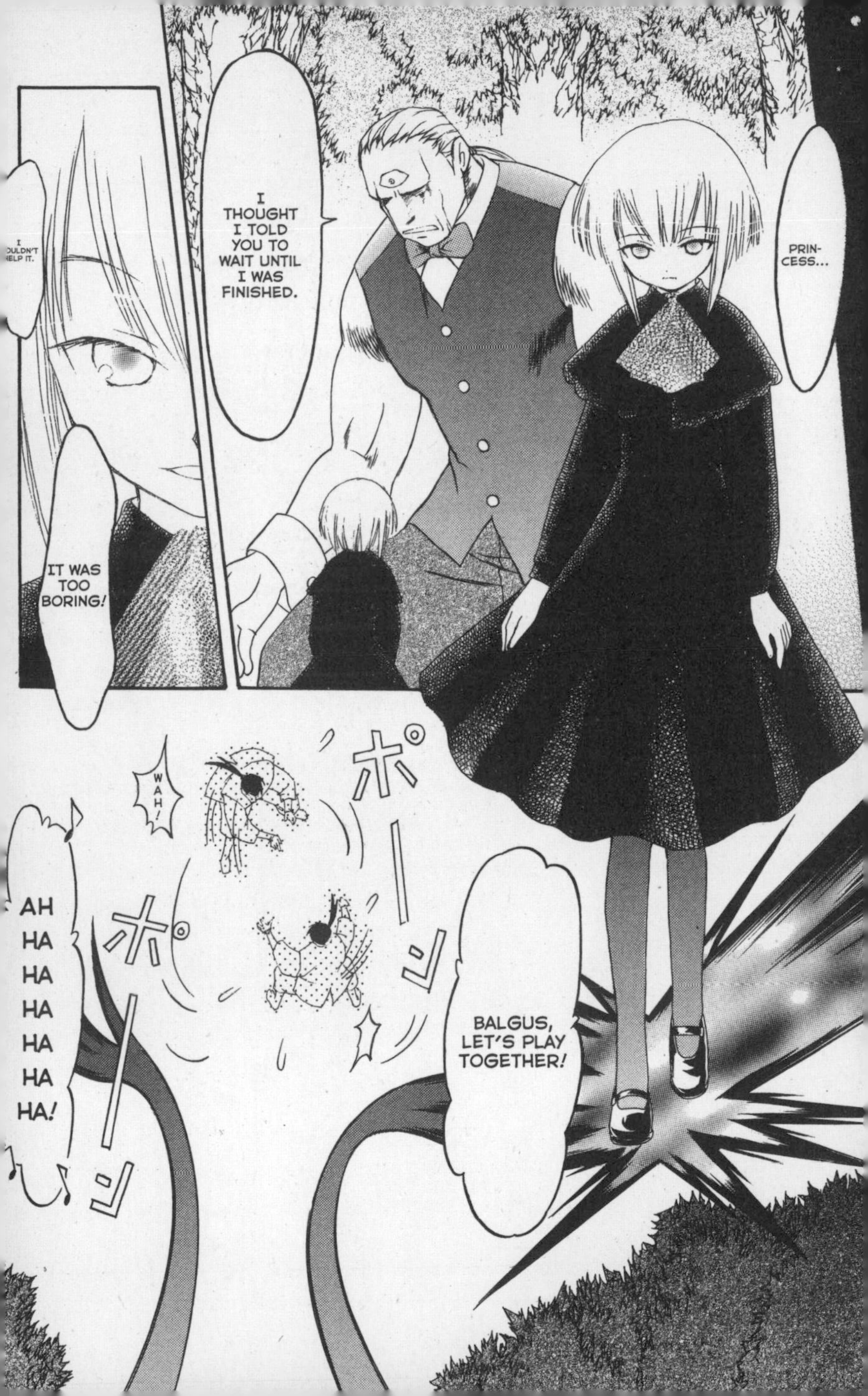
PRIN-CESS...
I THOUGHT I TOLD YOU TO WAIT UNTIL I WAS FINISHED.
IT WAS TOO BORING!
BALGUS, LET'S PLAY TOGETHER!
ポーン
WAH!
ポーン
AH HA HA HA HA HA HA HA!

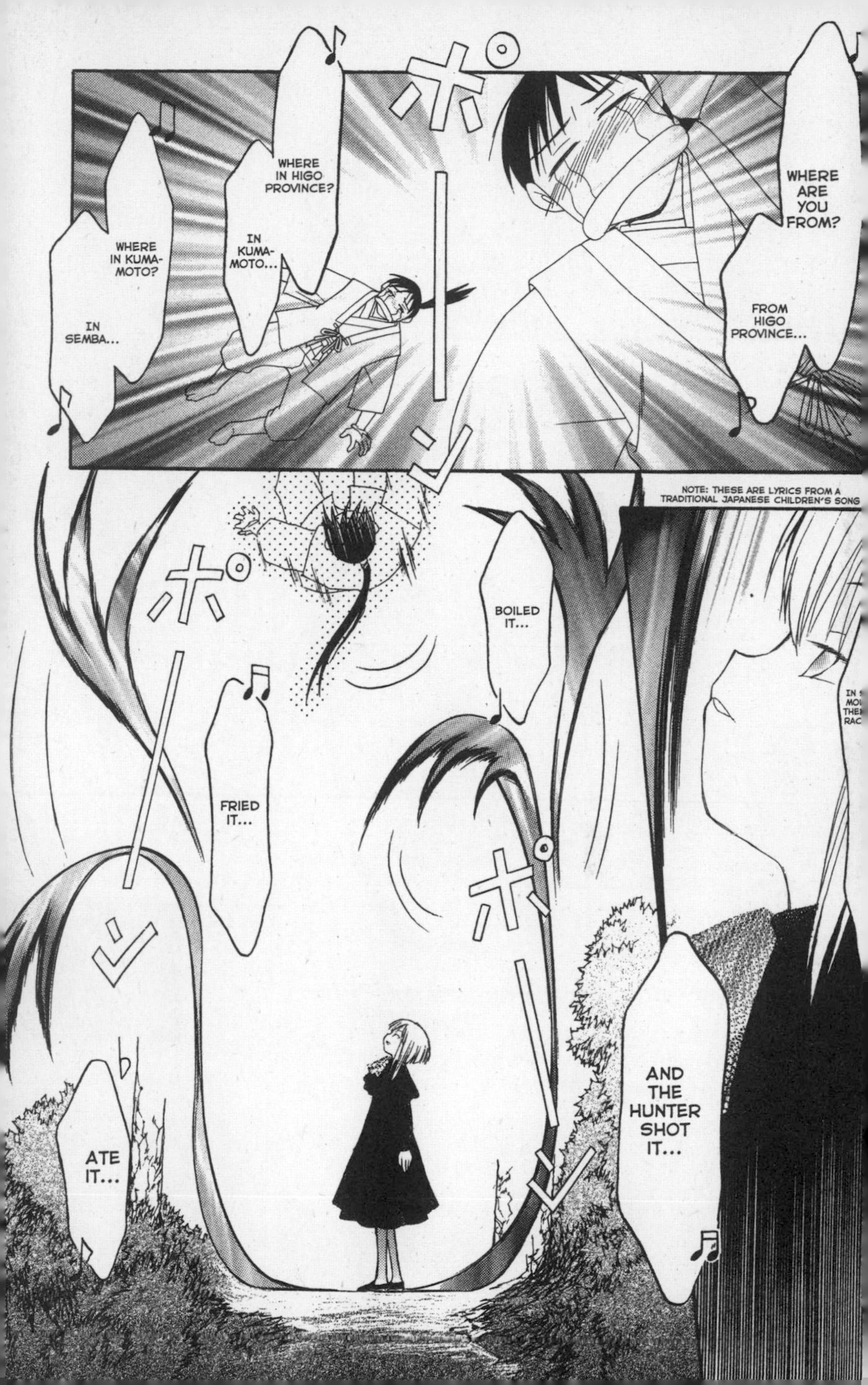
WHERE ARE YOU FROM?
FROM HIGO PROVINCE...
ポン
WHERE IN HIGO PROVINCE?
IN KUMAMOTO...
WHERE IN KUMAMOTO?
IN SEMBA...
NOTE: THESE ARE LYRICS FROM A TRADITIONAL JAPANESE CHILDREN'S SONG
AND THE HUNTER SHOT IT...
BOILED IT...
ポン
FRIED IT...
ポン
ATE IT...

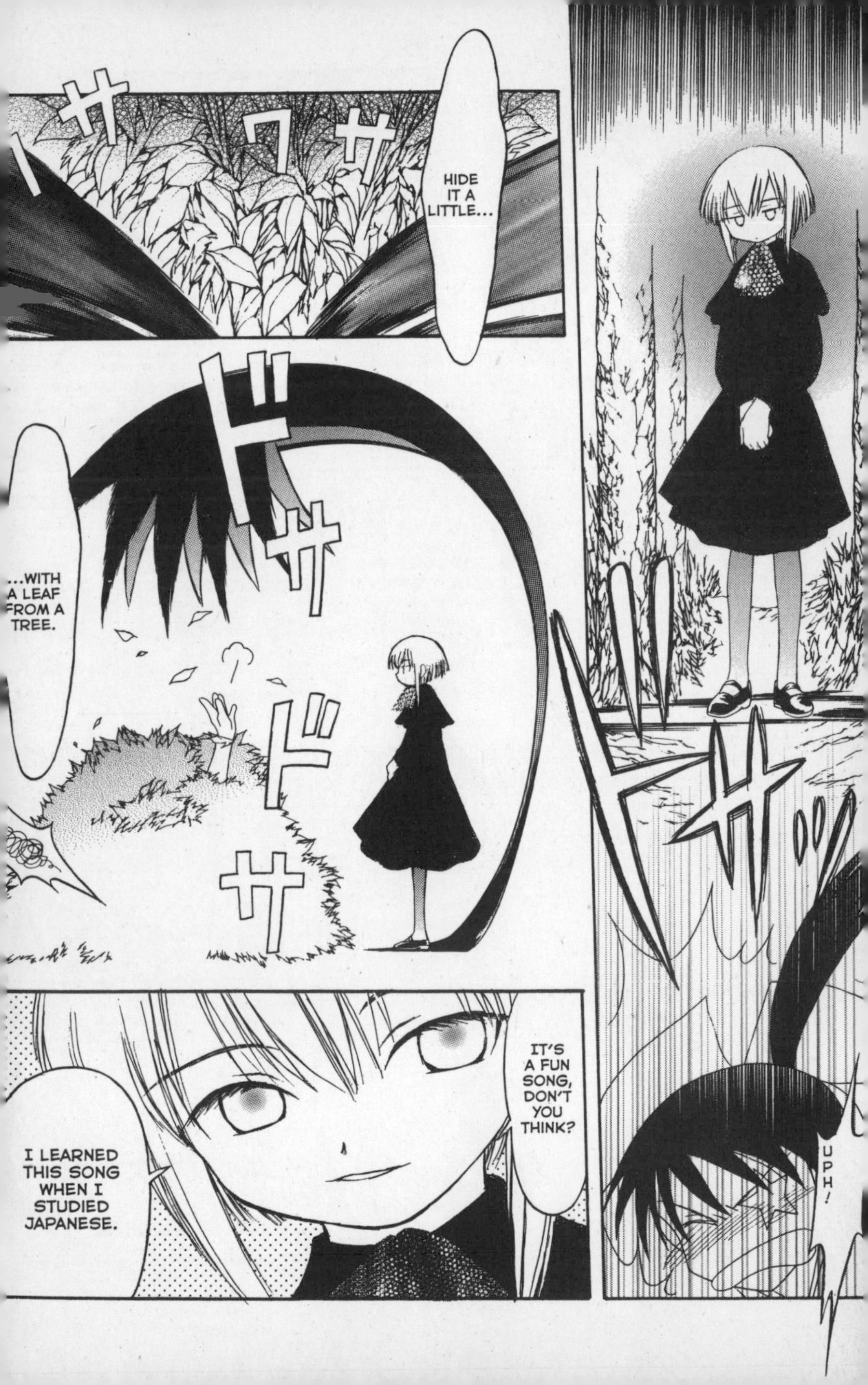
UPH!
ザワザ
HIDE IT A LITTLE...
ドザドザ
...WITH A LEAF FROM A TREE.
IT'S A FUN SONG, DON'T YOU THINK?
I LEARNED THIS SONG WHEN I STUDIED JAPANESE.

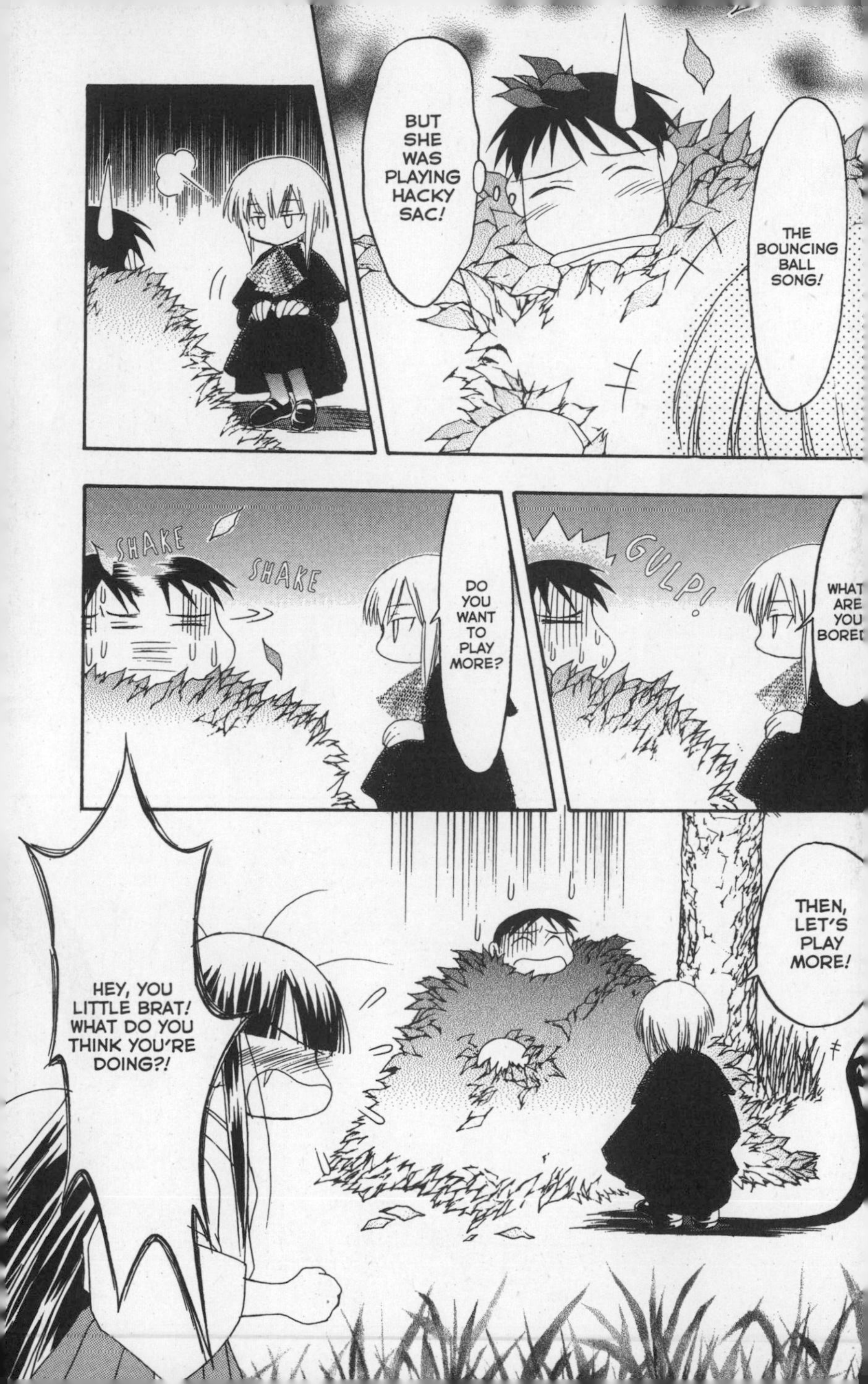
THE BOUNCING BALL SONG!
BUT SHE WAS PLAYING HACKY SAC!
WHAT ARE YOU BORED
GULP!
DO YOU WANT TO PLAY MORE?
SHAKE
SHAKE
THEN, LET'S PLAY MORE!
HEY, YOU LITTLE BRAT! WHAT DO YOU THINK YOU'RE DOING?!

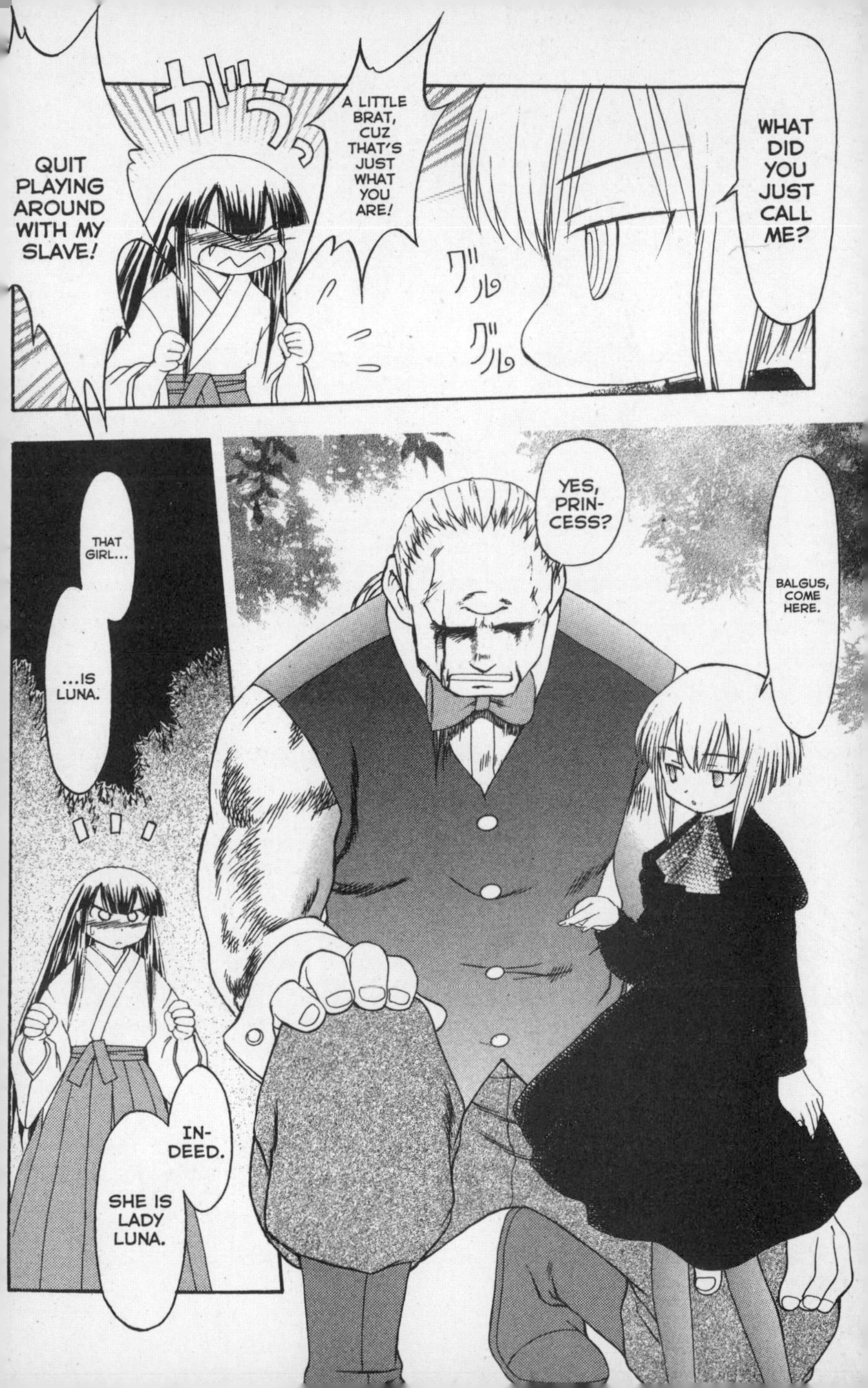
WHAT DID YOU JUST CALL ME?
A LITTLE BRAT, CUZ THAT'S JUST WHAT YOU ARE!
グル
グル
QUIT PLAYING AROUND WITH MY SLAVE!
BALGUS, COME HERE.
YES, PRIN-CESS?
THAT GIRL...
...IS LUNA.
IN-DEED.
SHE IS LADY LUNA.

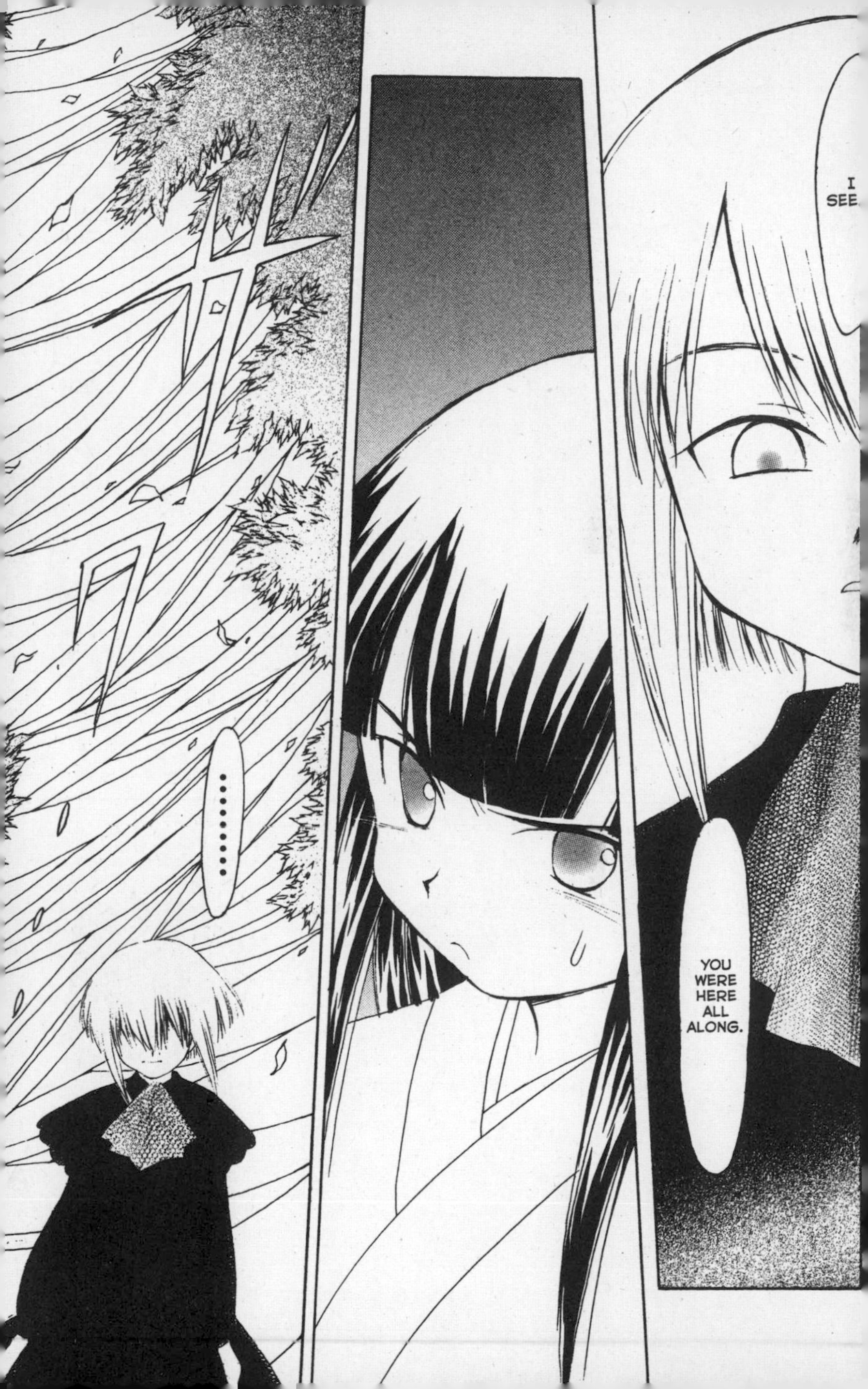
I SEE.
YOU WERE HERE ALL ALONG.
....

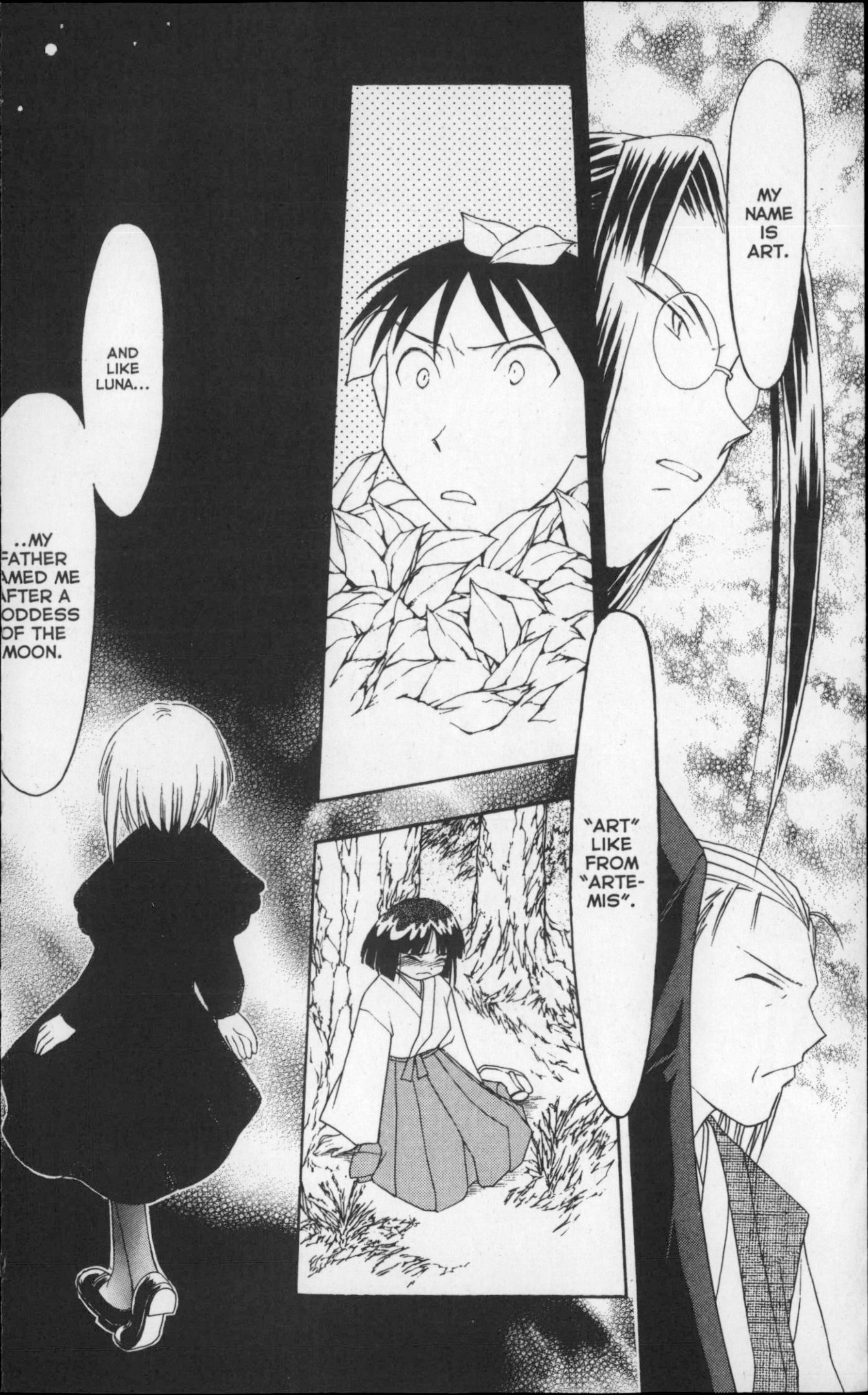
MY NAME IS ART.
"ART" LIKE FROM "ARTE-MIS".
AND LIKE LUNA...
..MY FATHER AMED ME AFTER A ODDESS OF THE MOON.

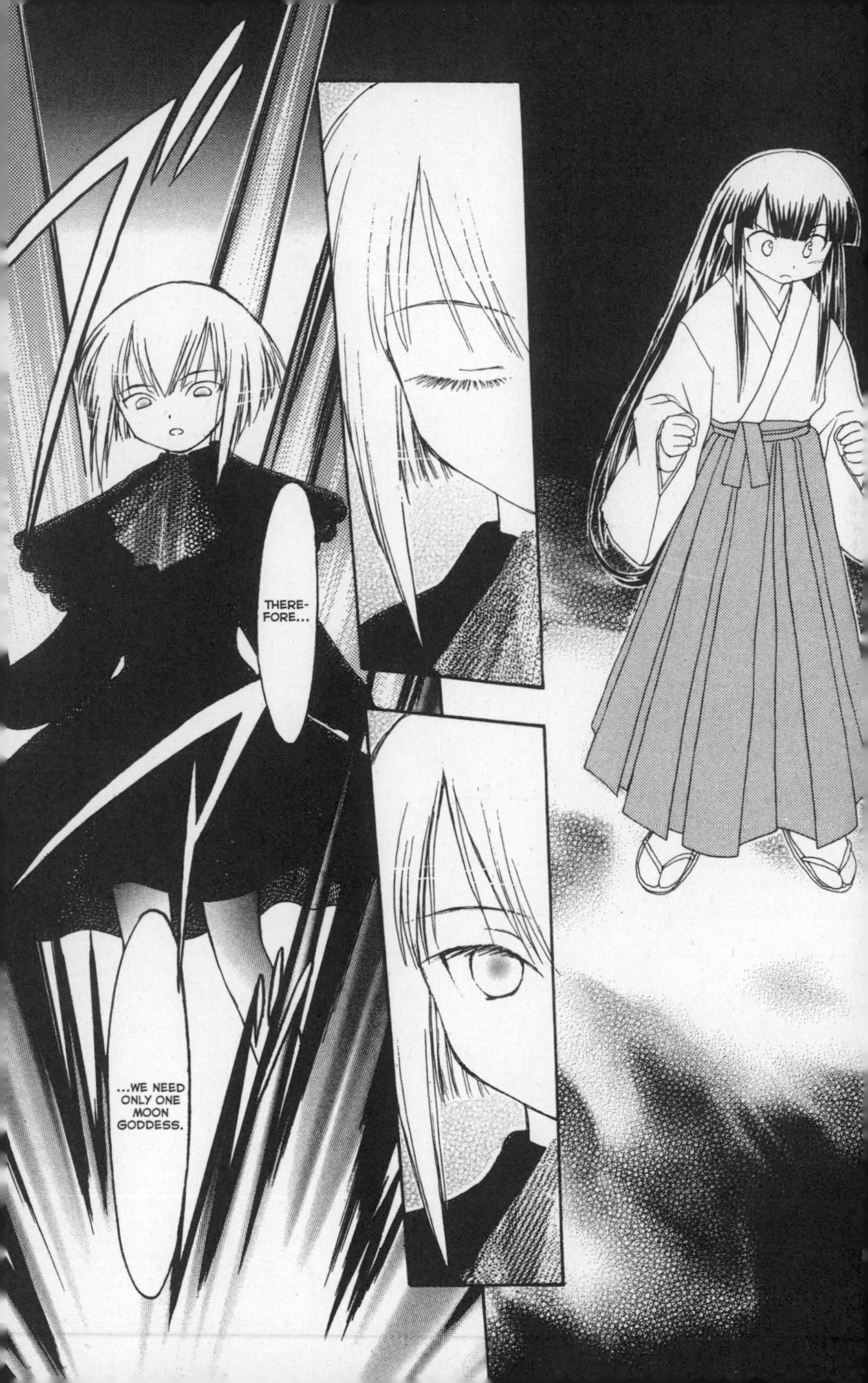
THERE-FORE...
...WE NEED ONLY ONE MOON GODDESS.

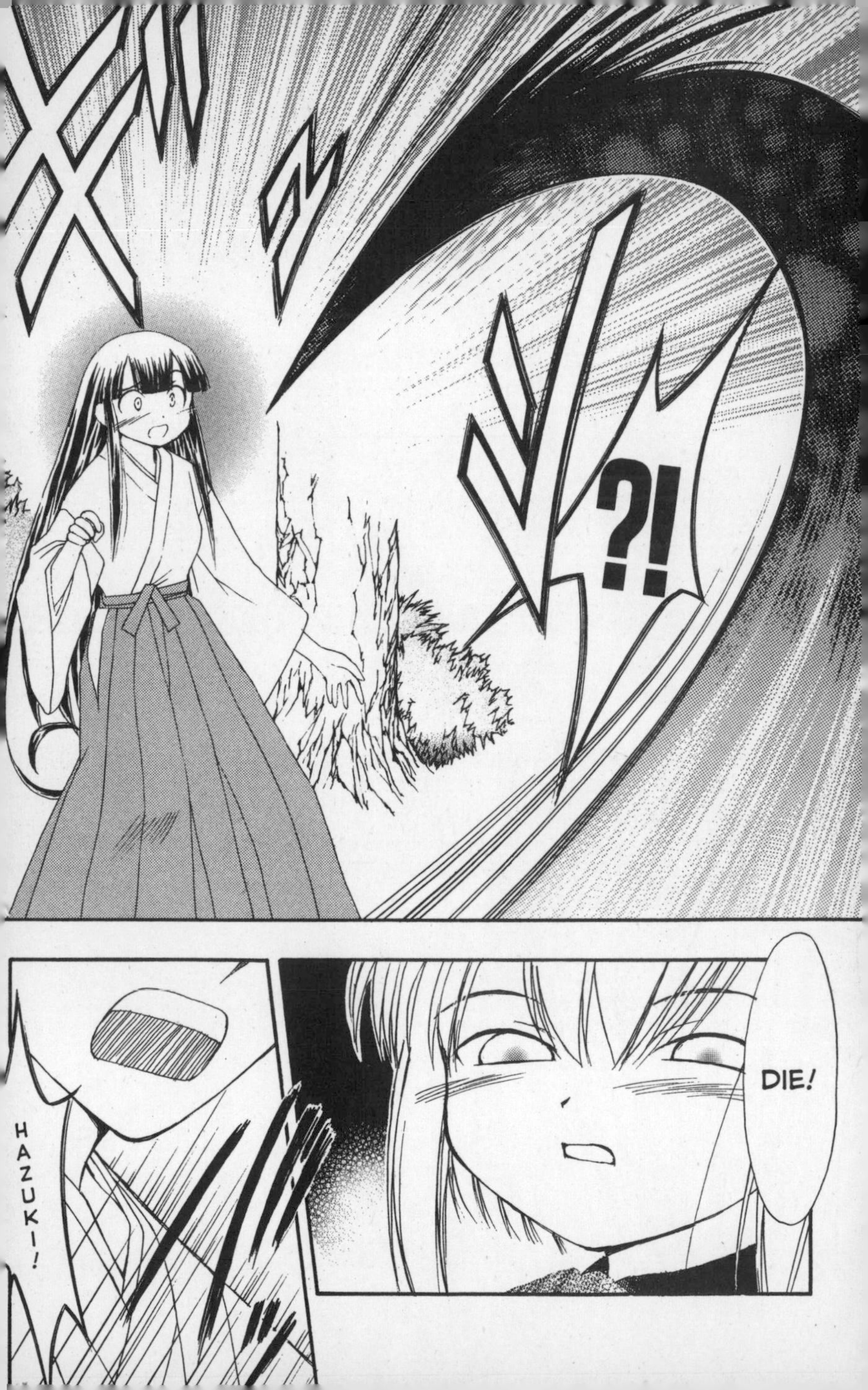
?!
DIE!
HAZUKI!

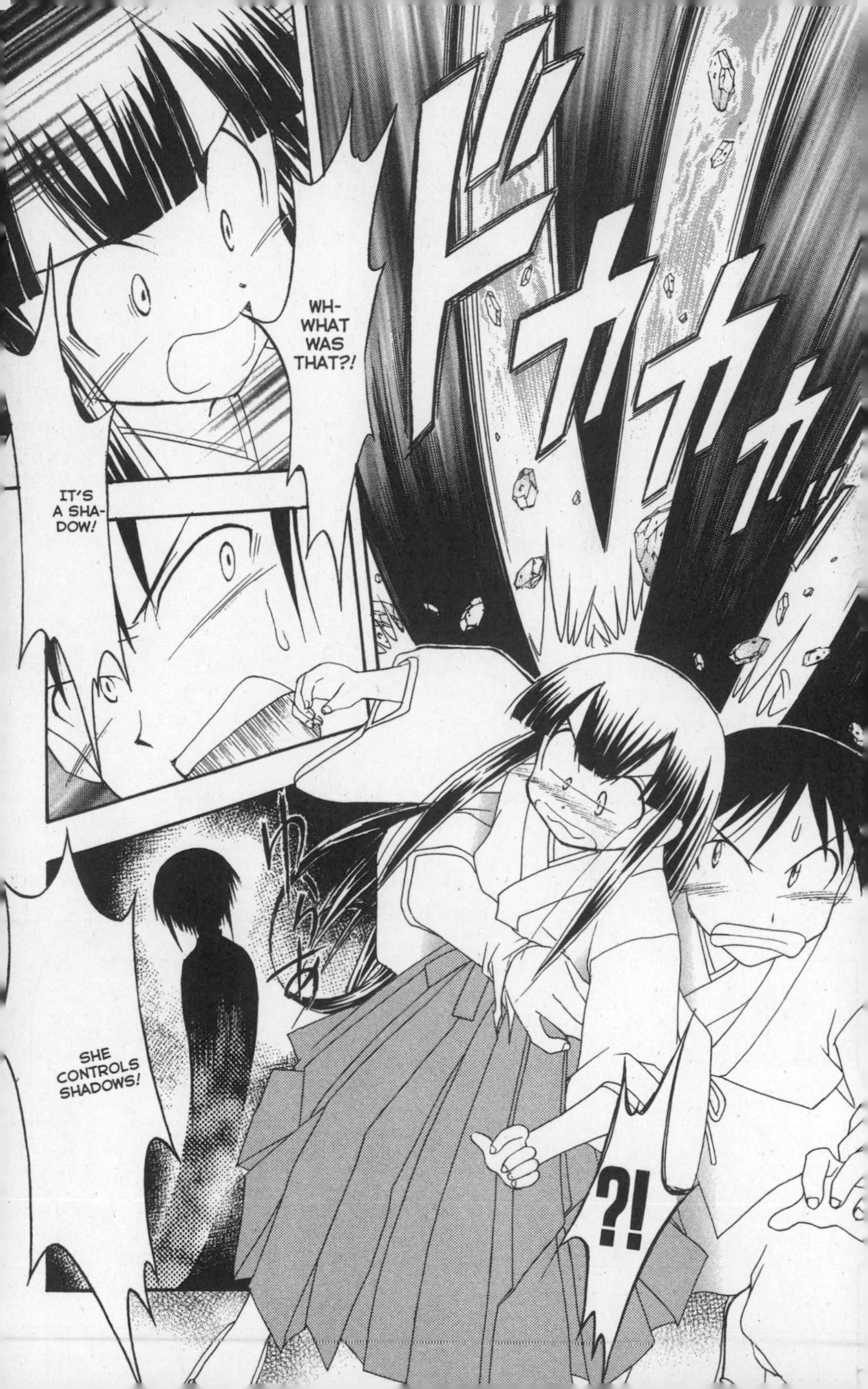
WH- WHAT WAS THAT?!
IT'S A SHA- DOW!
SHE CONTROLS SHADOWS!
?!

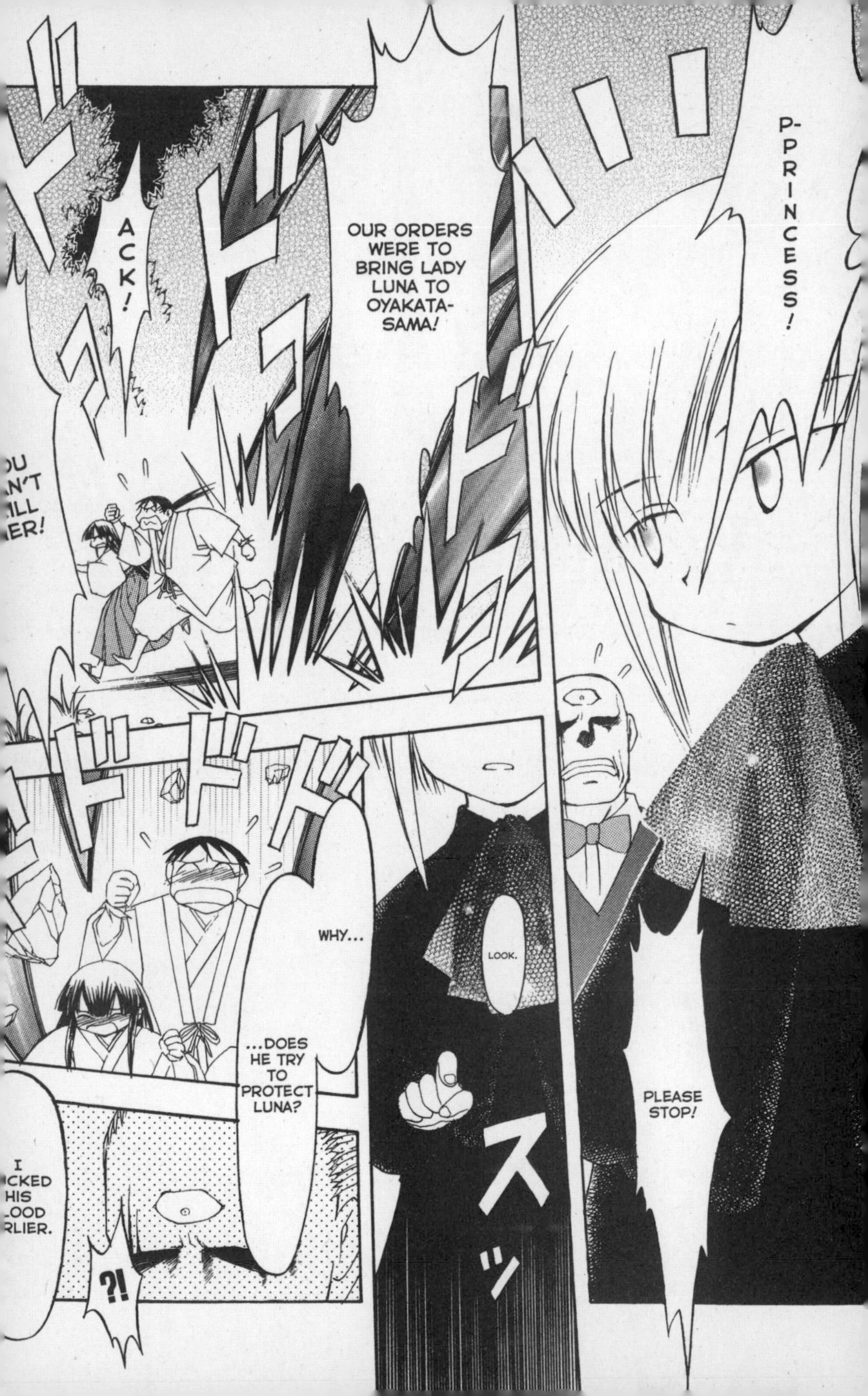
P-PRINCESS!
OUR ORDERS WERE TO BRING LADY LUNA TO OYAKATA-SAMA!
ACK!
PLEASE STOP!
スッ
LOOK.
WHY...
...DOES HE TRY TO PROTECT LUNA?
?!

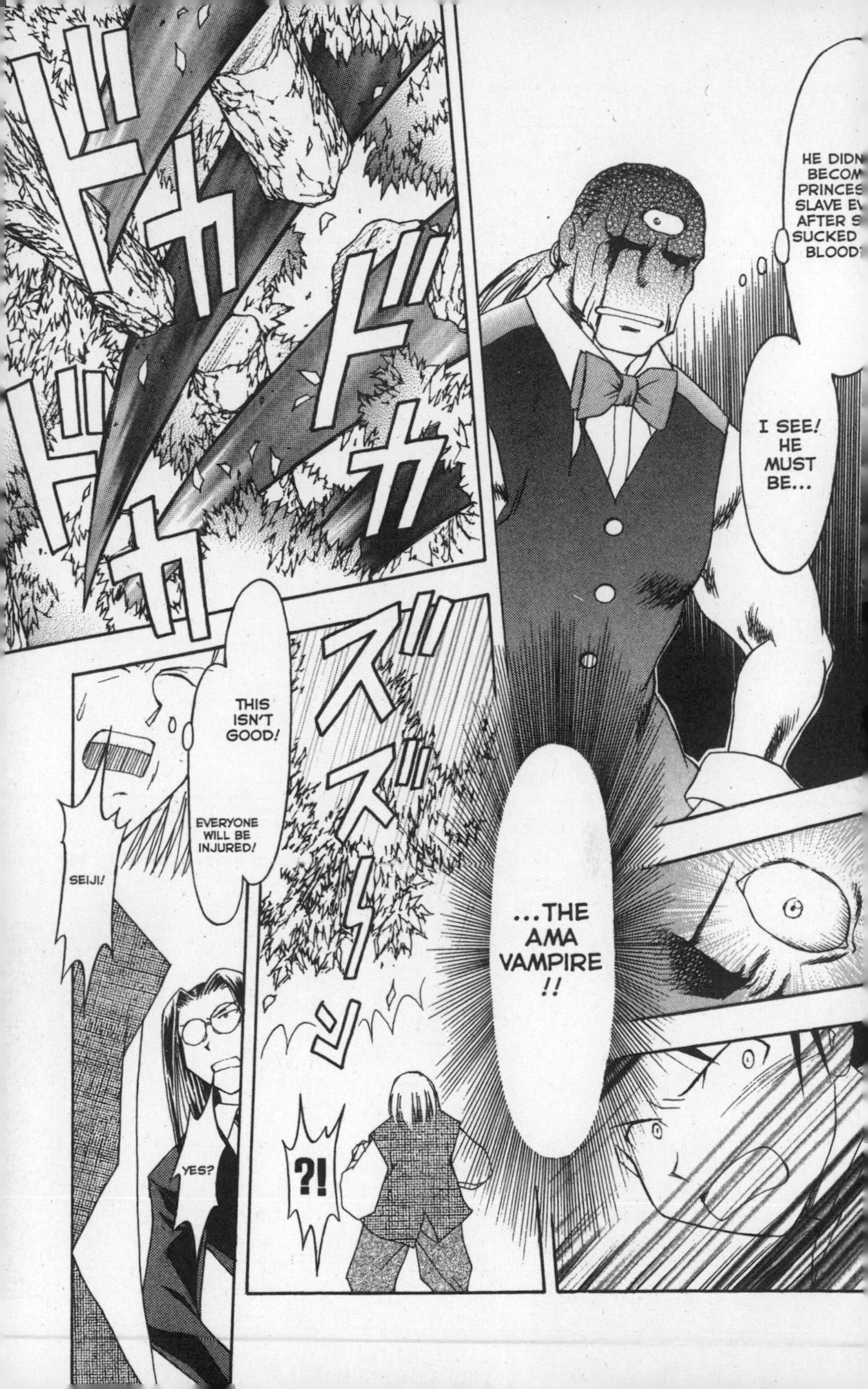

HE DIDN BECOM PRINCES SLAVE EV AFTER S SUCKED BLOOD?
I SEE! HE MUST BE...
...THE AMA VAMPIRE!!
ドカ
ドカ
ドカ
THIS ISN'T GOOD!
EVERYONE WILL BE INJURED!
ズズズン
?!
SEIJI!
YES?

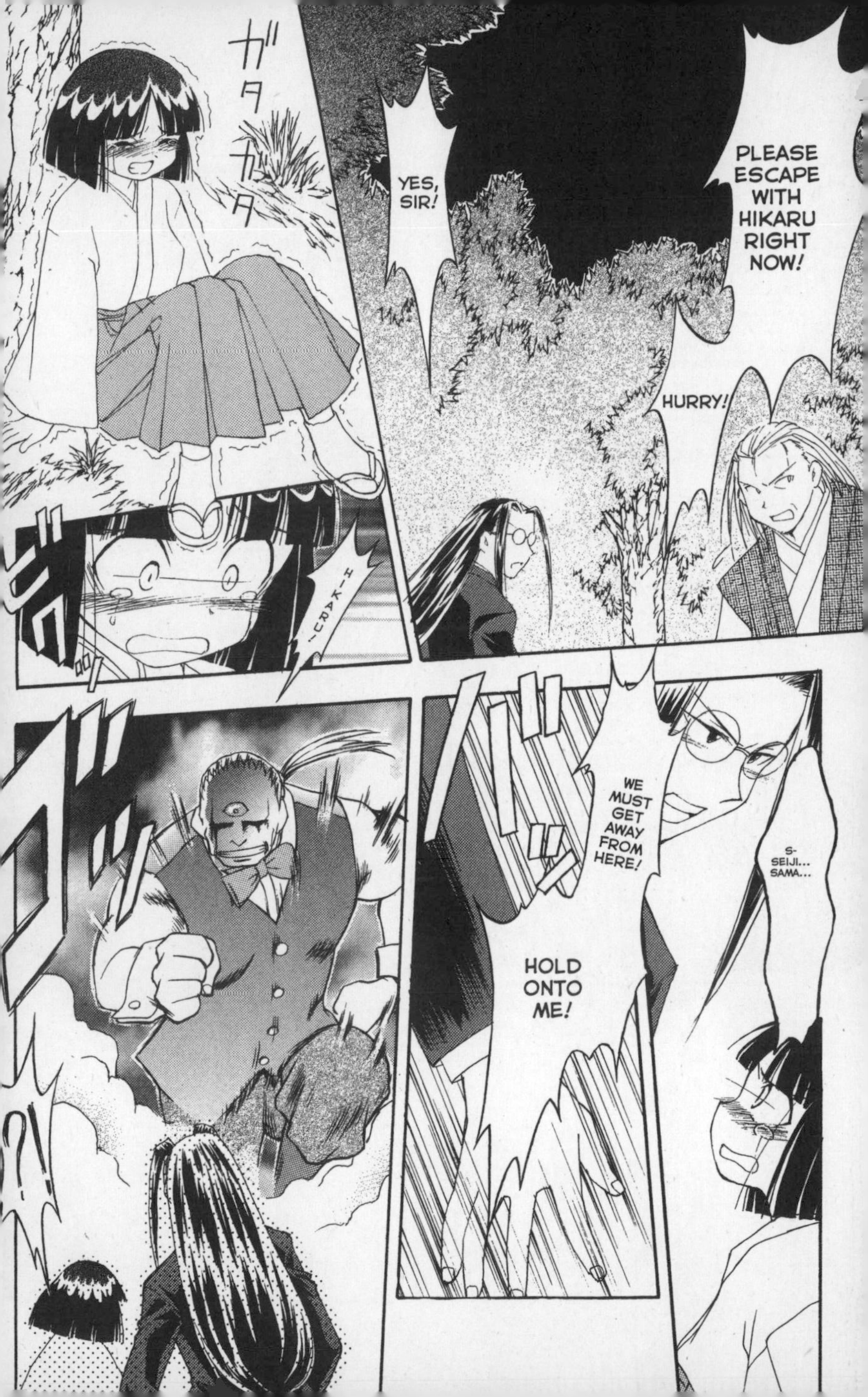
PLEASE ESCAPE WITH HIKARU RIGHT NOW!
YES, SIR!
HURRY!
ガタガタ
HIKARU!
WE MUST GET AWAY FROM HERE!
S-SEIJI... SAMA...
HOLD ONTO ME!
?!

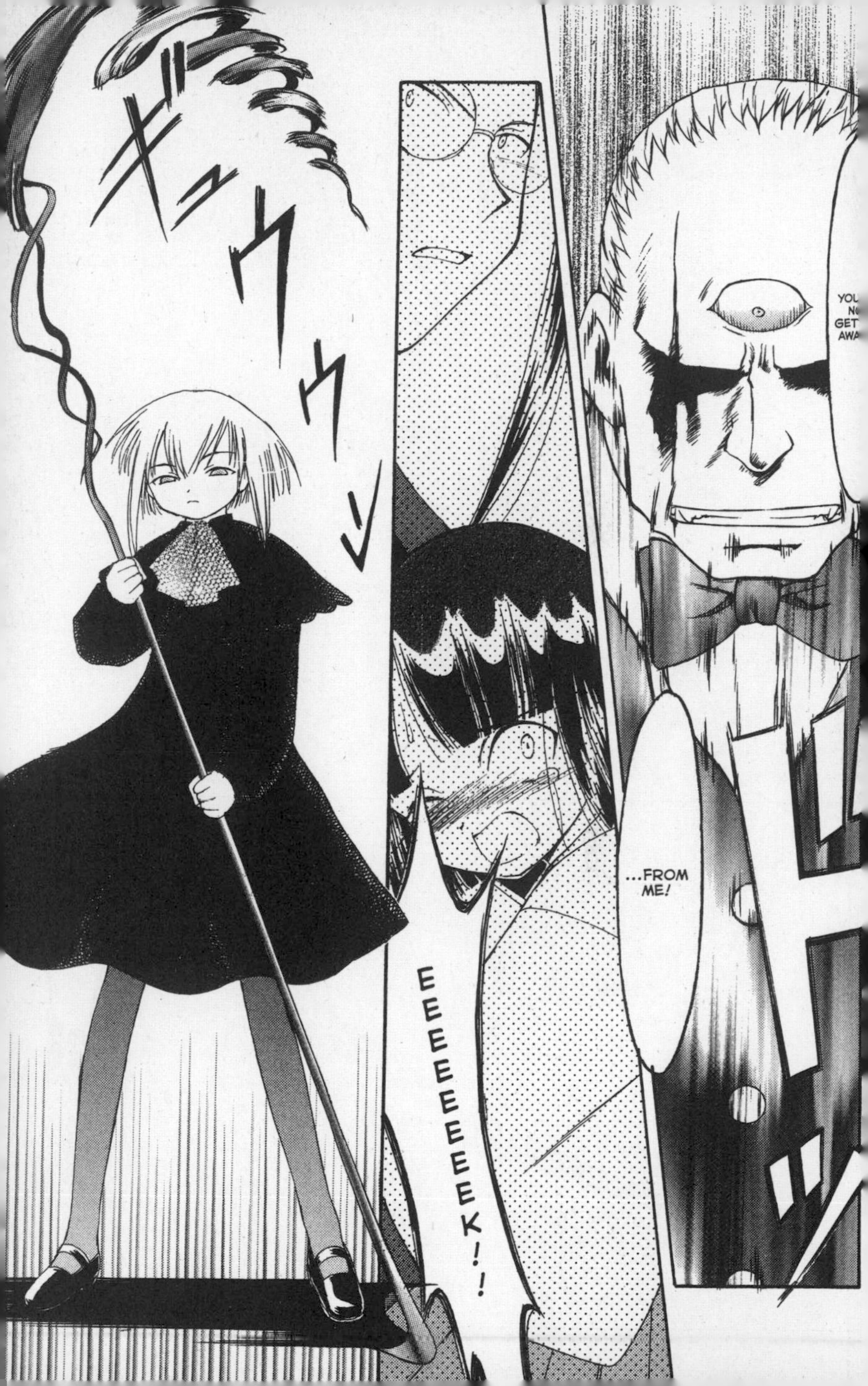
YOU NO GET AWA
...FROM ME!
EEEEEEEEEK!!
ギュウゥゥン

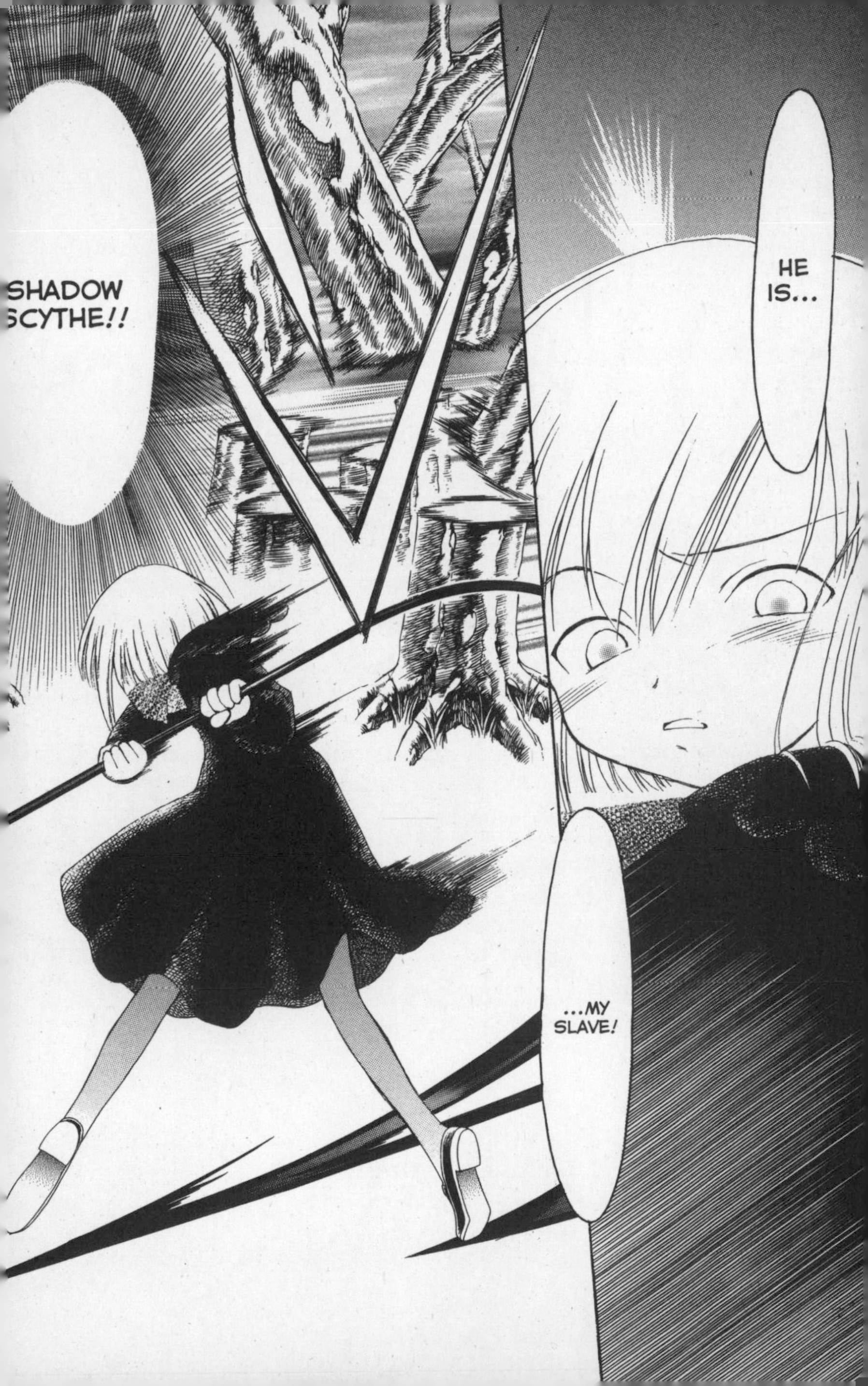
HE IS...
...MY SLAVE!
SHADOW SCYTHE!!

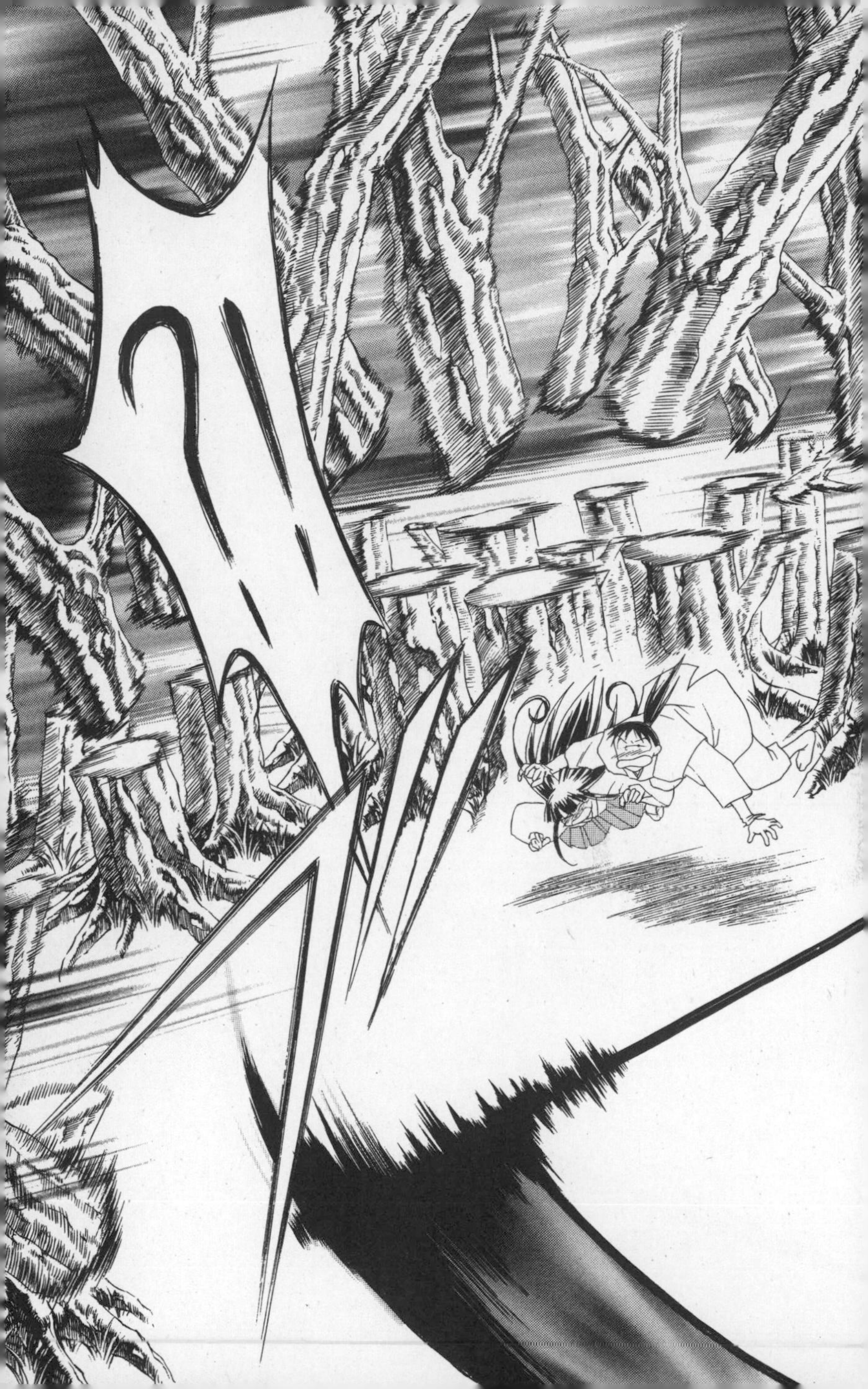

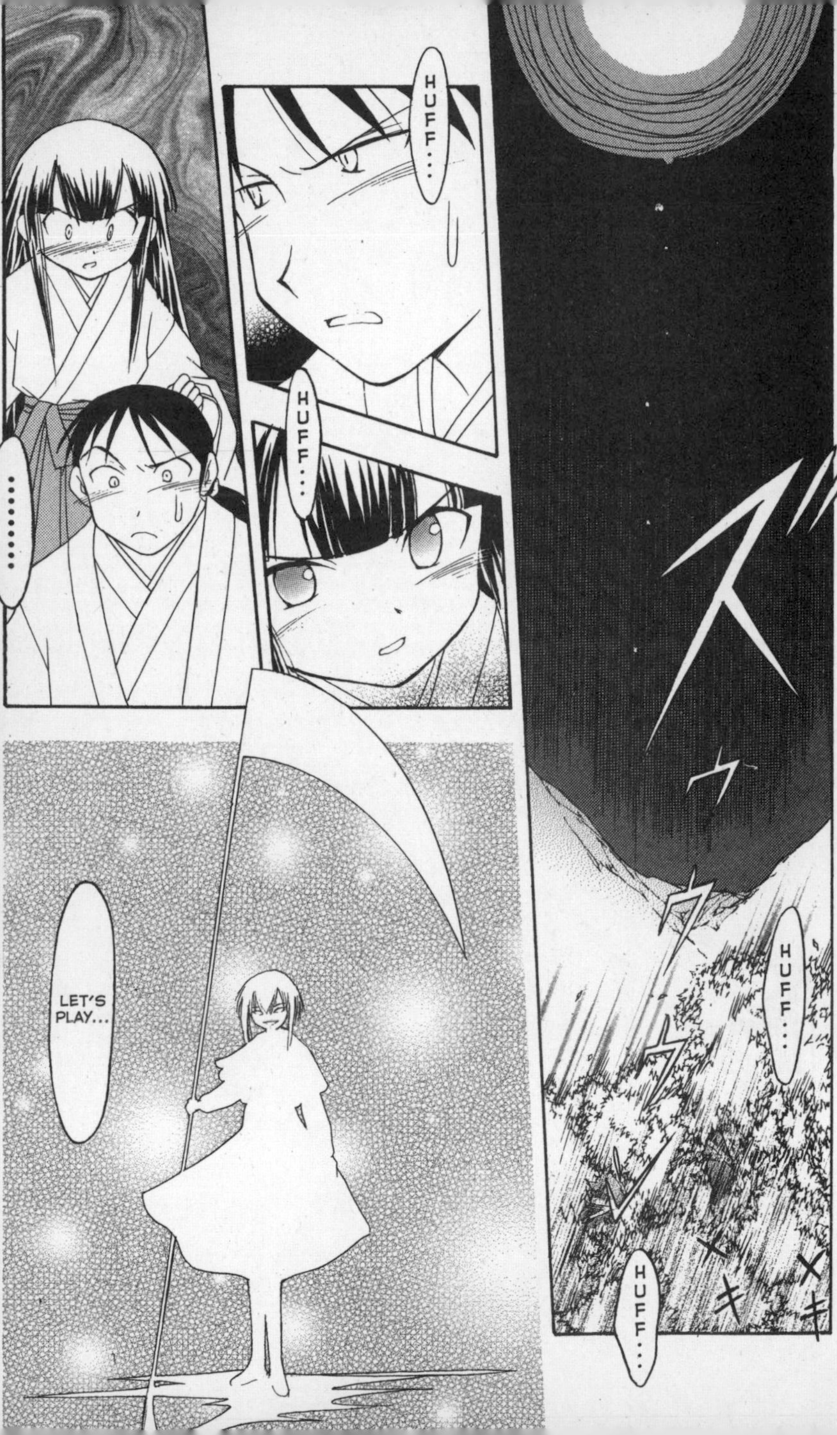

HUFF...
HUFF...
HUFF...
HUFF...
......
LET'S PLAY...

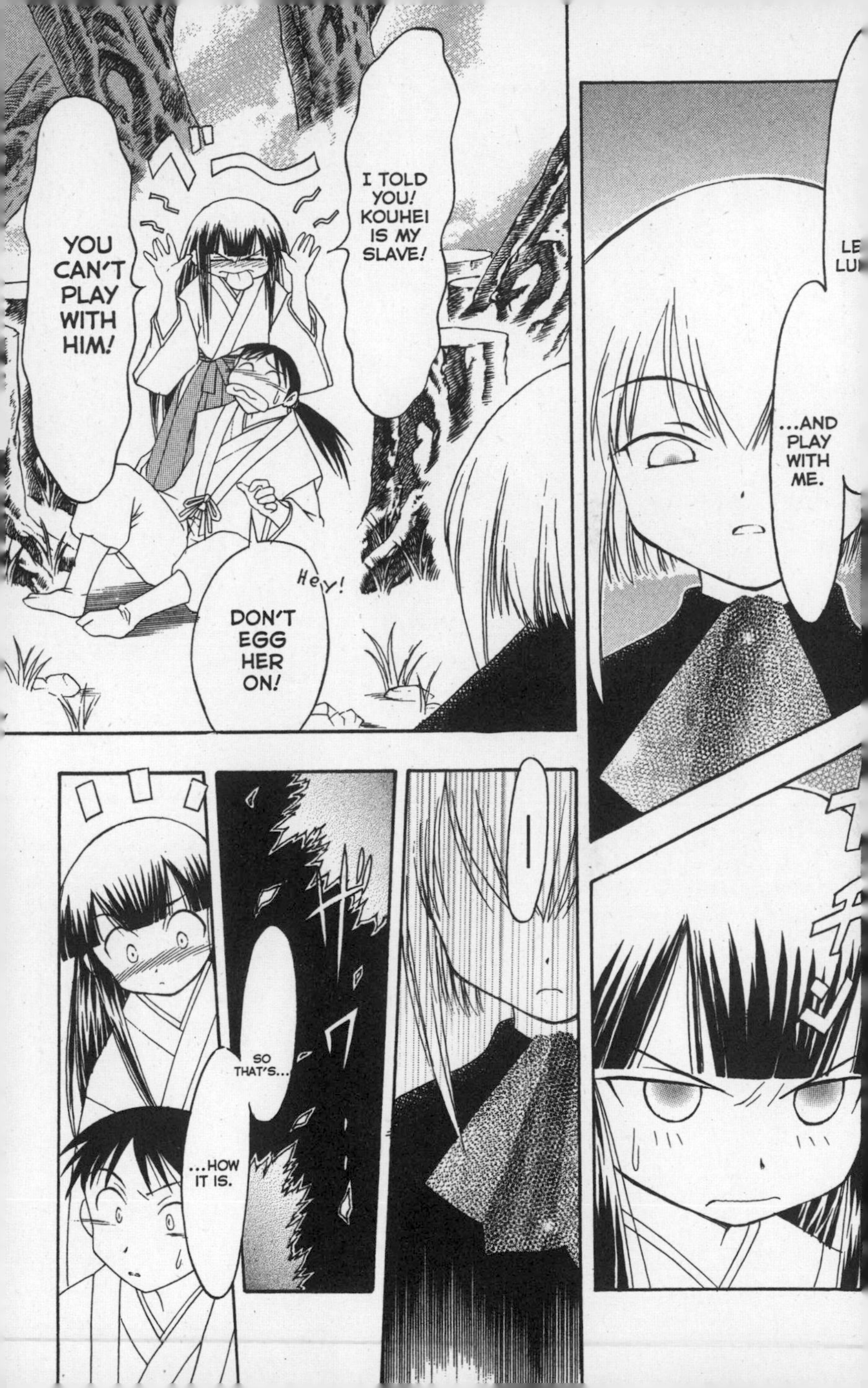
...AND PLAY WITH ME.
I TOLD YOU! KOUHEI IS MY SLAVE!
YOU CAN'T PLAY WITH HIM!
Hey!
DON'T EGG HER ON!
SO THAT'S...
...HOW IT IS.

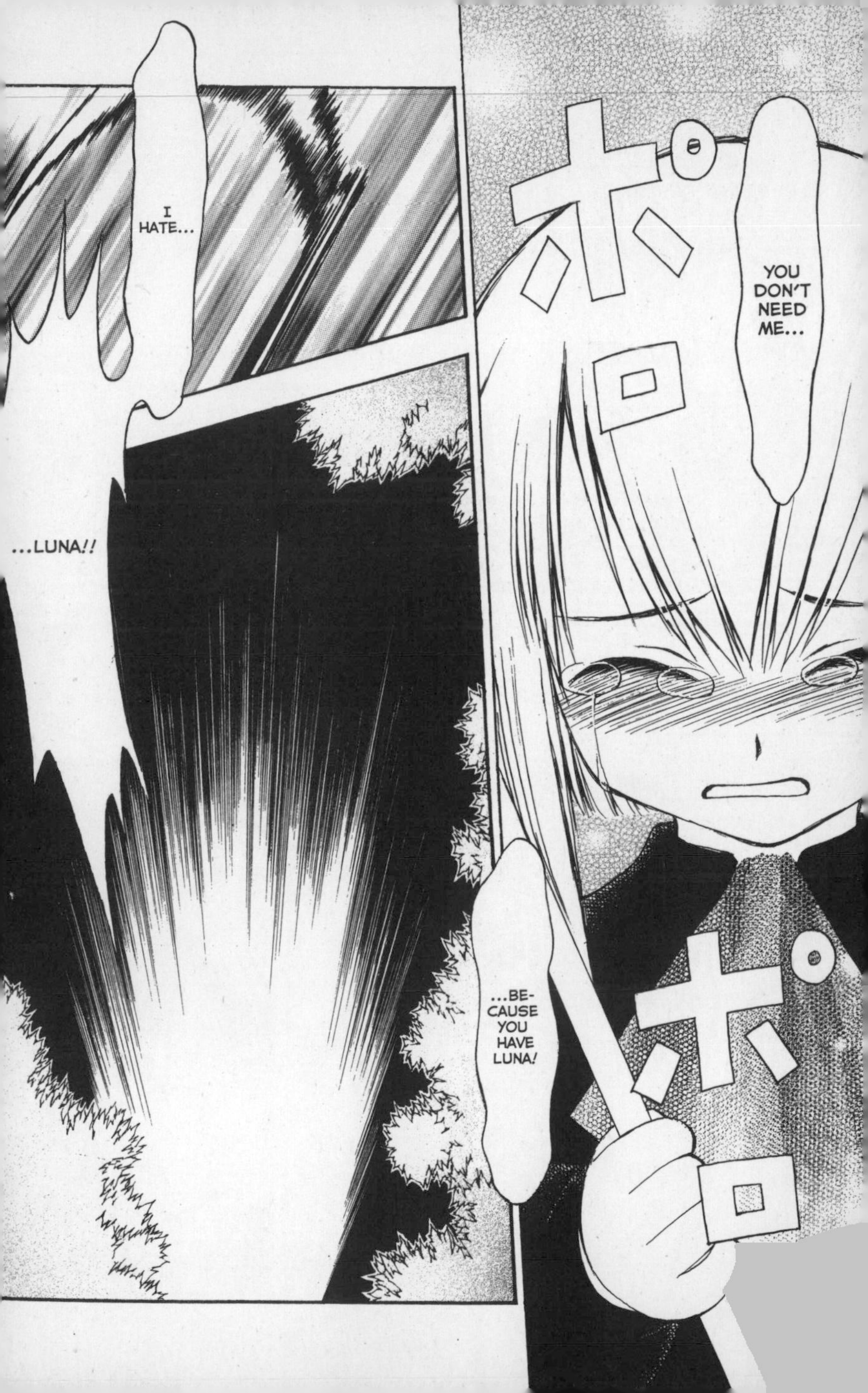
ポロ
YOU DON'T NEED ME...
ポロ
...BE-CAUSE YOU HAVE LUNA!
I HATE...
...LUNA!!

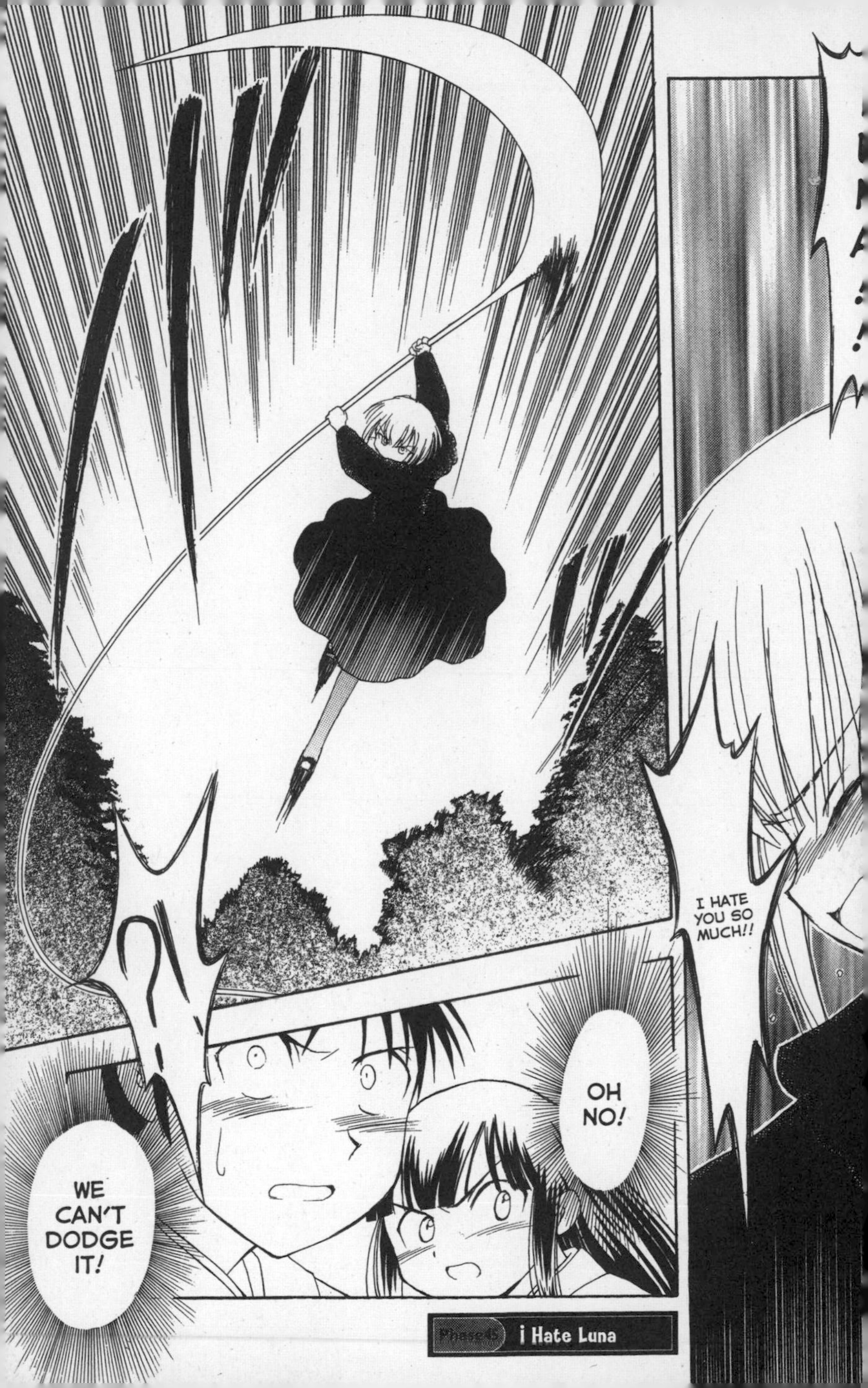
I HATE YOU SO MUCH!!
OH NO!
WE CAN'T DODGE IT!
Phase45 I Hate Luna

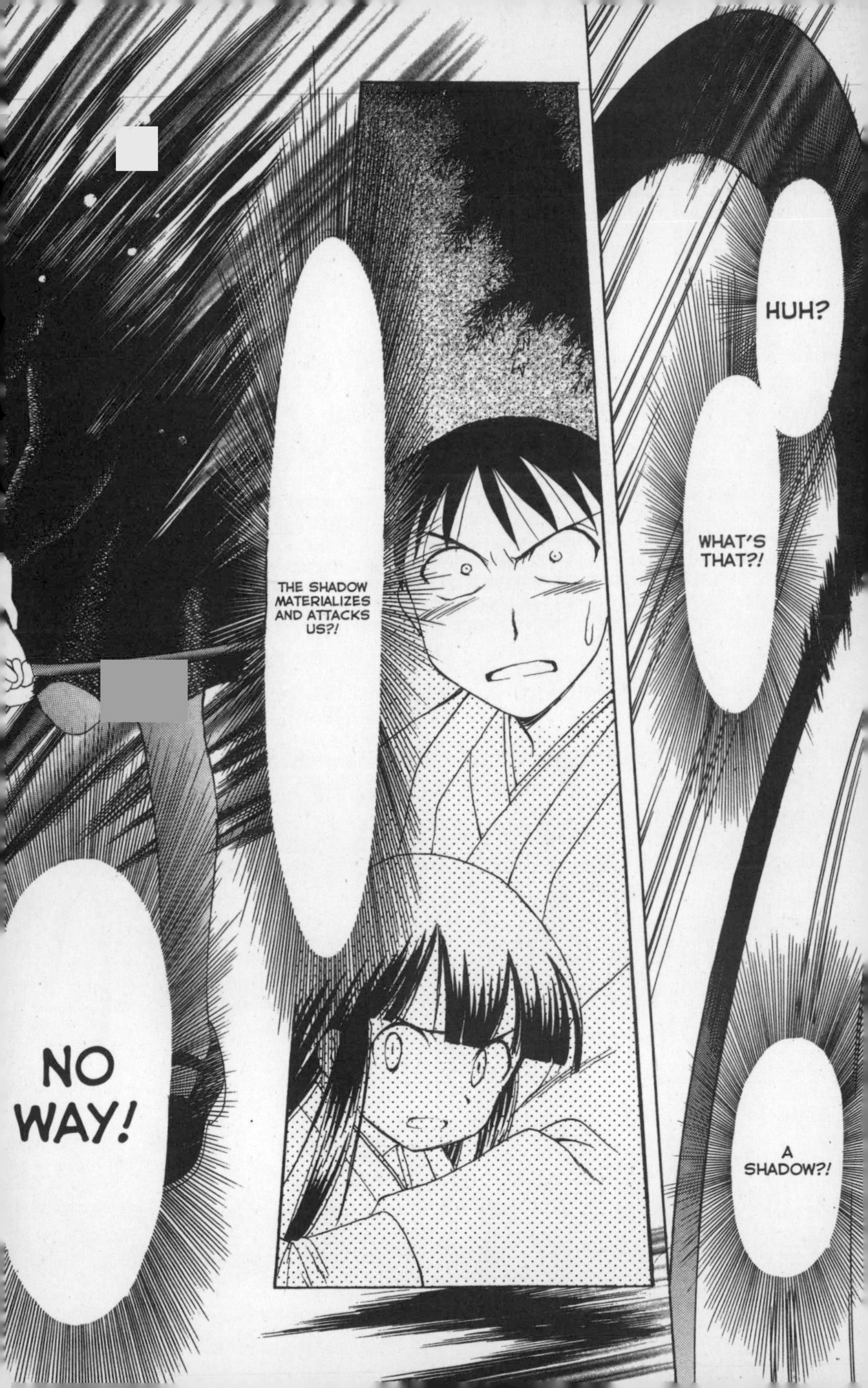
HUH?
WHAT'S THAT?!
A SHADOW?!
THE SHADOW MATERIALIZES AND ATTACKS US?!
NO WAY!

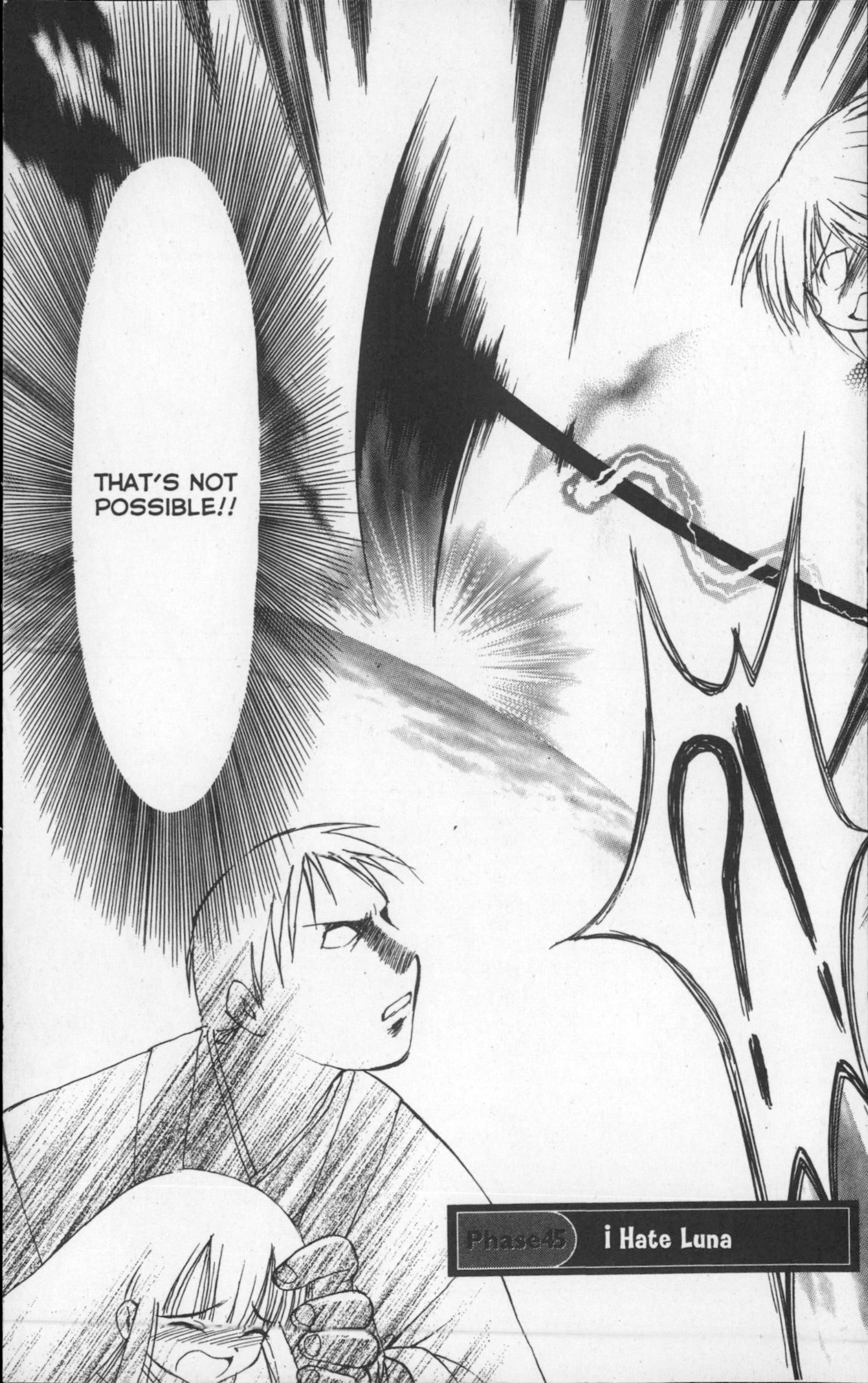
THAT'S NOT POSSIBLE!!
Phase45
i Hate Luna

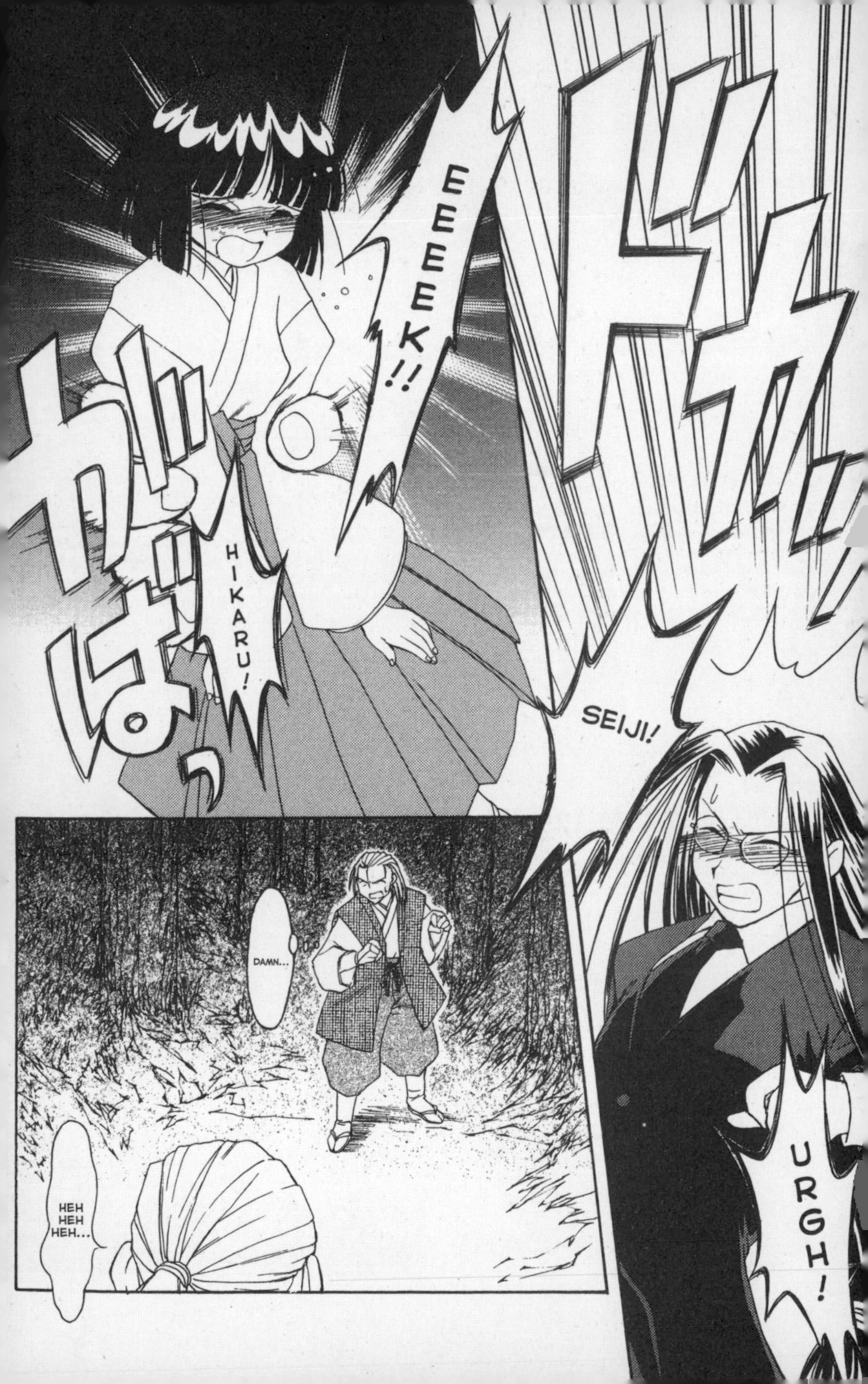
SEIJI!
URGH!
EEEEK!!
HIKARU!
DAMN...
HEH HEH HEH...

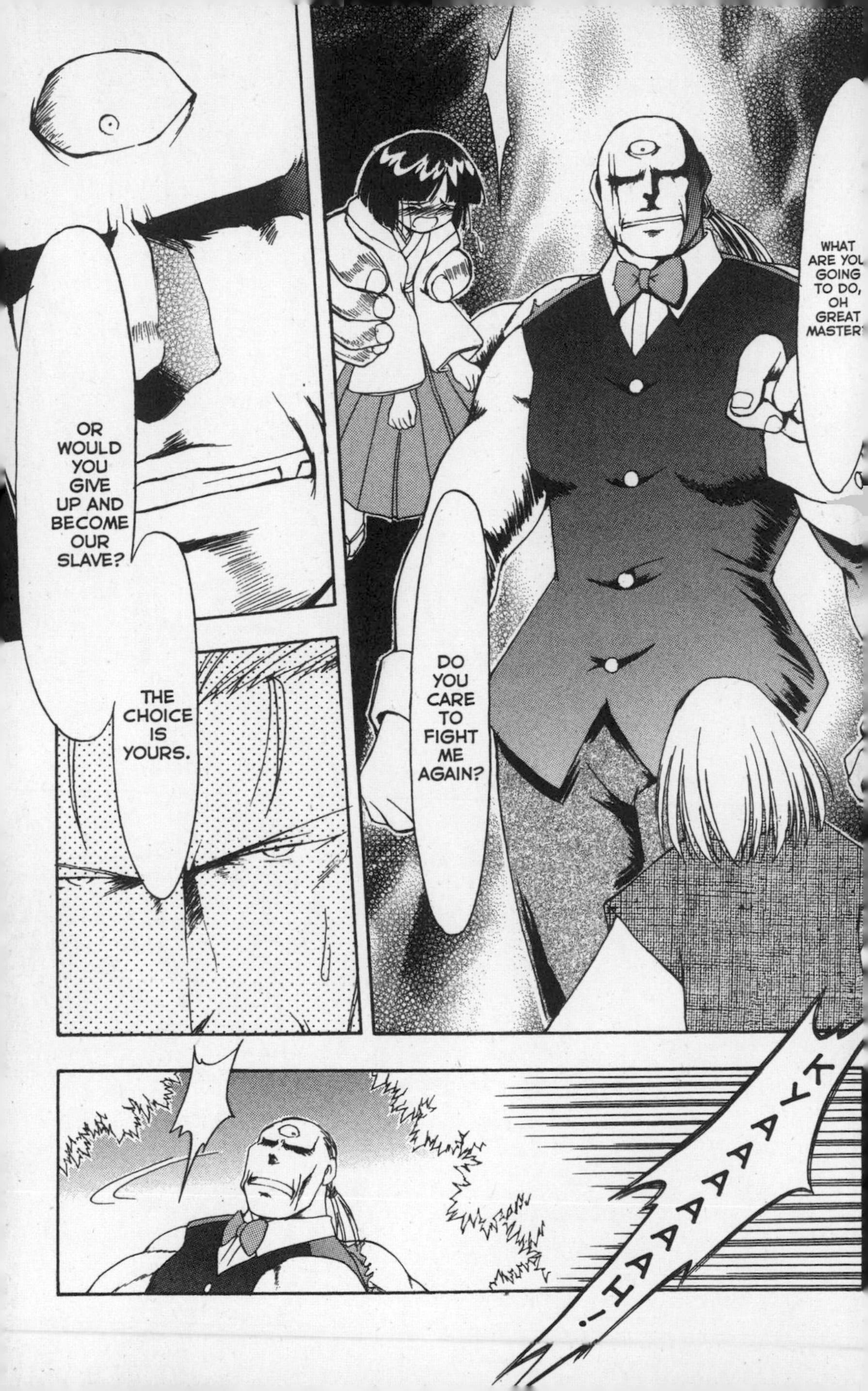
WHAT ARE YOU GOING TO DO, OH GREAT MASTER?
DO YOU CARE TO FIGHT ME AGAIN?
OR WOULD YOU GIVE UP AND BECOME OUR SLAVE?
THE CHOICE IS YOURS.
KYAAAAAAH!

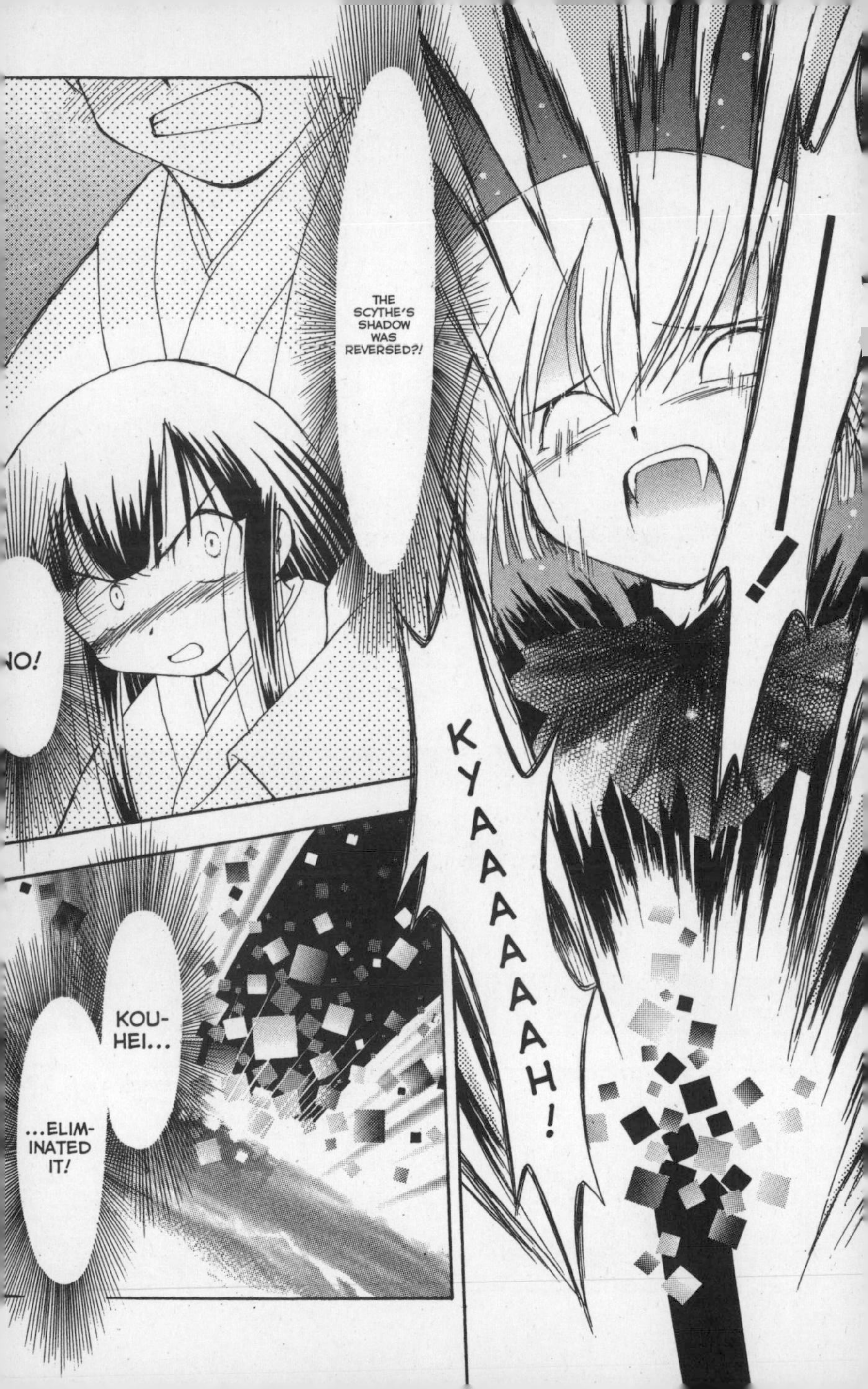
!
KYAAAAAH!
THE SCYTHE'S SHADOW WAS REVERSED?!
NO!
KOU-HEI...
...ELIM-INATED IT!

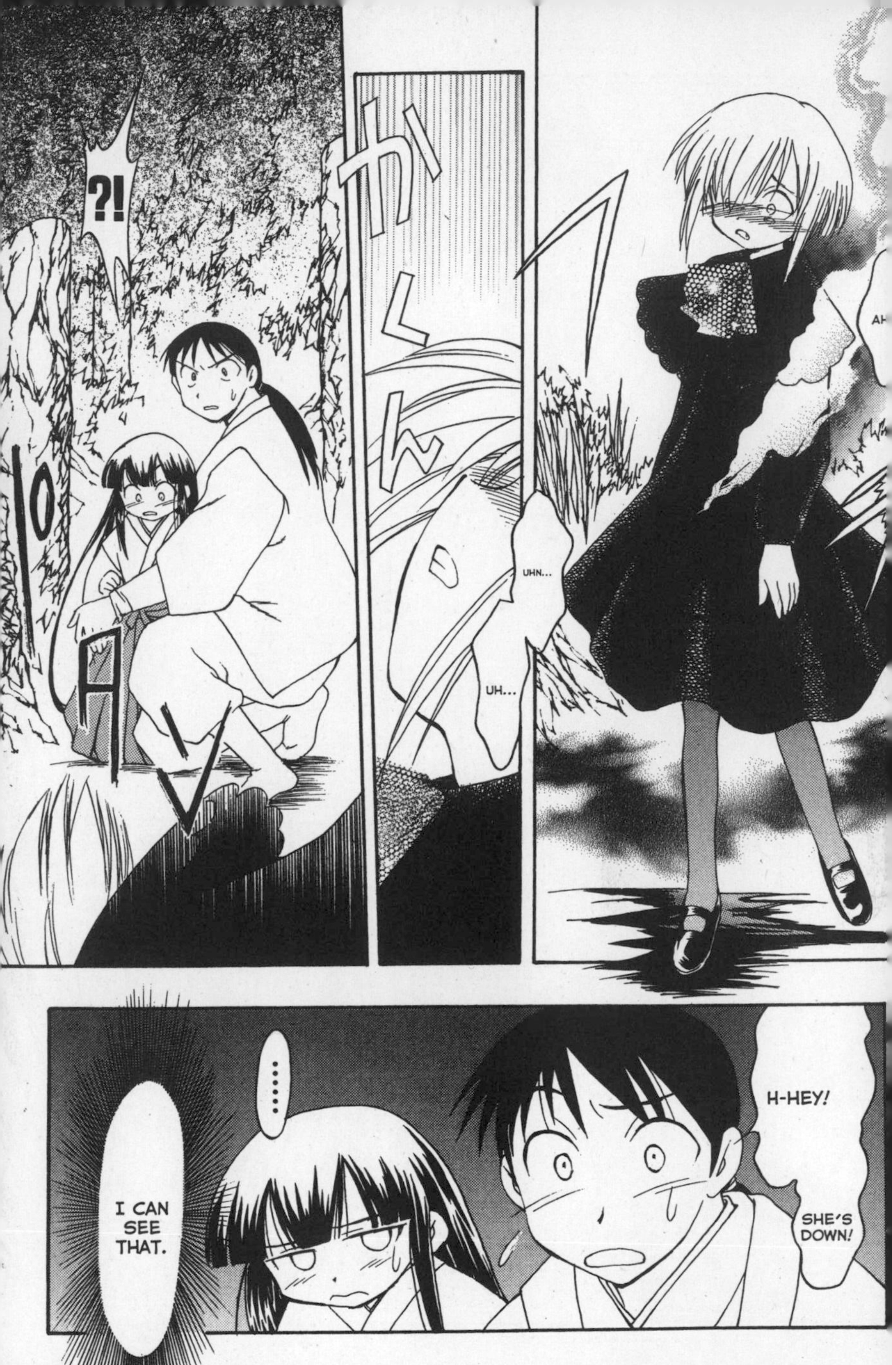
AH
UHN...
UH...
かくん
?!
H-HEY!
SHE'S DOWN!
......
I CAN SEE THAT.

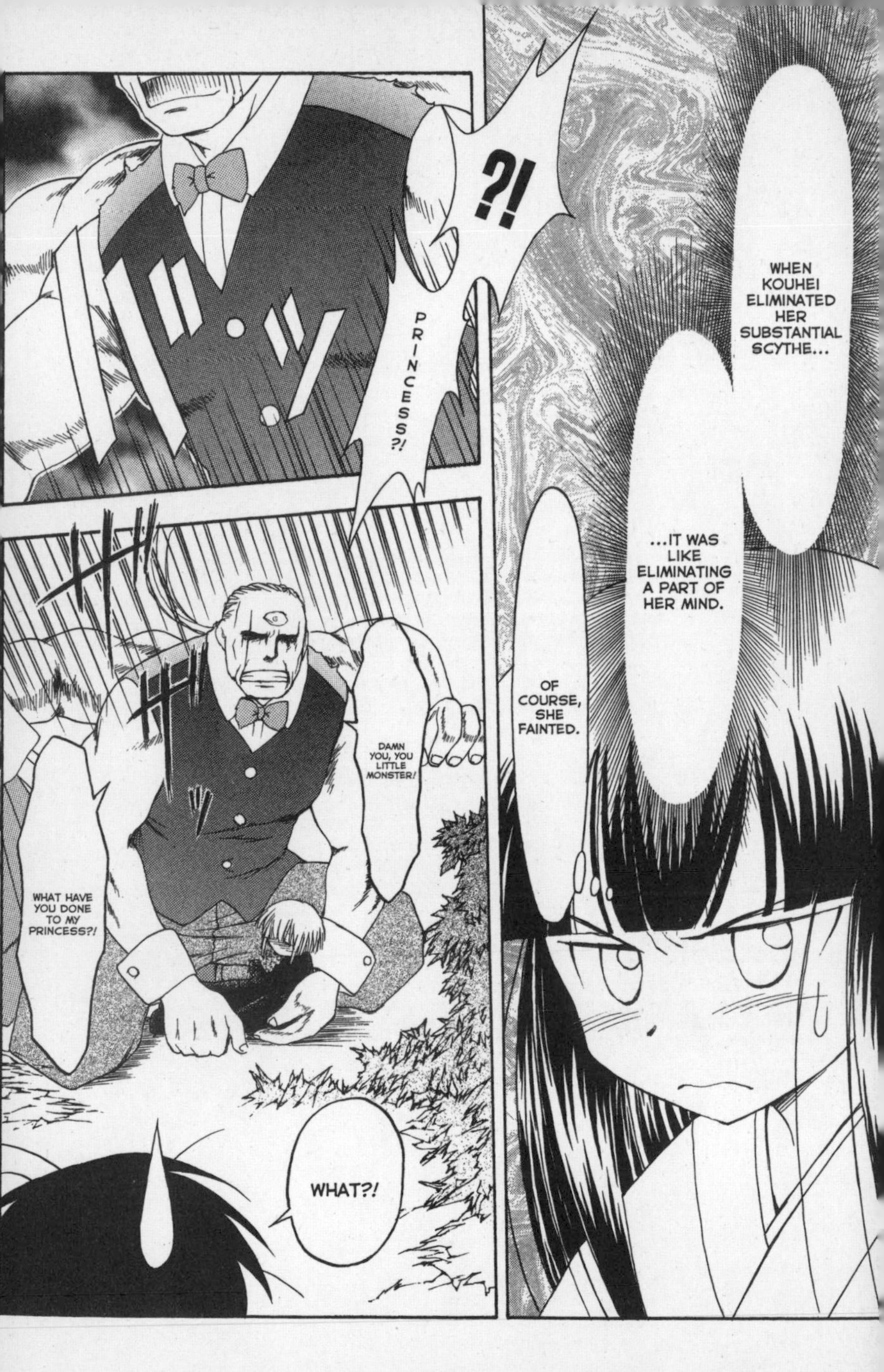
WHEN KOUHEI ELIMINATED HER SUBSTANTIAL SCYTHE...
...IT WAS LIKE ELIMINATING A PART OF HER MIND.
OF COURSE, SHE FAINTED.
?!
PRINCESS?!
DAMN YOU, YOU LITTLE MONSTER!
WHAT HAVE YOU DONE TO MY PRINCESS?!
WHAT?!

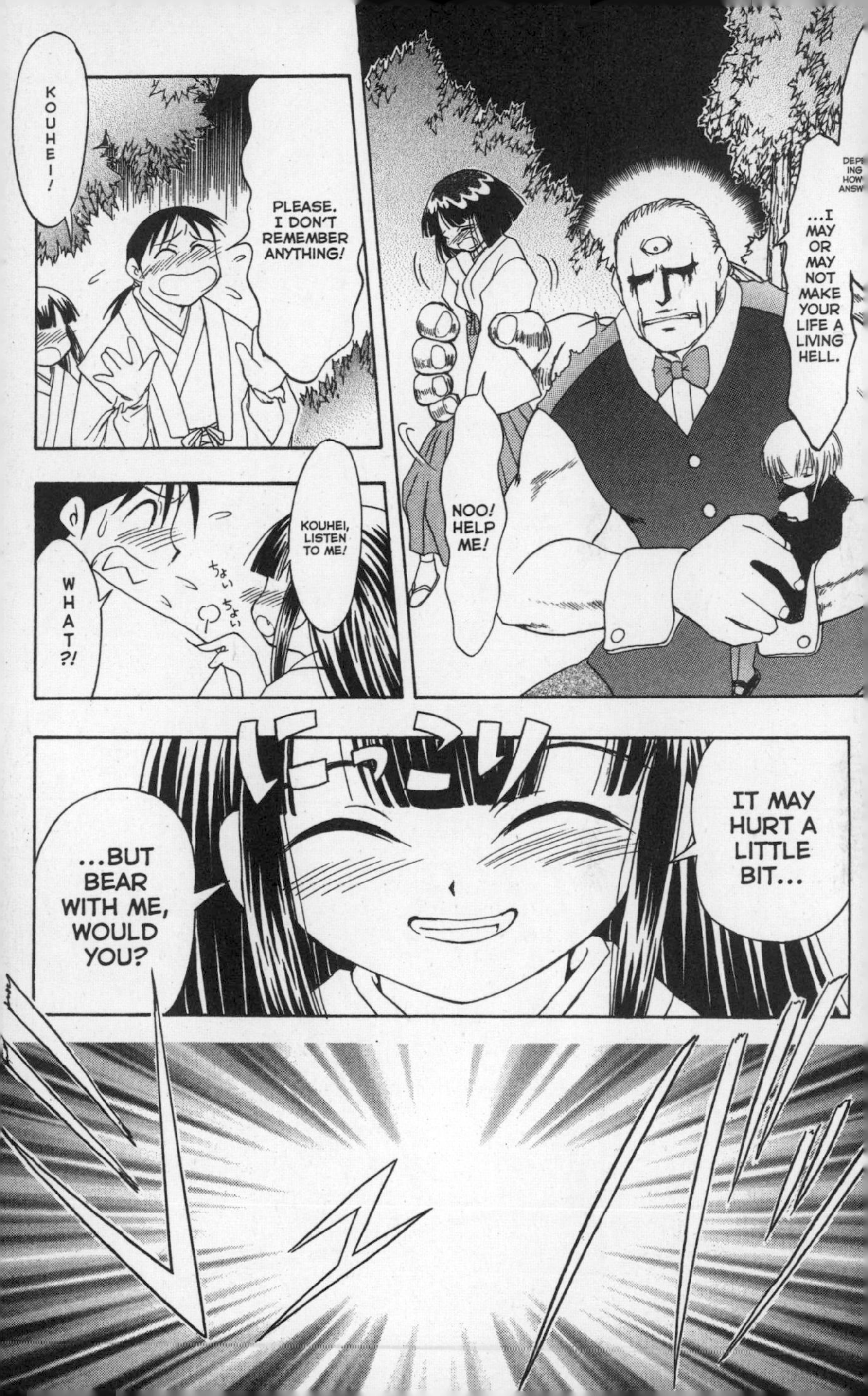
...I MAY OR MAY NOT MAKE YOUR LIFE A LIVING HELL.
NOO! HELP ME!
PLEASE. I DON'T REMEMBER ANYTHING!
KOUHEI!
KOUHEI, LISTEN TO ME!
ちょい ちょい
WHAT?!
にっこり
IT MAY HURT A LITTLE BIT...
...BUT BEAR WITH ME, WOULD YOU?

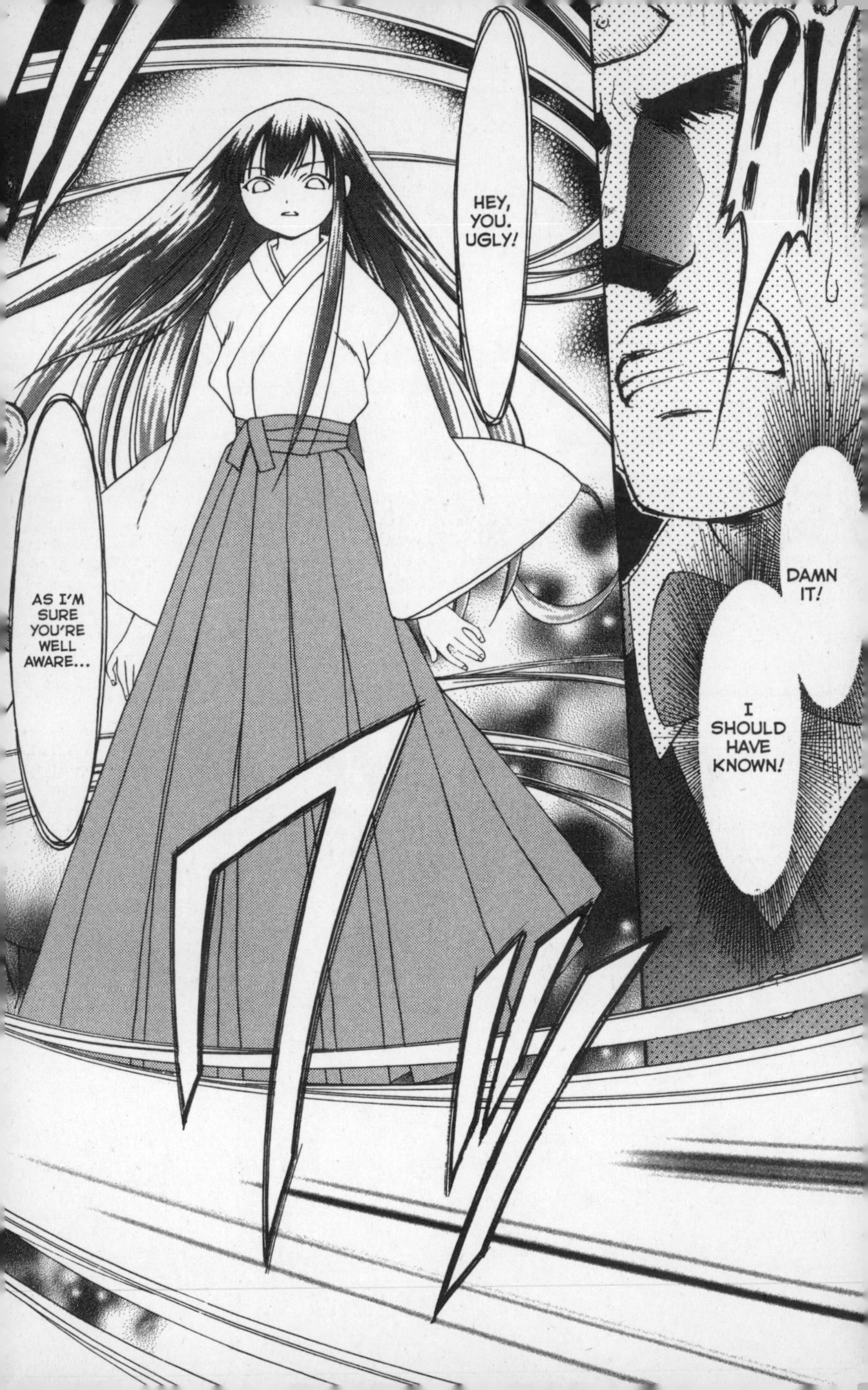
?!
DAMN IT!
I SHOULD HAVE KNOWN!
HEY, YOU. UGLY!
AS I'M SURE YOU'RE WELL AWARE...

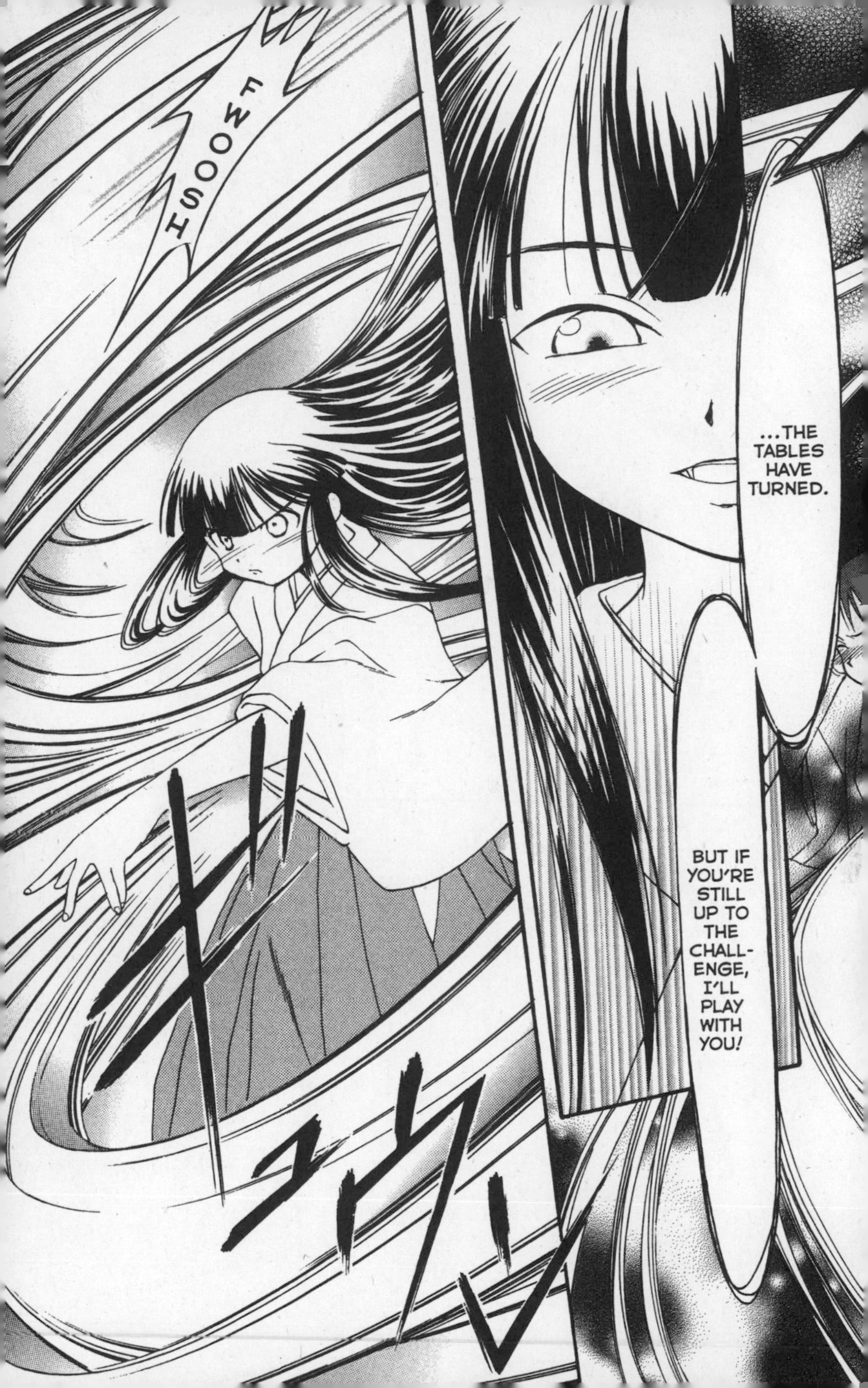
...THE TABLES HAVE TURNED.
BUT IF YOU'RE STILL UP TO THE CHALL-ENGE, I'LL PLAY WITH YOU!
FWOOSH

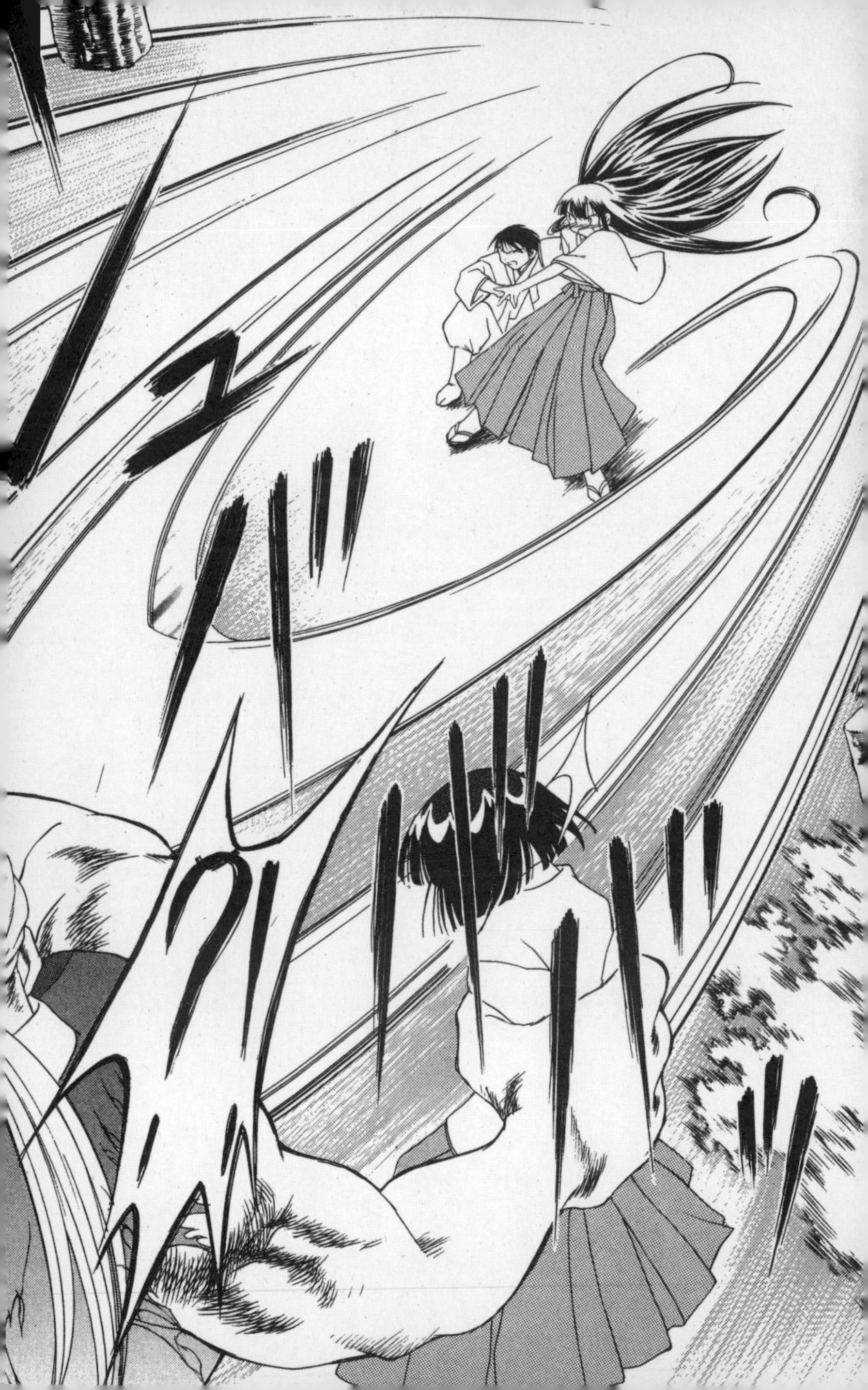

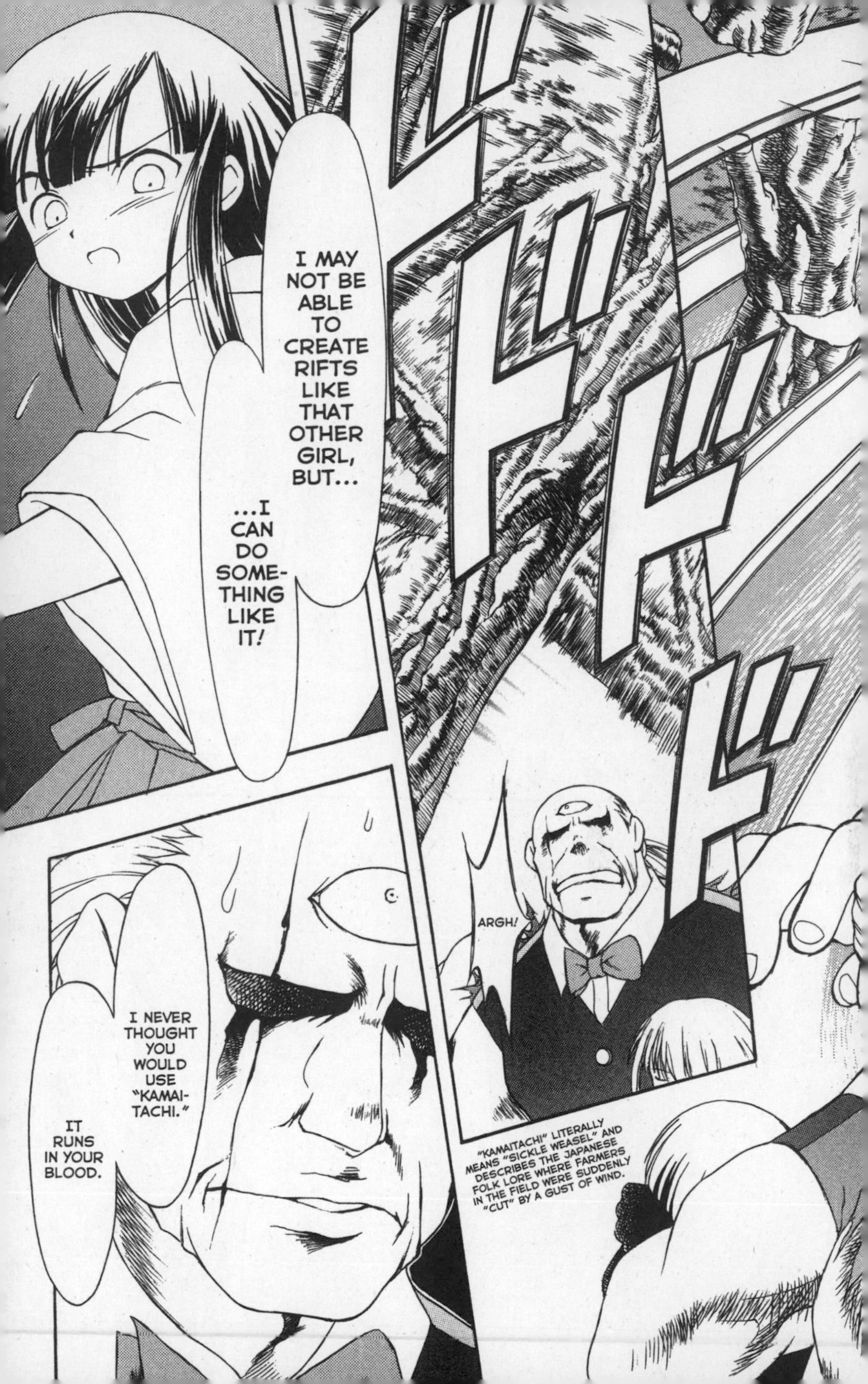
I MAY NOT BE ABLE TO CREATE RIFTS LIKE THAT OTHER GIRL, BUT...
...I CAN DO SOME-THING LIKE IT!
ARGH!
"KAMAITACHI" LITERALLY MEANS "SICKLE WEASEL" AND DESCRIBES THE JAPANESE FOLK LORE WHERE FARMERS IN THE FIELD WERE SUDDENLY "CUT" BY A GUST OF WIND.
I NEVER THOUGHT YOU WOULD USE "KAMAI-TACHI."
IT RUNS IN YOUR BLOOD.

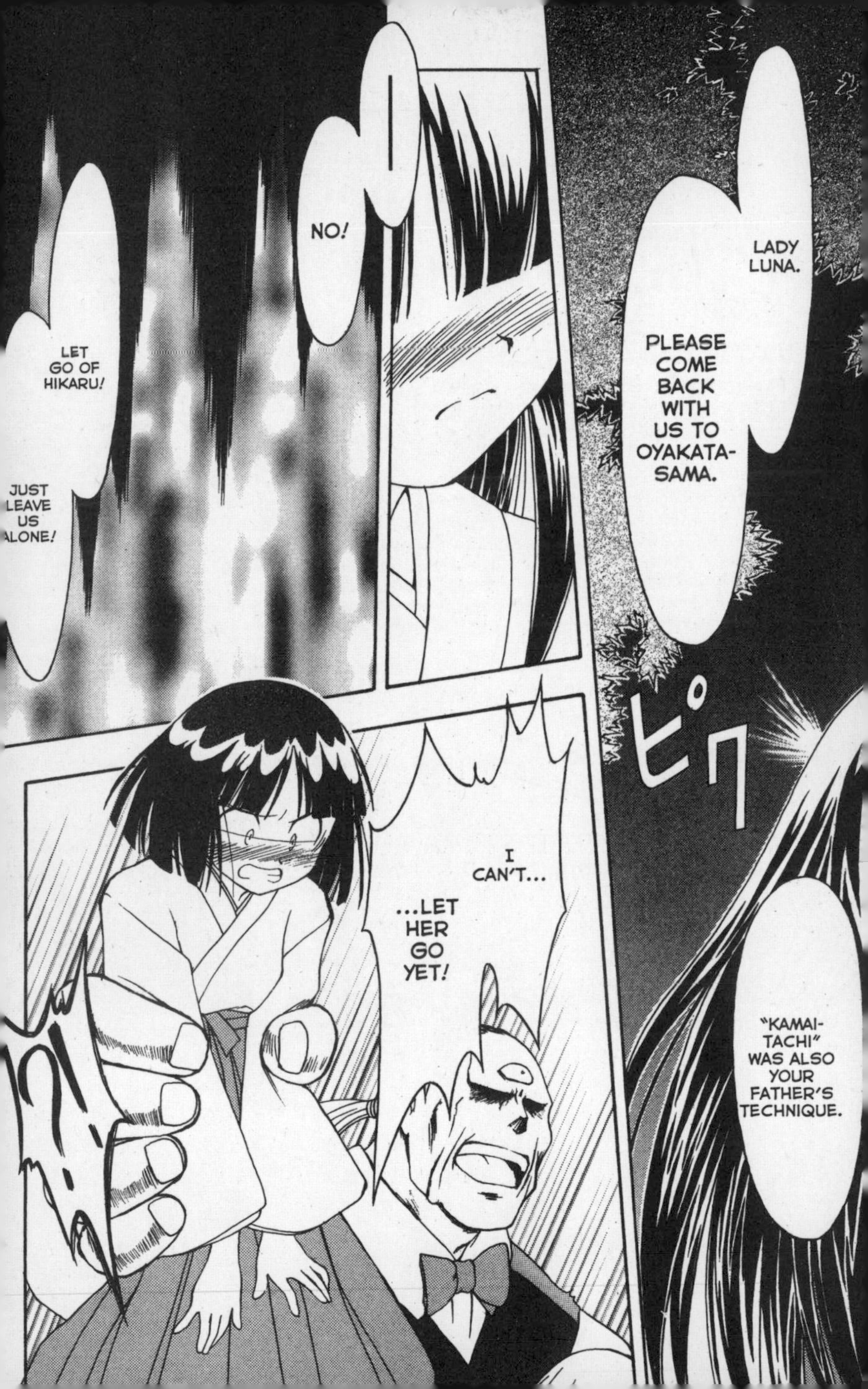
LADY LUNA.
PLEASE COME BACK WITH US TO OYAKATA-SAMA.
ピク
"KAMAI-TACHI" WAS ALSO YOUR FATHER'S TECHNIQUE.
NO!
LET GO OF HIKARU!
JUST LEAVE US ALONE!
I CAN'T...
...LET HER GO YET!
!?

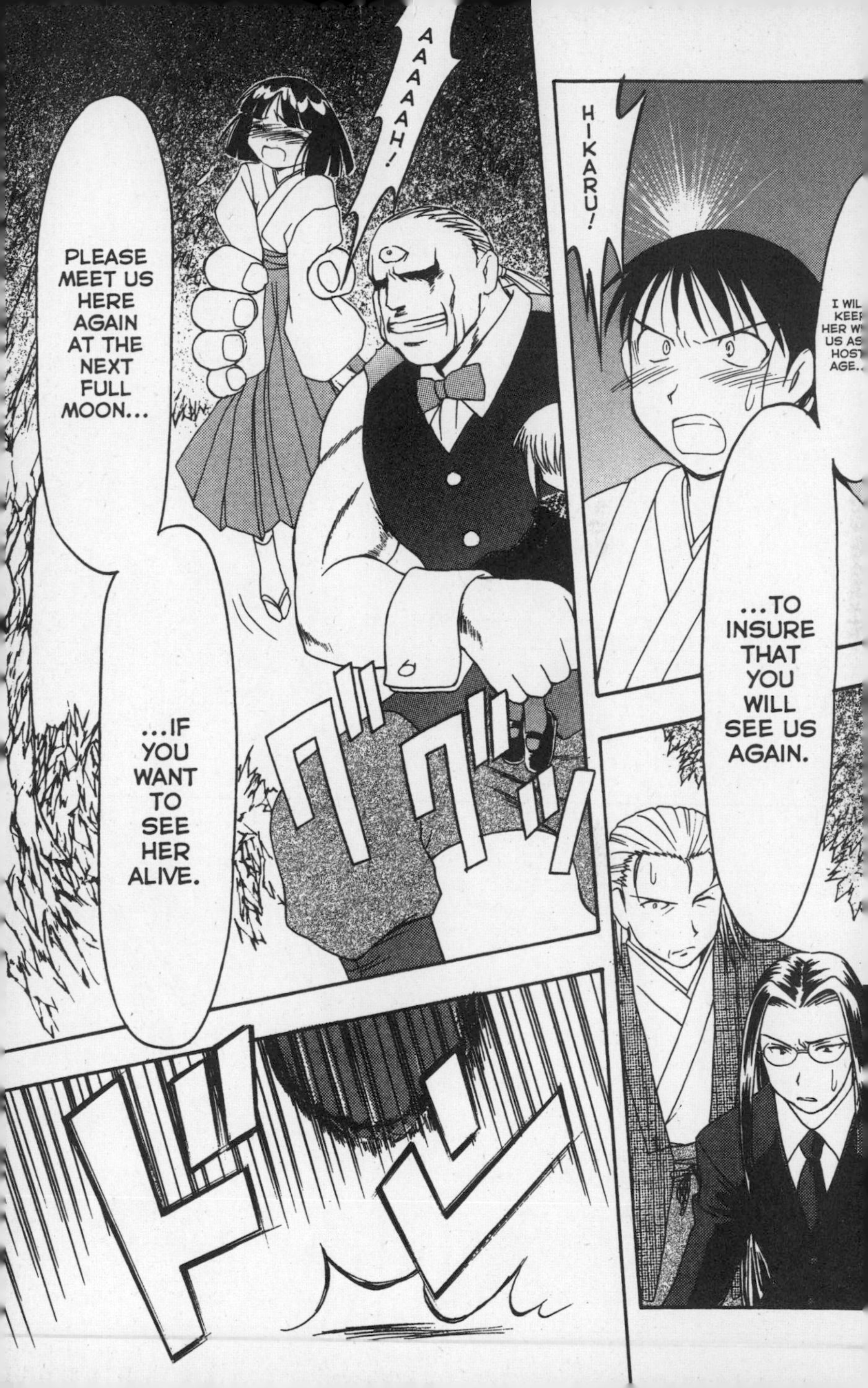
HIKARU!
I WIL KEEP HER W US AS HOST AGE..
...TO INSURE THAT YOU WILL SEE US AGAIN.
AAAAAAH!
PLEASE MEET US HERE AGAIN AT THE NEXT FULL MOON...
...IF YOU WANT TO SEE HER ALIVE.

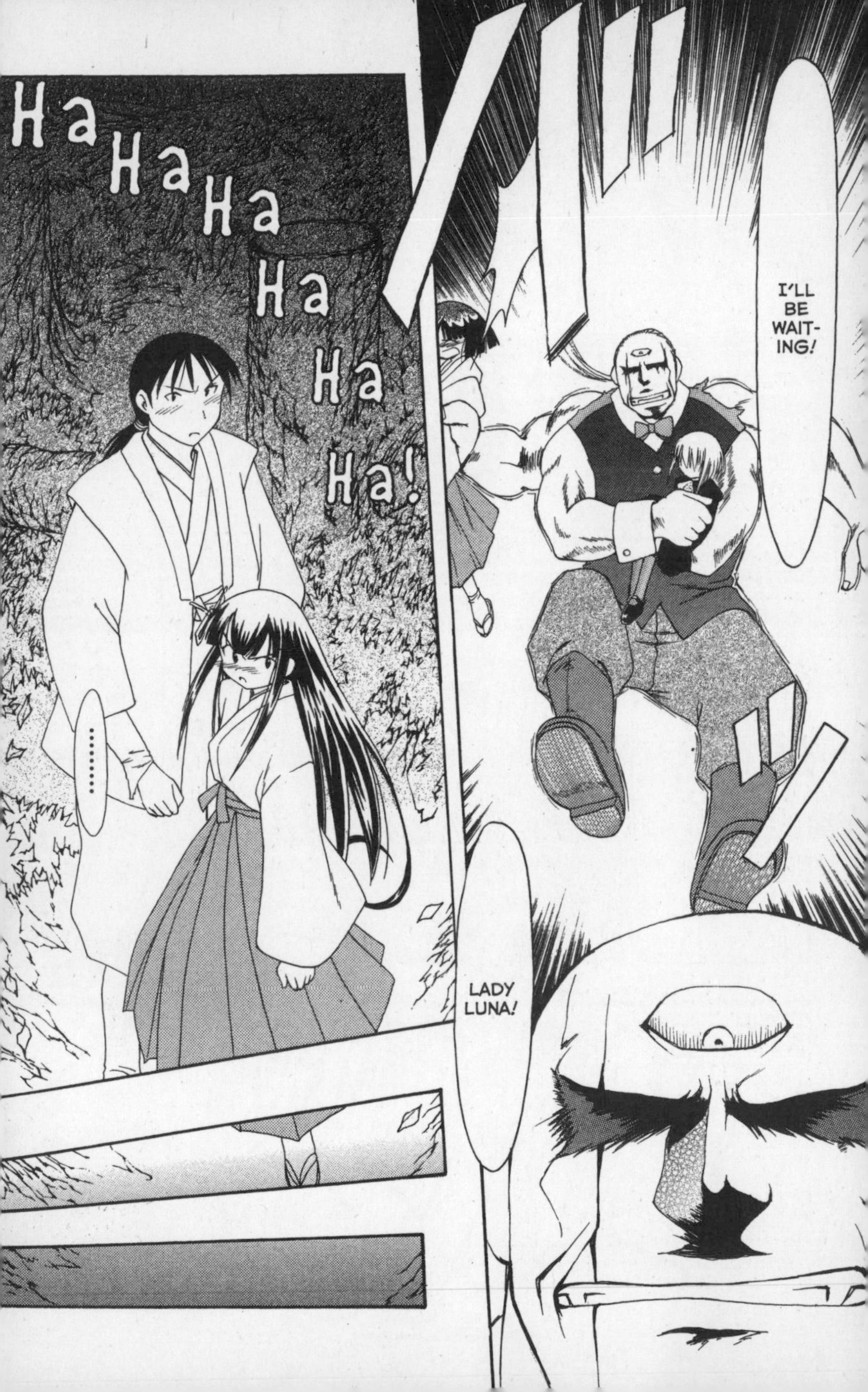
I'LL BE WAITING!
LADY LUNA!
Ha Ha Ha Ha Ha Ha!
......

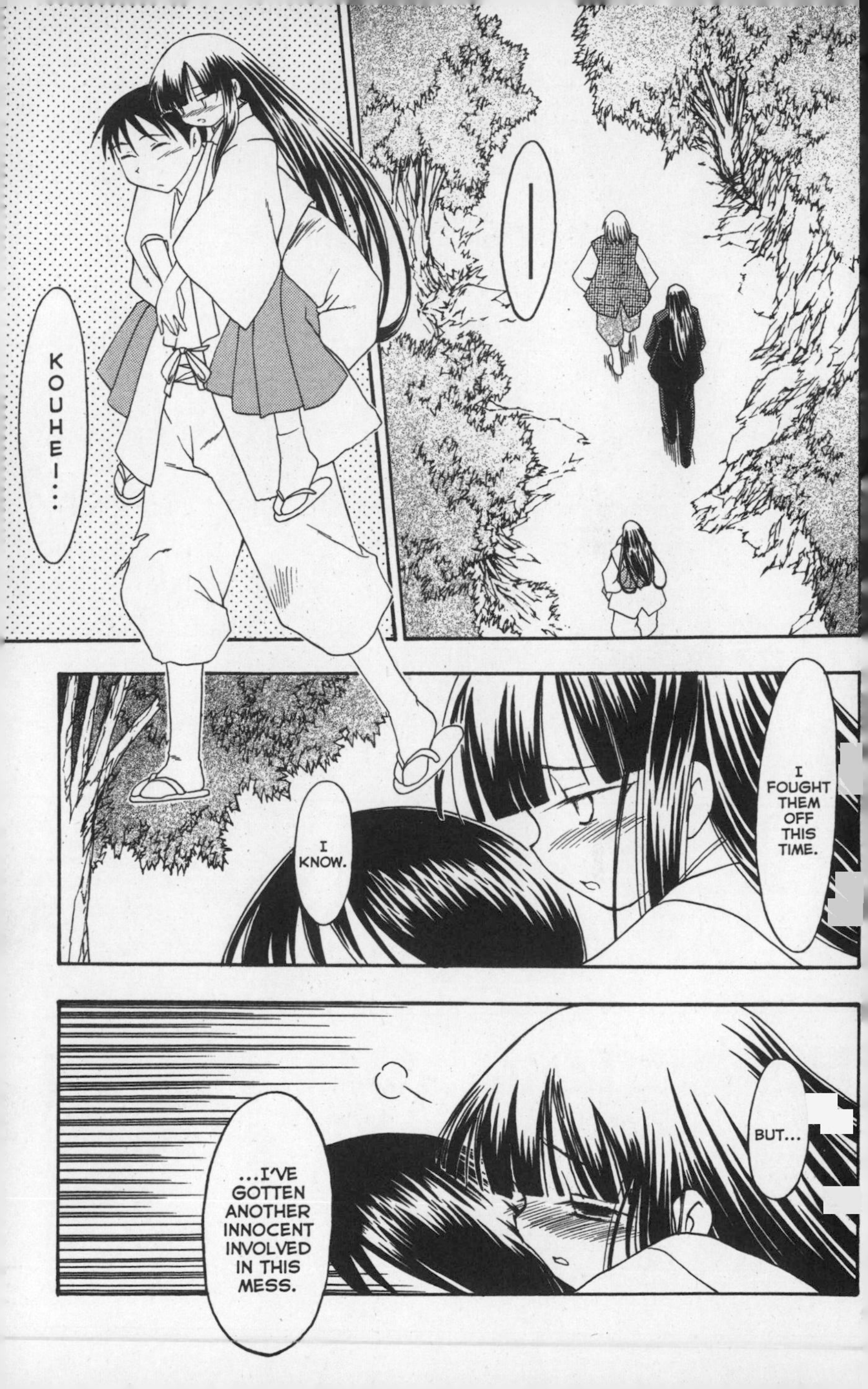
—
KOUHEI!...
I FOUGHT THEM OFF THIS TIME.
I KNOW.
BUT...
...I'VE GOTTEN ANOTHER INNOCENT INVOLVED IN THIS MESS.

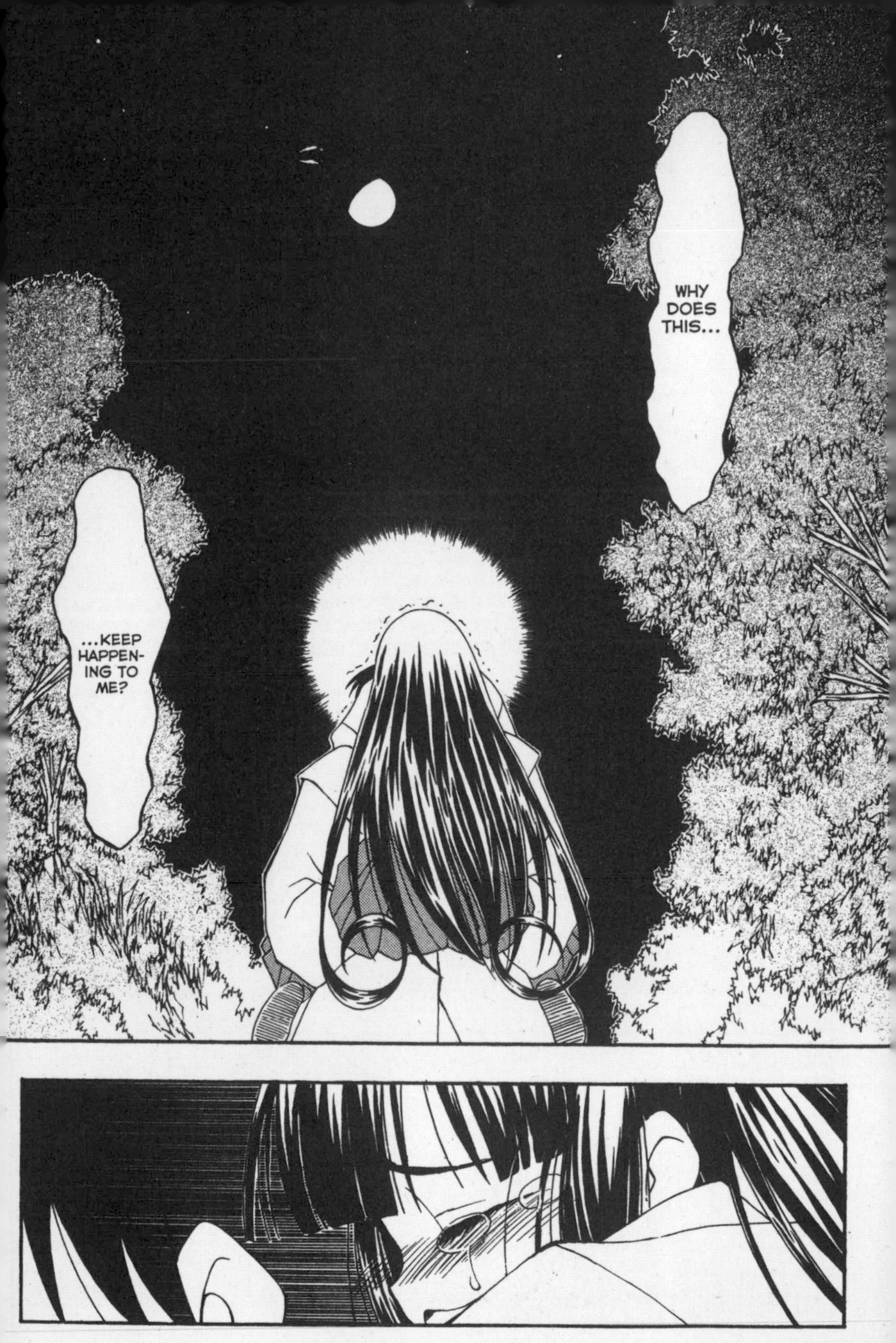
WHY DOES THIS...
...KEEP HAPPEN-ING TO ME?

Moon 月詠 Phase

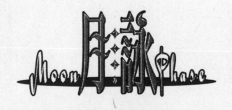

Moon Phase Yomoyama Story

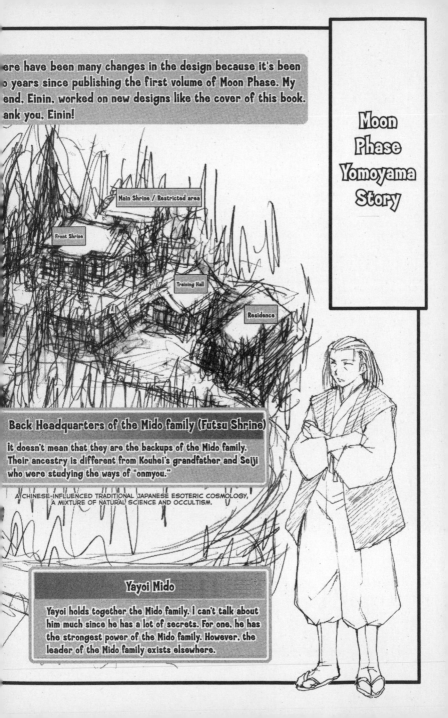

ere have been many changes in the design because it's been
o years since publishing the first volume of Moon Phase. My
end, Einin, worked on new designs like the cover of this book.
ank you, Einin!

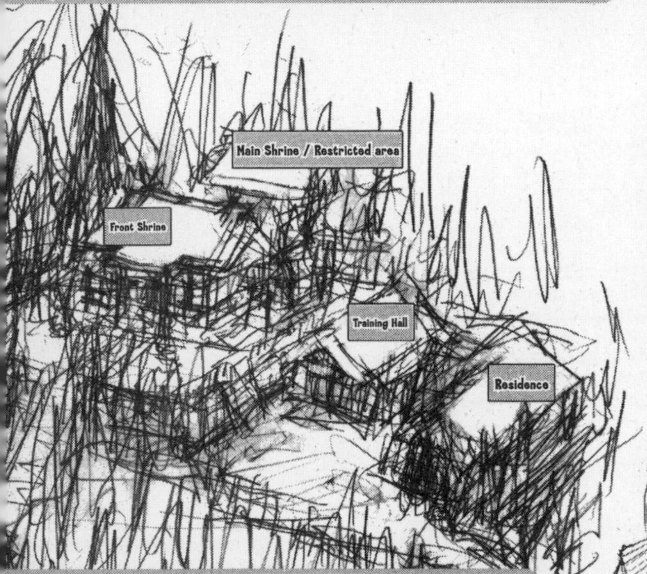

Main Shrine / Restricted area
Front Shrine
Training Hall
Residence

Back Headquarters of the Mido family (Futsu Shrine)

it doesn't mean that they are the backups of the Mido family. Their ancestry is different from Kouhei's grandfather and Seiji who were studying the ways of "onmyou."

A CHINESE-INFLUENCED TRADITIONAL JAPANESE ESOTERIC COSMOLOGY, A MIXTURE OF NATURAL SCIENCE AND OCCULTISM.

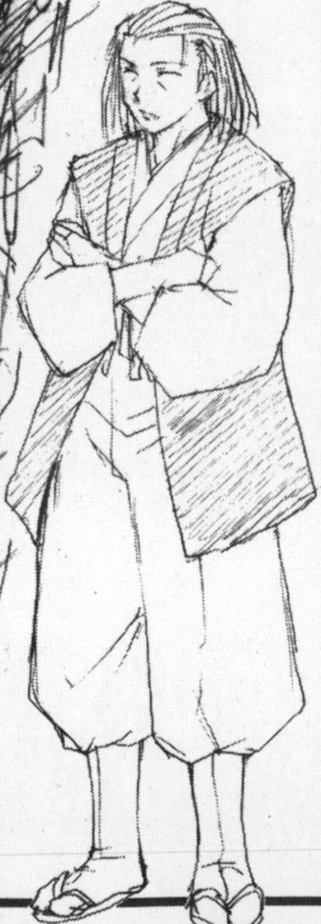

Yayoi Mido

Yayoi holds together the Mido family. I can't talk about him much since he has a lot of secrets. For one, he has the strongest power of the Mido family. However, the leader of the Mido family exists elsewhere.

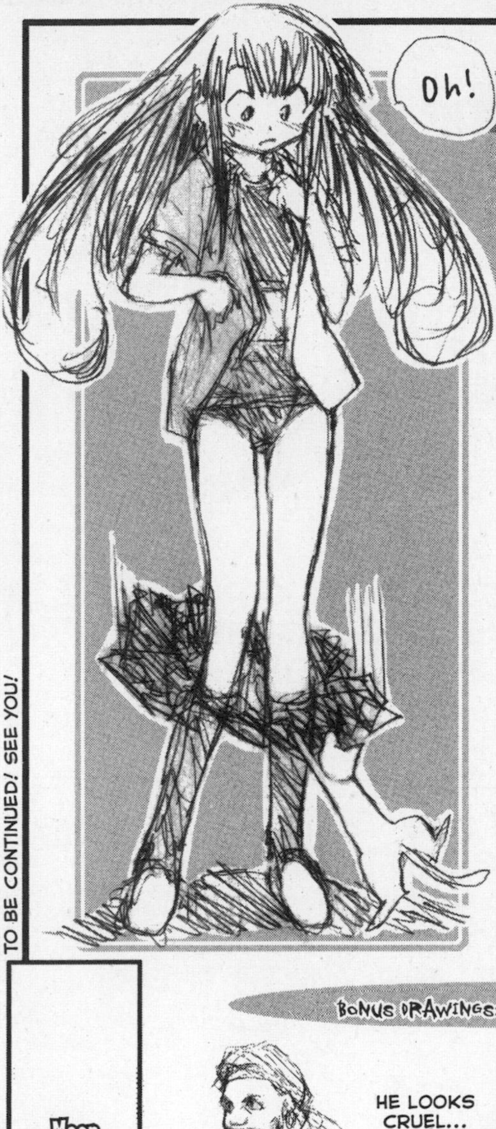
Oh!

School Bathing Suit

i just wanted to draw this for no reason (Laugh) Readers may think that Hazuki doesn't grow up much in these two year But she is 5cm taller and her chest is getting bigger in my mind.

Hikaru Mido & Kaoru Mido

Kouhei's twin cousins. They each have their own special skills. Back in volum two, when Seiji mentions, "it's been ki of noisey over there," he's referring these two.

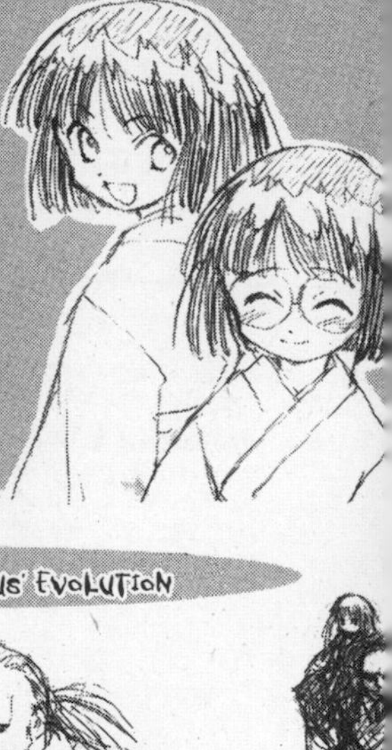

TO BE CONTINUED! SEE YOU!

Moon Phase Yomoyama Story

BONUS DRAWINGS: BALGUS' EVOLUTION

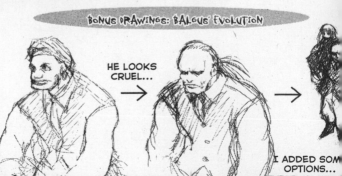

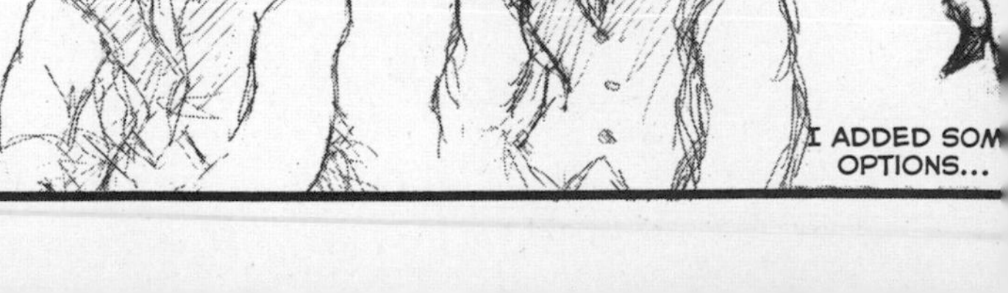
HE LOOKS CRUEL...
I ADDED SOM OPTIONS...

IN THE NEXT

TSUKUYOMI
Moon Phase 月詠

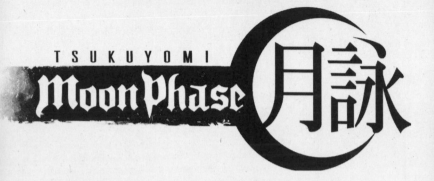

WITH HIS COUSIN, HIKARU, TAKEN HOSTAGE, KOUHEI PUTS HIS OWN LIFE ON THE LINE TO GET HER BACK! TOO BAD THIS HEROIC ACTION COMES WITH A HEAVY PRICE--ONE THAT MAY TEAR THE SPECIAL BOND BETWEEN HAZUKI AND KOUHEI! WHAT'S A GUY TO DO WHEN THE GIRL HE LOVES FILLS HIM WITH THE GREATEST FEAR OF ALL?!

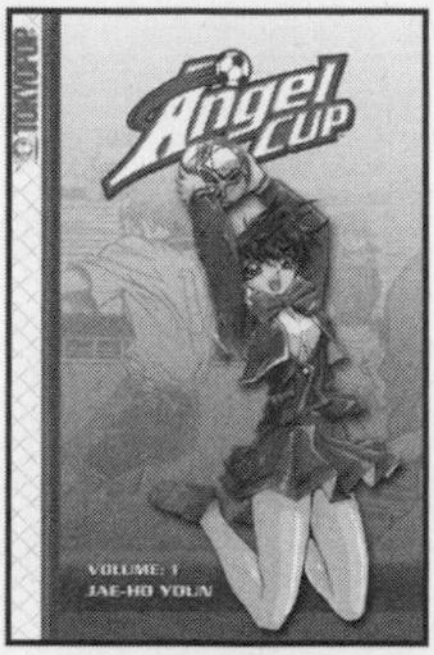
TOKYOPOP
Angel Cup
VOLUME: 1
JAE-HO YOUN

ACTION

T TEEN AGE 13+

ANGEL CUP

BY JAE-HO YOUN

Who's the newest bouncing broad that bends it like Beckam better than Braz—er, you get the idea? So-jin of the hit Korean manhwa, *Angel Cup!* She and her misfit team of athletic Amazons tear up the soccer field, whether it's to face up against the boys' team, or wear their ribbons with pride against a rival high school. While the feminist in me cheers for So-jin and the gang, the more perverted side of me drools buckets over the sexy bust-shots and scandalous camera angles... But from any and every angle, *Angel Cup* will be sure to tantalize the soccer fan in you... or perv. Whichever!

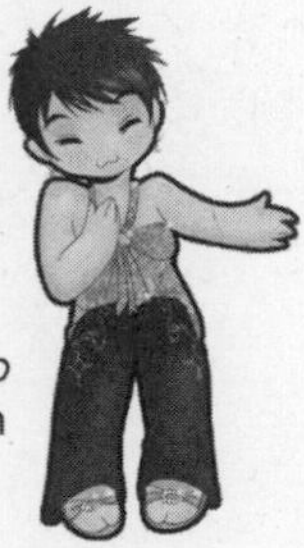

~Katherine Schilling, Jr. Editor

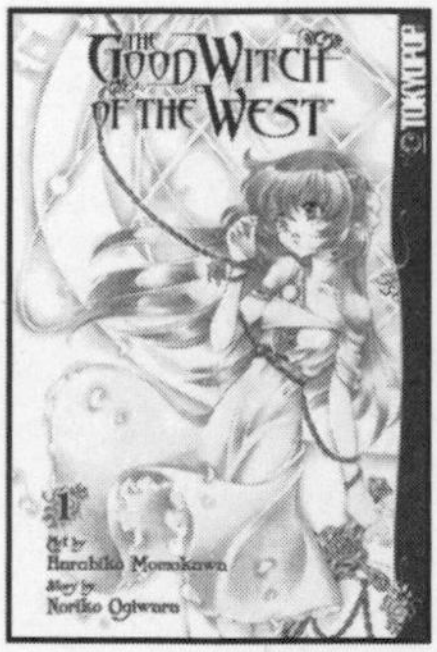
THE GOOD WITCH OF THE WEST
TOKYOPOP
1
Art by Haruhiko Momokawa
Story by Noriko Ogiwara

FANTASY

T TEEN AGE 13+

GOOD WITCH OF THE WEST

BY NORIKO OGIWARA AND HARUHIKO MOMOKAWA

For any dreamers who ever wanted more out of a fairytale, indulge yourself with *Good Witch*. Although there's lots of familiar territory fairytale-wise—peasant girl learns she's a princess—you'll be surprised as Firiel Dee's enemies turn out to be as diverse as religious fanaticism, evil finishing school student councils and dinosaurs. This touching, sophisticated tale will pull at your heartstrings while astounding you with breathtaking art. *Good Witch* has big shoes to fill, and it takes off running.

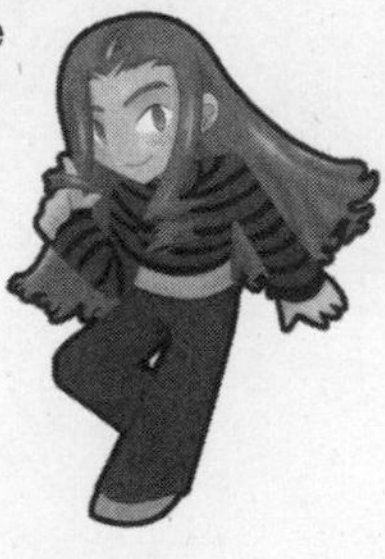

~Hope Donovan, Jr. Editor

EDITORS' PICKS TOKYOPOP MANGA SUPPLEMENT

SAKURA TAISEN
BY OHJI HIROI, IKKU MASA AND KOSUKE FUJISHIMA

I really, really like this series. I'm a sucker for steampunk-type stories, and 1920s Japanese fashion, and throw in demon invaders, robot battles and references to Japanese popular theater? Sold! There's lots of fun tidbits for the clever reader to pick up in this series (all the characters have flower names, for one, and the fact that all the Floral Assault divisions are named after branches of the Takarazuka Review, Japan's sensational all-female theater troupe!), but the consistently stylish and clean art will appeal even to the most casual fan.

~Lillian Diaz-Przybyl, Editor

BATTLE ROYALE
BY KOUSHUN TAKAMI AND MASAYUKI TAGUCHI

As far as cautionary tales go, you couldn't get any timelier than *Battle Royale*. Telling the bleak story of a class of middle school students who are forced to fight each other to the death on national television, Koushun Takami and Masayuki Taguchi have created a dark satire that's sickening, yet undeniably exciting as well. And if we have that reaction reading it, it becomes alarmingly clear how the students could so easily be swayed into doing it.

~Tim Beedle, Editor

Sakura Taisen © SEGA © RED © Ikku Masa. Battle Royale © Koushun Takami/Masayuki Taguchi/AKITA SHOTEN

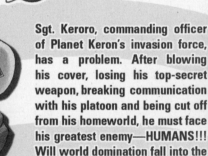

KING of THORN

YUJI IWAHARA

ACTION

OT OLDER TEEN AGE 16+

WARNING
Virus outbrea

Kasumi and h
sister, Shizuk
are infected wi
the fatal Medu
virus. There is
cure, but Kasu
is selected to
into a cryoger
freezer unti
cure is foun
But wh
Kasumi awaken
she must strugg
to survive i
treachero
world if sl
hopes
discover wh
happened
her sist

From Yuji Iwaha
the creator
the popu
Chikyu Misa
and *Koudelk*

© YUJI IWAH

STOP!

This is the back of the book.
You wouldn't want to spoil a great ending!

This book is printed "manga-style," in the authentic Japanese right-to-left format. Since none of the artwork has been flipped or altered, readers get to experience the story just as the creator intended. You've been asking for it, so TOKYOPOP® delivered: authentic, hot-off-the-press, and far more fun!

DIRECTIONS

If this is your first time reading manga-style, here's a quick guide to help you understand how it works.

It's easy... just start in the top right panel and follow the numbers. Have fun, and look for more 100% authentic manga from TOKYOPOP®!